30 DAYS OF NIGHT™:
BLOODSUCKER TALES

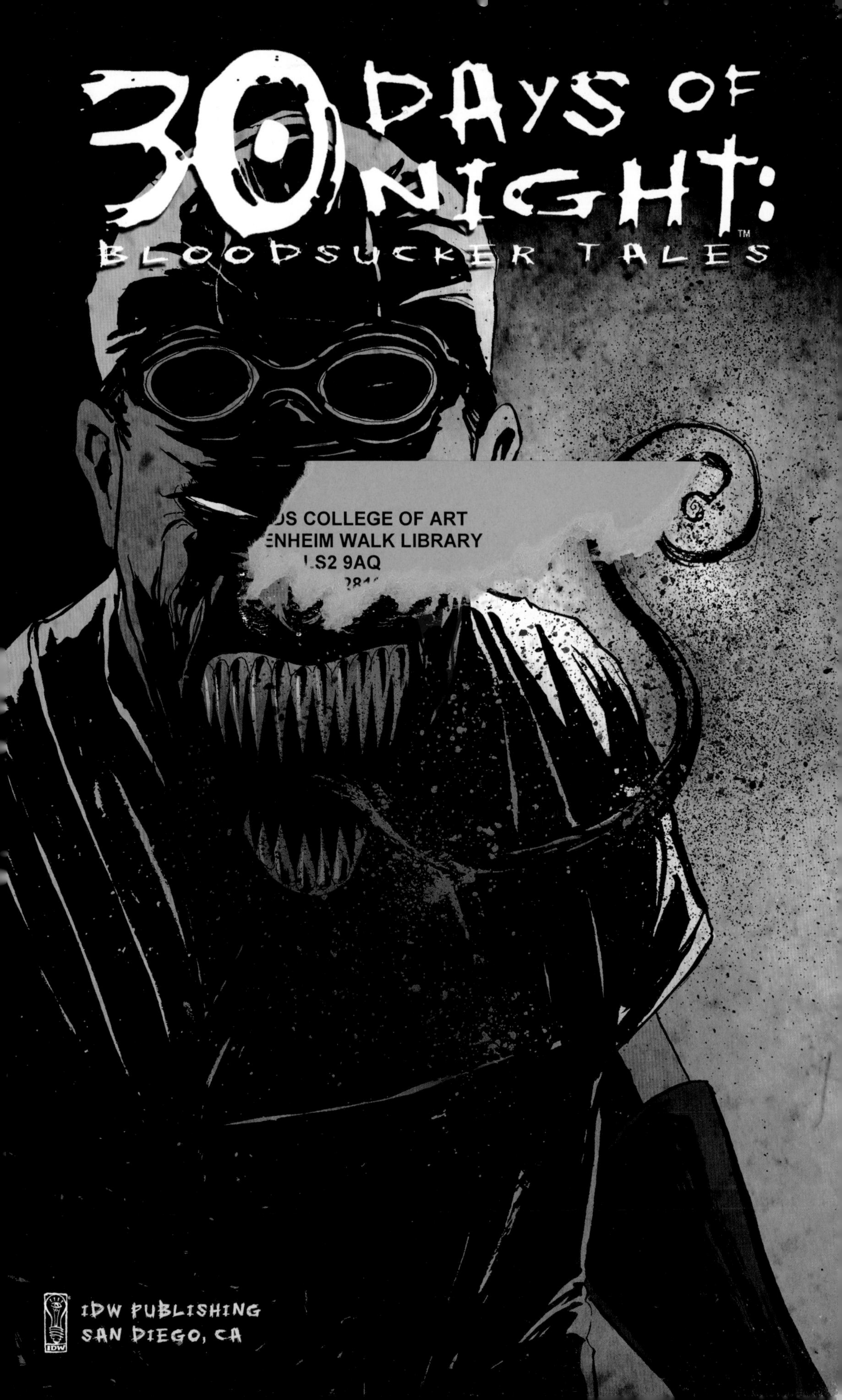
30 DAYS OF NIGHT:
BLOODSUCKER TALES
IDW PUBLISHING
SAN DIEGO, CA

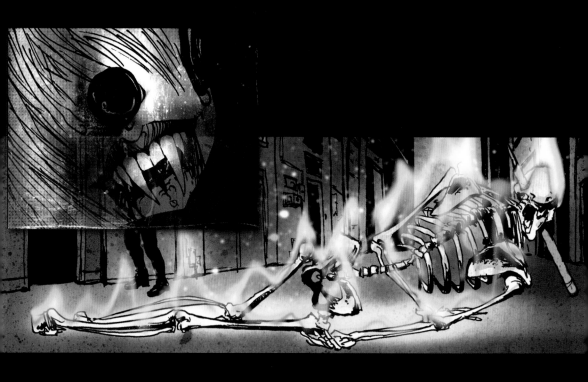

ISBN: 978-1-932382-78-5

10 09 08 07   3 4 5 6 7

www.idwpublishing.com

IDW Publishing is:
Ted Adams, President
Robbie Robbins, EVP/Sr. Graphic Artist
Clifford Meth, EVP of Strategies/Editorial
Chris Ryall, Publisher/Editor-in-Chief
Alan Payne, VP of Sales
Neil Uyetake, Art Director
Dan Taylor, Editor
Justin Eisinger, Assistant Editor
Tom Waltz, Assistant Editor
Chris Mowry, Graphic Artist
Amauri Osorio, Graphic Artist
Matthew Ruzicka, CPA, Controller
Alonzo Simon, Shipping Manager
Kris Oprisko, Editor/Foreign Lic. Rep.

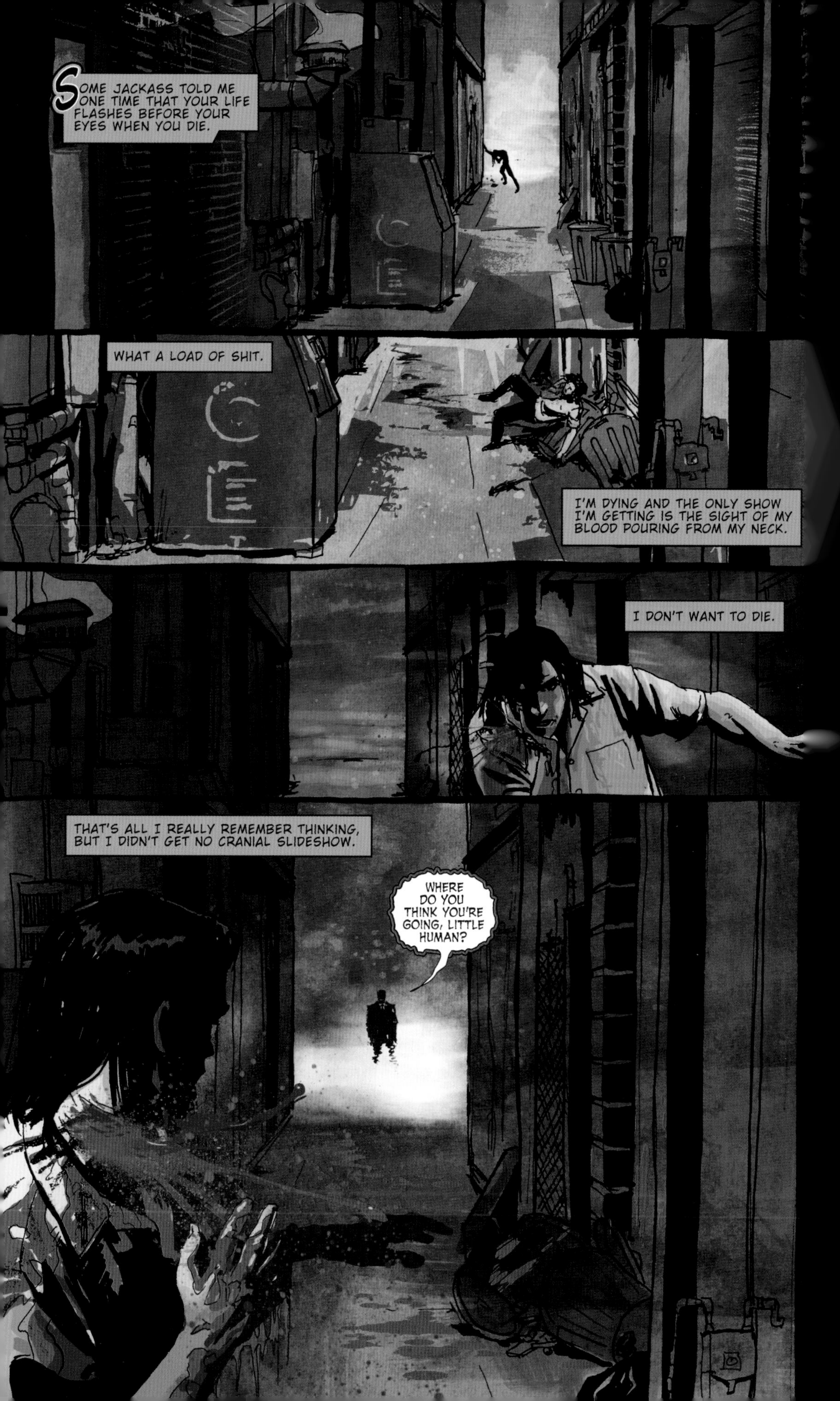
SOME JACKASS TOLD ME ONE TIME THAT YOUR LIFE FLASHES BEFORE YOUR EYES WHEN YOU DIE.
WHAT A LOAD OF SHIT.
I'M DYING AND THE ONLY SHOW I'M GETTING IS THE SIGHT OF MY BLOOD POURING FROM MY NECK.
I DON'T WANT TO DIE.
THAT'S ALL I REALLY REMEMBER THINKING, BUT I DIDN'T GET NO CRANIAL SLIDESHOW.
WHERE DO YOU THINK YOU'RE GOING, LITTLE HUMAN?

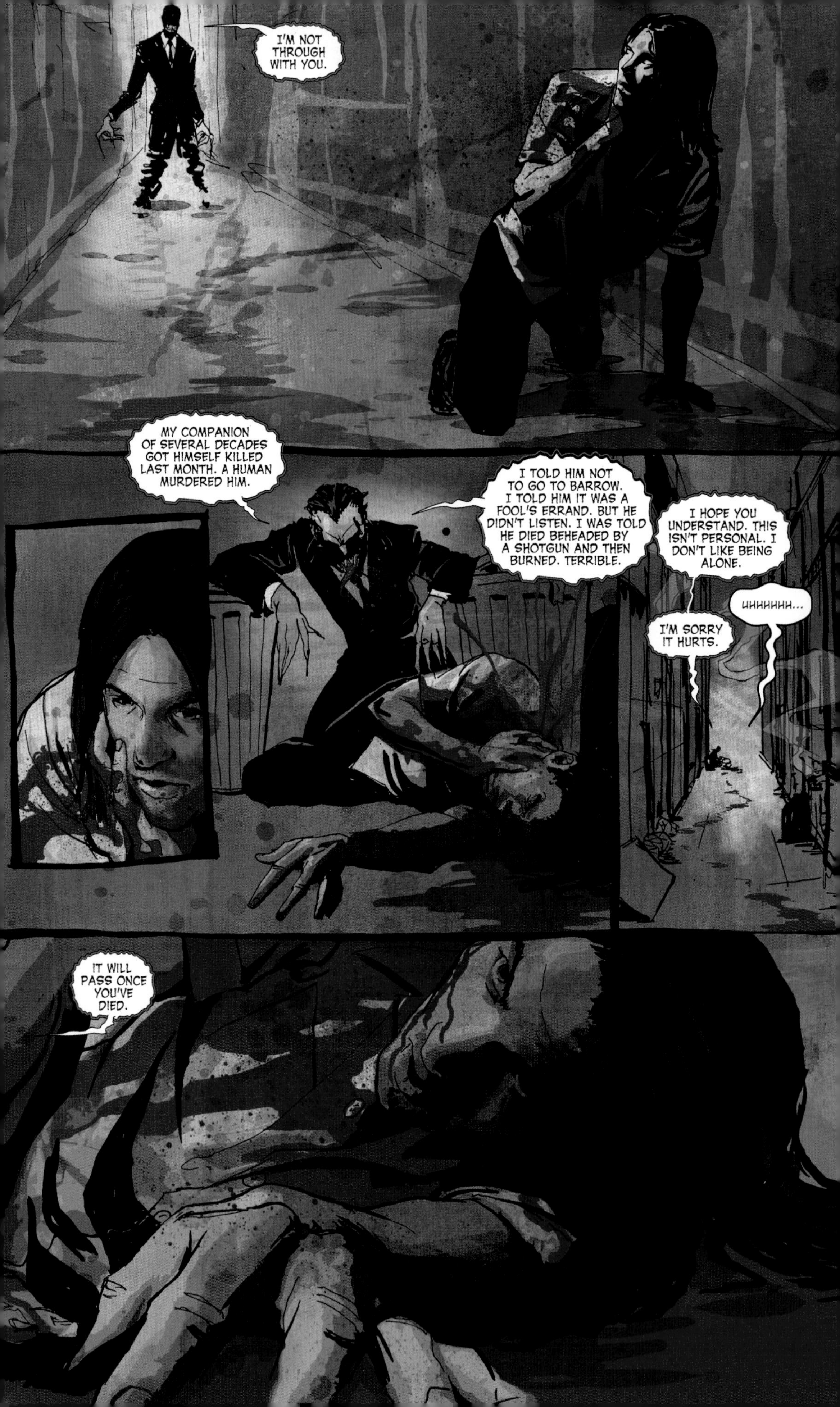

I'M NOT THROUGH WITH YOU.
MY COMPANION OF SEVERAL DECADES GOT HIMSELF KILLED LAST MONTH. A HUMAN MURDERED HIM.
I TOLD HIM NOT TO GO TO BARROW. I TOLD HIM IT WAS A FOOL'S ERRAND. BUT HE DIDN'T LISTEN. I WAS TOLD HE DIED BEHEADED BY A SHOTGUN AND THEN BURNED. TERRIBLE.
I HOPE YOU UNDERSTAND. THIS ISN'T PERSONAL. I DON'T LIKE BEING ALONE.
UHHHHHH...
I'M SORRY IT HURTS.
IT WILL PASS ONCE YOU'VE DIED.

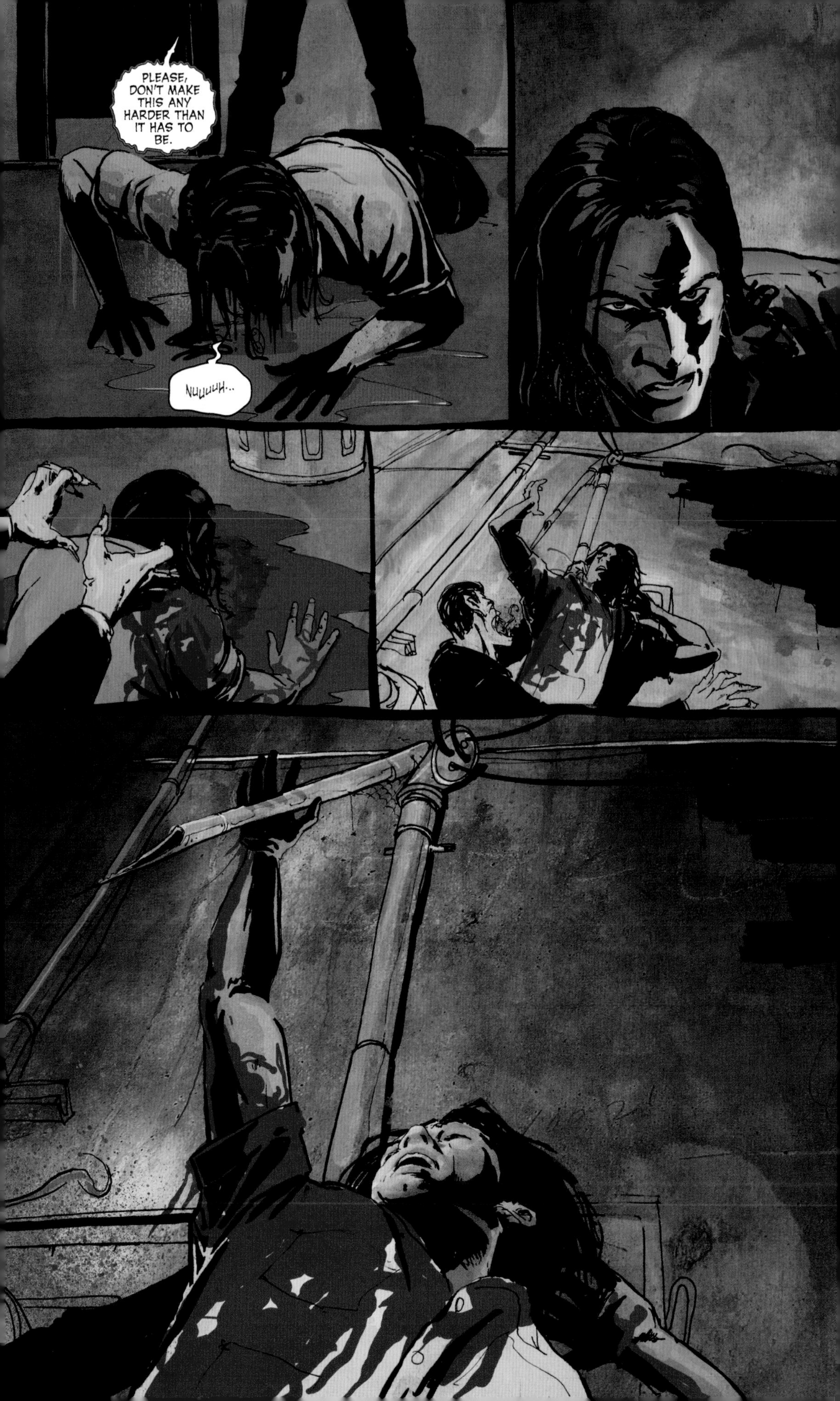
PLEASE, DON'T MAKE THIS ANY HARDER THAN IT HAS TO BE.
NUUUUH...

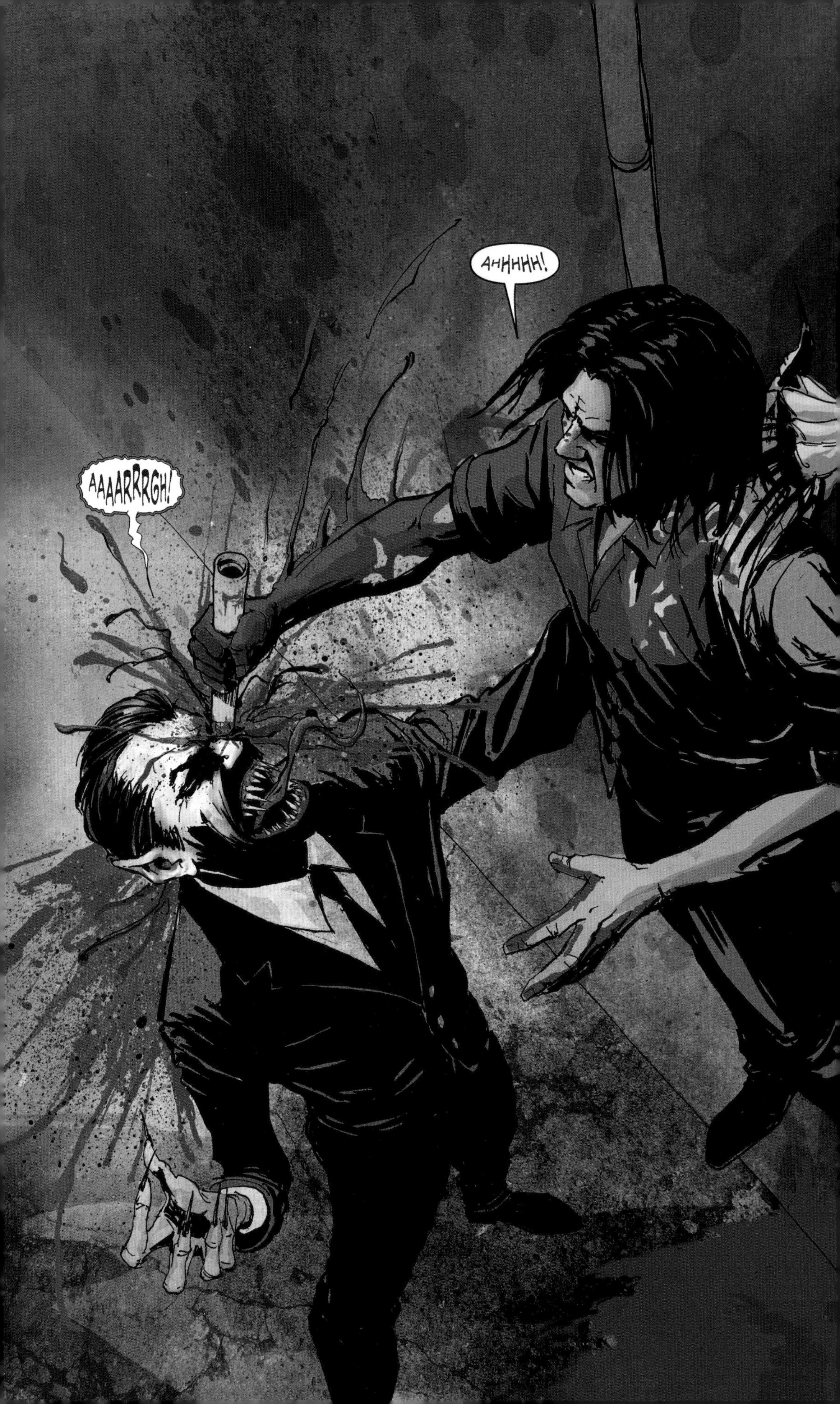
AAAARRRGH!
AHHHHH!

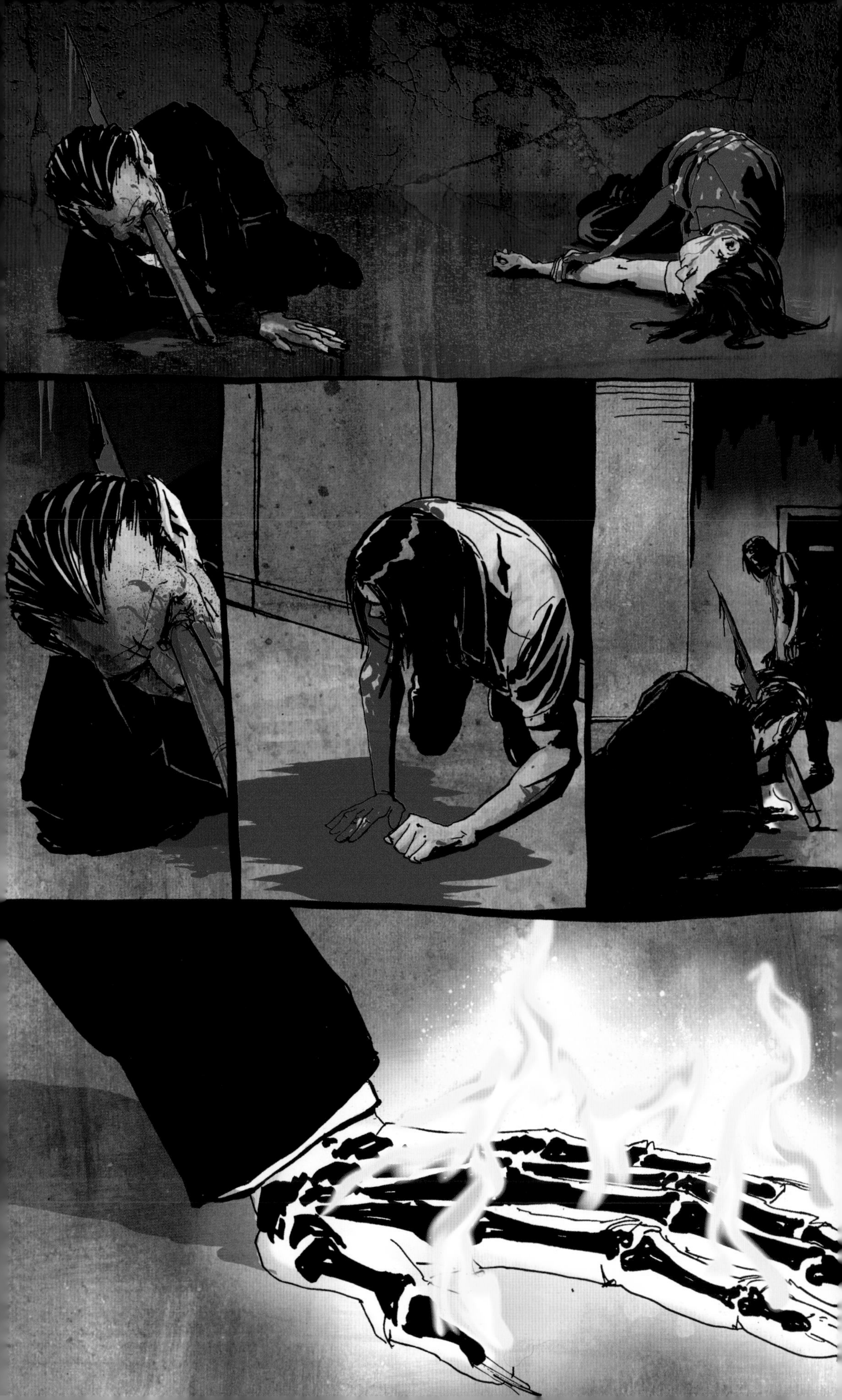

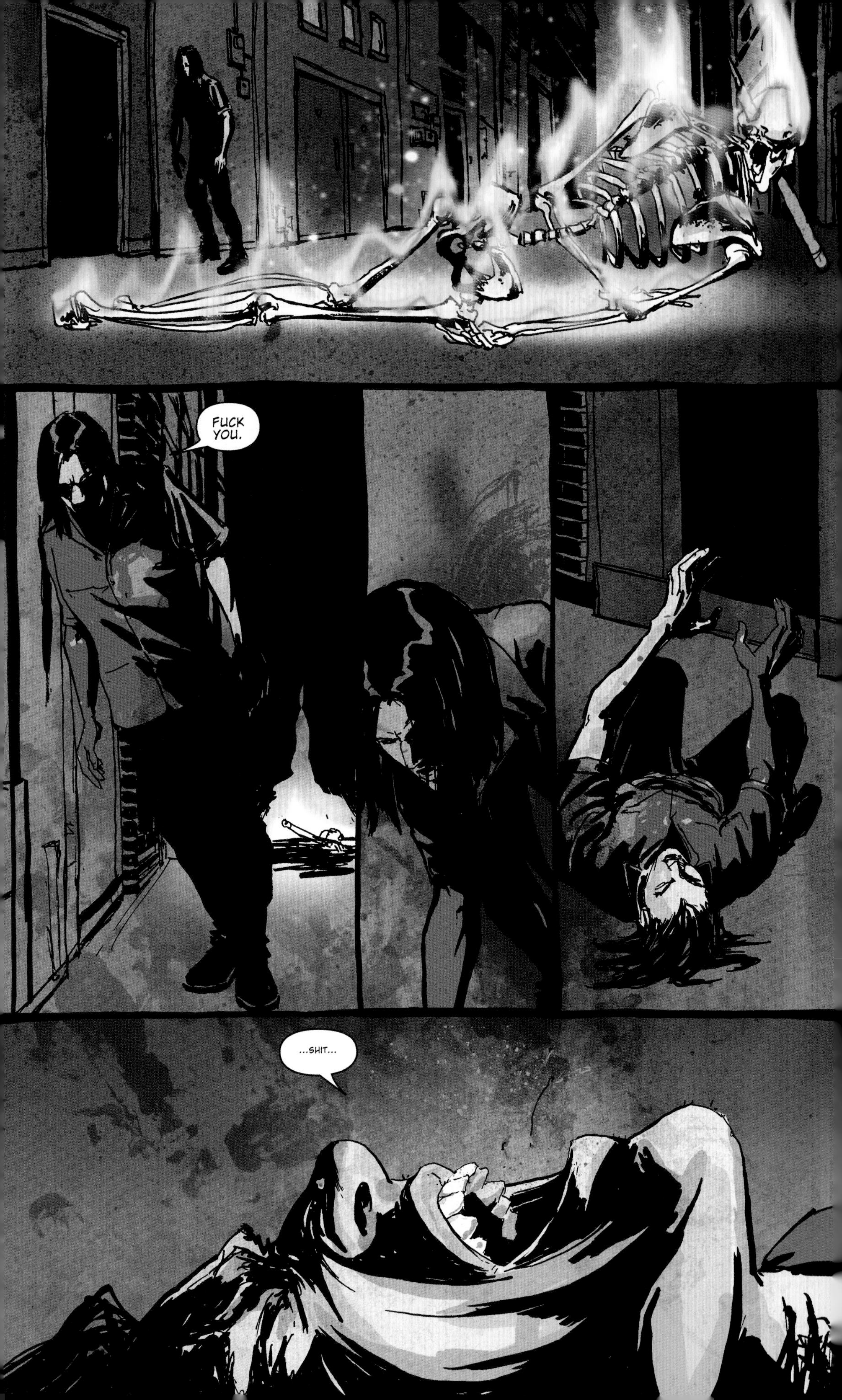
FUCK YOU.
...SHIT...

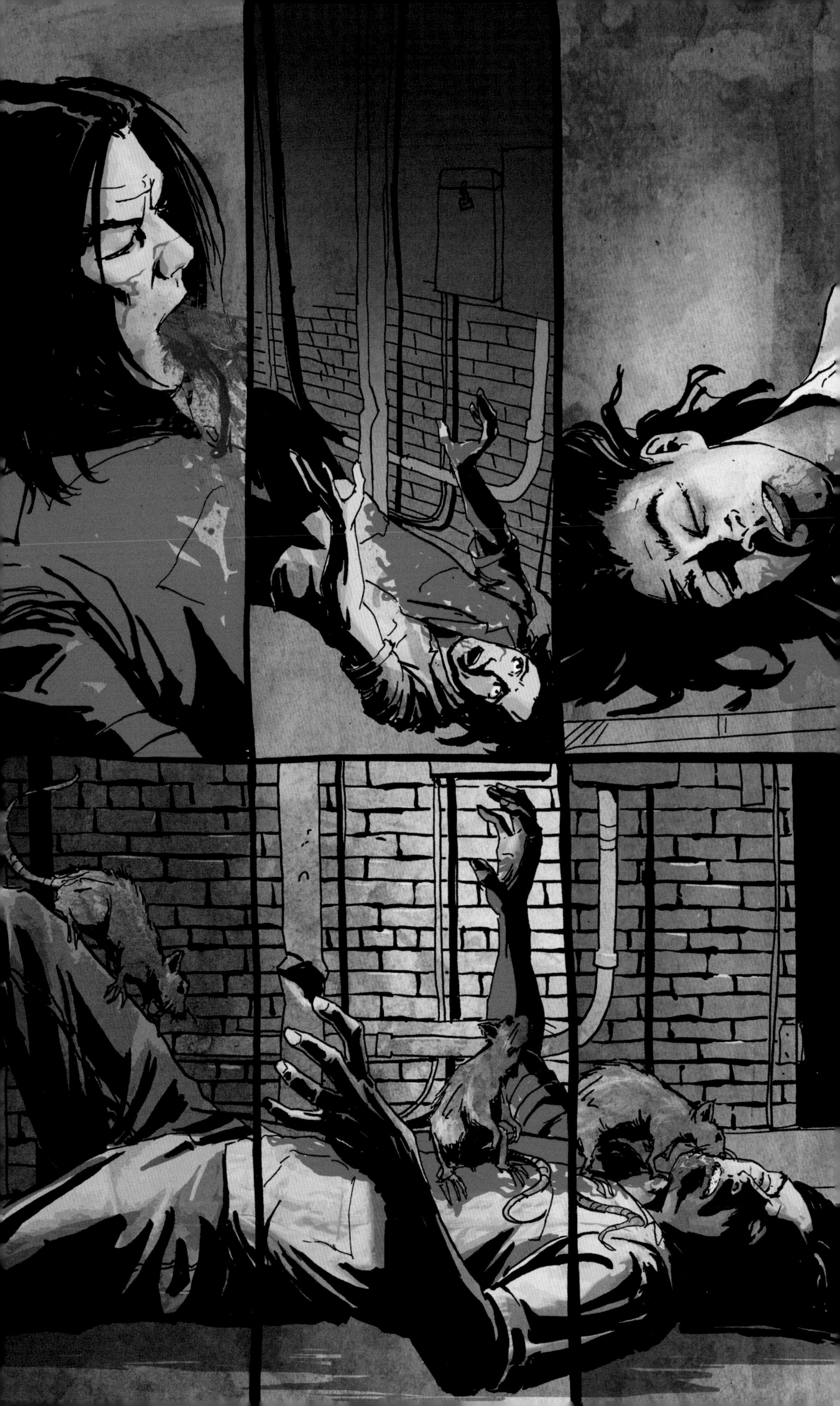

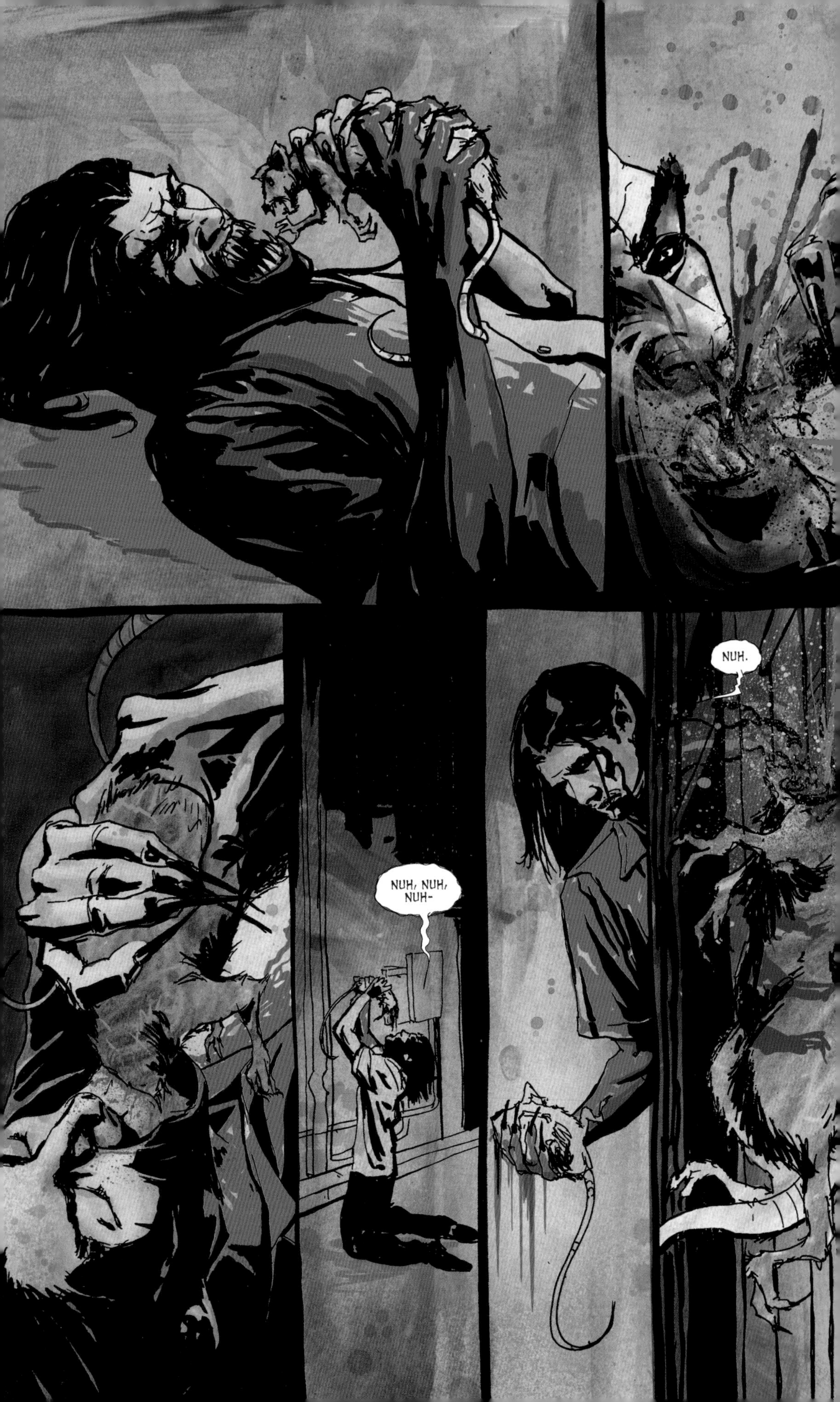
NUH, NUH, NUH-
NUH.

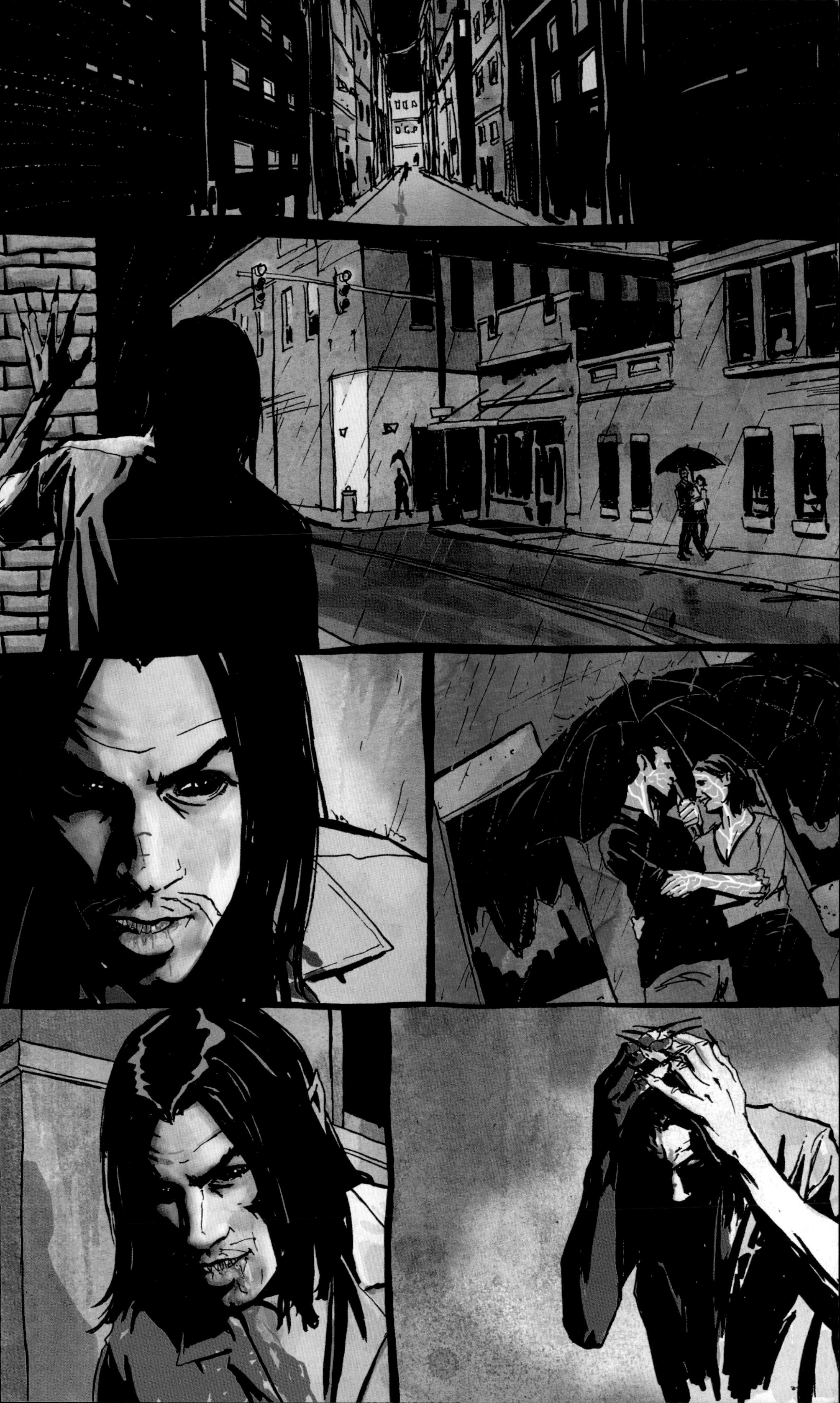

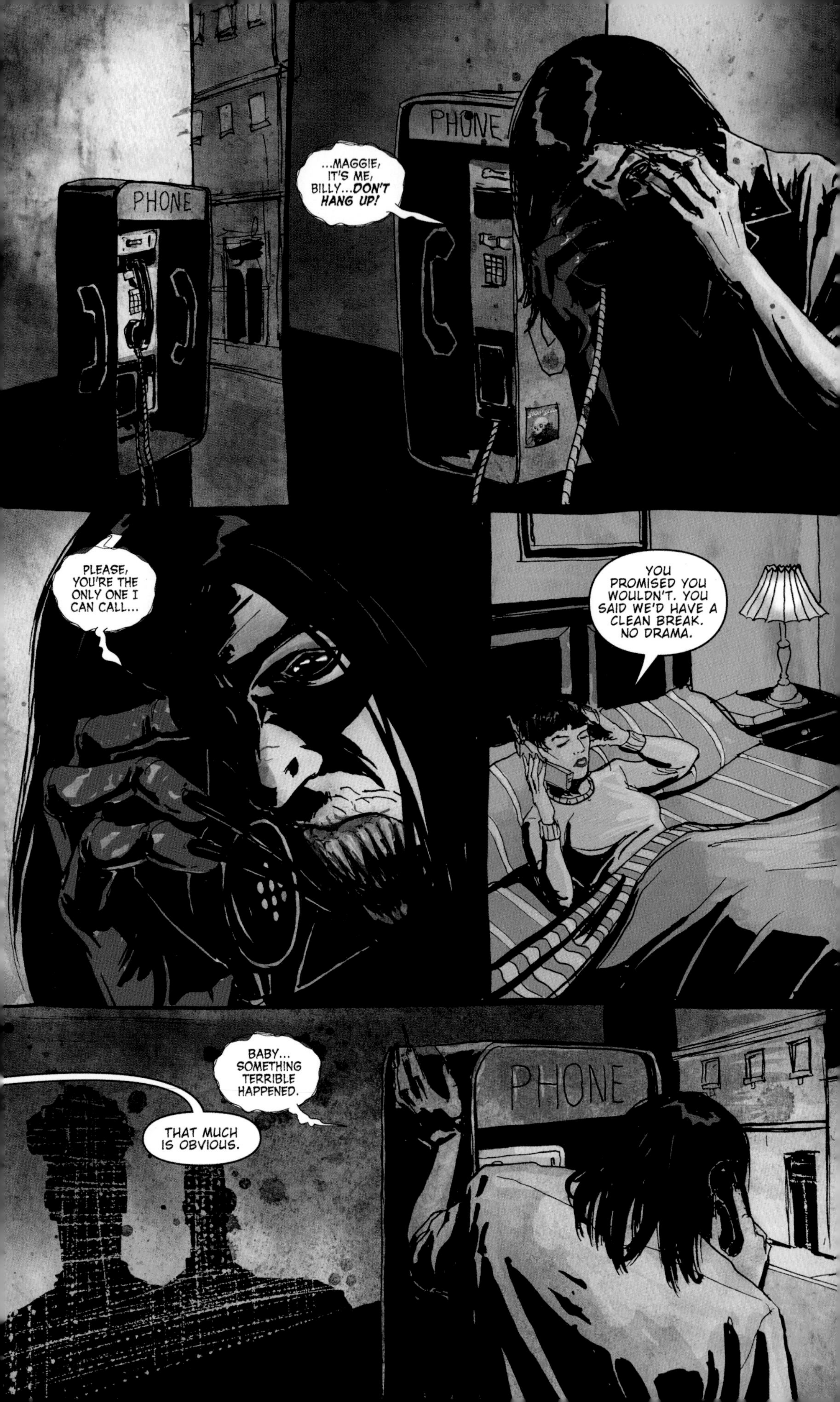
PHONE
PHONE
...MAGGIE, IT'S ME, BILLY...**DON'T HANG UP!**
PLEASE, YOU'RE THE ONLY ONE I CAN CALL...
YOU PROMISED YOU WOULDN'T. YOU SAID WE'D HAVE A CLEAN BREAK. NO DRAMA.
PHONE
BABY... SOMETHING TERRIBLE HAPPENED.
THAT MUCH IS OBVIOUS.

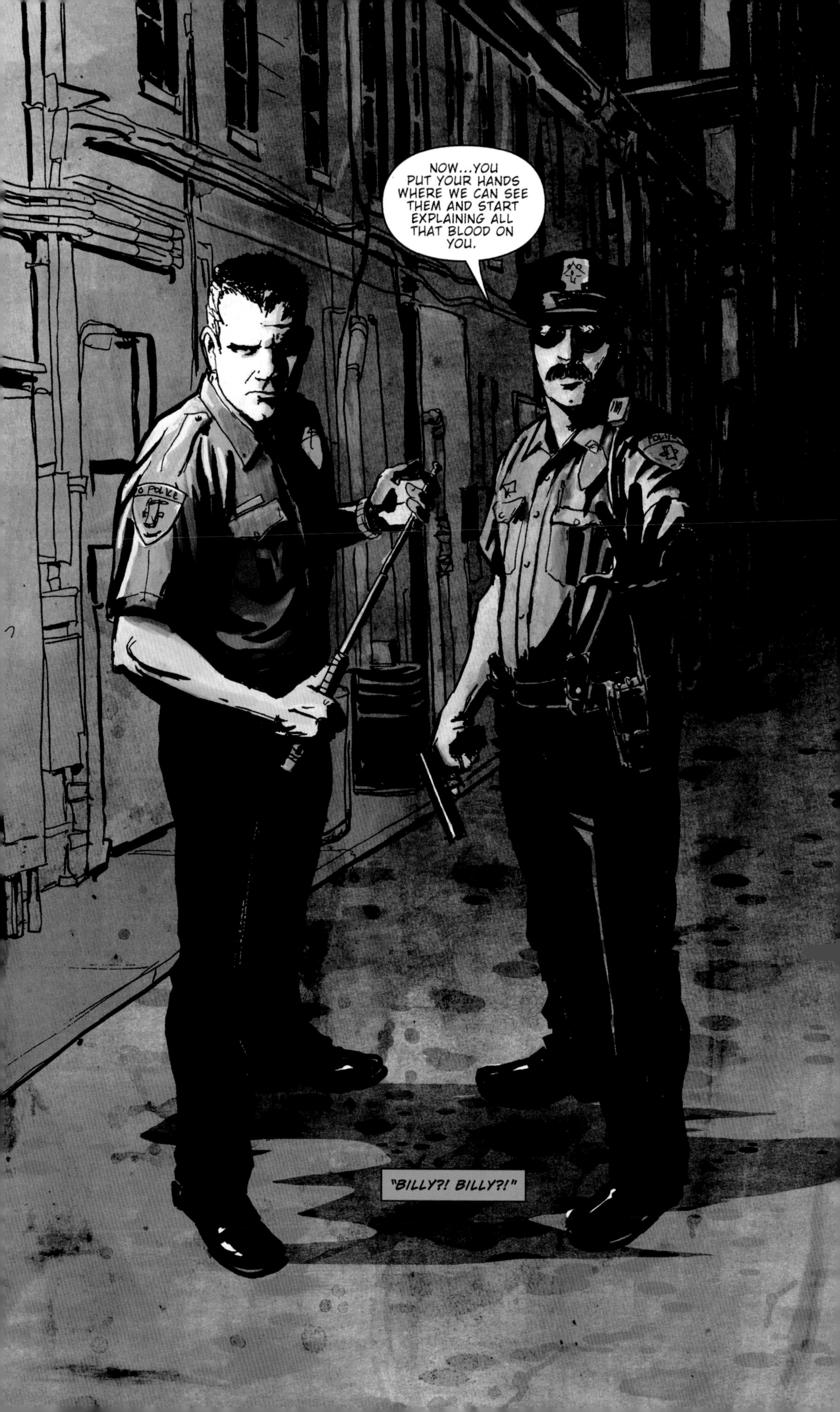
NOW...YOU PUT YOUR HANDS WHERE WE CAN SEE THEM AND START EXPLAINING ALL THAT BLOOD ON YOU.
"BILLY?! BILLY?!"

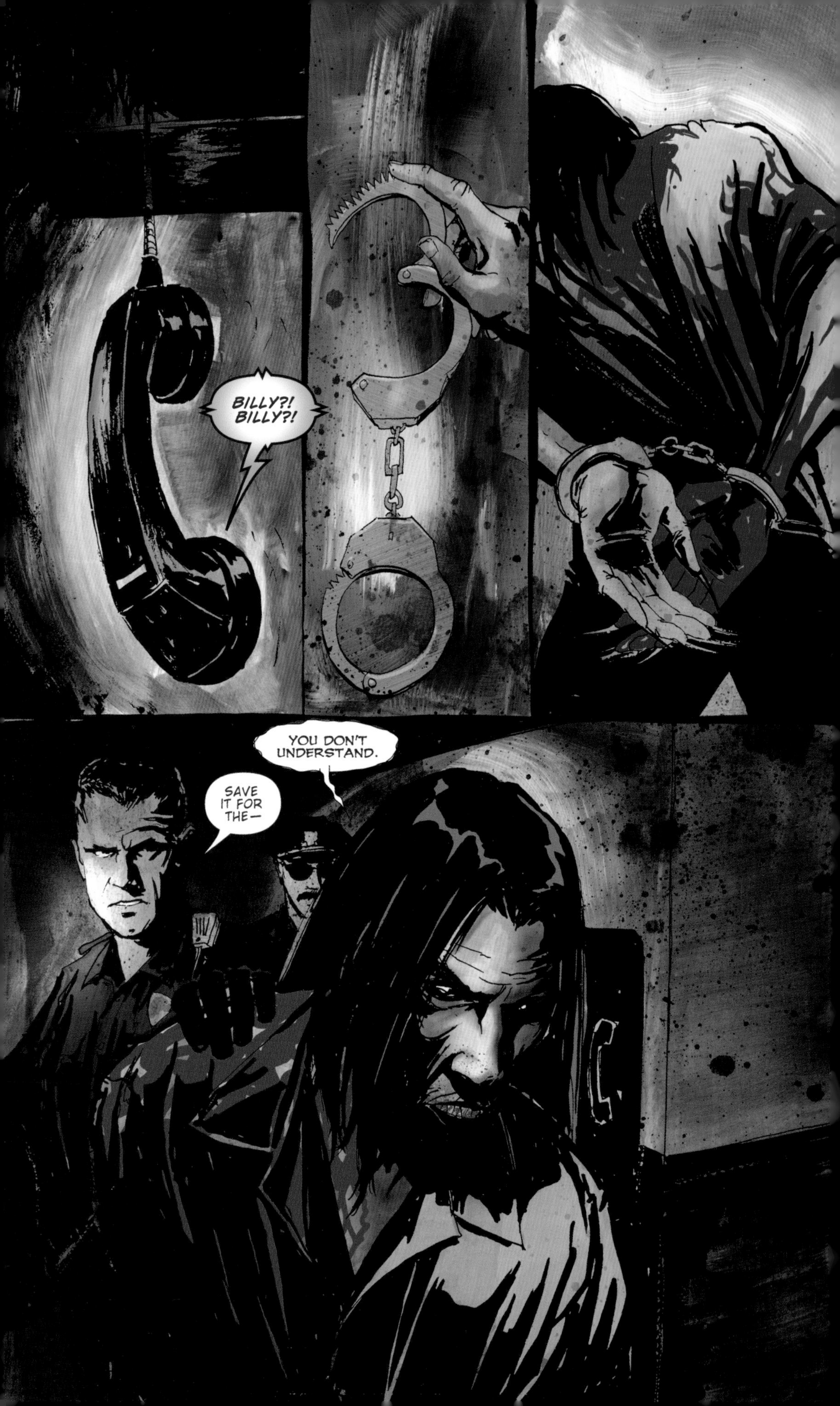
BILLY?! BILLY?!
SAVE IT FOR THE—
YOU DON'T UNDERSTAND.

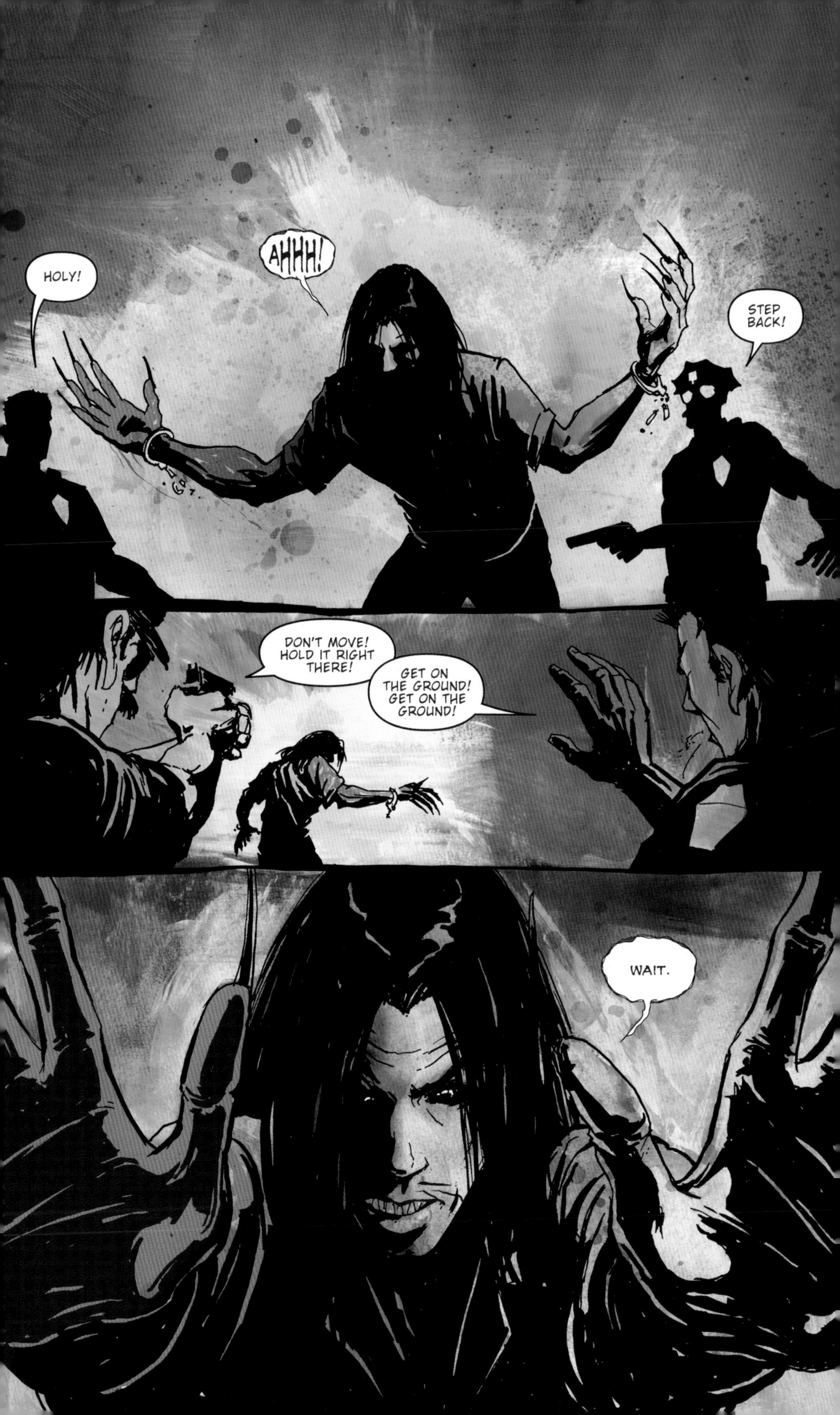
HOLY!
AHHH!
STEP BACK!
DON'T MOVE! HOLD IT RIGHT THERE!
GET ON THE GROUND! GET ON THE GROUND!
WAIT.

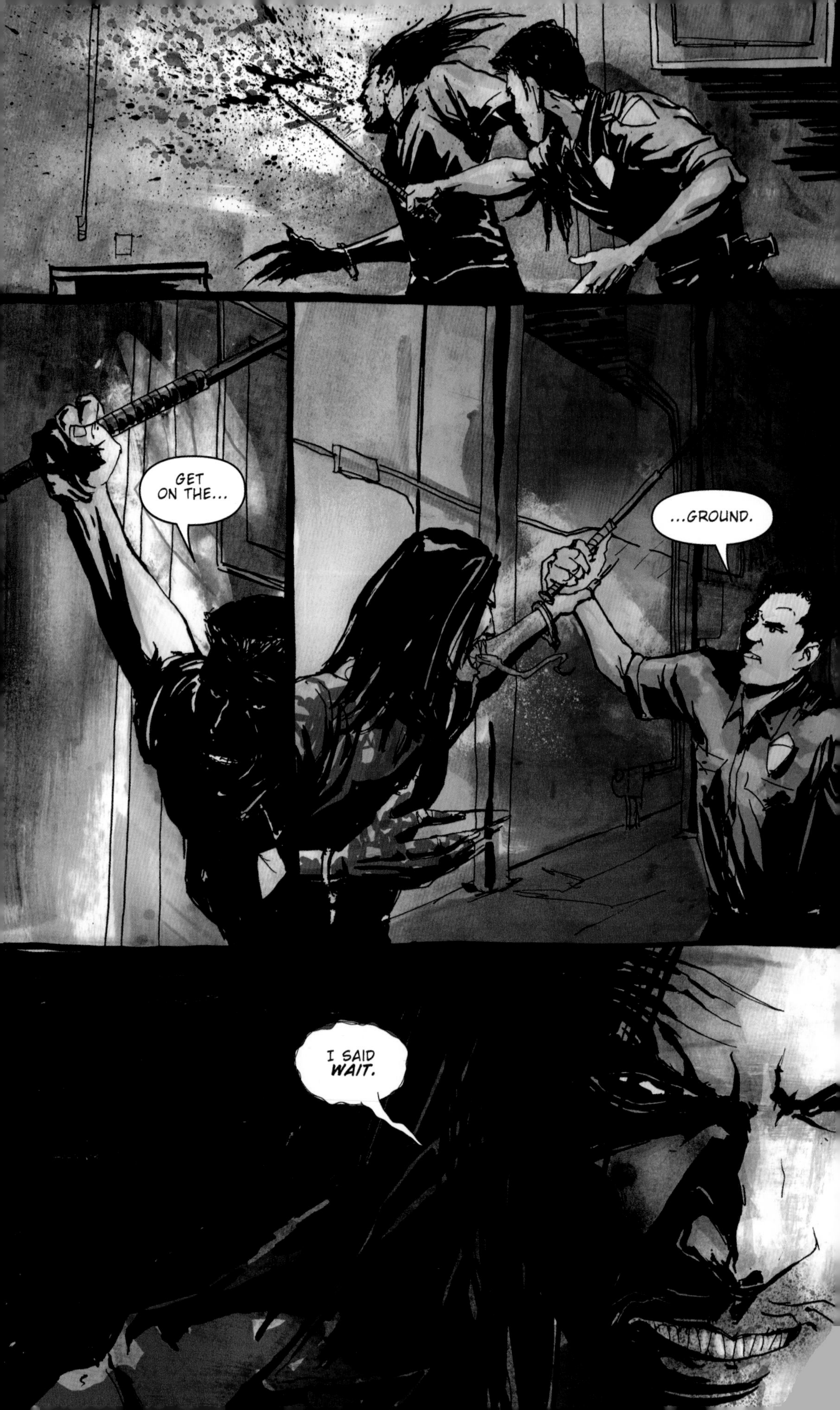
GET ON THE...
...GROUND.
I SAID WAIT.

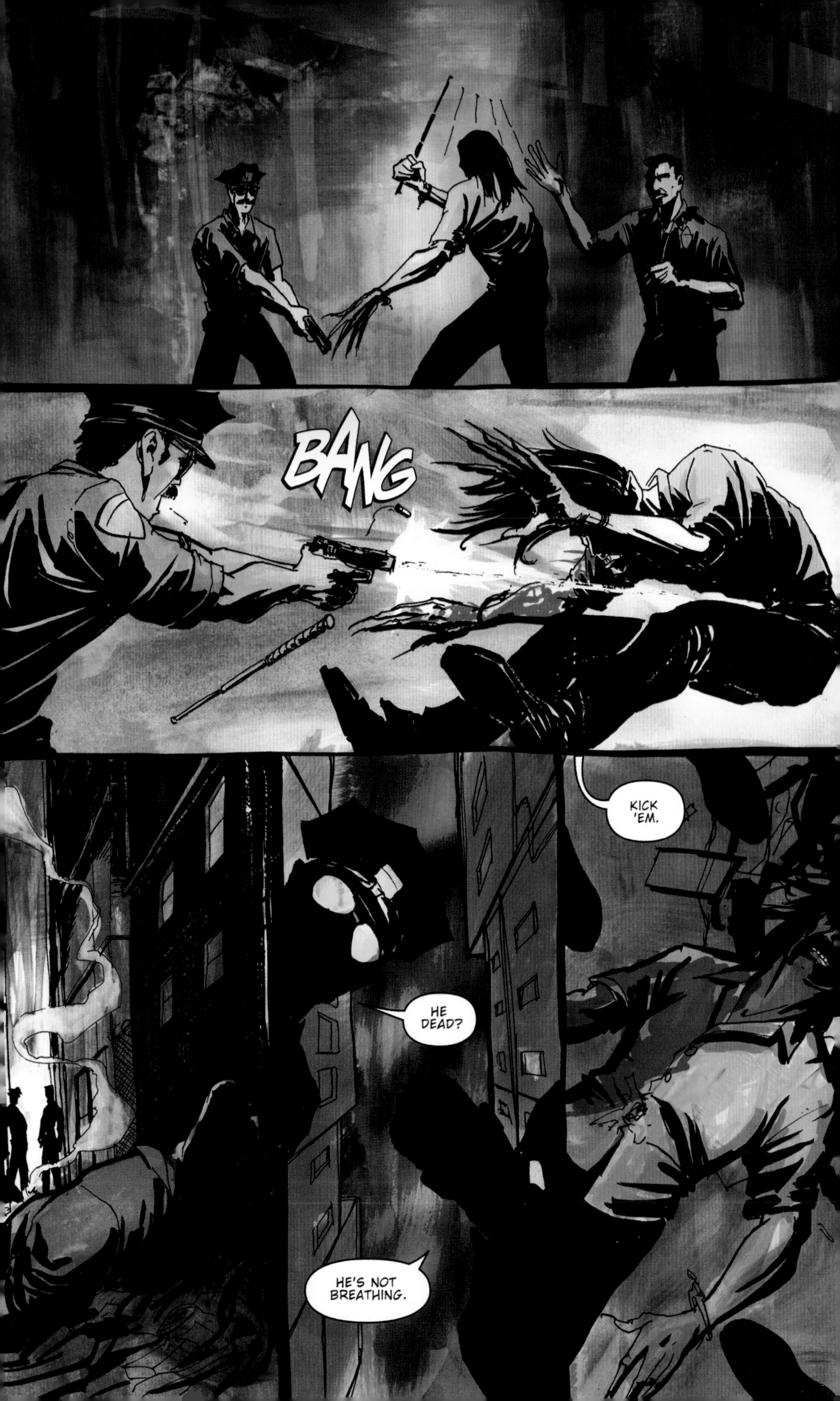
BANG
KICK 'EM.
HE DEAD?
HE'S NOT BREATHING.

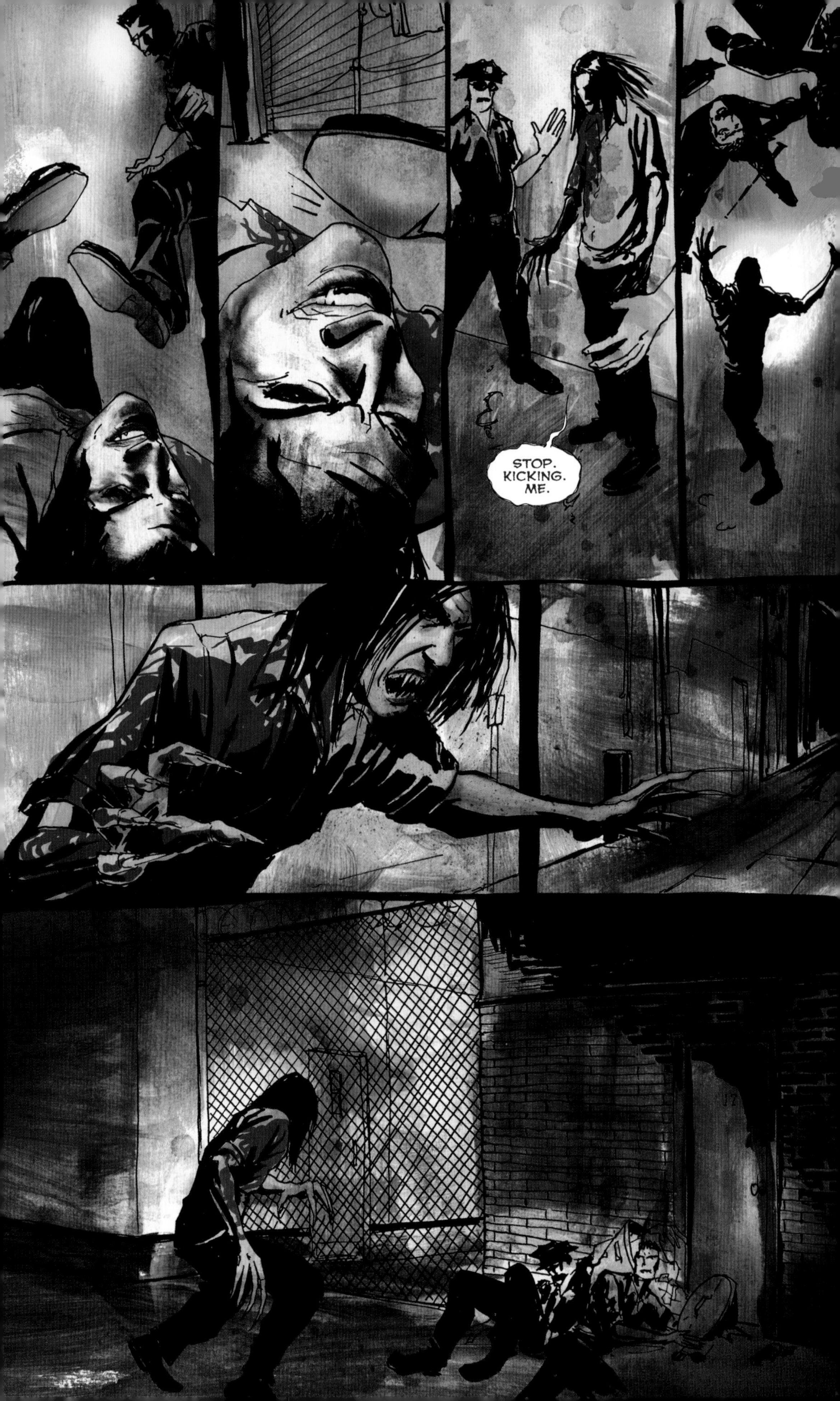
STOP.
KICKING.
ME.

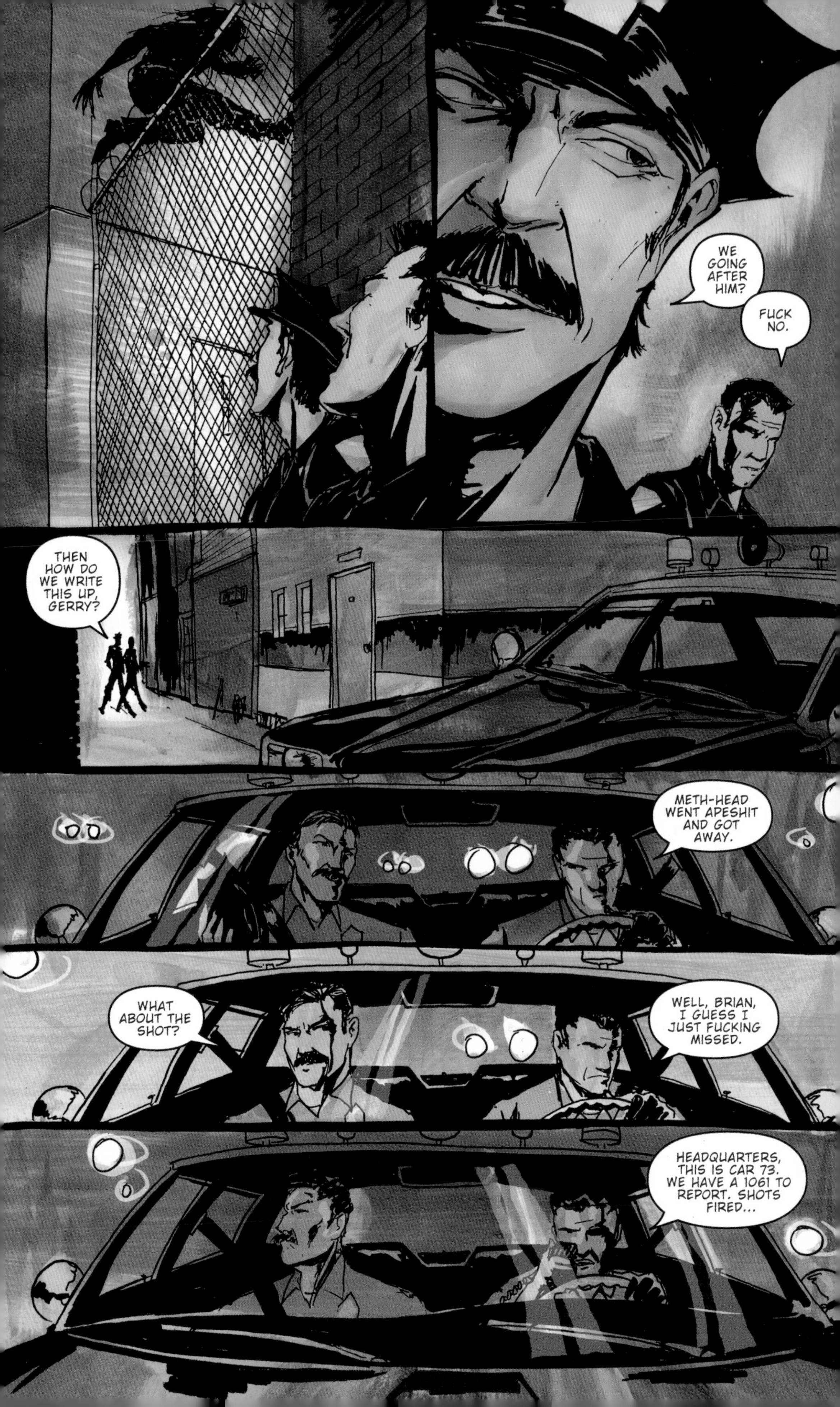

WE GOING AFTER HIM?
FUCK NO.
THEN HOW DO WE WRITE THIS UP, GERRY?
METH-HEAD WENT APESHIT AND GOT AWAY.
WHAT ABOUT THE SHOT?
WELL, BRIAN, I GUESS I JUST FUCKING MISSED.
HEADQUARTERS, THIS IS CAR 73. WE HAVE A 1061 TO REPORT. SHOTS FIRED...

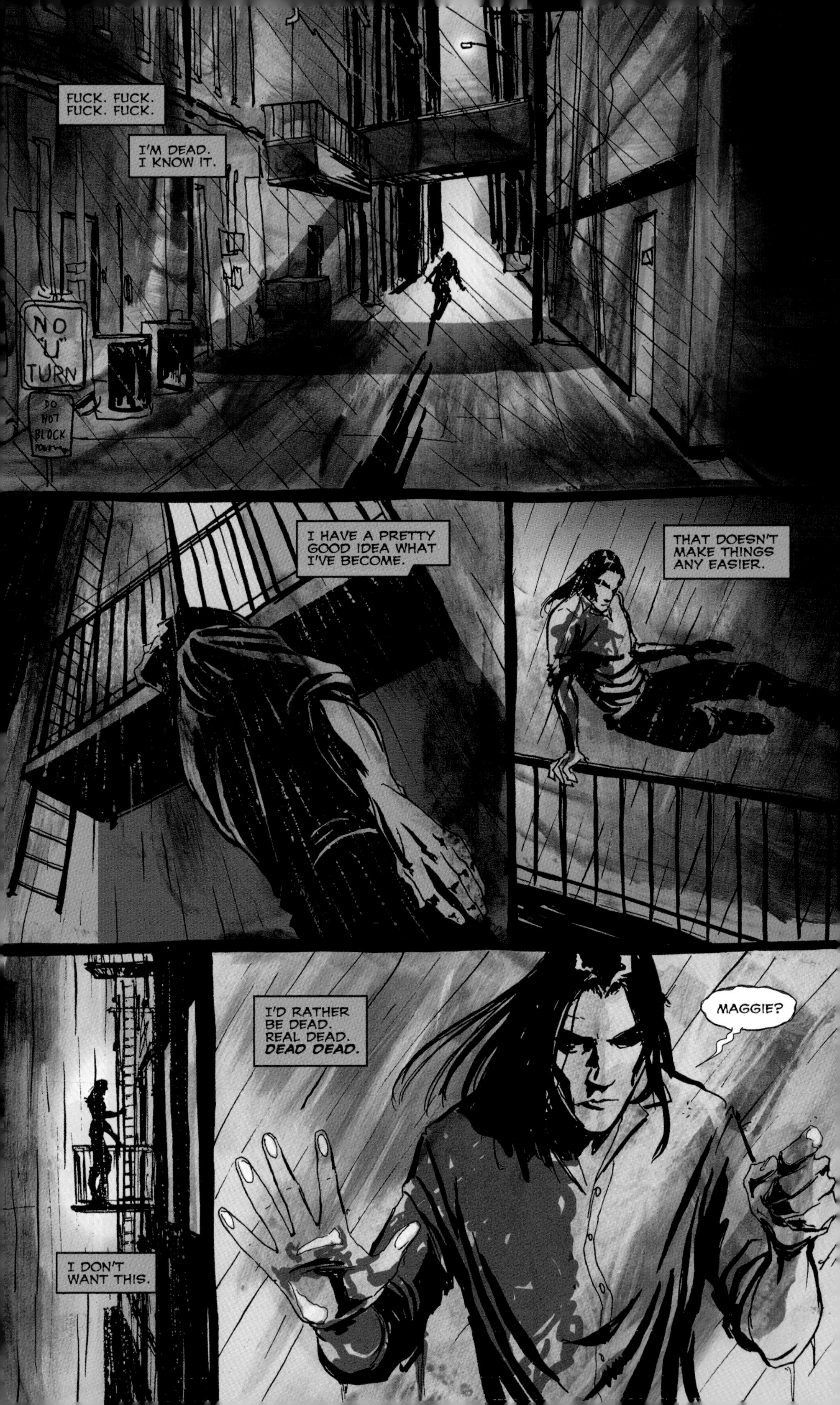
FUCK. FUCK. FUCK. FUCK.
I'M DEAD. I KNOW IT.
NO "U" TURN
DO NOT BLOCK
I HAVE A PRETTY GOOD IDEA WHAT I'VE BECOME.
THAT DOESN'T MAKE THINGS ANY EASIER.
I DON'T WANT THIS.
I'D RATHER BE DEAD. REAL DEAD. *DEAD DEAD.*
MAGGIE?

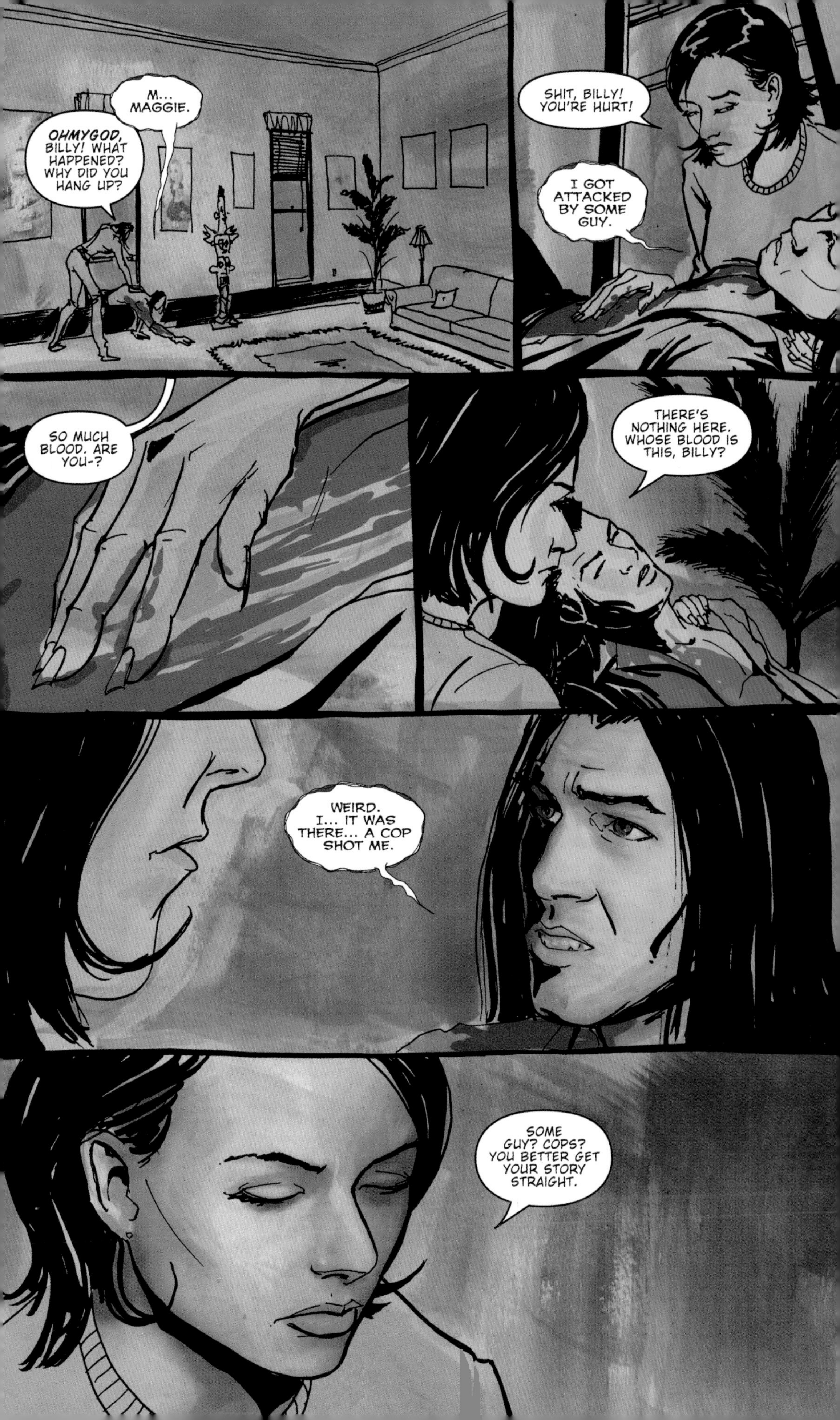
M... MAGGIE.
OHMYGOD, BILLY! WHAT HAPPENED? WHY DID YOU HANG UP?
SHIT, BILLY! YOU'RE HURT!
I GOT ATTACKED BY SOME GUY.
SO MUCH BLOOD. ARE YOU-?
THERE'S NOTHING HERE. WHOSE BLOOD IS THIS, BILLY?
WEIRD. I... IT WAS THERE... A COP SHOT ME.
SOME GUY? COPS? YOU BETTER GET YOUR STORY STRAIGHT.

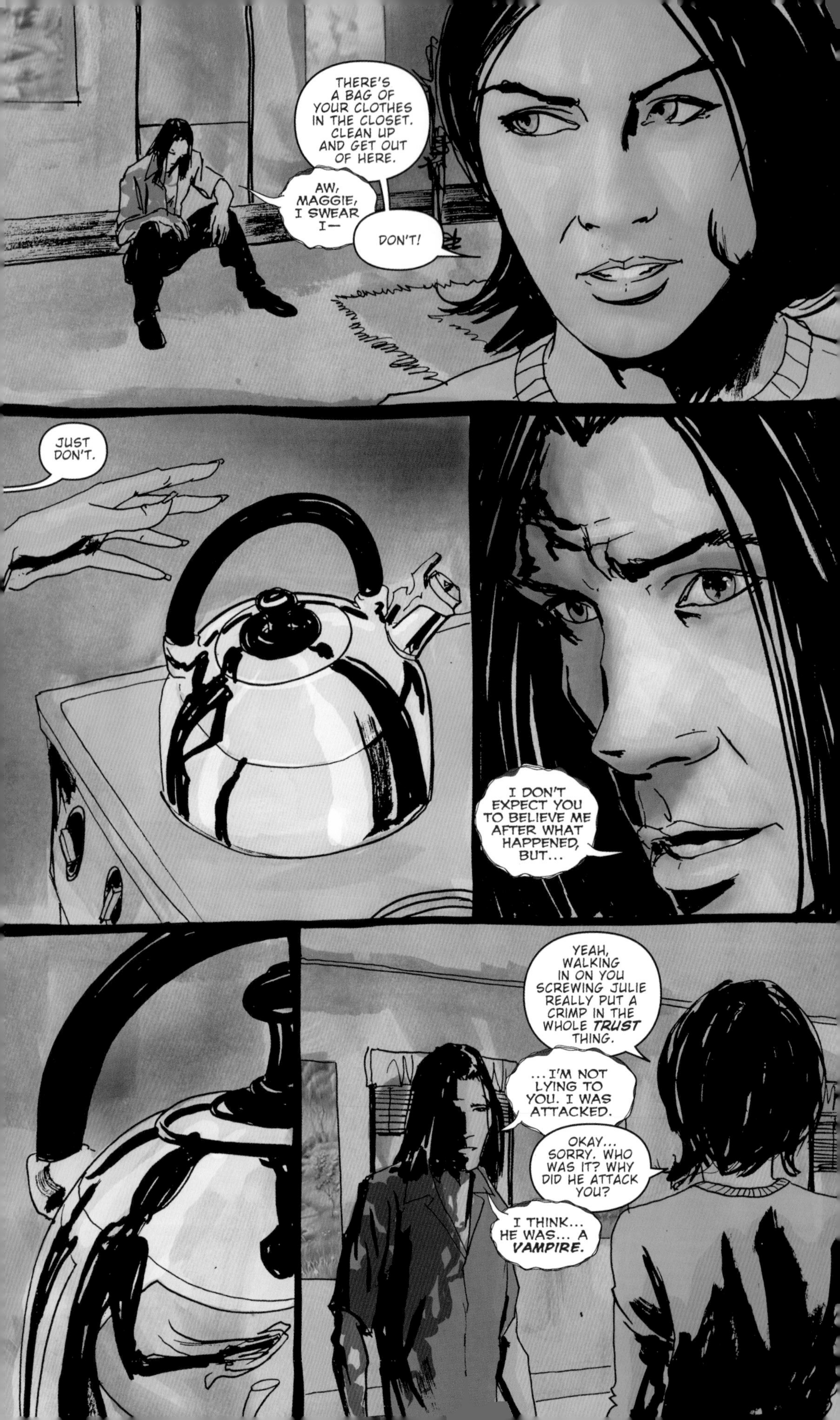
THERE'S A BAG OF YOUR CLOTHES IN THE CLOSET. CLEAN UP AND GET OUT OF HERE.
AW, MAGGIE, I SWEAR I—
DON'T!
JUST DON'T.
I DON'T EXPECT YOU TO BELIEVE ME AFTER WHAT HAPPENED, BUT...
YEAH, WALKING IN ON YOU SCREWING JULIE REALLY PUT A CRIMP IN THE WHOLE *TRUST* THING.
...I'M NOT LYING TO YOU. I WAS ATTACKED.
OKAY... SORRY. WHO WAS IT? WHY DID HE ATTACK YOU?
I THINK... HE WAS... A *VAMPIRE.*

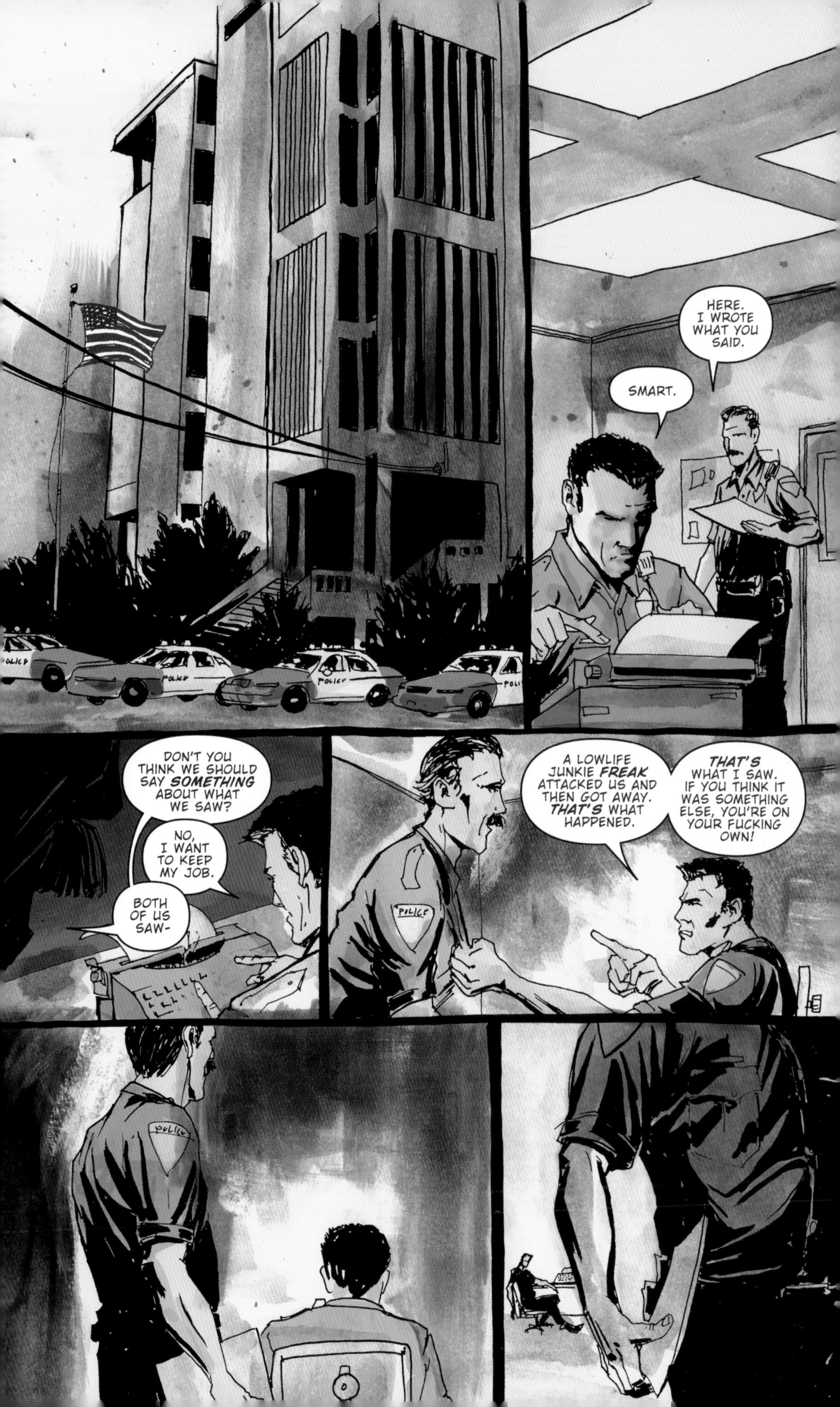

HERE. I WROTE WHAT YOU SAID.
SMART.
DON'T YOU THINK WE SHOULD SAY SOMETHING ABOUT WHAT WE SAW?
NO, I WANT TO KEEP MY JOB.
BOTH OF US SAW-
A LOWLIFE JUNKIE FREAK ATTACKED US AND THEN GOT AWAY. THAT'S WHAT HAPPENED.
THAT'S WHAT I SAW. IF YOU THINK IT WAS SOMETHING ELSE, YOU'RE ON YOUR FUCKING OWN!

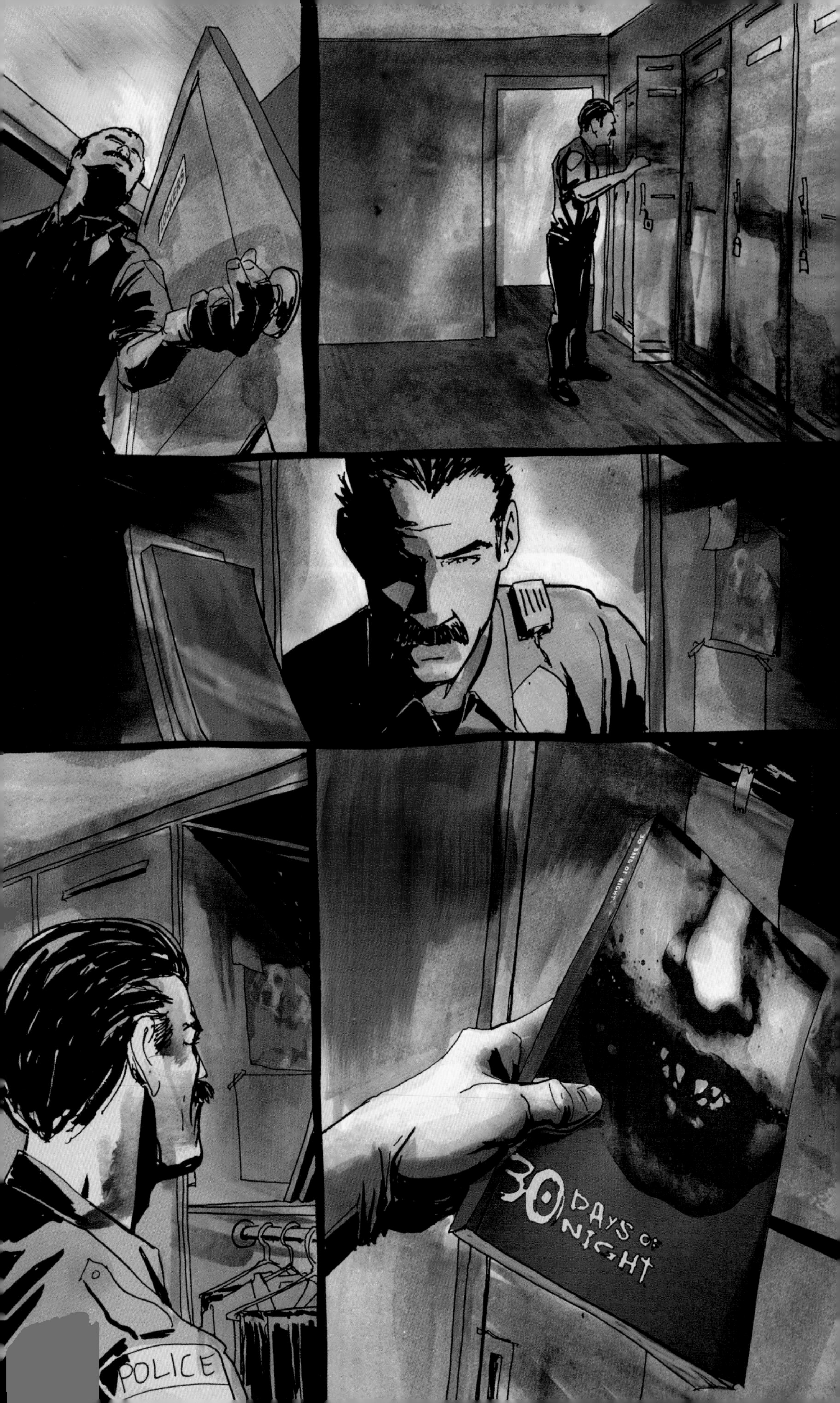
30 DAYS OF NIGHT
POLICE

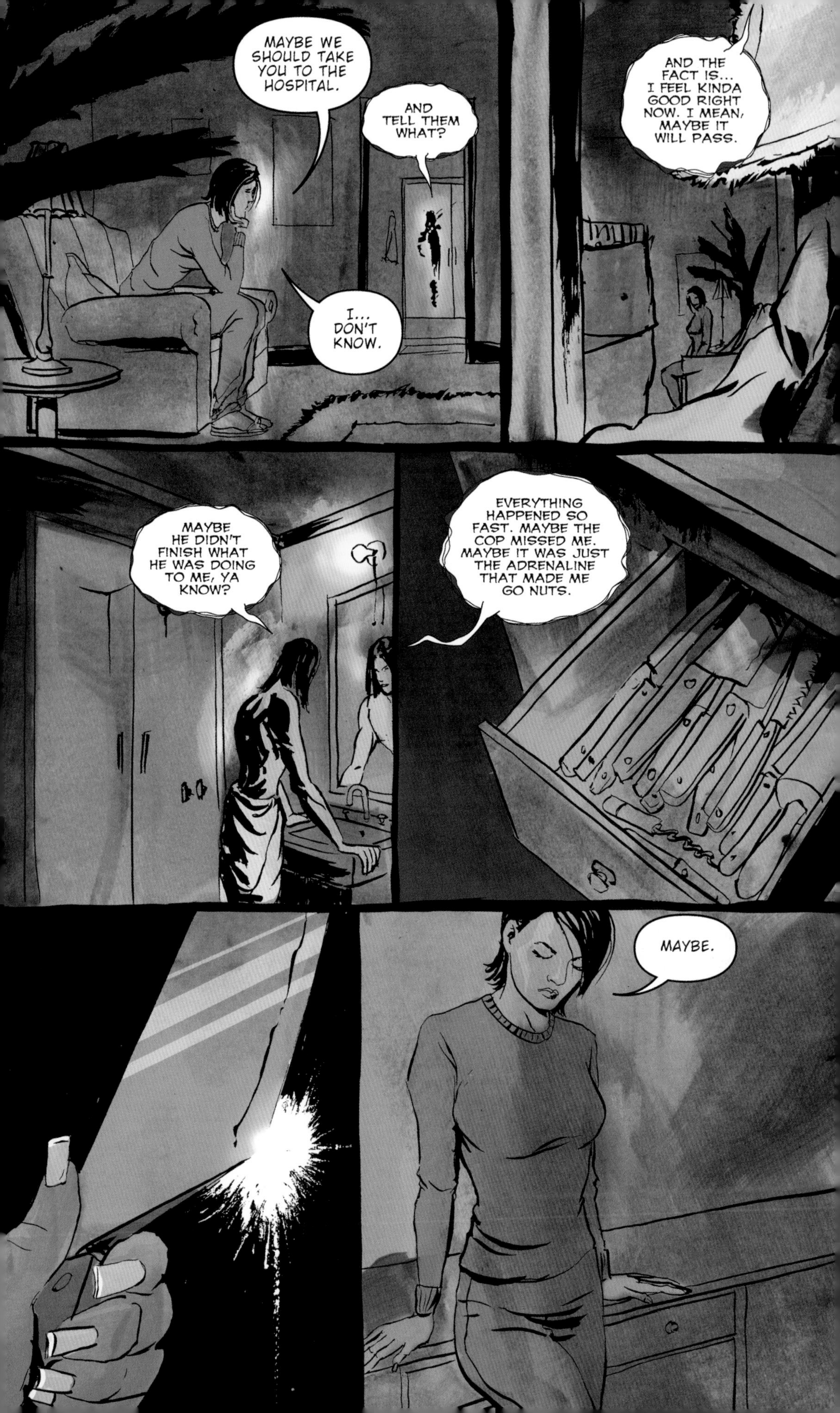
MAYBE WE SHOULD TAKE YOU TO THE HOSPITAL.
AND TELL THEM WHAT?
I... DON'T KNOW.
AND THE FACT IS... I FEEL KINDA GOOD RIGHT NOW. I MEAN, MAYBE IT WILL PASS.
MAYBE HE DIDN'T FINISH WHAT HE WAS DOING TO ME, YA KNOW?
EVERYTHING HAPPENED SO FAST. MAYBE THE COP MISSED ME. MAYBE IT WAS JUST THE ADRENALINE THAT MADE ME GO NUTS.
MAYBE.

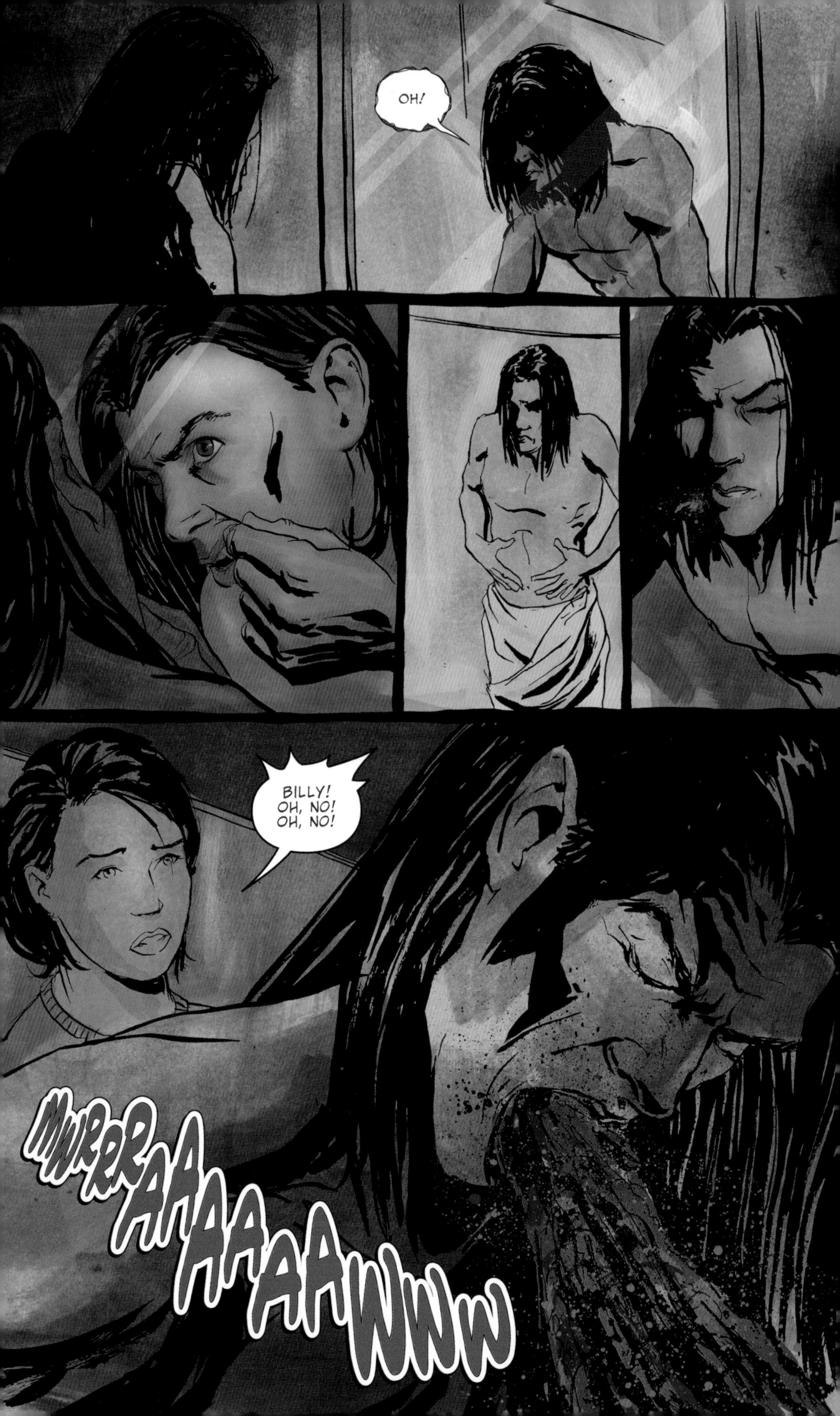
OH!
BILLY! OH, NO! OH, NO!
MWRRRAAAAAAWWWW

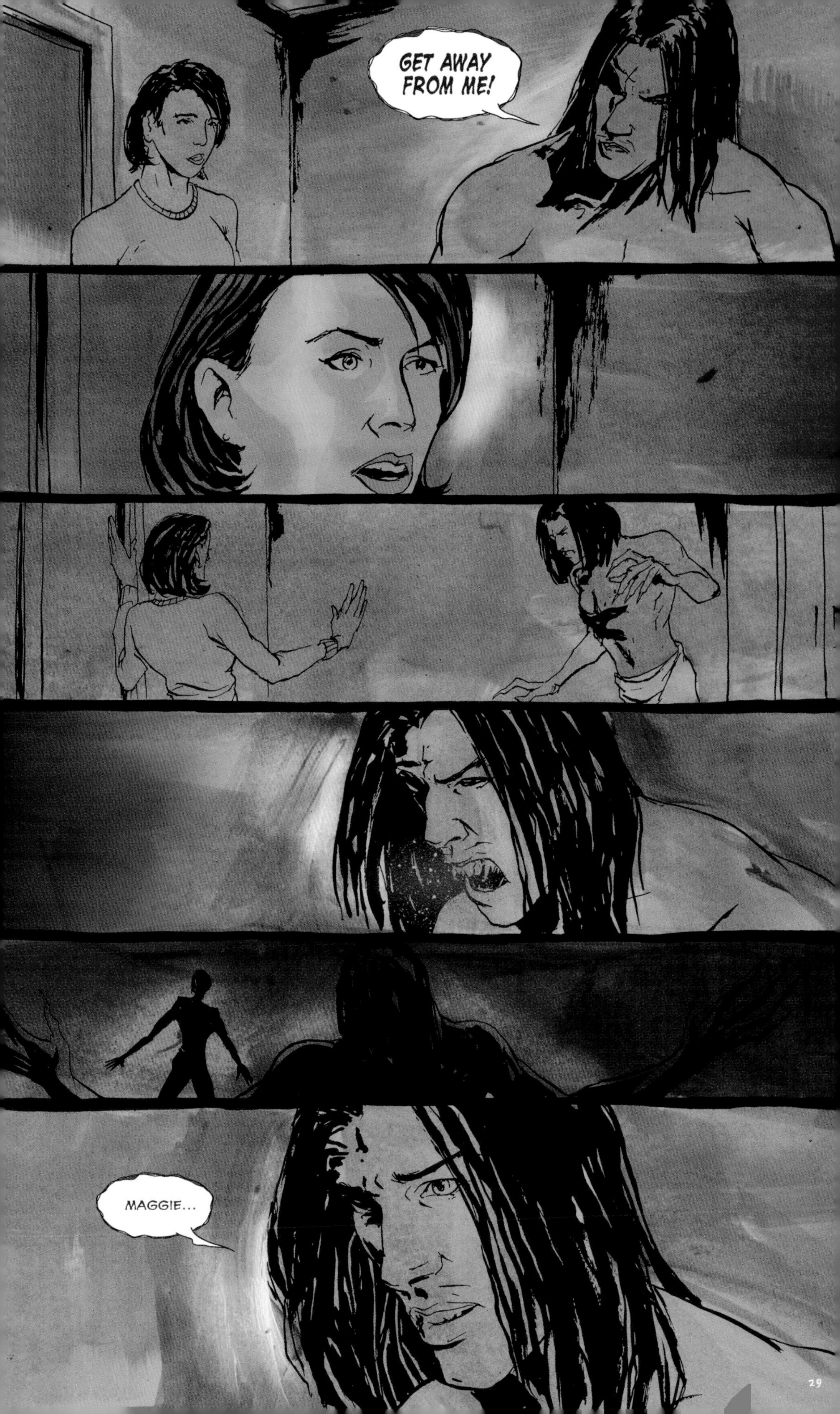
GET AWAY FROM ME!
MAGGIE...

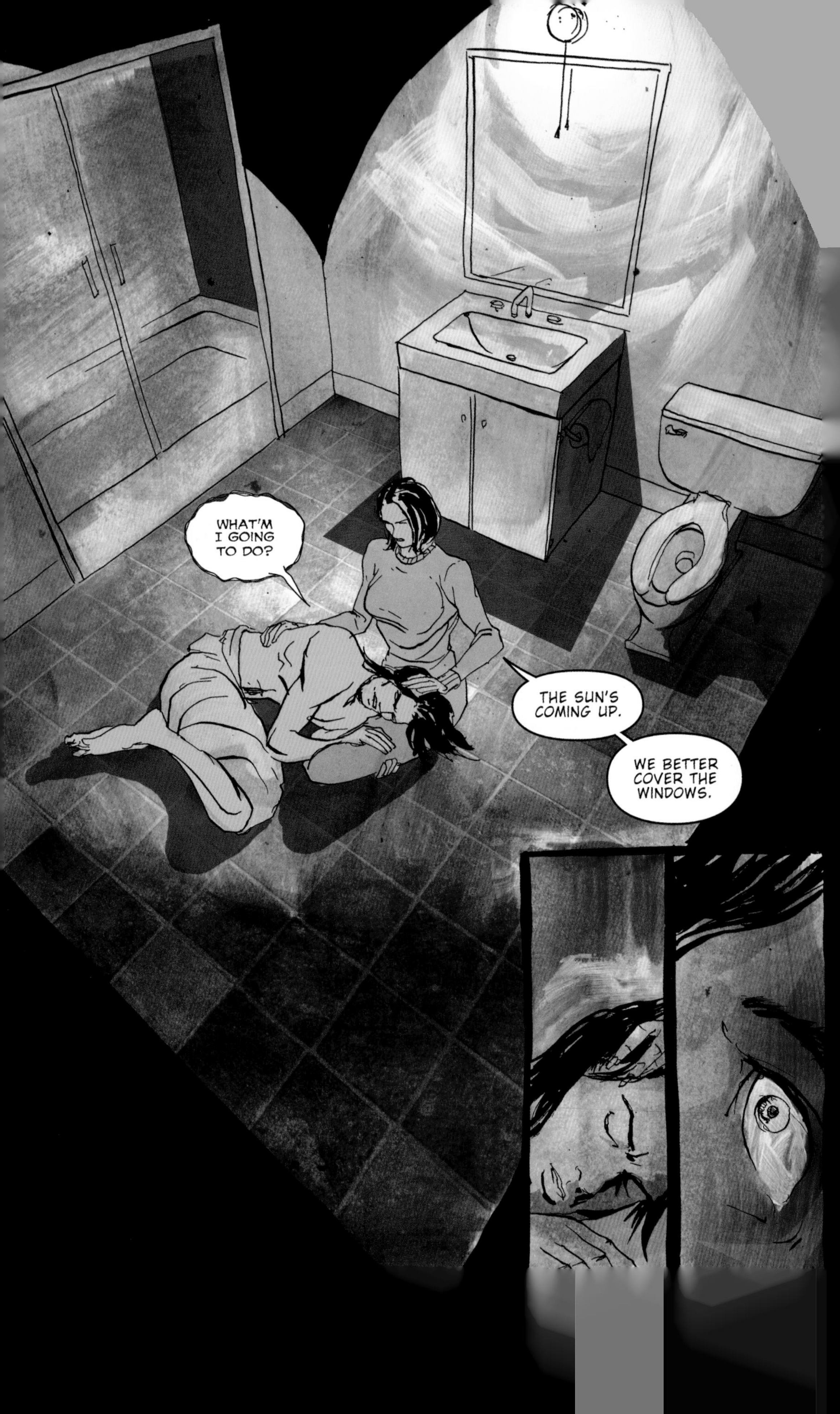
WHAT'M I GOING TO DO?
THE SUN'S COMING UP.
WE BETTER COVER THE WINDOWS.

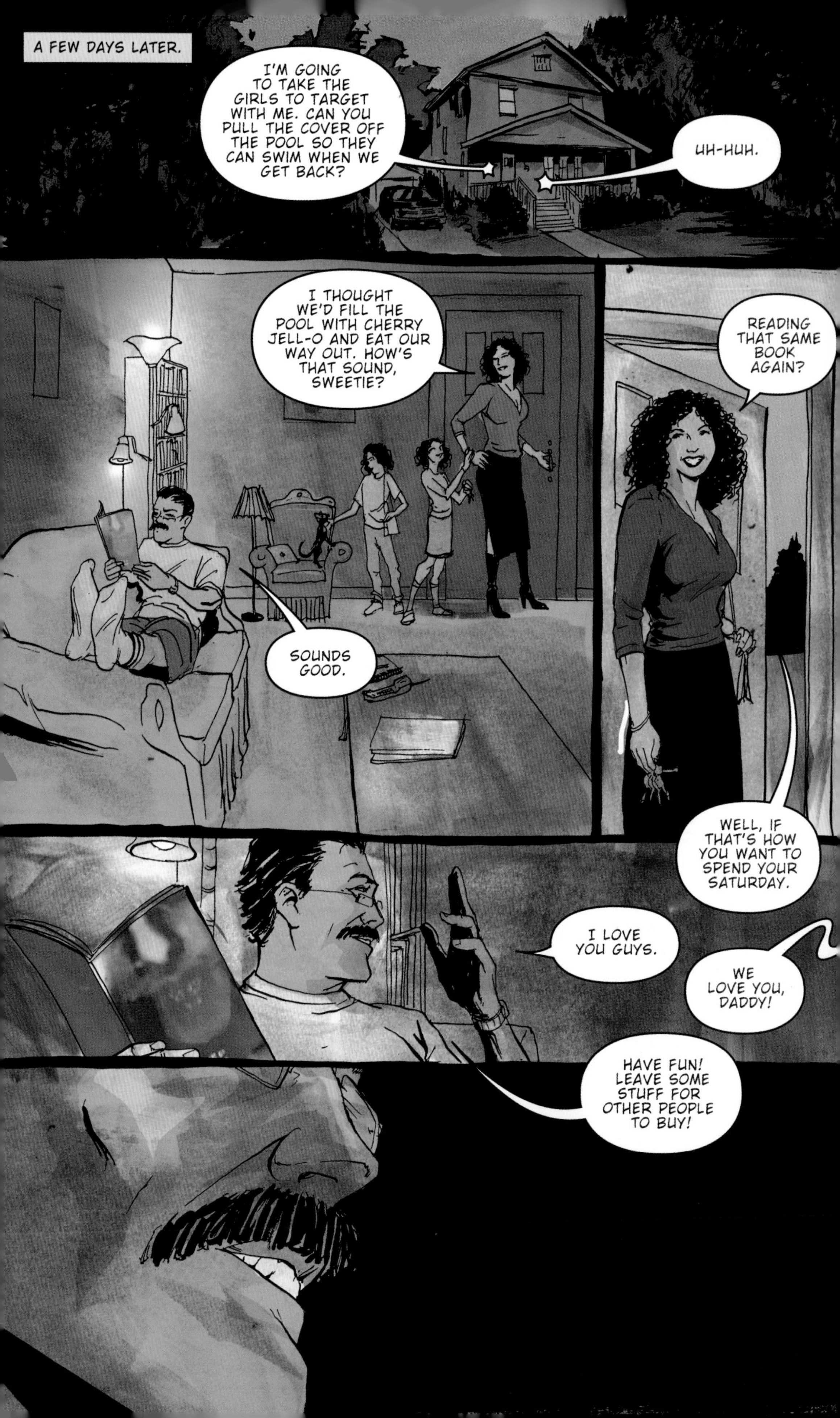

A FEW DAYS LATER.
I'M GOING TO TAKE THE GIRLS TO TARGET WITH ME. CAN YOU PULL THE COVER OFF THE POOL SO THEY CAN SWIM WHEN WE GET BACK?
UH-HUH.
I THOUGHT WE'D FILL THE POOL WITH CHERRY JELL-O AND EAT OUR WAY OUT. HOW'S THAT SOUND, SWEETIE?
SOUNDS GOOD.
READING THAT SAME BOOK AGAIN?
WELL, IF THAT'S HOW YOU WANT TO SPEND YOUR SATURDAY.
I LOVE YOU GUYS.
WE LOVE YOU, DADDY!
HAVE FUN! LEAVE SOME STUFF FOR OTHER PEOPLE TO BUY!

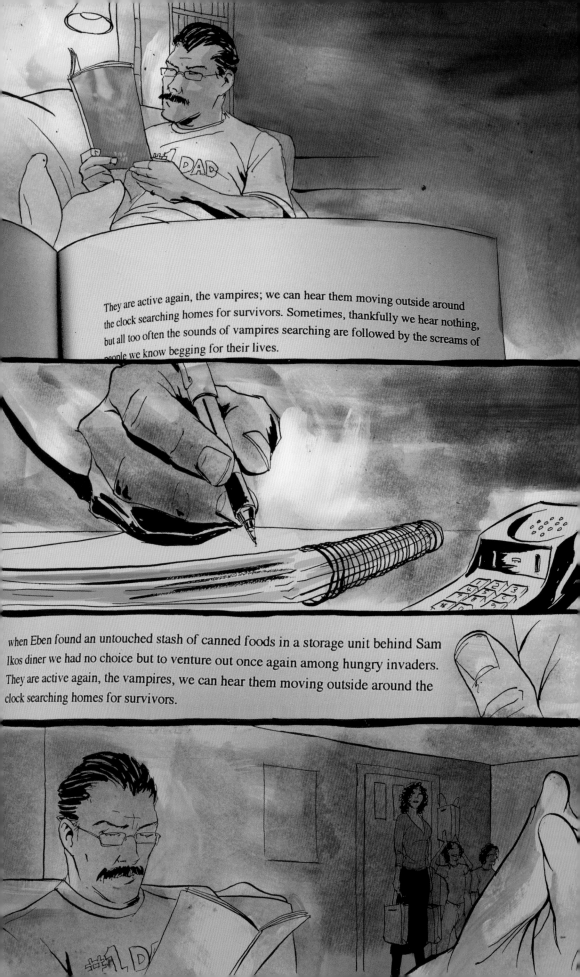

They are active again, the vampires; we can hear them moving outside around the clock searching homes for survivors. Sometimes, thankfully we hear nothing, but all too often the sounds of vampires searching are followed by the screams of people we know begging for their lives.

when Eben found an untouched stash of canned foods in a storage unit behind Sam Ikos diner we had no choice but to venture out once again among hungry invaders. They are active again, the vampires, we can hear them moving outside around the clock searching homes for survivors.

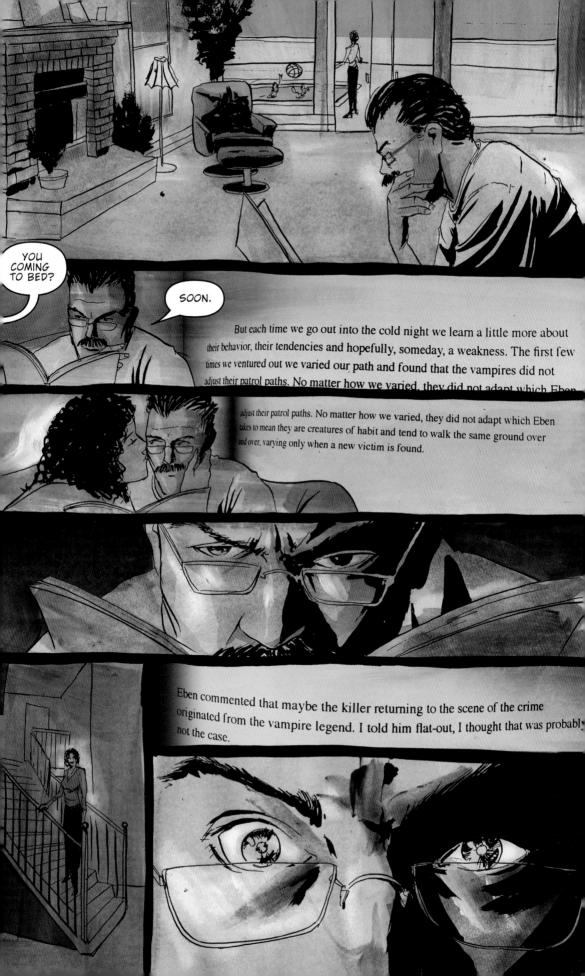

YOU COMING TO BED?

SOON.

But each time we go out into the cold night we learn a little more about their behavior, their tendencies and hopefully, someday, a weakness. The first few times we ventured out we varied our path and found that the vampires did not adjust their patrol paths. No matter how we varied, they did not adapt which Eben

adjust their patrol paths. No matter how we varied, they did not adapt which Eben takes to mean they are creatures of habit and tend to walk the same ground over and over, varying only when a new victim is found.

Eben commented that maybe the killer returning to the scene of the crime originated from the vampire legend. I told him flat-out, I thought that was probably not the case.

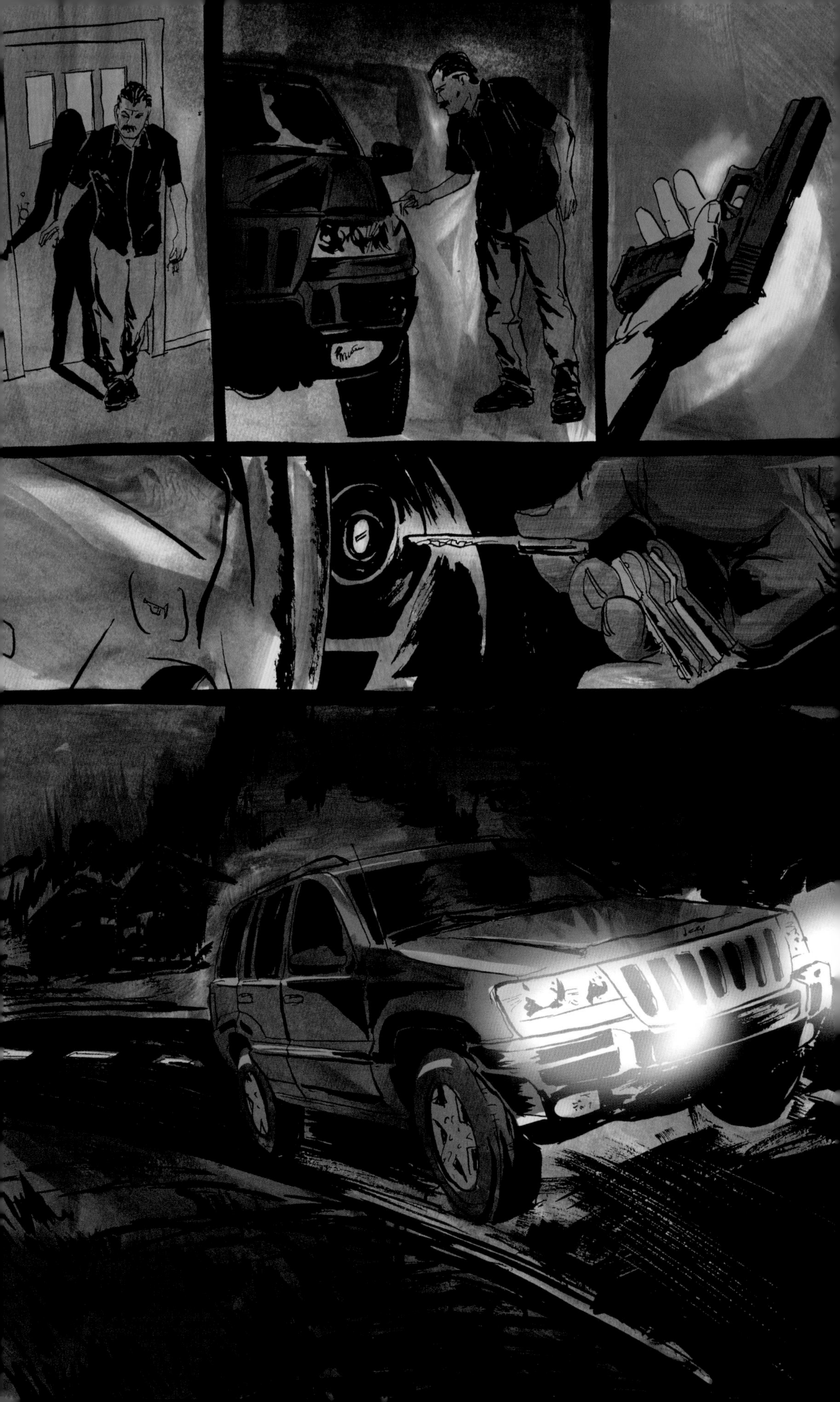

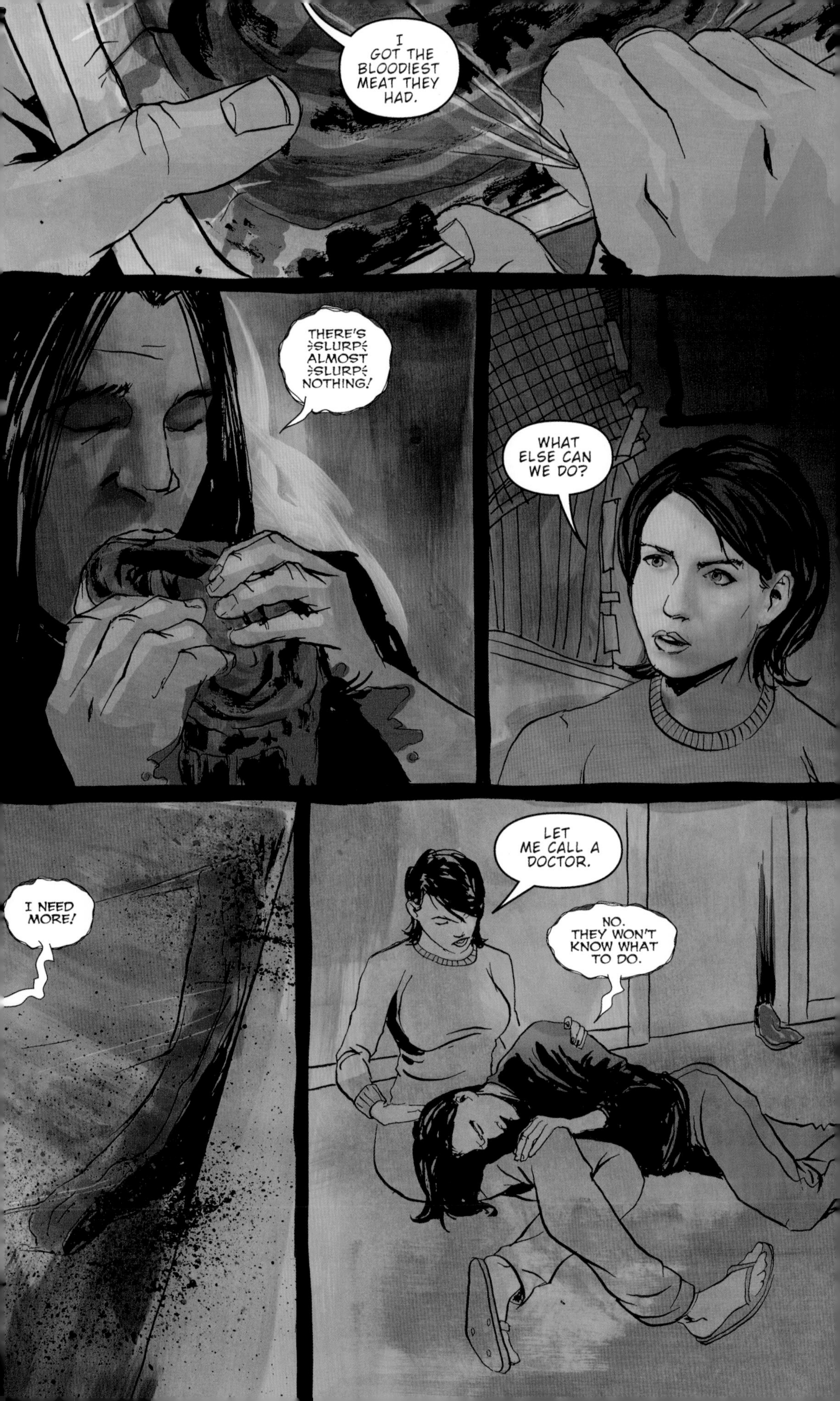

I GOT THE BLOODIEST MEAT THEY HAD.
THERE'S *SLURP* ALMOST *SLURP* NOTHING!
WHAT ELSE CAN WE DO?
I NEED MORE!
LET ME CALL A DOCTOR.
NO. THEY WON'T KNOW WHAT TO DO.

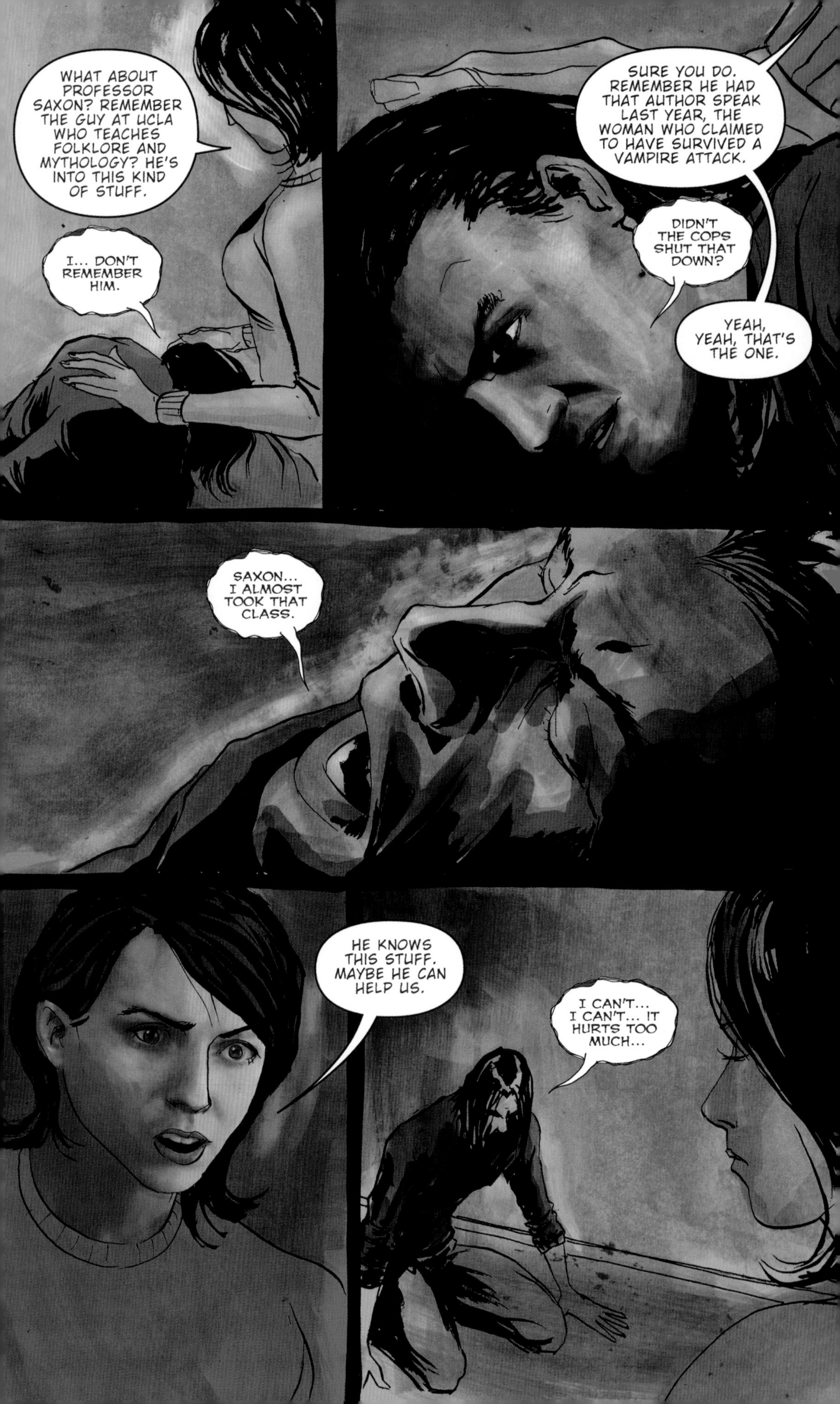
WHAT ABOUT PROFESSOR SAXON? REMEMBER THE GUY AT UCLA WHO TEACHES FOLKLORE AND MYTHOLOGY? HE'S INTO THIS KIND OF STUFF.
I... DON'T REMEMBER HIM.
SURE YOU DO. REMEMBER HE HAD THAT AUTHOR SPEAK LAST YEAR, THE WOMAN WHO CLAIMED TO HAVE SURVIVED A VAMPIRE ATTACK.
DIDN'T THE COPS SHUT THAT DOWN?
YEAH, YEAH, THAT'S THE ONE.
SAXON... I ALMOST TOOK THAT CLASS.
HE KNOWS THIS STUFF. MAYBE HE CAN HELP US.
I CAN'T... I CAN'T... IT HURTS TOO MUCH...

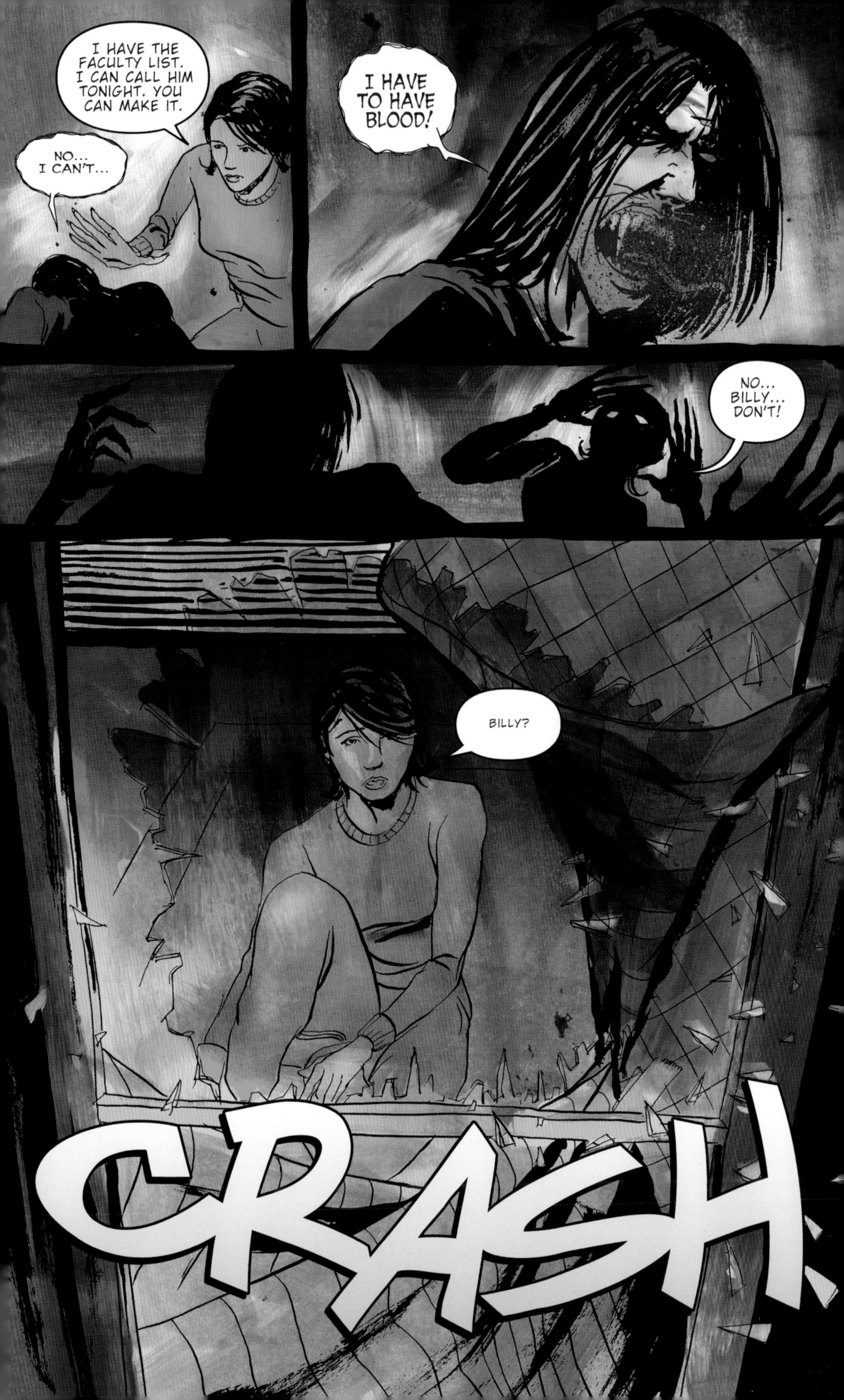

I HAVE THE FACULTY LIST. I CAN CALL HIM TONIGHT. YOU CAN MAKE IT.
NO... I CAN'T...
I HAVE TO HAVE BLOOD!
NO... BILLY... DON'T!
BILLY?
CRASH!

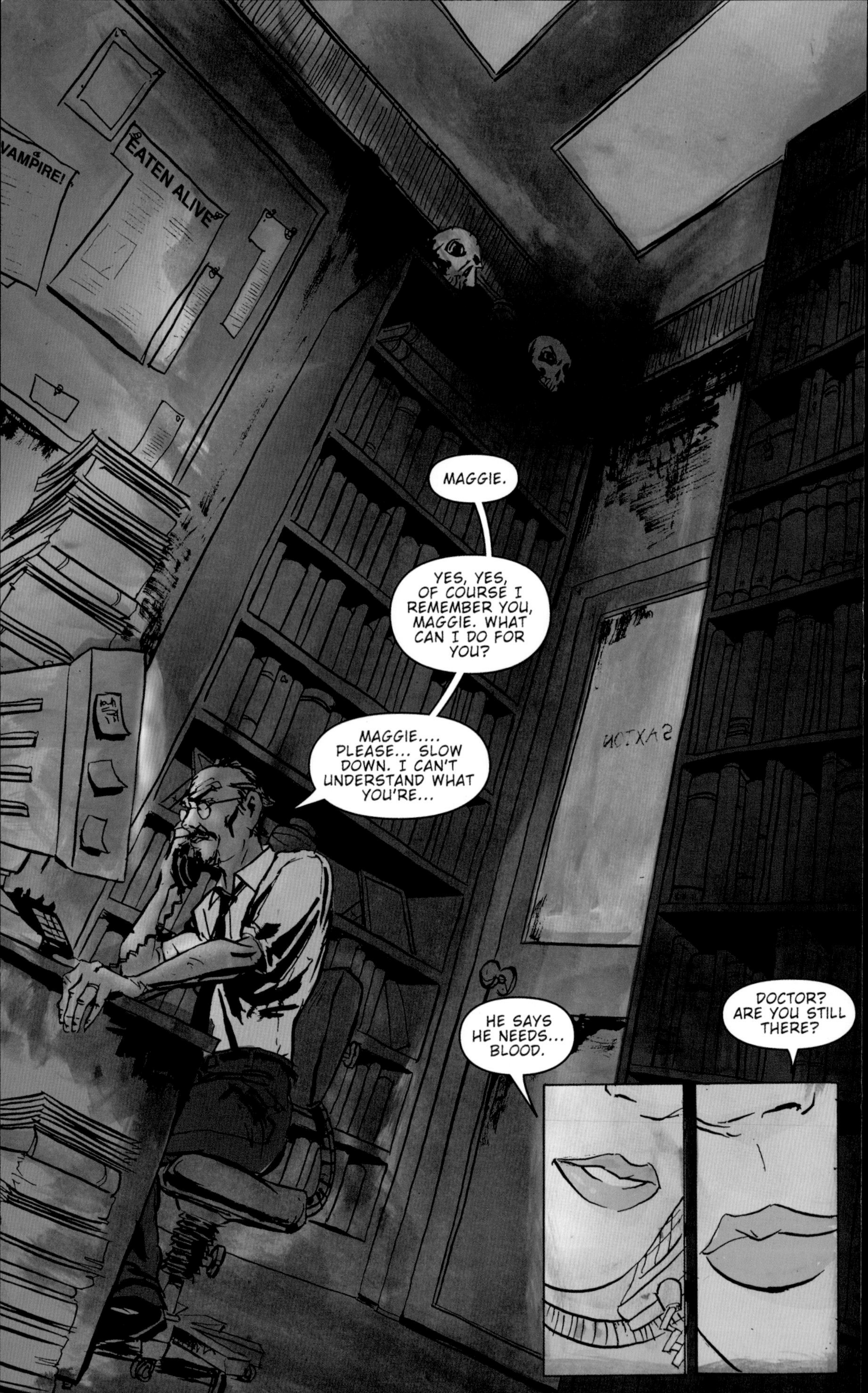
VAMPIRE!
EATEN ALIVE
SAXTON
MAGGIE.
YES, YES, OF COURSE I REMEMBER YOU, MAGGIE. WHAT CAN I DO FOR YOU?
MAGGIE.... PLEASE... SLOW DOWN. I CAN'T UNDERSTAND WHAT YOU'RE...
HE SAYS HE NEEDS... BLOOD.
DOCTOR? ARE YOU STILL THERE?

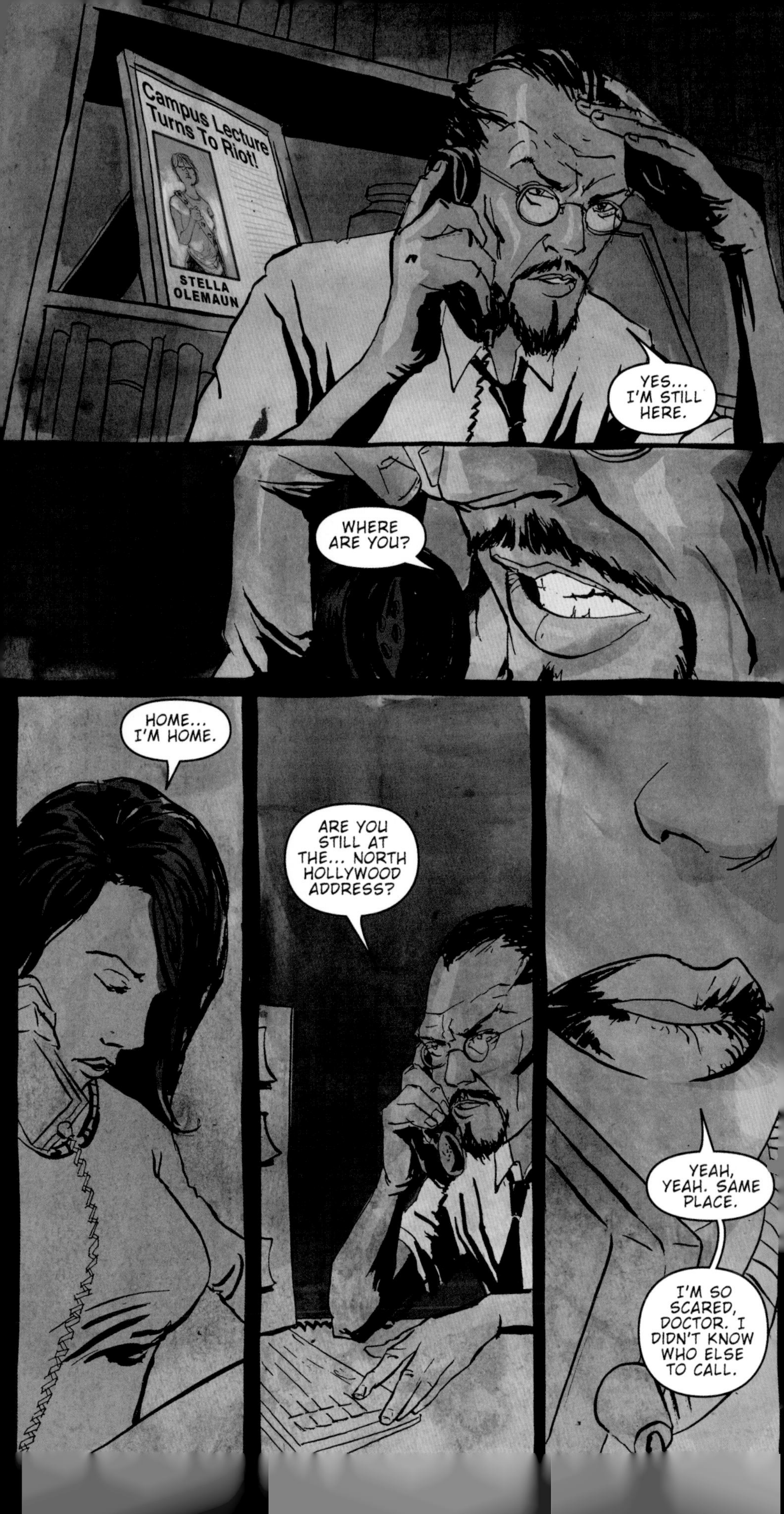
Campus Lecture Turns To Riot!
STELLA OLEMAUN
YES... I'M STILL HERE.
WHERE ARE YOU?
HOME... I'M HOME.
ARE YOU STILL AT THE... NORTH HOLLYWOOD ADDRESS?
YEAH, YEAH. SAME PLACE.
I'M SO SCARED, DOCTOR. I DIDN'T KNOW WHO ELSE TO CALL.

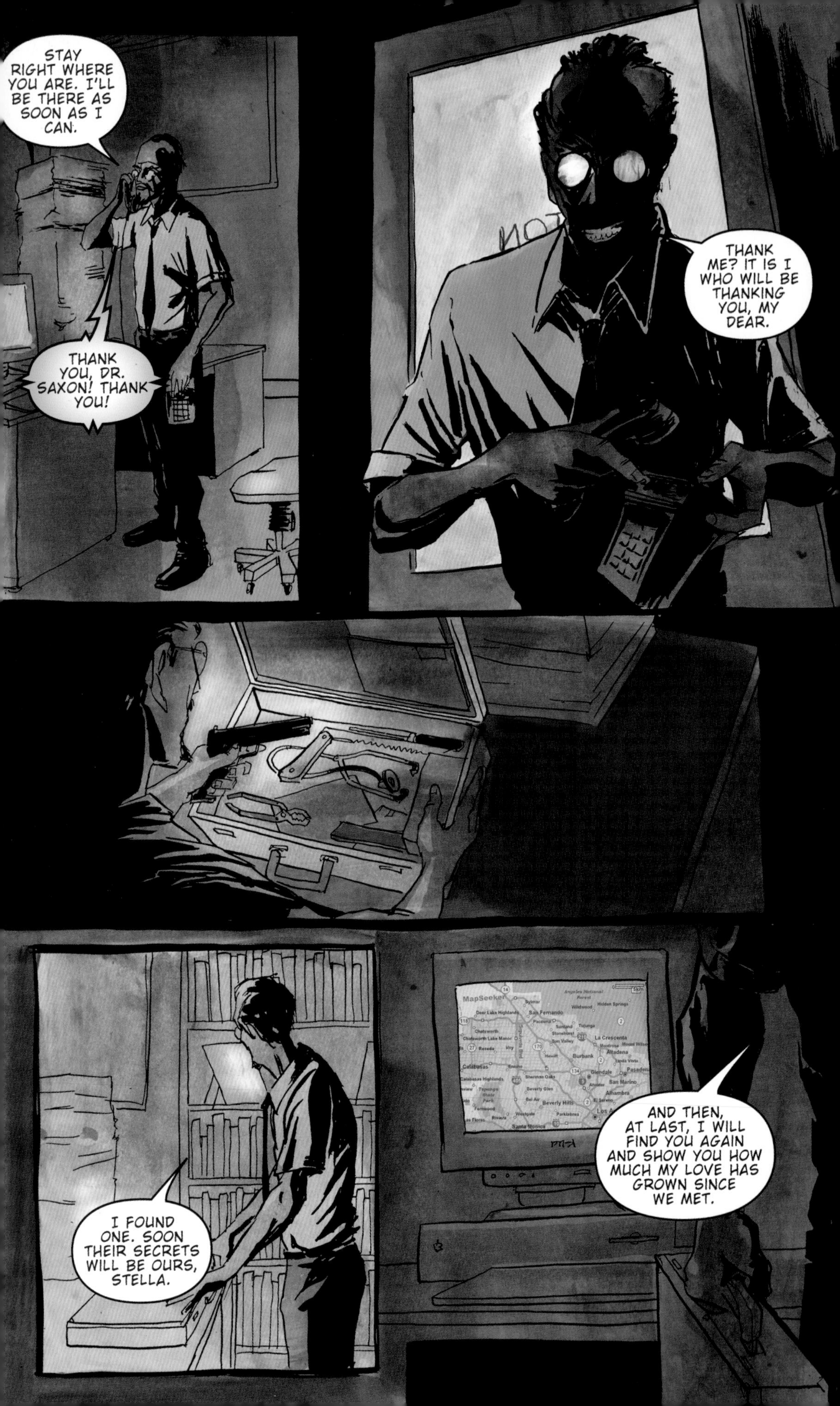
STAY RIGHT WHERE YOU ARE. I'LL BE THERE AS SOON AS I CAN.
THANK YOU, DR. SAXON! THANK YOU!
THANK ME? IT IS I WHO WILL BE THANKING YOU, MY DEAR.
I FOUND ONE. SOON THEIR SECRETS WILL BE OURS, STELLA.
AND THEN, AT LAST, I WILL FIND YOU AGAIN AND SHOW YOU HOW MUCH MY LOVE HAS GROWN SINCE WE MET.

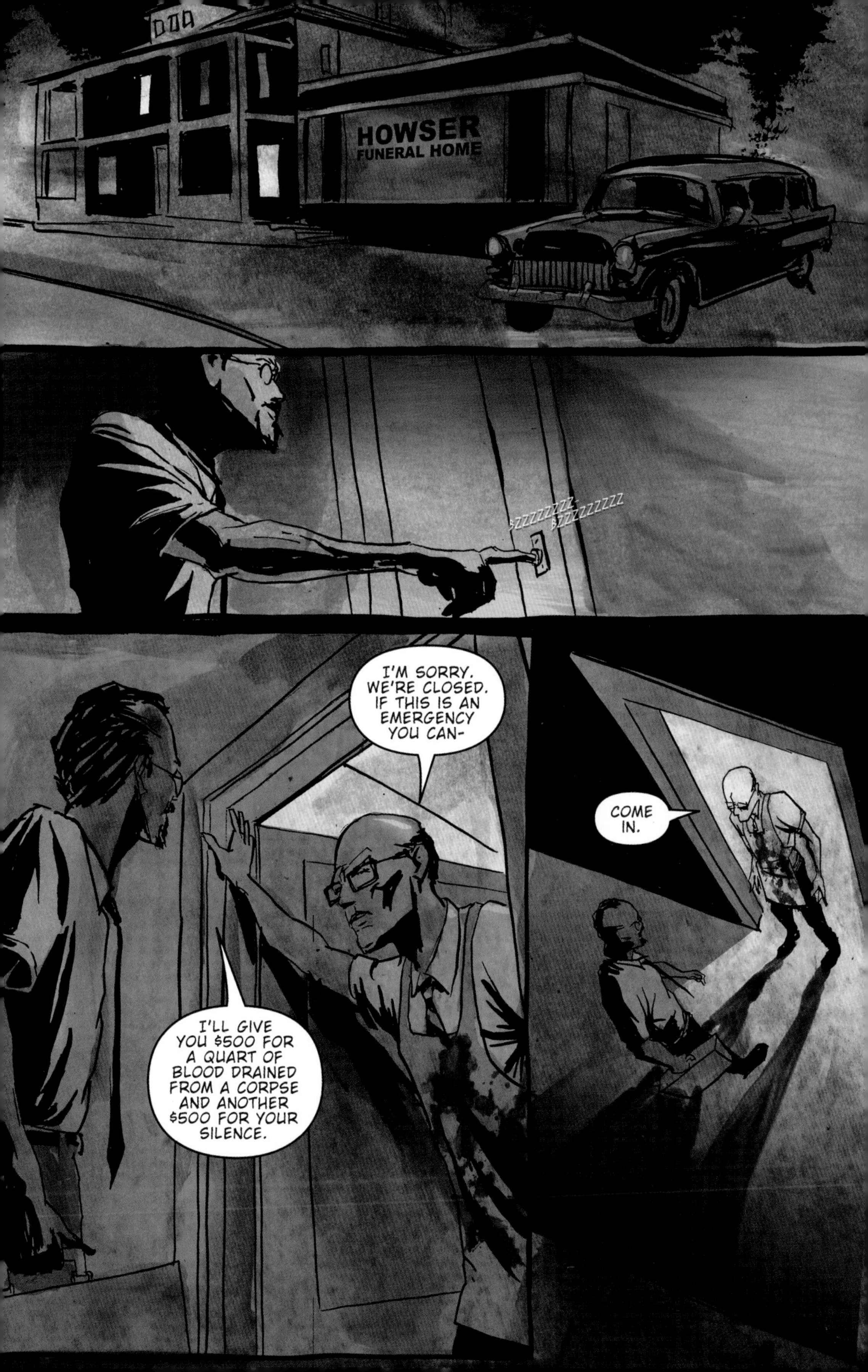
HOWSER
FUNERAL HOME
BZZZZZZZZZ-
BZZZZZZZZZZ
I'M SORRY. WE'RE CLOSED. IF THIS IS AN EMERGENCY YOU CAN-
I'LL GIVE YOU $500 FOR A QUART OF BLOOD DRAINED FROM A CORPSE AND ANOTHER $500 FOR YOUR SILENCE.
COME IN.

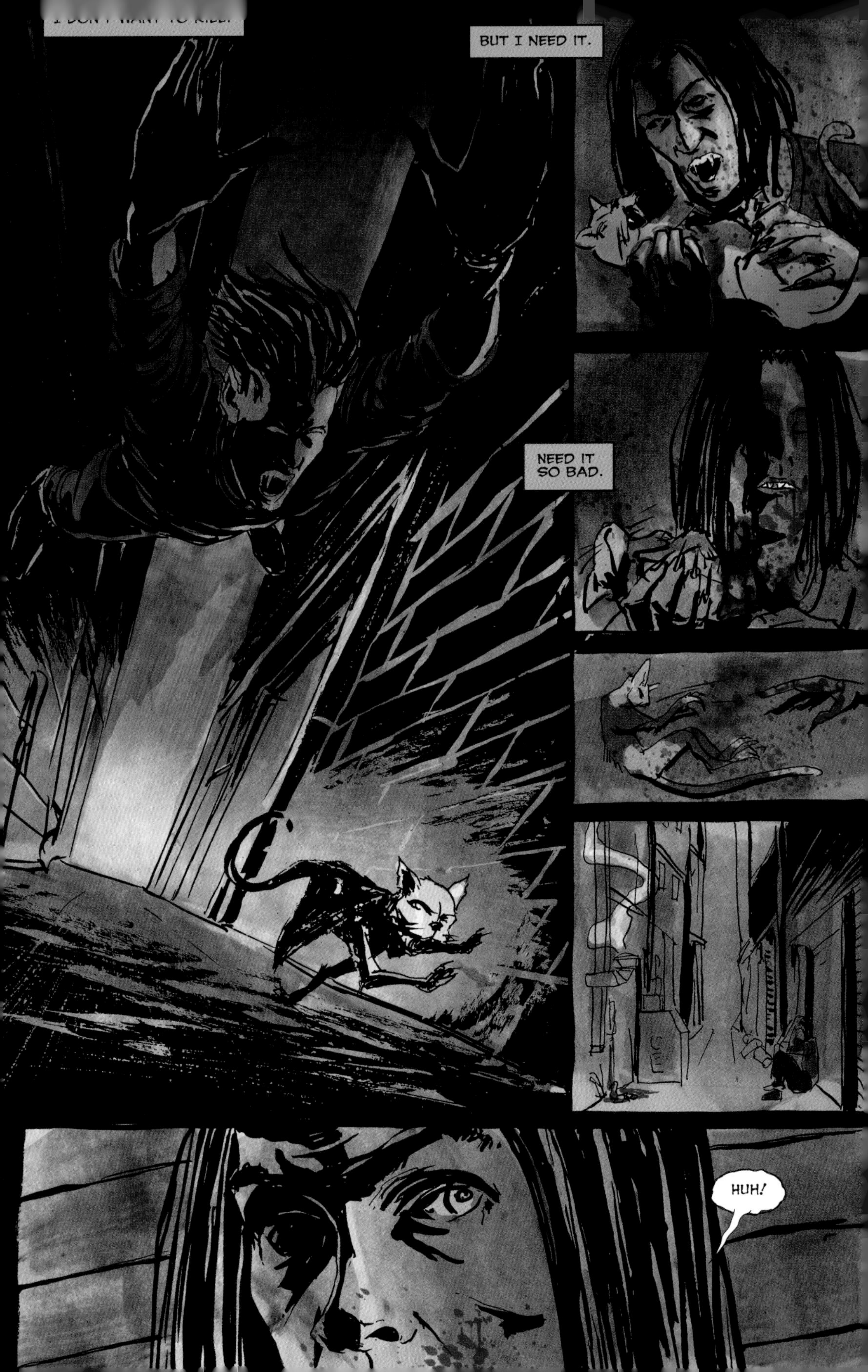

BUT I NEED IT.
NEED IT SO BAD.
HUH!

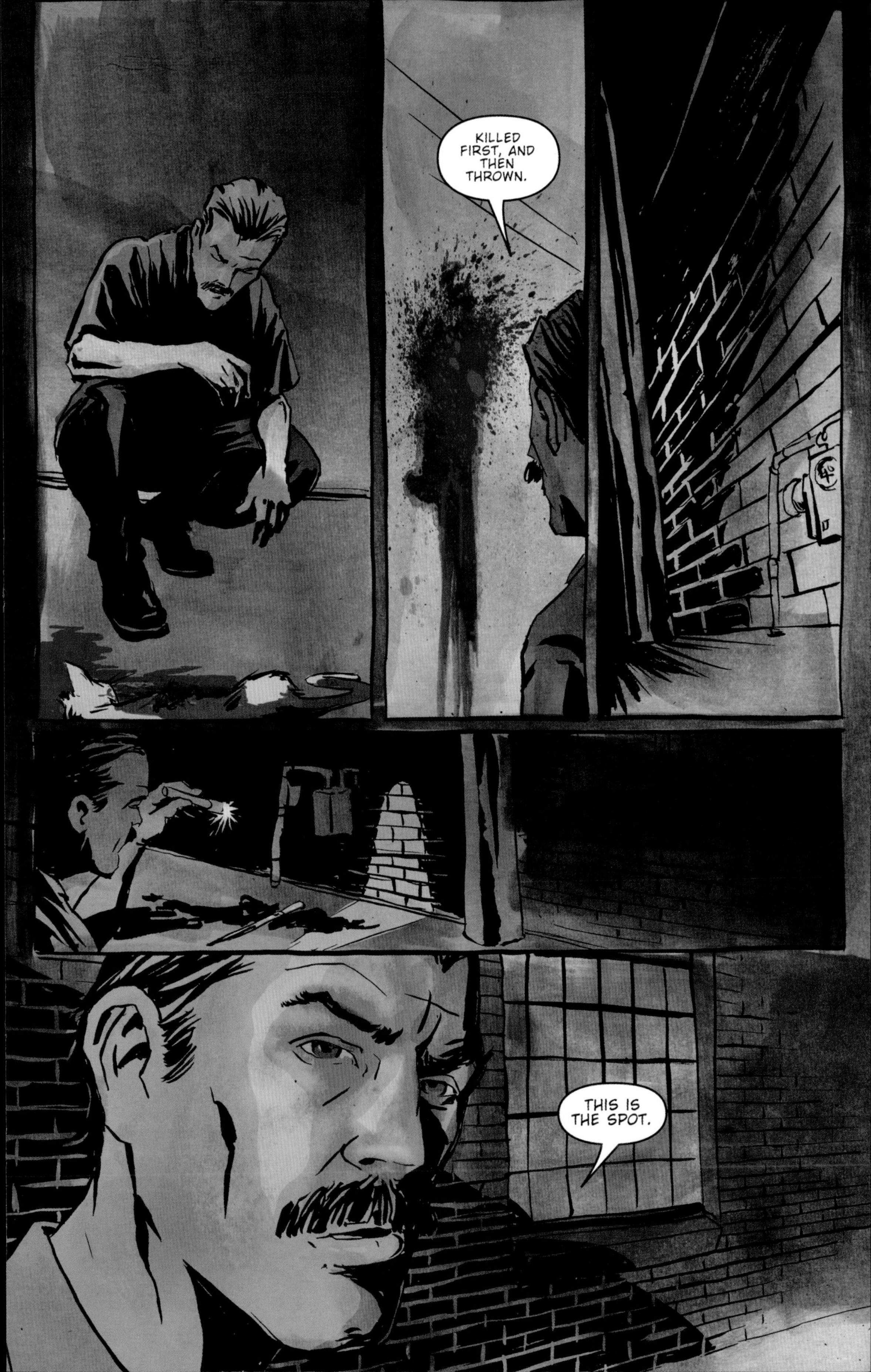
KILLED FIRST, AND THEN THROWN.
THIS IS THE SPOT.

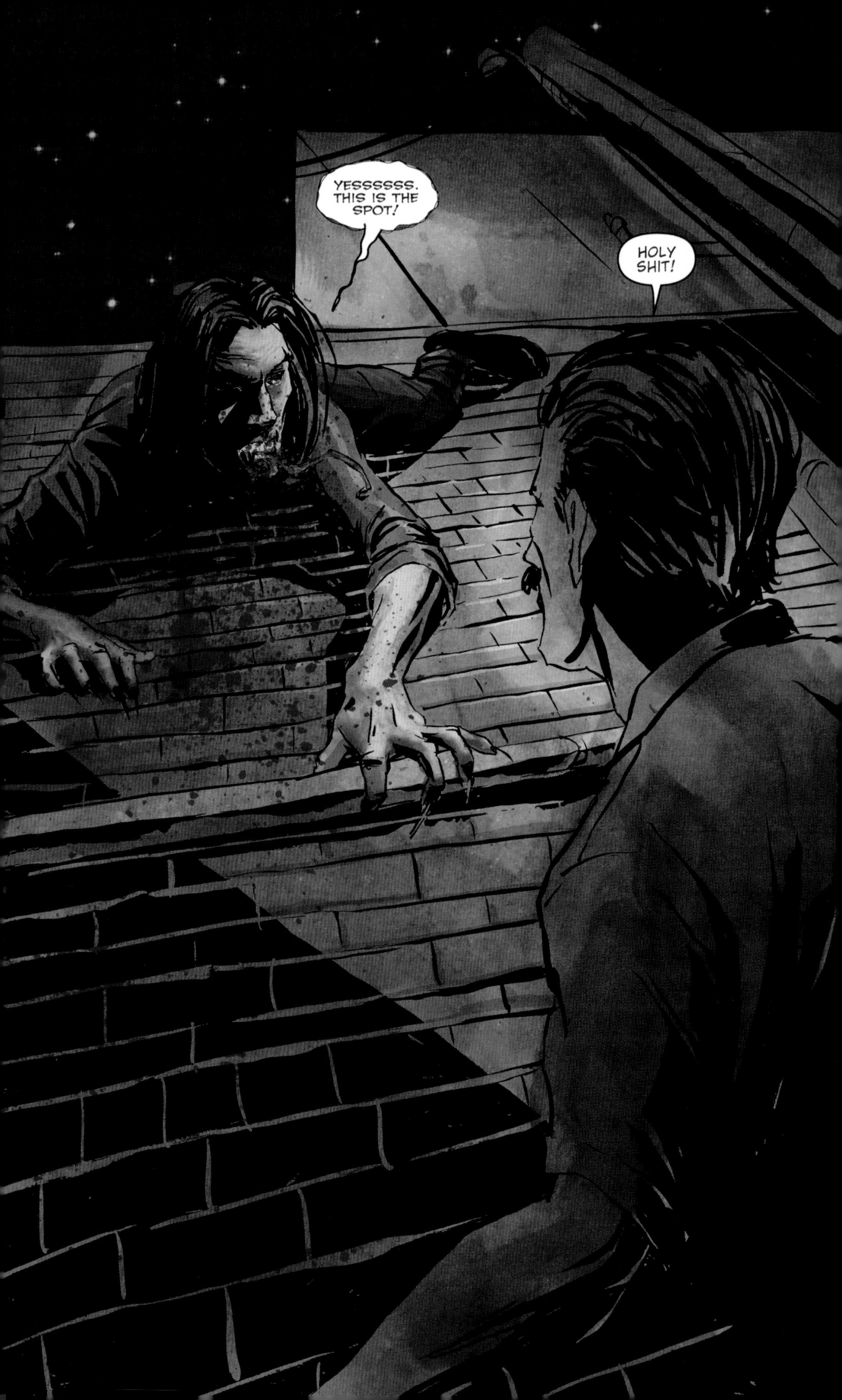

YESSSSSS. THIS IS THE SPOT!
HOLY SHIT!

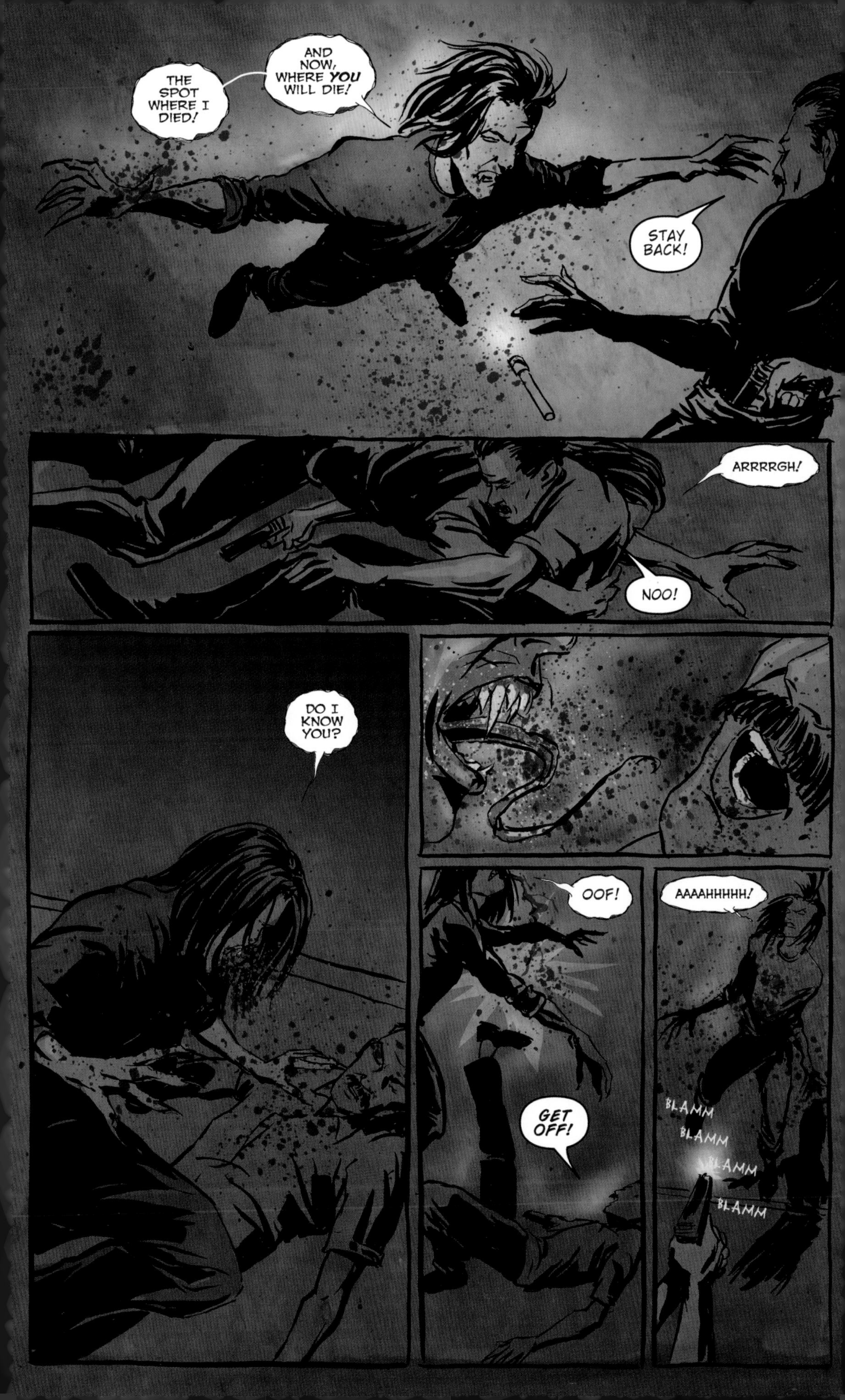
THE SPOT WHERE I DIED!
AND NOW, WHERE YOU WILL DIE!
STAY BACK!
ARRRRGH!
NOO!
DO I KNOW YOU?
OOF!
GET OFF!
AAAAHHHHH!
BLAMM
BLAMM
BLAMM
BLAMM

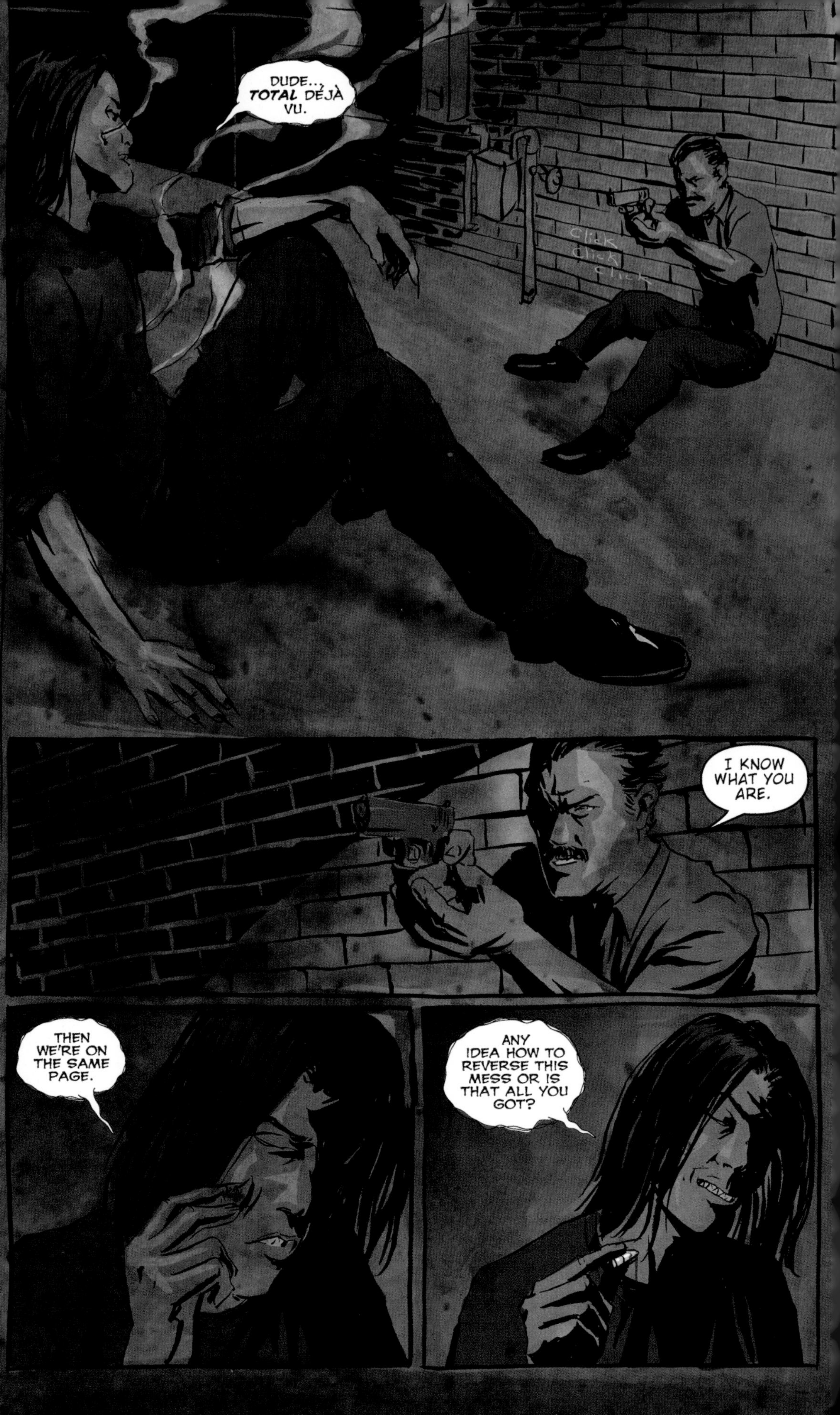
DUDE..., TOTAL DÉJÀ VU.
click click click
I KNOW WHAT YOU ARE.
THEN WE'RE ON THE SAME PAGE.
ANY IDEA HOW TO REVERSE THIS MESS OR IS THAT ALL YOU GOT?

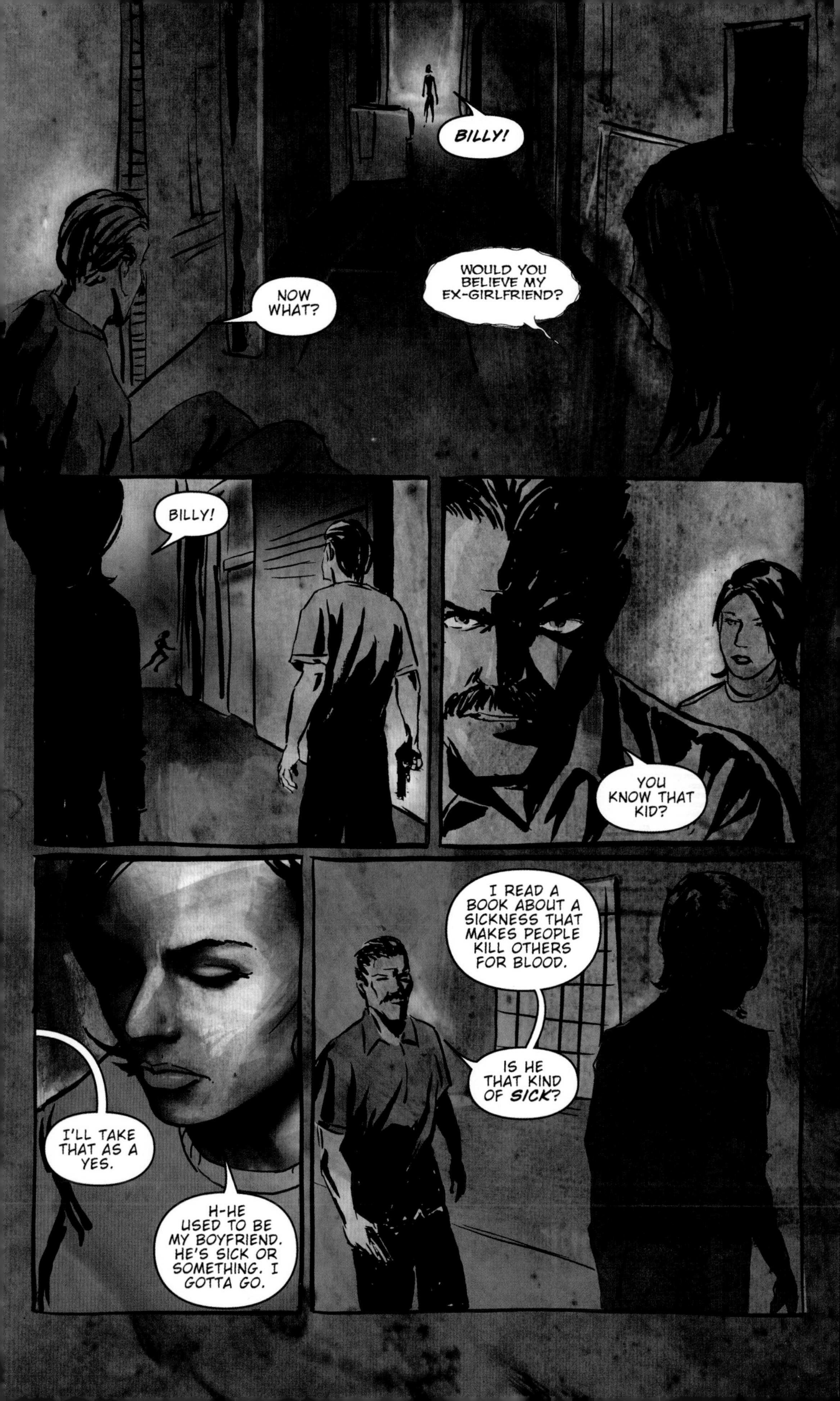
BILLY!
NOW WHAT?
WOULD YOU BELIEVE MY EX-GIRLFRIEND?
BILLY!
YOU KNOW THAT KID?
I'LL TAKE THAT AS A YES.
H-HE USED TO BE MY BOYFRIEND. HE'S SICK OR SOMETHING. I GOTTA GO.
I READ A BOOK ABOUT A SICKNESS THAT MAKES PEOPLE KILL OTHERS FOR BLOOD.
IS HE THAT KIND OF SICK?

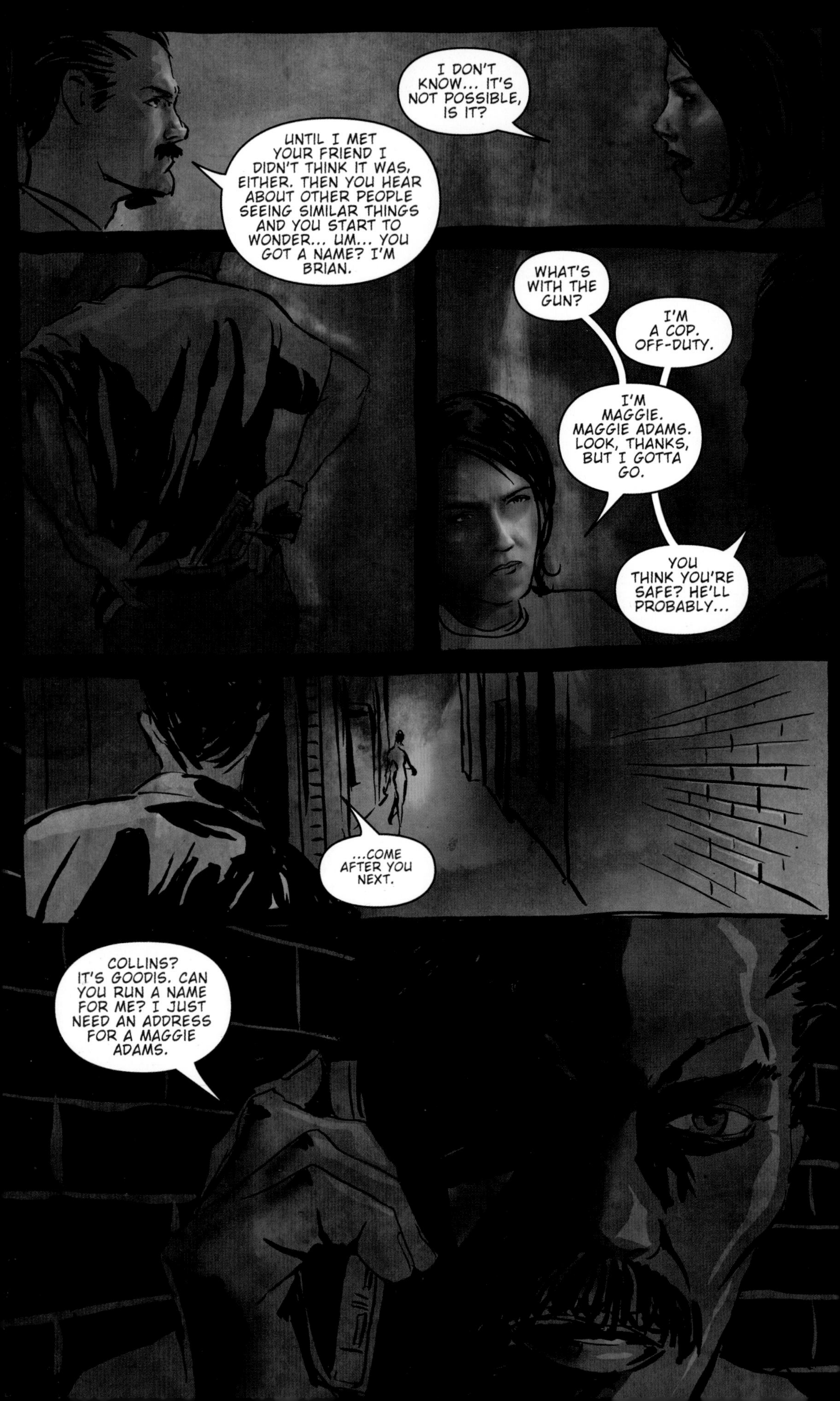

I DON'T KNOW... IT'S NOT POSSIBLE, IS IT?
UNTIL I MET YOUR FRIEND I DIDN'T THINK IT WAS, EITHER. THEN YOU HEAR ABOUT OTHER PEOPLE SEEING SIMILAR THINGS AND YOU START TO WONDER... UM... YOU GOT A NAME? I'M BRIAN.
WHAT'S WITH THE GUN?
I'M A COP. OFF-DUTY.
I'M MAGGIE. MAGGIE ADAMS. LOOK, THANKS, BUT I GOTTA GO.
YOU THINK YOU'RE SAFE? HE'LL PROBABLY...
...COME AFTER YOU NEXT.
COLLINS? IT'S GOODIS. CAN YOU RUN A NAME FOR ME? I JUST NEED AN ADDRESS FOR A MAGGIE ADAMS.

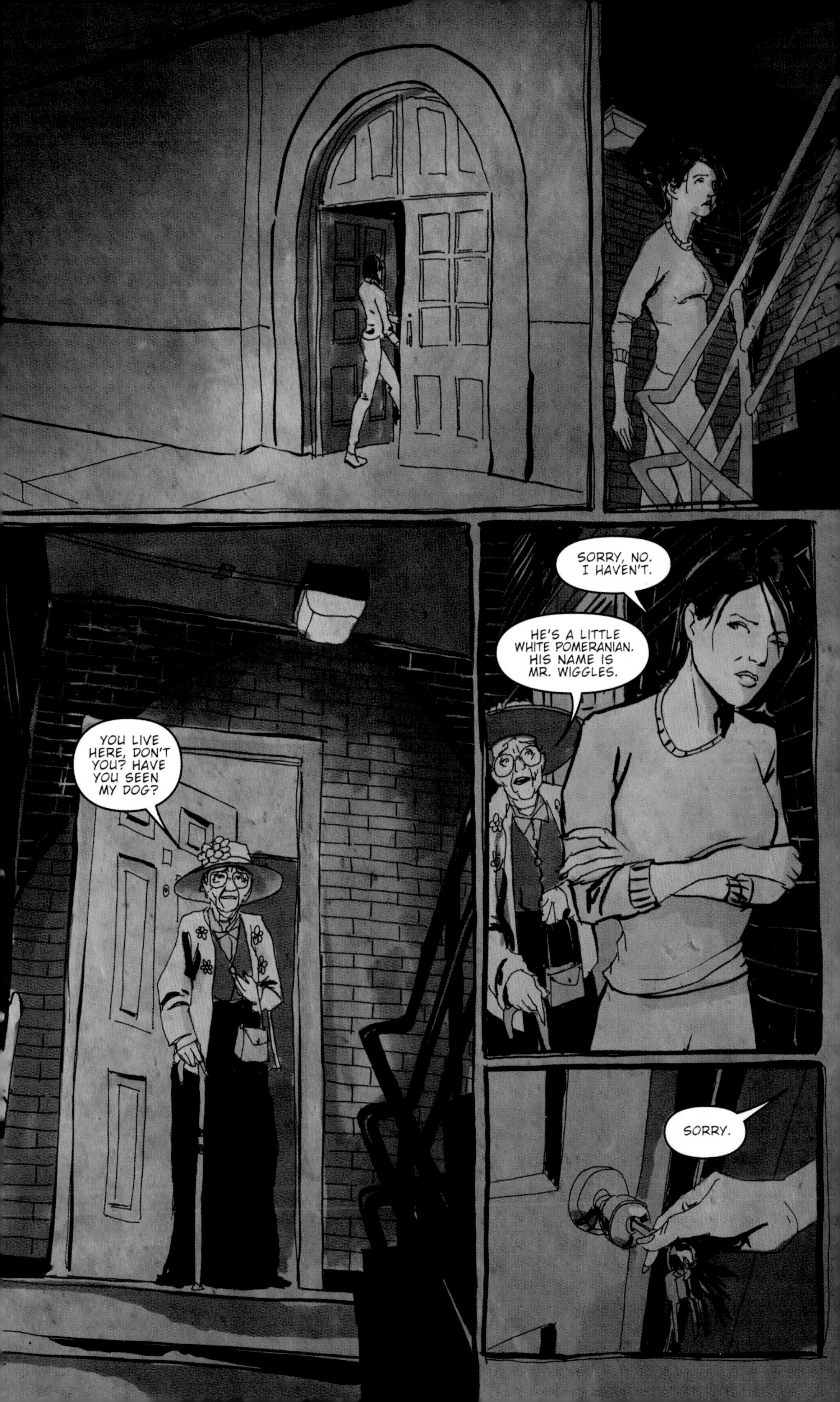
YOU LIVE HERE, DON'T YOU? HAVE YOU SEEN MY DOG?
SORRY, NO. I HAVEN'T.
HE'S A LITTLE WHITE POMERANIAN. HIS NAME IS MR. WIGGLES.
SORRY.

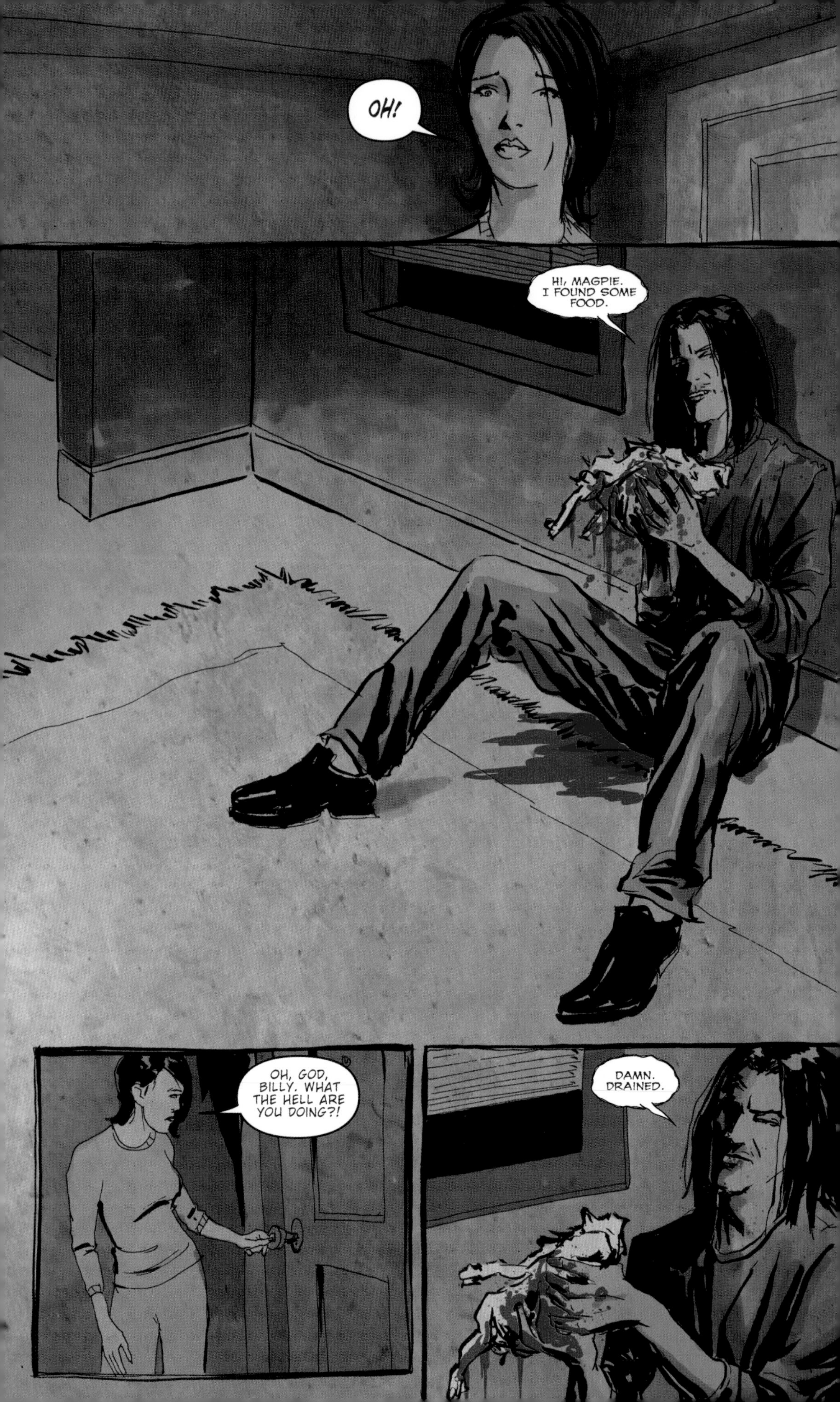
OH!
HI, MAGPIE. I FOUND SOME FOOD.
OH, GOD, BILLY. WHAT THE HELL ARE YOU DOING?!
DAMN. DRAINED.

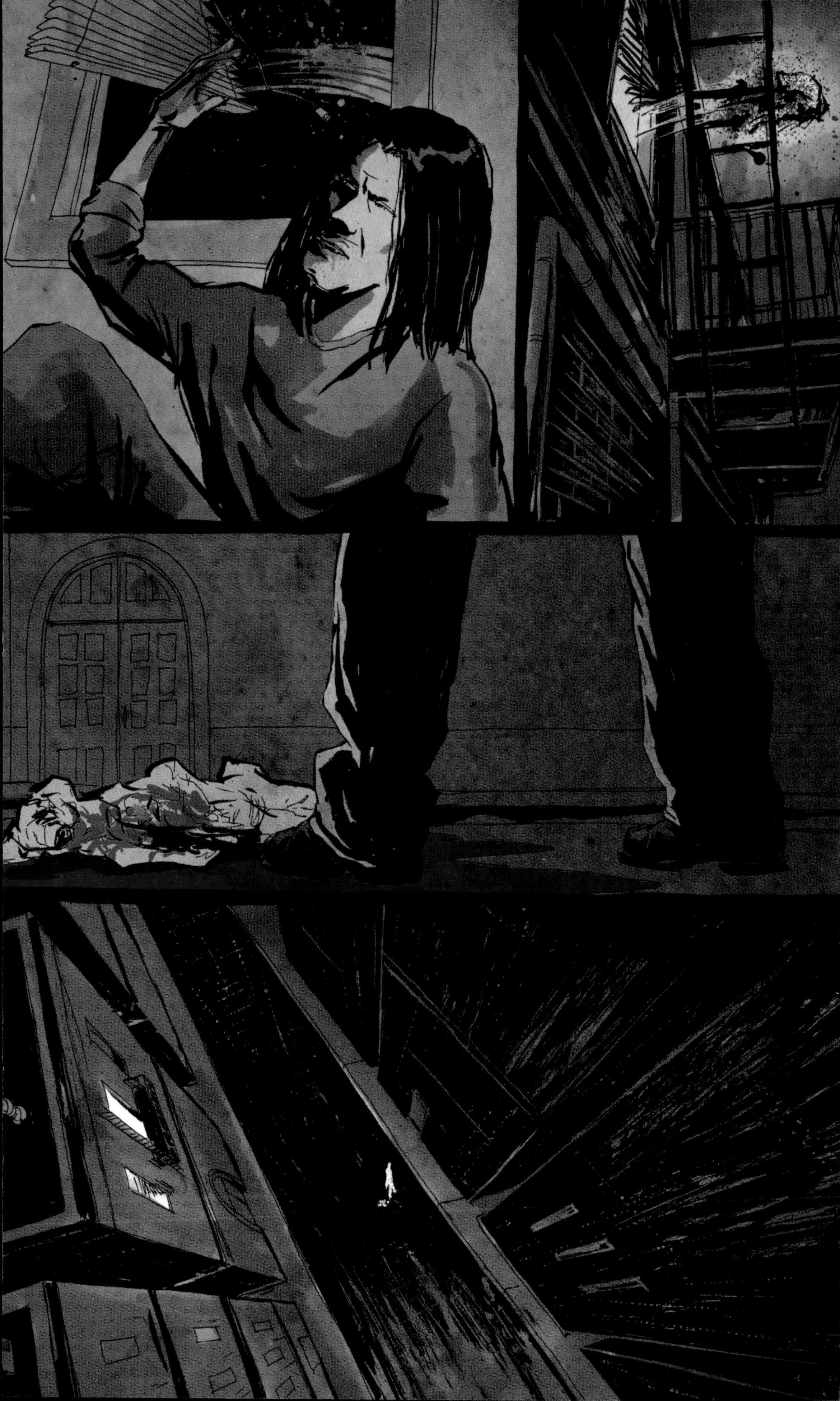

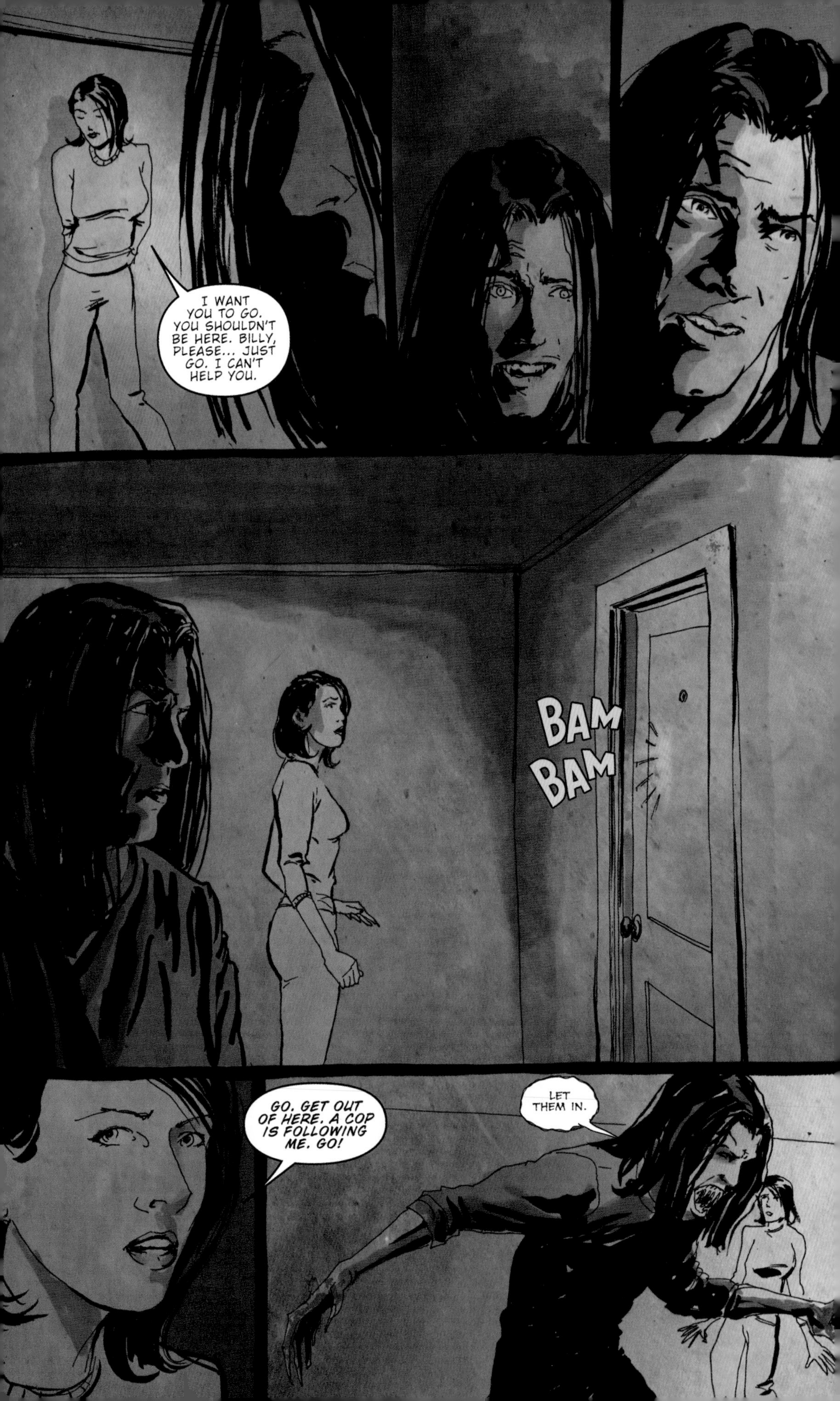
I WANT YOU TO GO. YOU SHOULDN'T BE HERE. BILLY, PLEASE... JUST GO. I CAN'T HELP YOU.
BAM BAM
GO. GET OUT OF HERE. A COP IS FOLLOWING ME. GO!
LET THEM IN.

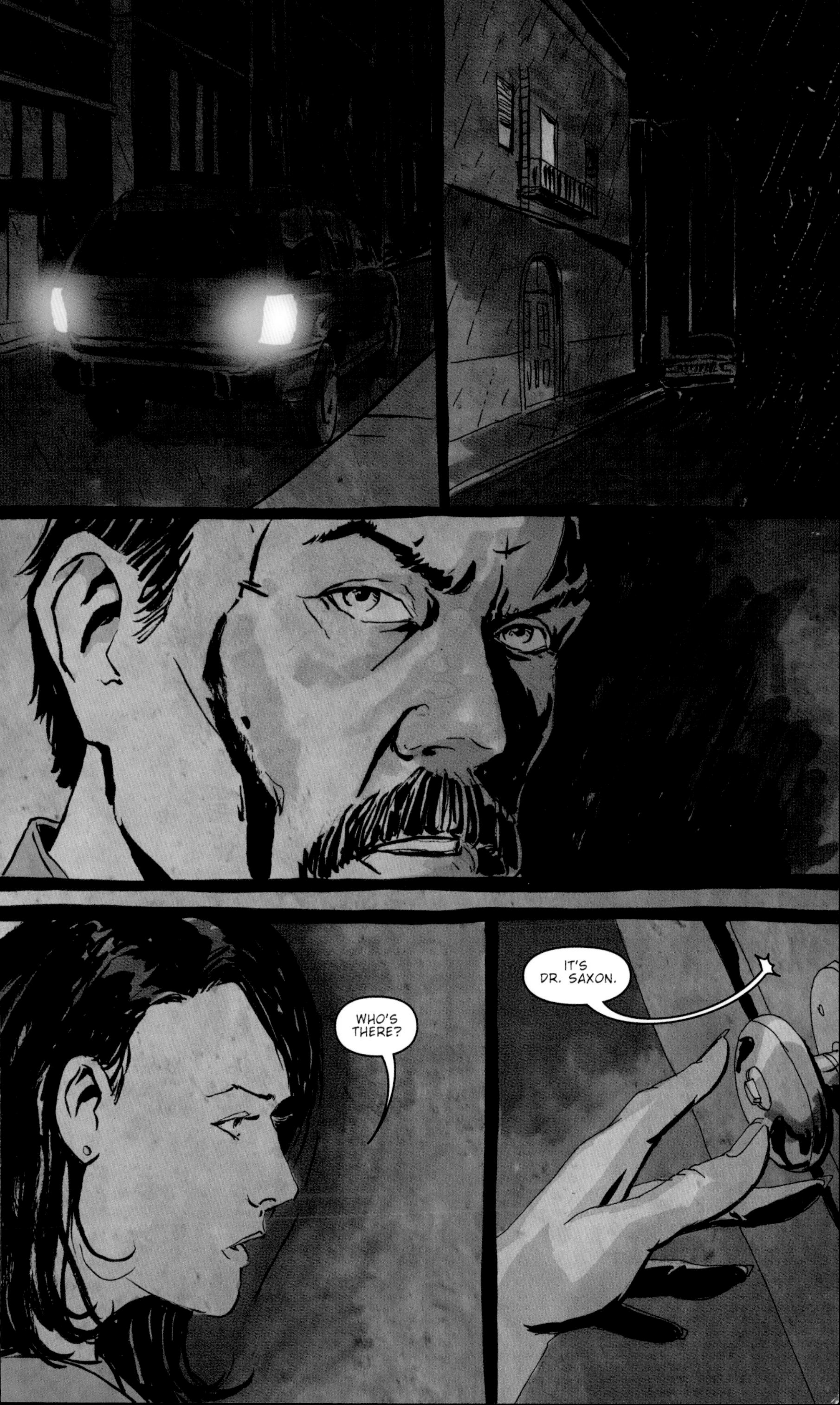
WHO'S THERE?
IT'S DR. SAXON.

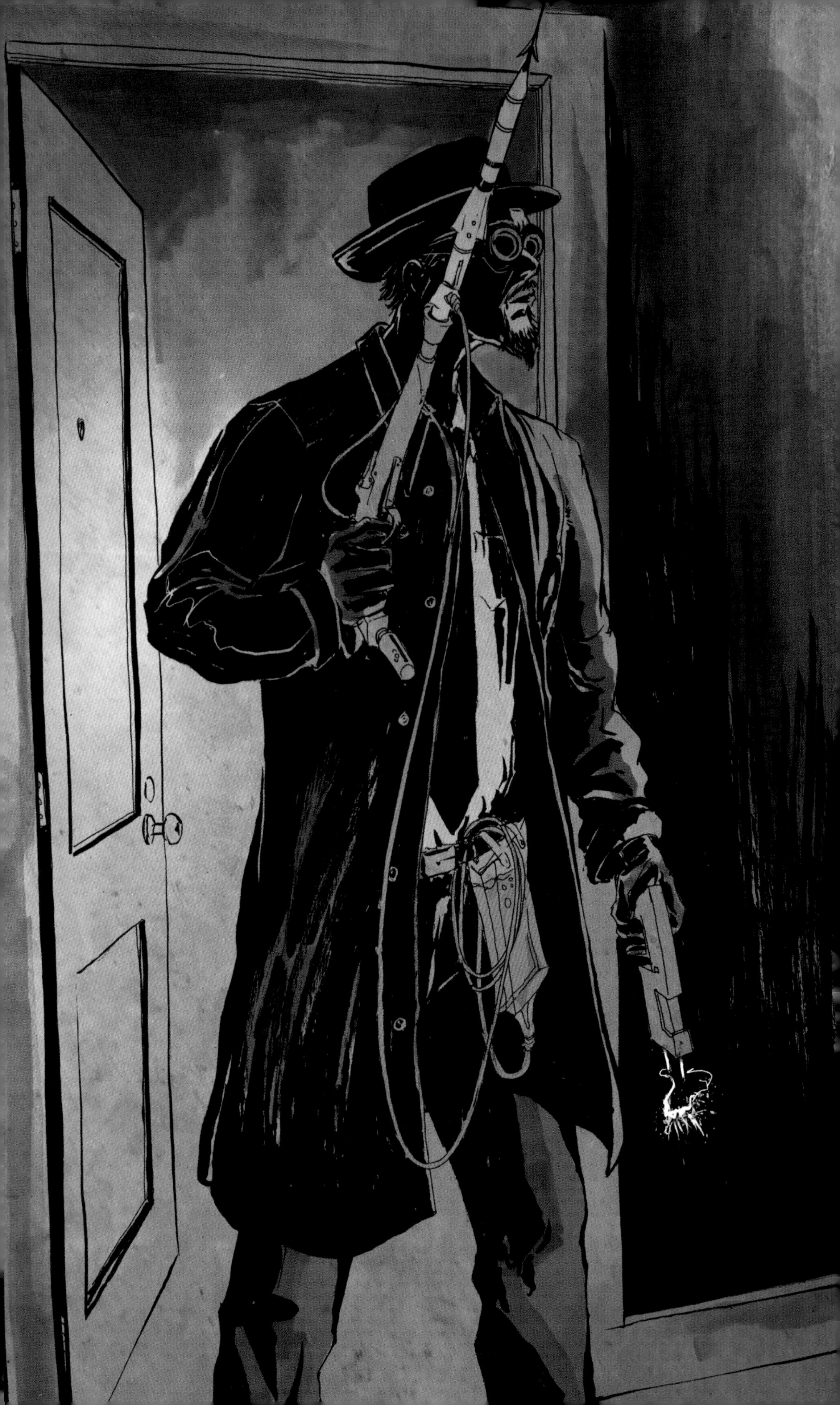

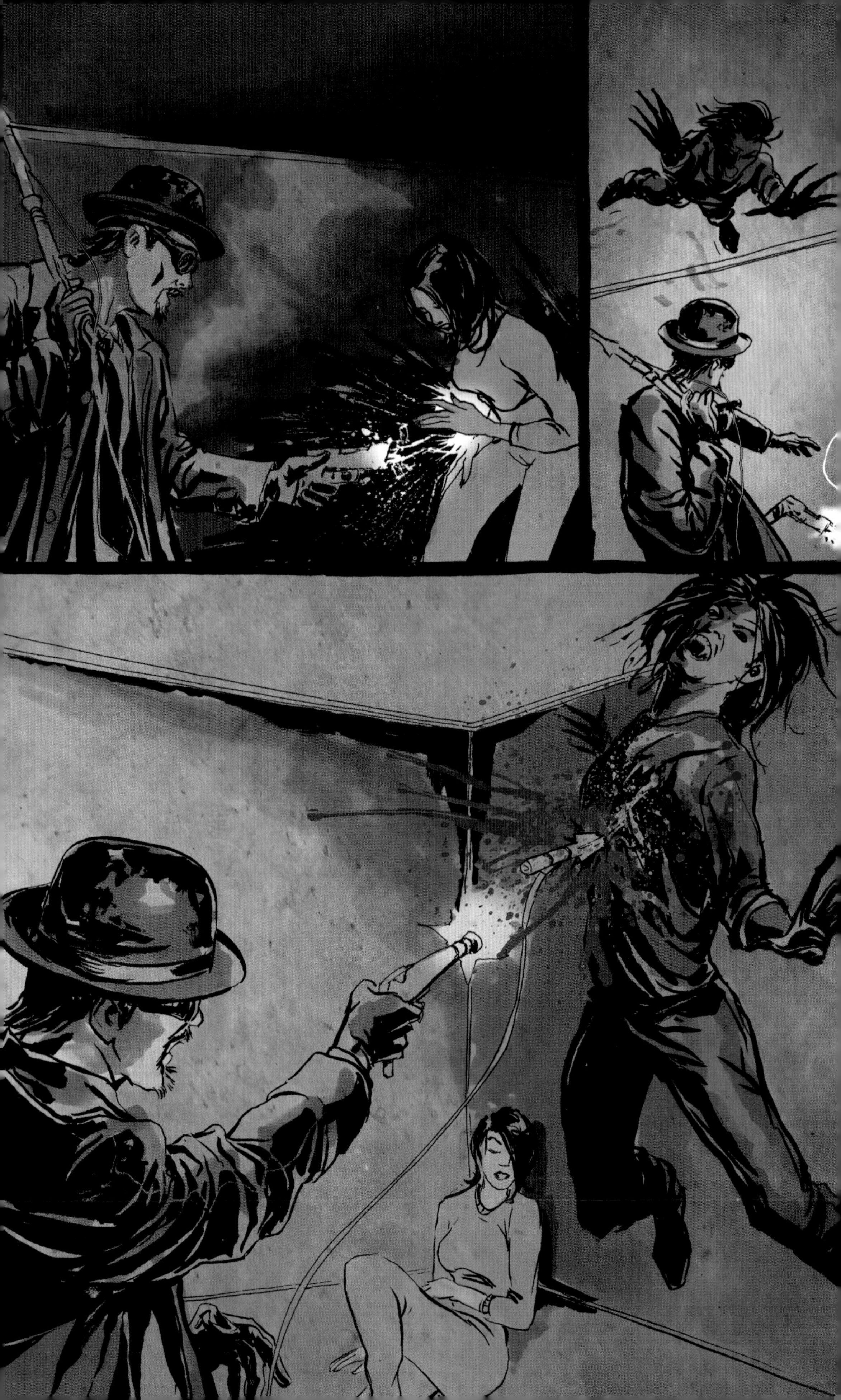

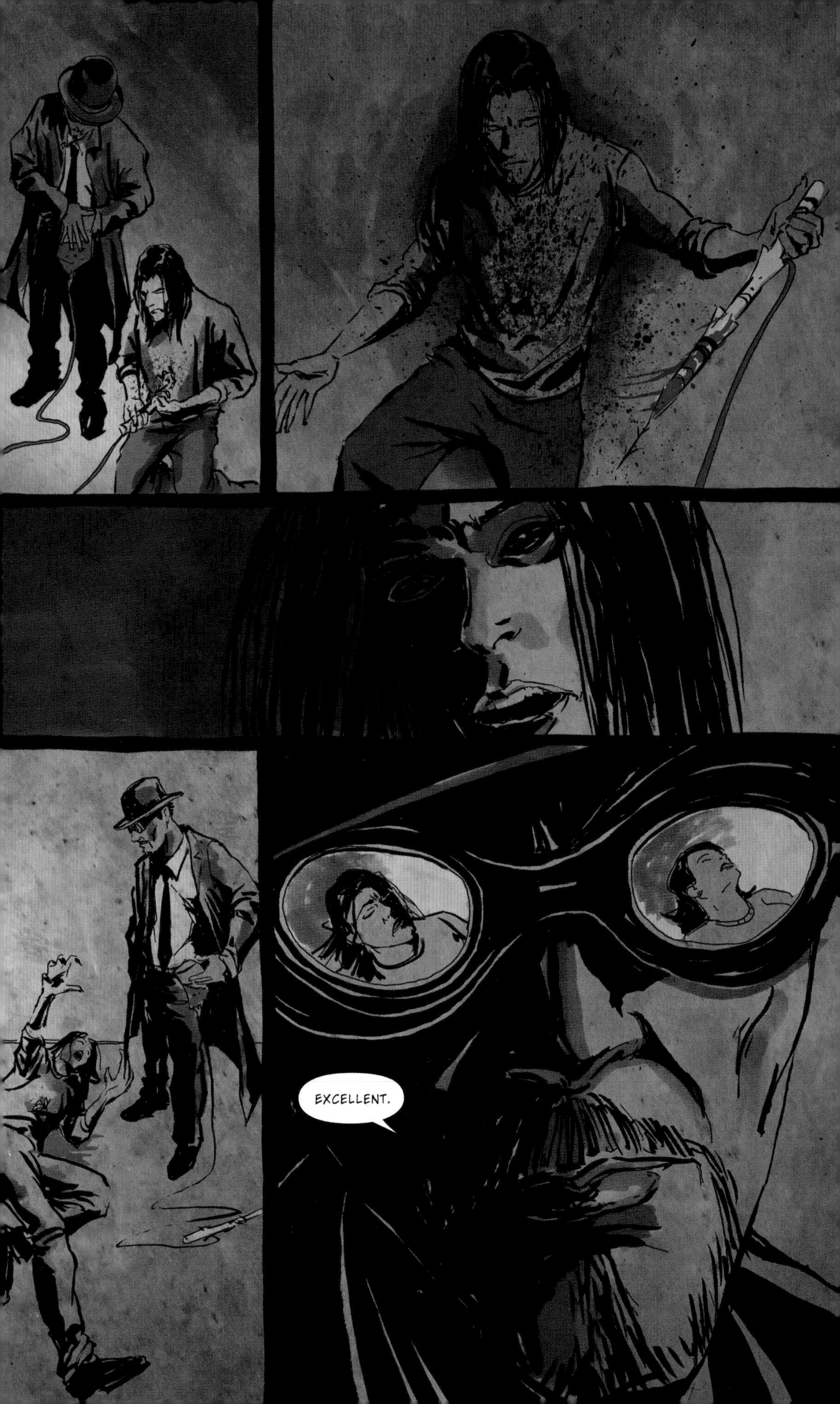
EXCELLENT.

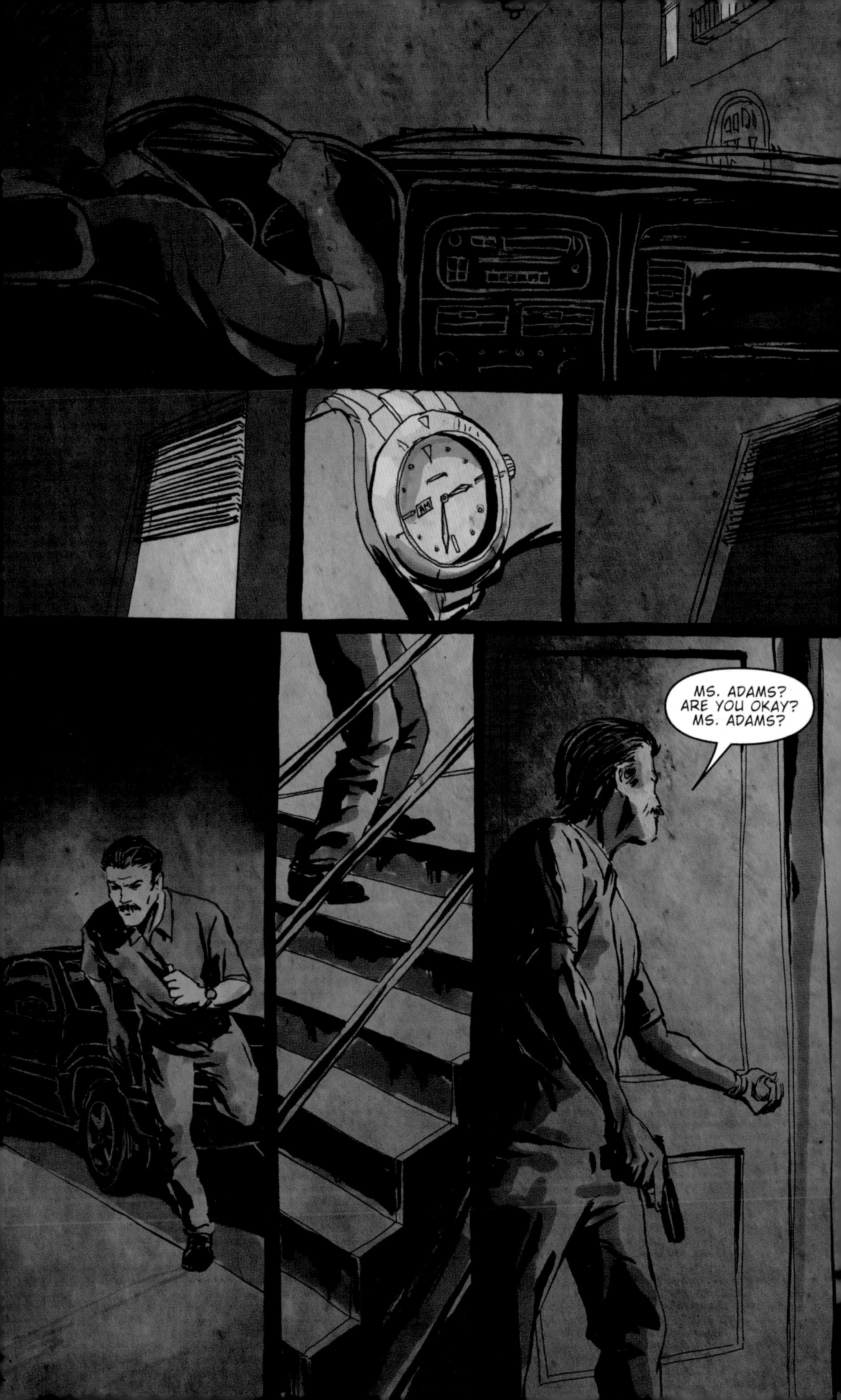

AM
MS. ADAMS?
ARE YOU OKAY?
MS. ADAMS?

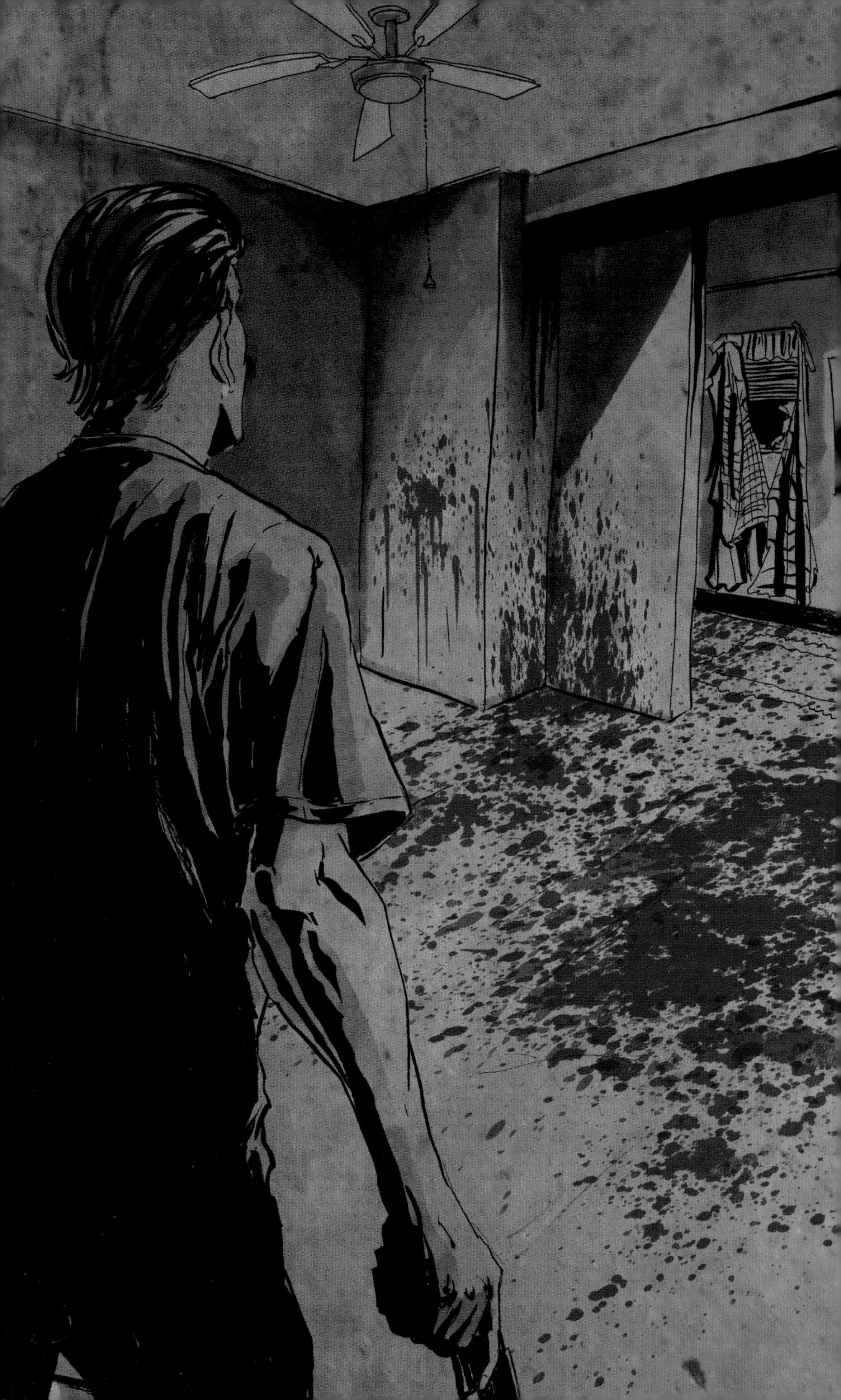

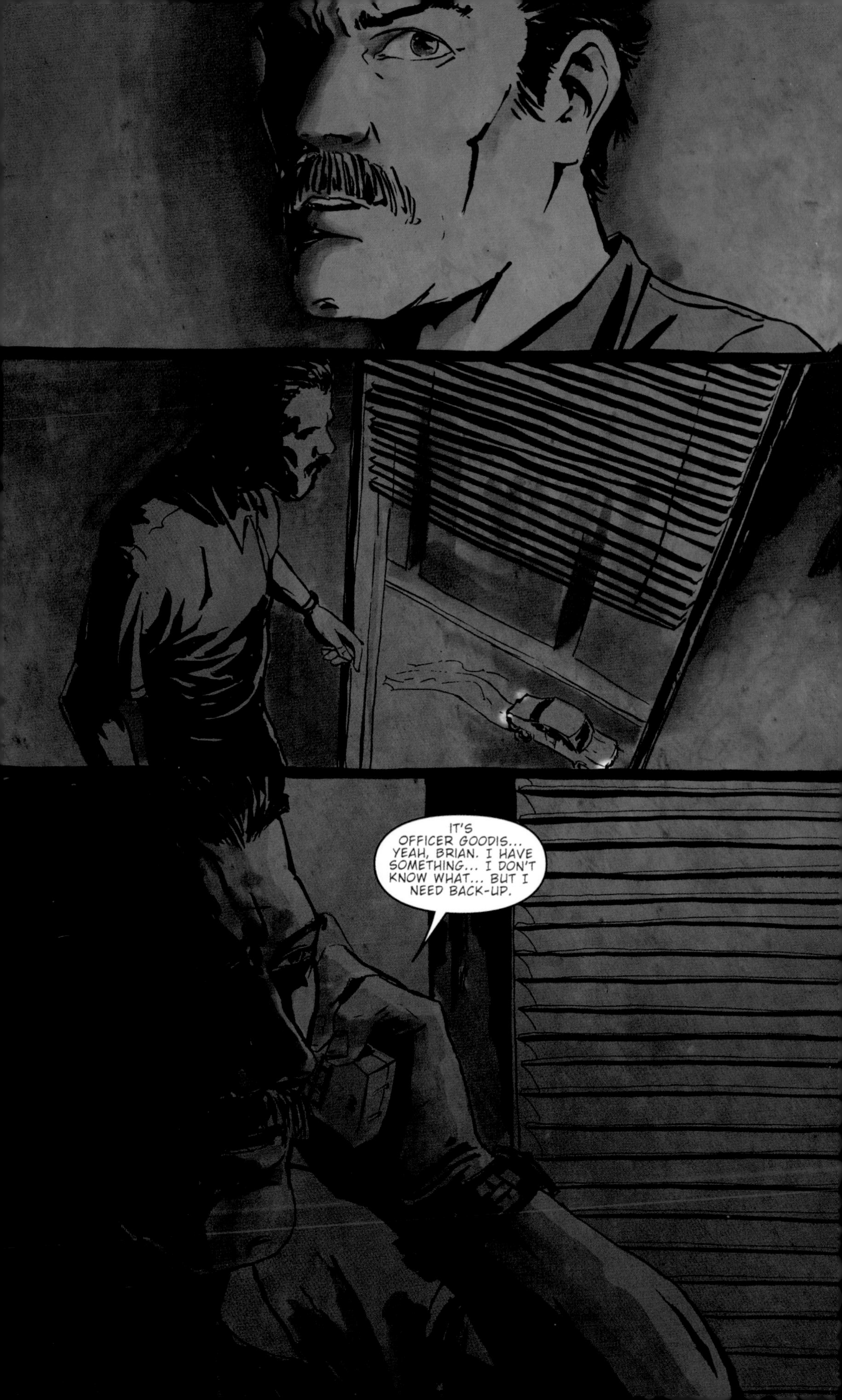
IT'S OFFICER GOODIS... YEAH, BRIAN. I HAVE SOMETHING... I DON'T KNOW WHAT... BUT I NEED BACK-UP.

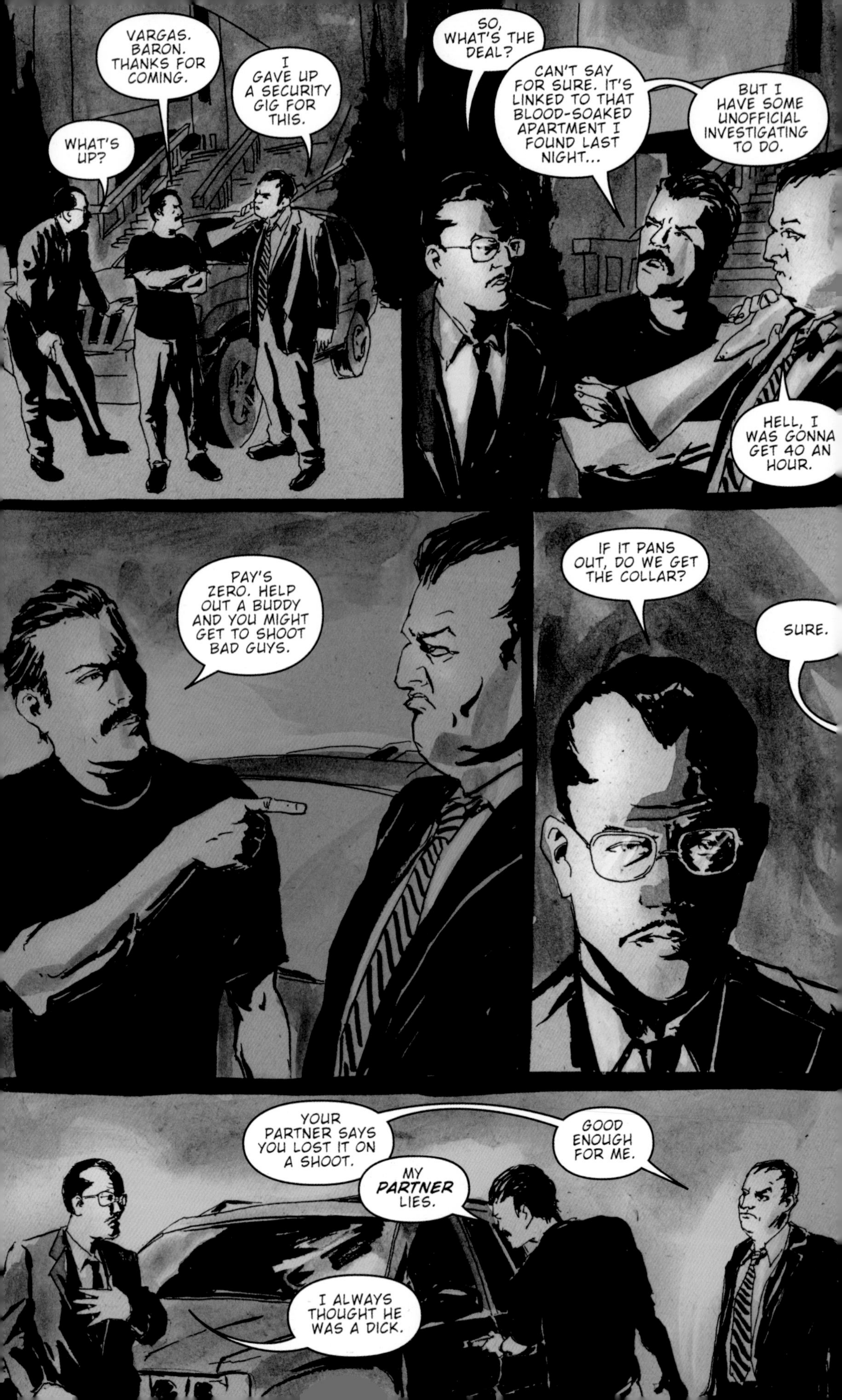
VARGAS. BARON. THANKS FOR COMING.
WHAT'S UP?
I GAVE UP A SECURITY GIG FOR THIS.
SO, WHAT'S THE DEAL?
CAN'T SAY FOR SURE. IT'S LINKED TO THAT BLOOD-SOAKED APARTMENT I FOUND LAST NIGHT...
BUT I HAVE SOME UNOFFICIAL INVESTIGATING TO DO.
HELL, I WAS GONNA GET 40 AN HOUR.
PAY'S ZERO. HELP OUT A BUDDY AND YOU MIGHT GET TO SHOOT BAD GUYS.
IF IT PANS OUT, DO WE GET THE COLLAR?
SURE.
YOUR PARTNER SAYS YOU LOST IT ON A SHOOT.
GOOD ENOUGH FOR ME.
MY PARTNER LIES.
I ALWAYS THOUGHT HE WAS A DICK.

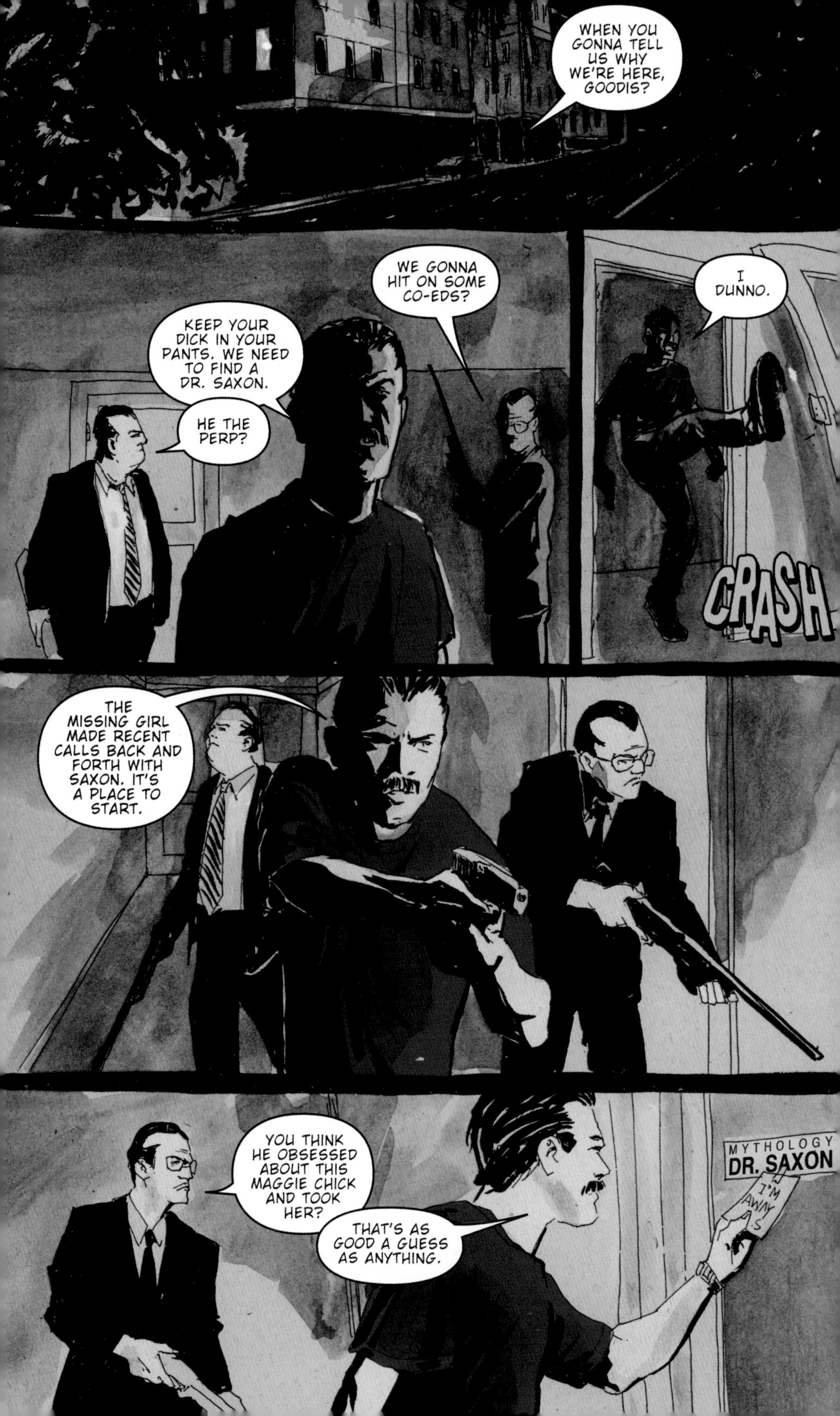
WHEN YOU GONNA TELL US WHY WE'RE HERE, GOODIS?
KEEP YOUR DICK IN YOUR PANTS. WE NEED TO FIND A DR. SAXON.
HE THE PERP?
WE GONNA HIT ON SOME CO-EDS?
I DUNNO.
CRASH
THE MISSING GIRL MADE RECENT CALLS BACK AND FORTH WITH SAXON. IT'S A PLACE TO START.
YOU THINK HE OBSESSED ABOUT THIS MAGGIE CHICK AND TOOK HER?
THAT'S AS GOOD A GUESS AS ANYTHING.
MYTHOLOGY
DR. SAXON
I'M AWAY

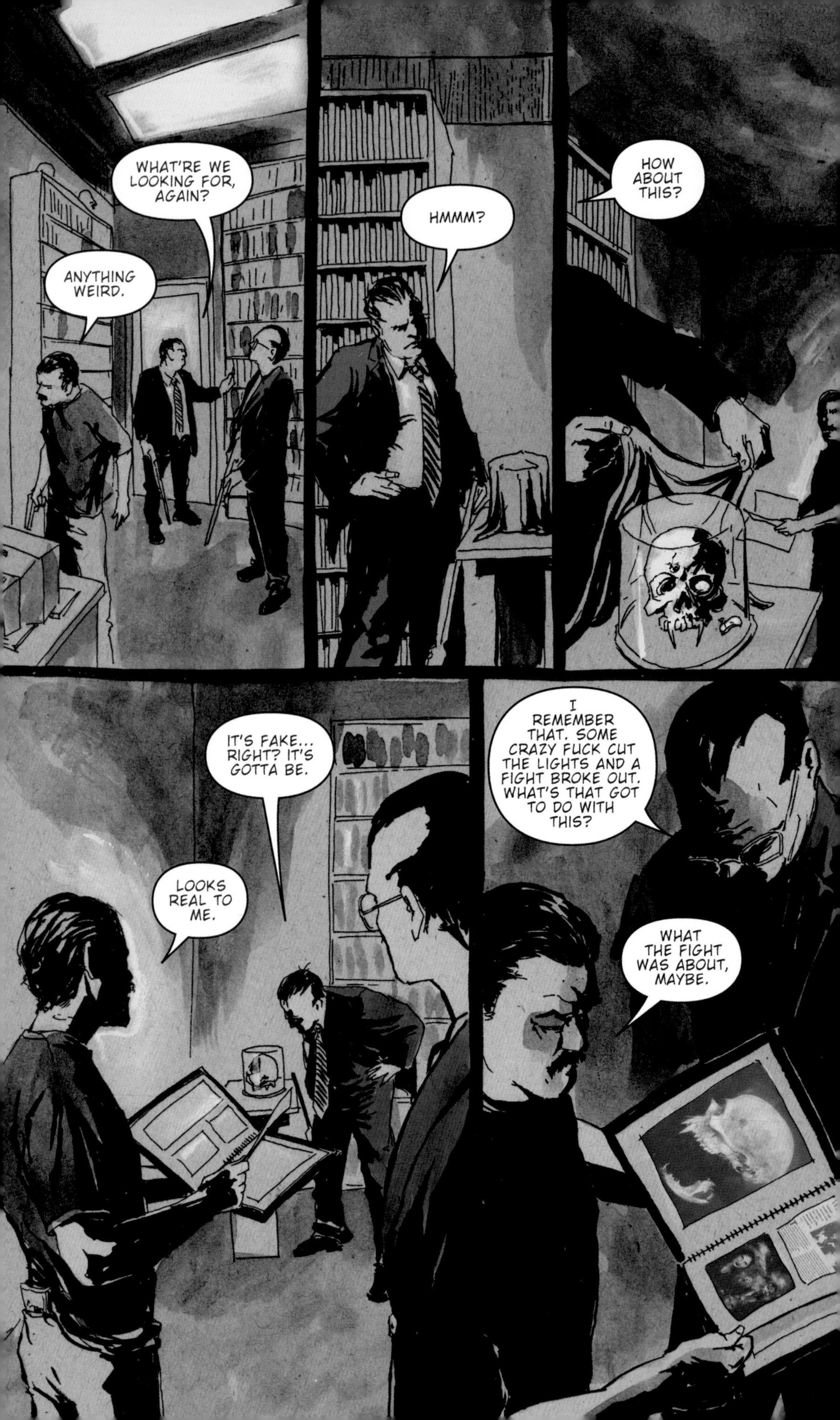
WHAT'RE WE LOOKING FOR, AGAIN?
ANYTHING WEIRD.
HMMM?
HOW ABOUT THIS?
IT'S FAKE... RIGHT? IT'S GOTTA BE.
LOOKS REAL TO ME.
I REMEMBER THAT. SOME CRAZY FUCK CUT THE LIGHTS AND A FIGHT BROKE OUT. WHAT'S THAT GOT TO DO WITH THIS?
WHAT THE FIGHT WAS ABOUT, MAYBE.

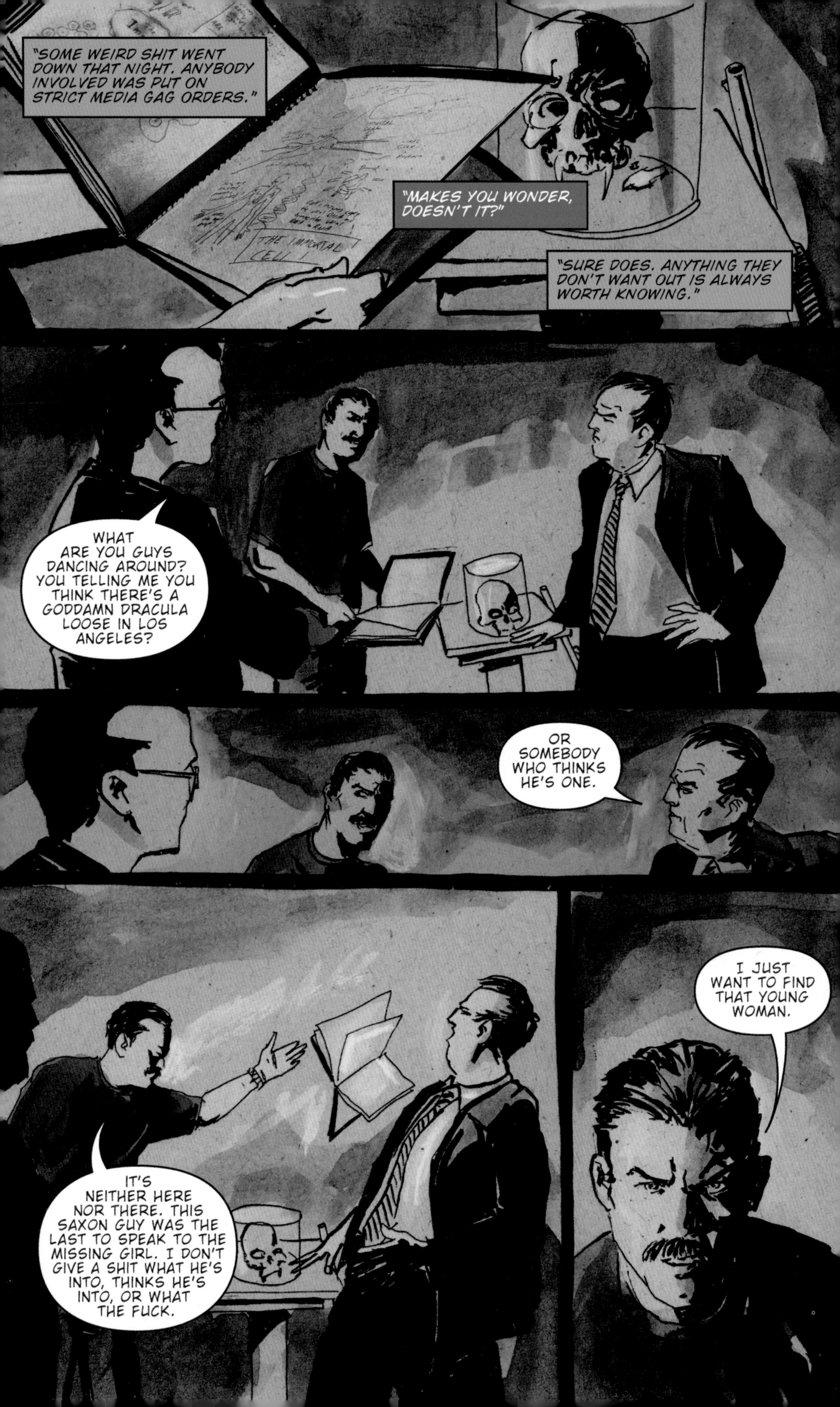
"SOME WEIRD SHIT WENT DOWN THAT NIGHT. ANYBODY INVOLVED WAS PUT ON STRICT MEDIA GAG ORDERS."
"MAKES YOU WONDER, DOESN'T IT?"
"SURE DOES. ANYTHING THEY DON'T WANT OUT IS ALWAYS WORTH KNOWING."
WHAT ARE YOU GUYS DANCING AROUND? YOU TELLING ME YOU THINK THERE'S A GODDAMN DRACULA LOOSE IN LOS ANGELES?
OR SOMEBODY WHO THINKS HE'S ONE.
IT'S NEITHER HERE NOR THERE. THIS SAXON GUY WAS THE LAST TO SPEAK TO THE MISSING GIRL. I DON'T GIVE A SHIT WHAT HE'S INTO, THINKS HE'S INTO, OR WHAT THE FUCK.
I JUST WANT TO FIND THAT YOUNG WOMAN.

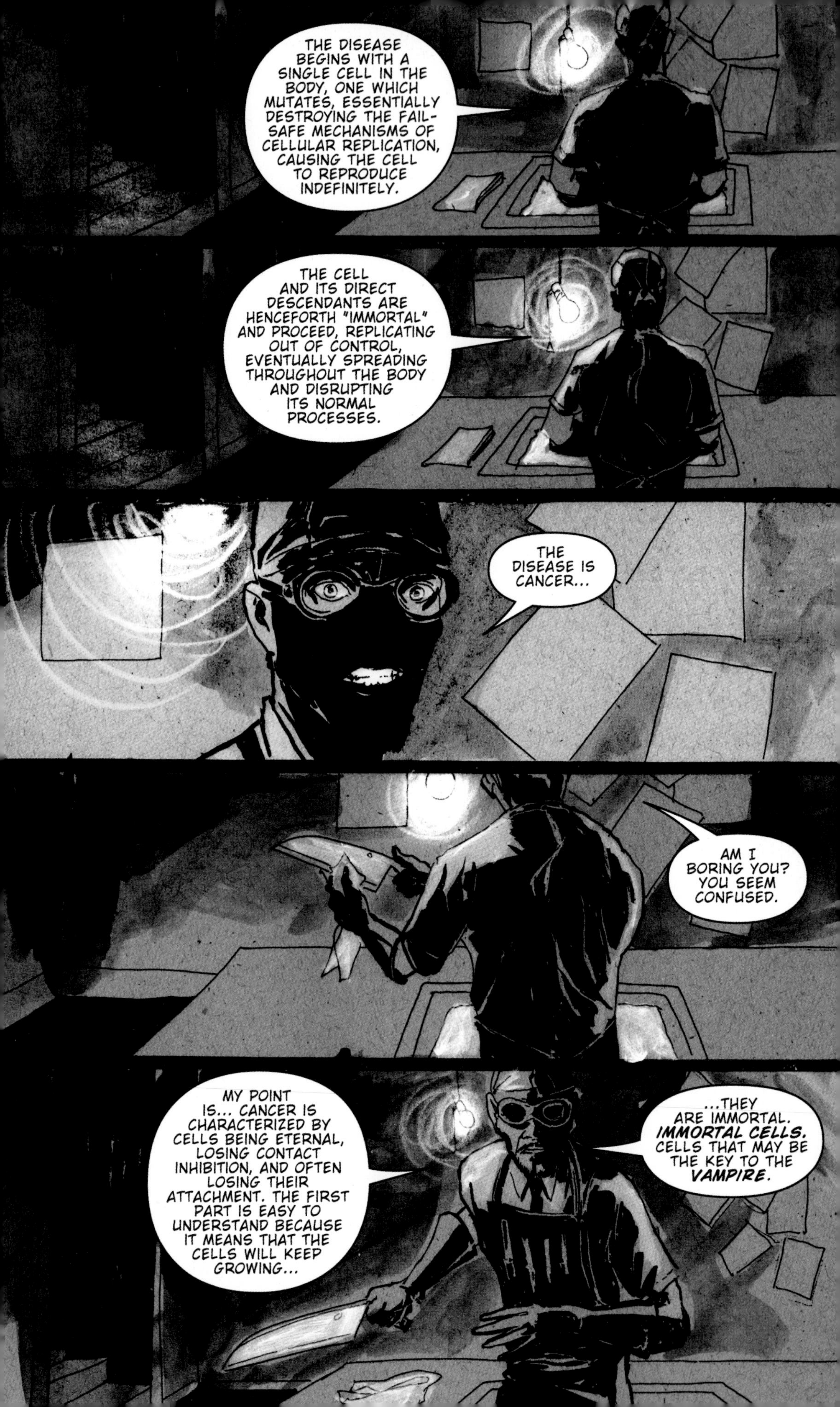
THE DISEASE BEGINS WITH A SINGLE CELL IN THE BODY, ONE WHICH MUTATES, ESSENTIALLY DESTROYING THE FAIL-SAFE MECHANISMS OF CELLULAR REPLICATION, CAUSING THE CELL TO REPRODUCE INDEFINITELY.
THE CELL AND ITS DIRECT DESCENDANTS ARE HENCEFORTH "IMMORTAL" AND PROCEED, REPLICATING OUT OF CONTROL, EVENTUALLY SPREADING THROUGHOUT THE BODY AND DISRUPTING ITS NORMAL PROCESSES.
THE DISEASE IS CANCER...
AM I BORING YOU? YOU SEEM CONFUSED.
MY POINT IS... CANCER IS CHARACTERIZED BY CELLS BEING ETERNAL, LOSING CONTACT INHIBITION, AND OFTEN LOSING THEIR ATTACHMENT. THE FIRST PART IS EASY TO UNDERSTAND BECAUSE IT MEANS THAT THE CELLS WILL KEEP GROWING...
...THEY ARE IMMORTAL. ***IMMORTAL CELLS.*** CELLS THAT MAY BE THE KEY TO THE ***VAMPIRE***.

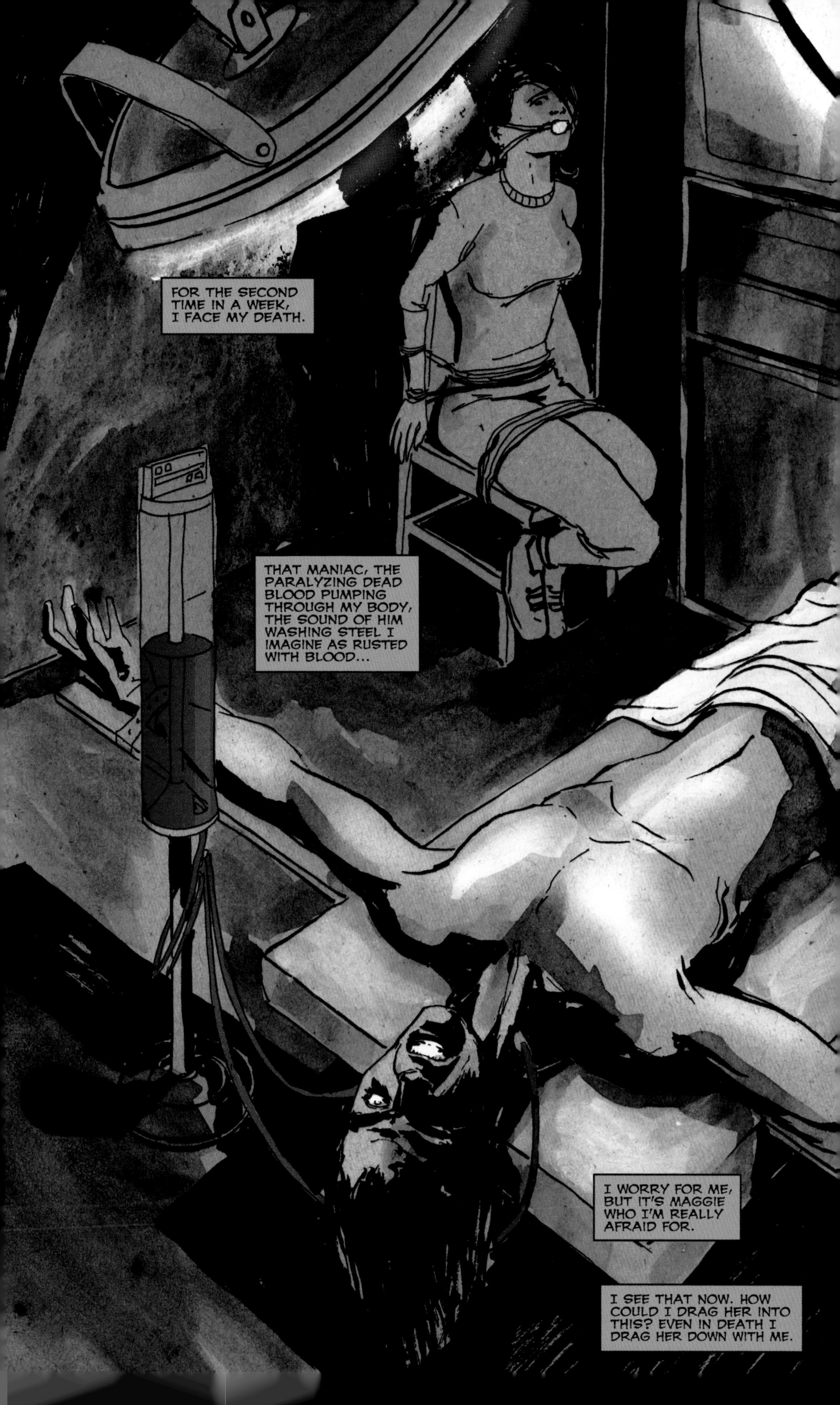
FOR THE SECOND TIME IN A WEEK, I FACE MY DEATH.
THAT MANIAC, THE PARALYZING DEAD BLOOD PUMPING THROUGH MY BODY, THE SOUND OF HIM WASHING STEEL I IMAGINE AS RUSTED WITH BLOOD...
I WORRY FOR ME, BUT IT'S MAGGIE WHO I'M REALLY AFRAID FOR.
I SEE THAT NOW. HOW COULD I DRAG HER INTO THIS? EVEN IN DEATH I DRAG HER DOWN WITH ME.

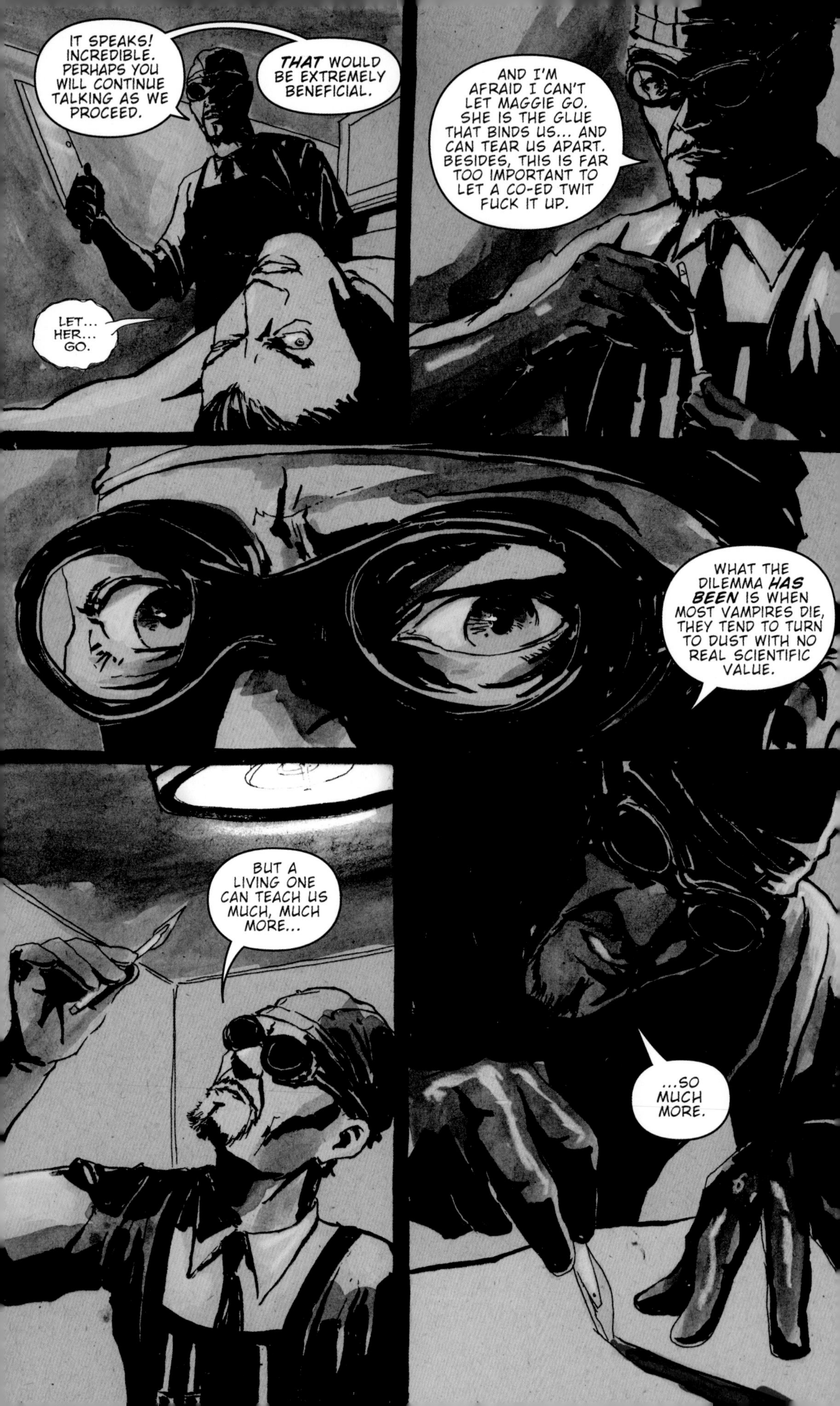
IT SPEAKS! INCREDIBLE. PERHAPS YOU WILL CONTINUE TALKING AS WE PROCEED.
THAT WOULD BE EXTREMELY BENEFICIAL.
LET... HER... GO.
AND I'M AFRAID I CAN'T LET MAGGIE GO. SHE IS THE GLUE THAT BINDS US... AND CAN TEAR US APART. BESIDES, THIS IS FAR TOO IMPORTANT TO LET A CO-ED TWIT FUCK IT UP.
WHAT THE DILEMMA HAS BEEN IS WHEN MOST VAMPIRES DIE, THEY TEND TO TURN TO DUST WITH NO REAL SCIENTIFIC VALUE.
BUT A LIVING ONE CAN TEACH US MUCH, MUCH MORE...
...SO MUCH MORE.

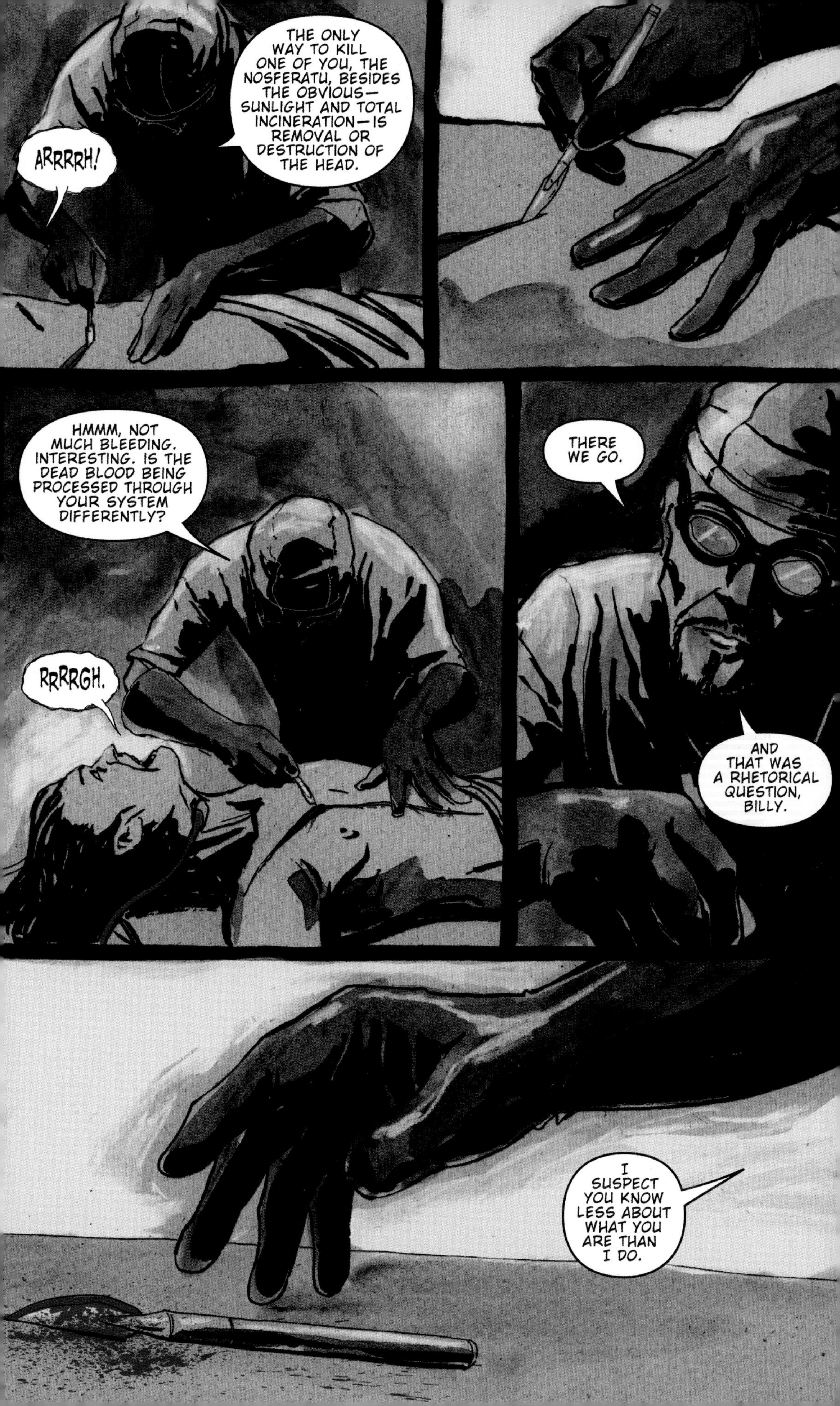
THE ONLY WAY TO KILL ONE OF YOU, THE NOSFERATU, BESIDES THE OBVIOUS— SUNLIGHT AND TOTAL INCINERATION—IS REMOVAL OR DESTRUCTION OF THE HEAD.
ARRRRH!
HMMM, NOT MUCH BLEEDING. INTERESTING. IS THE DEAD BLOOD BEING PROCESSED THROUGH YOUR SYSTEM DIFFERENTLY?
RRRRGH.
THERE WE GO.
AND THAT WAS A RHETORICAL QUESTION, BILLY.
I SUSPECT YOU KNOW LESS ABOUT WHAT YOU ARE THAN I DO.

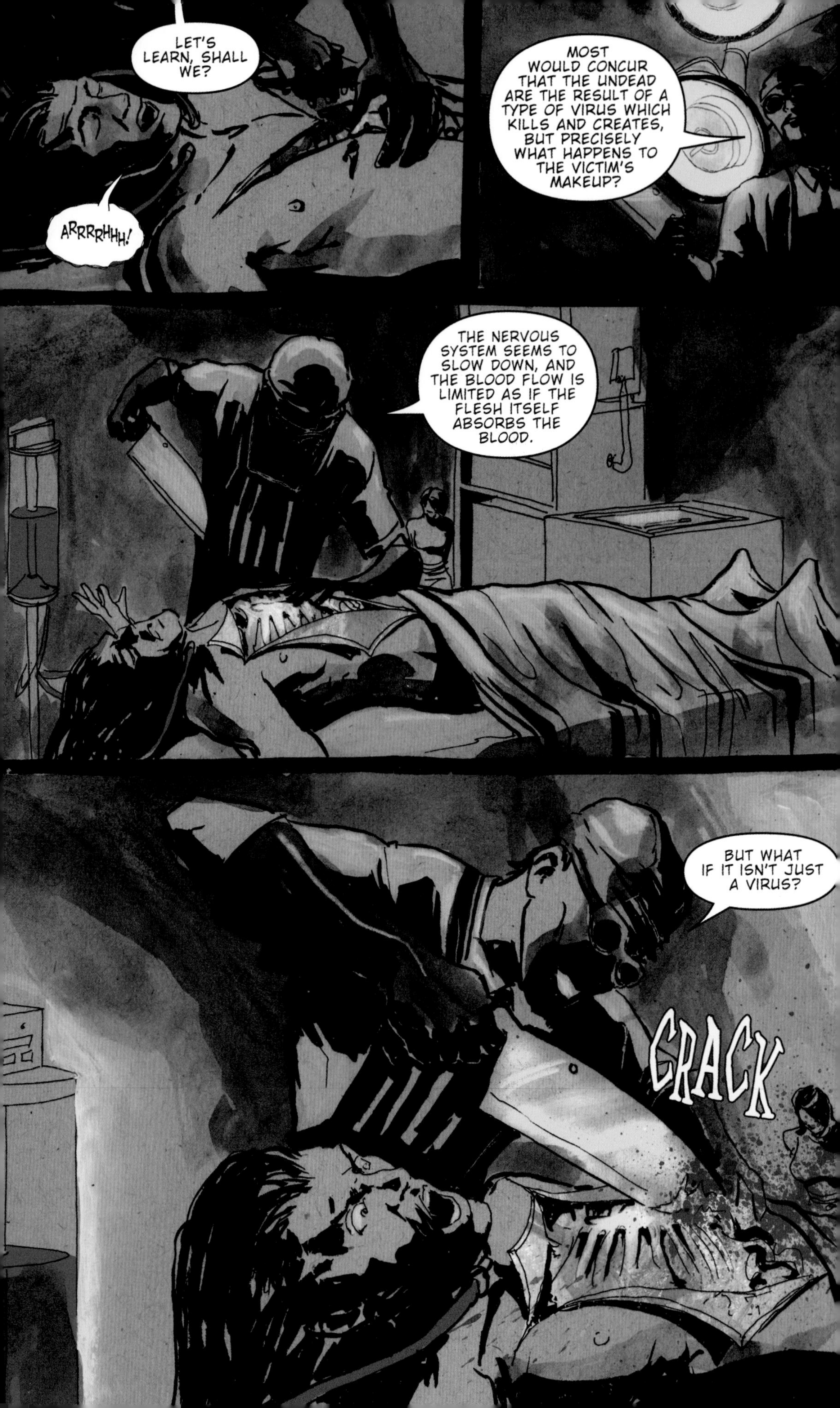
LET'S LEARN, SHALL WE?
ARRRRHHH!
MOST WOULD CONCUR THAT THE UNDEAD ARE THE RESULT OF A TYPE OF VIRUS WHICH KILLS AND CREATES, BUT PRECISELY WHAT HAPPENS TO THE VICTIM'S MAKEUP?
THE NERVOUS SYSTEM SEEMS TO SLOW DOWN, AND THE BLOOD FLOW IS LIMITED AS IF THE FLESH ITSELF ABSORBS THE BLOOD.
BUT WHAT IF IT ISN'T JUST A VIRUS?
CRACK

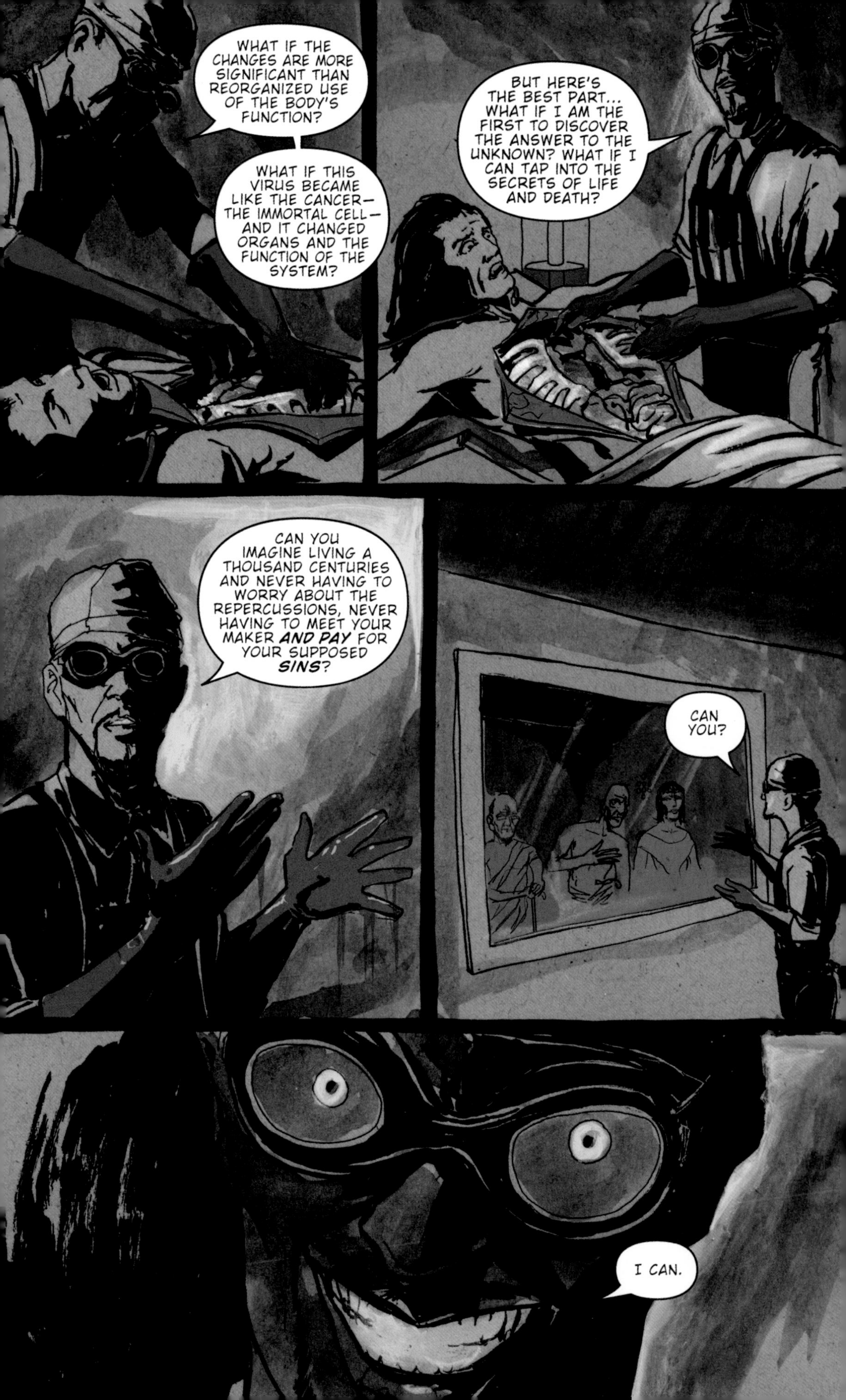
WHAT IF THE CHANGES ARE MORE SIGNIFICANT THAN REORGANIZED USE OF THE BODY'S FUNCTION?
WHAT IF THIS VIRUS BECAME LIKE THE CANCER— THE IMMORTAL CELL— AND IT CHANGED ORGANS AND THE FUNCTION OF THE SYSTEM?
BUT HERE'S THE BEST PART... WHAT IF I AM THE FIRST TO DISCOVER THE ANSWER TO THE UNKNOWN? WHAT IF I CAN TAP INTO THE SECRETS OF LIFE AND DEATH?
CAN YOU IMAGINE LIVING A THOUSAND CENTURIES AND NEVER HAVING TO WORRY ABOUT THE REPERCUSSIONS, NEVER HAVING TO MEET YOUR MAKER ***AND PAY*** FOR YOUR SUPPOSED ***SINS***?
CAN YOU?
I CAN.

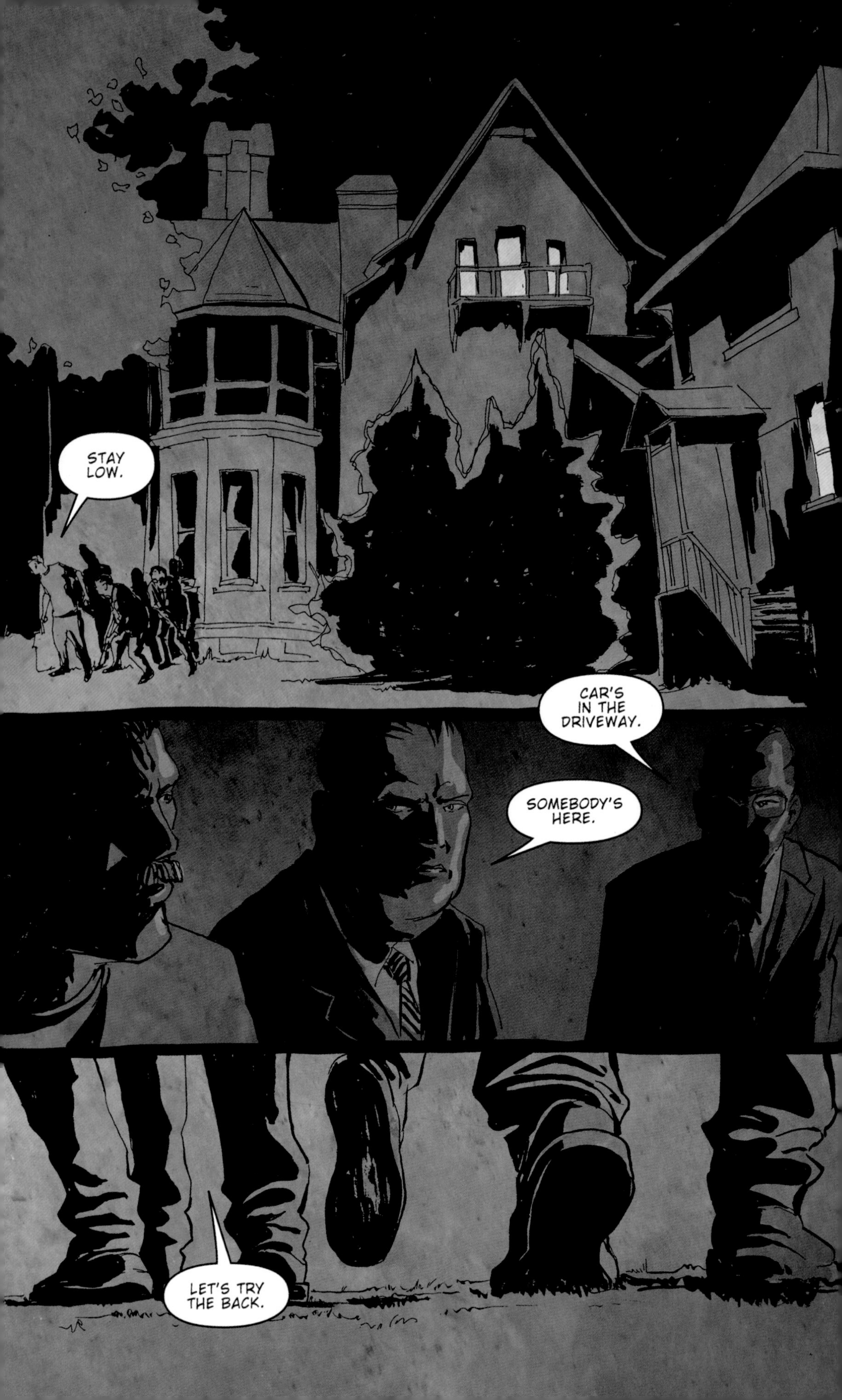
STAY LOW.
CAR'S IN THE DRIVEWAY.
SOMEBODY'S HERE.
LET'S TRY THE BACK.

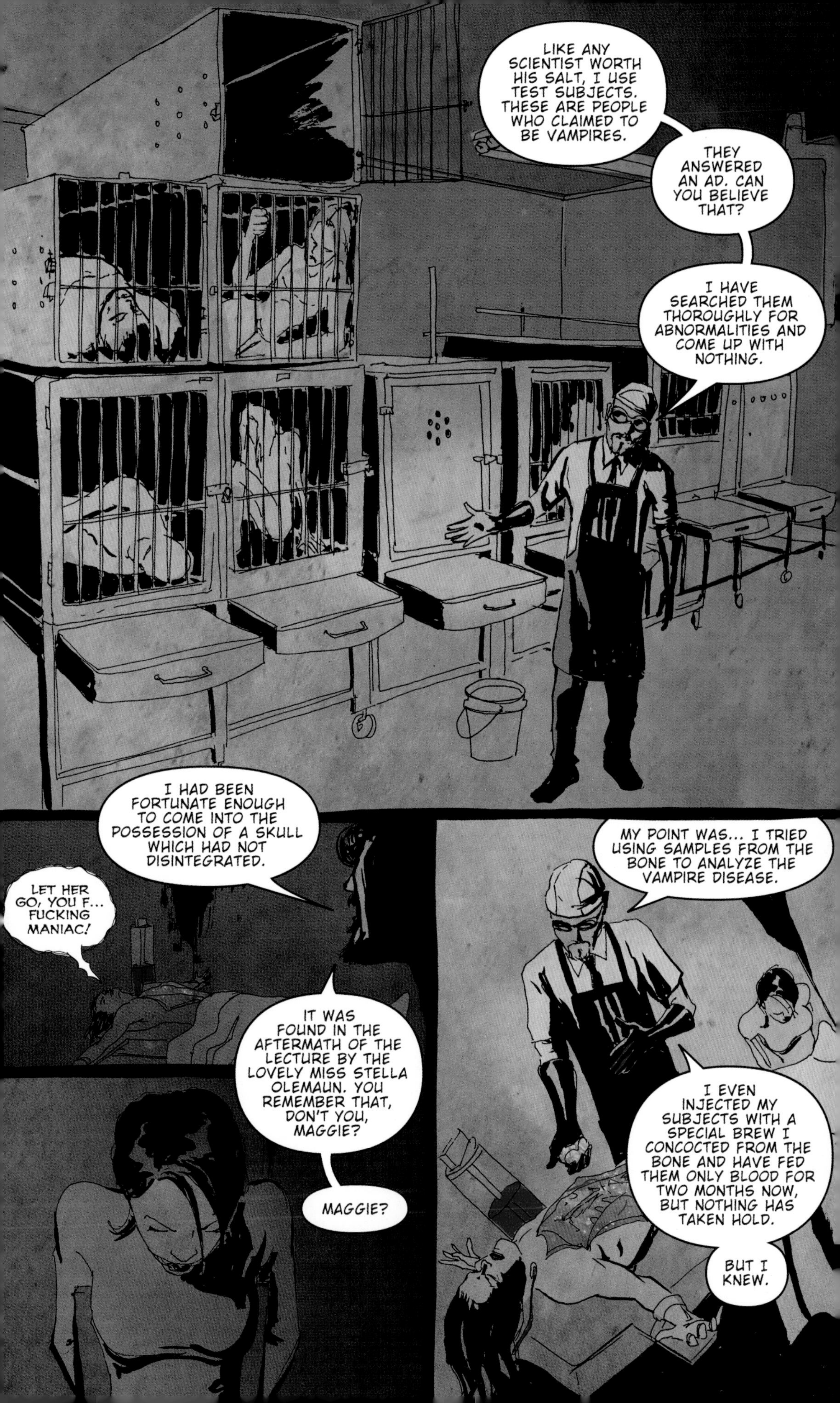
LIKE ANY SCIENTIST WORTH HIS SALT, I USE TEST SUBJECTS. THESE ARE PEOPLE WHO CLAIMED TO BE VAMPIRES.
THEY ANSWERED AN AD. CAN YOU BELIEVE THAT?
I HAVE SEARCHED THEM THOROUGHLY FOR ABNORMALITIES AND COME UP WITH NOTHING.
I HAD BEEN FORTUNATE ENOUGH TO COME INTO THE POSSESSION OF A SKULL WHICH HAD NOT DISINTEGRATED.
LET HER GO, YOU F... FUCKING MANIAC!
IT WAS FOUND IN THE AFTERMATH OF THE LECTURE BY THE LOVELY MISS STELLA OLEMAUN. YOU REMEMBER THAT, DON'T YOU, MAGGIE?
MAGGIE?
MY POINT WAS... I TRIED USING SAMPLES FROM THE BONE TO ANALYZE THE VAMPIRE DISEASE.
I EVEN INJECTED MY SUBJECTS WITH A SPECIAL BREW I CONCOCTED FROM THE BONE AND HAVE FED THEM ONLY BLOOD FOR TWO MONTHS NOW, BUT NOTHING HAS TAKEN HOLD.
BUT I KNEW.

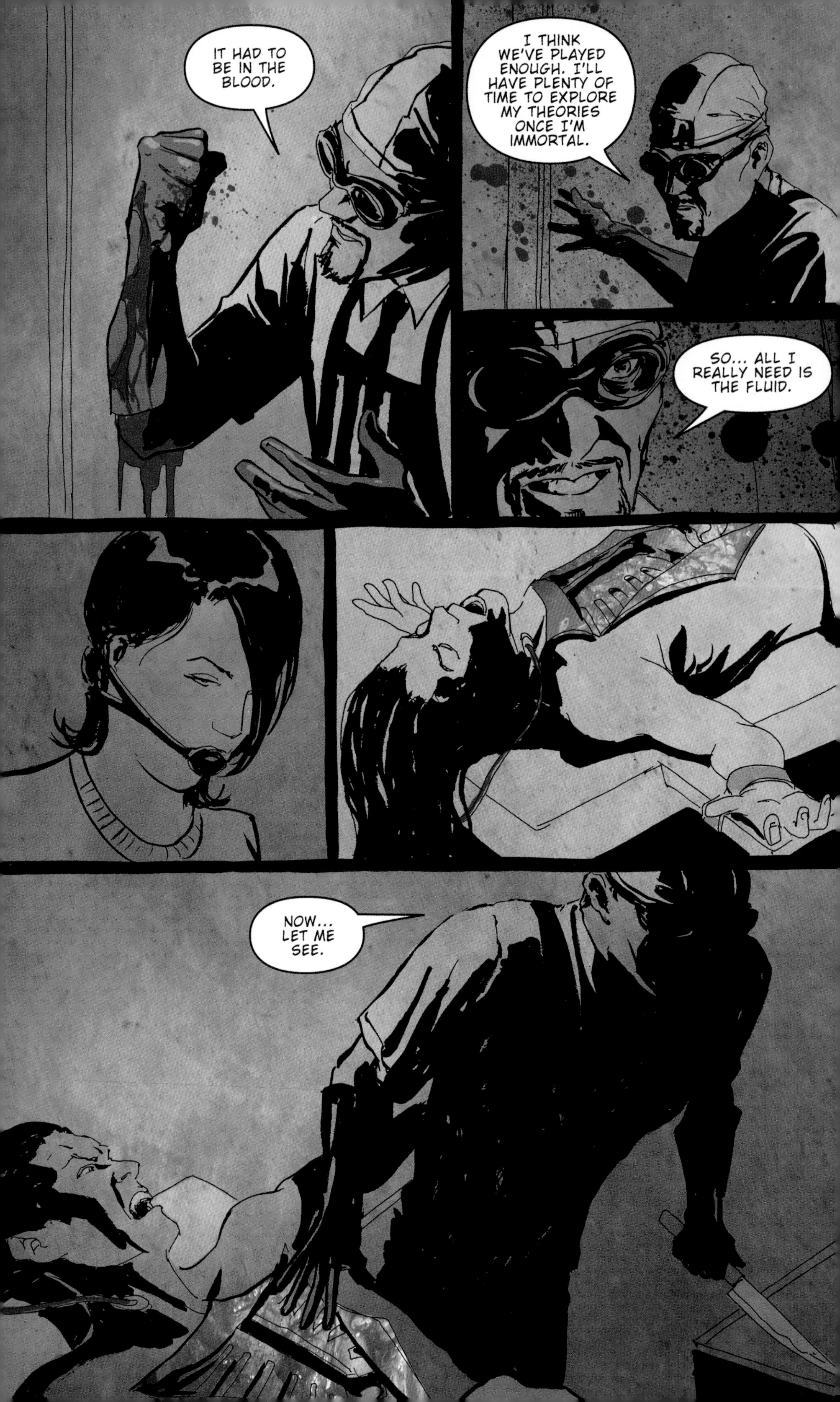
IT HAD TO BE IN THE BLOOD.
I THINK WE'VE PLAYED ENOUGH. I'LL HAVE PLENTY OF TIME TO EXPLORE MY THEORIES ONCE I'M IMMORTAL.
SO... ALL I REALLY NEED IS THE FLUID.
NOW... LET ME SEE.

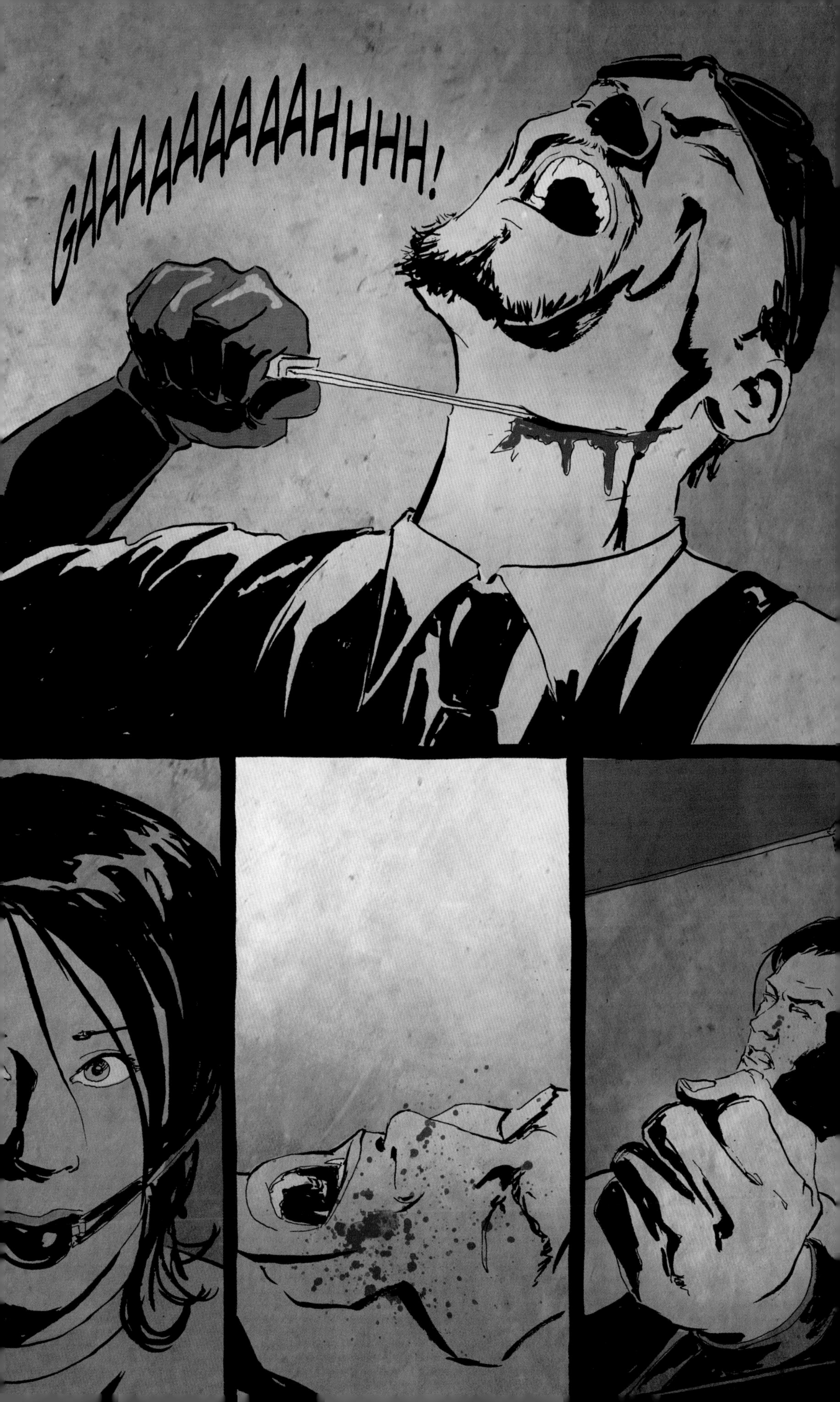
GAAAAAAAAHHHH!

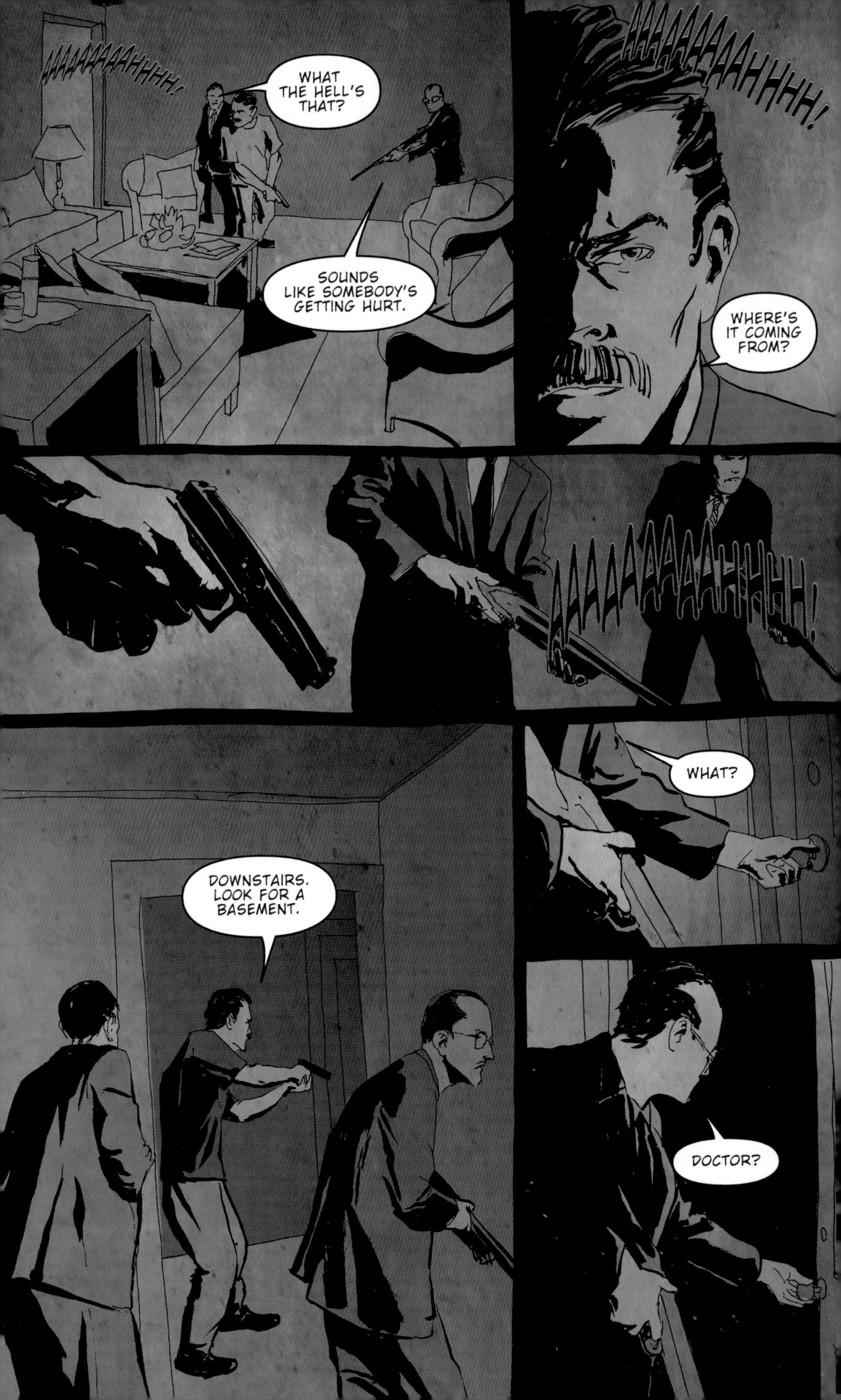
AAAAAAAAAHHHH!
WHAT THE HELL'S THAT?
SOUNDS LIKE SOMEBODY'S GETTING HURT.
AAAAAAAAAAAHHHH!
WHERE'S IT COMING FROM?
AAAAAAAAAAAHHHH!
DOWNSTAIRS. LOOK FOR A BASEMENT.
WHAT?
DOCTOR?

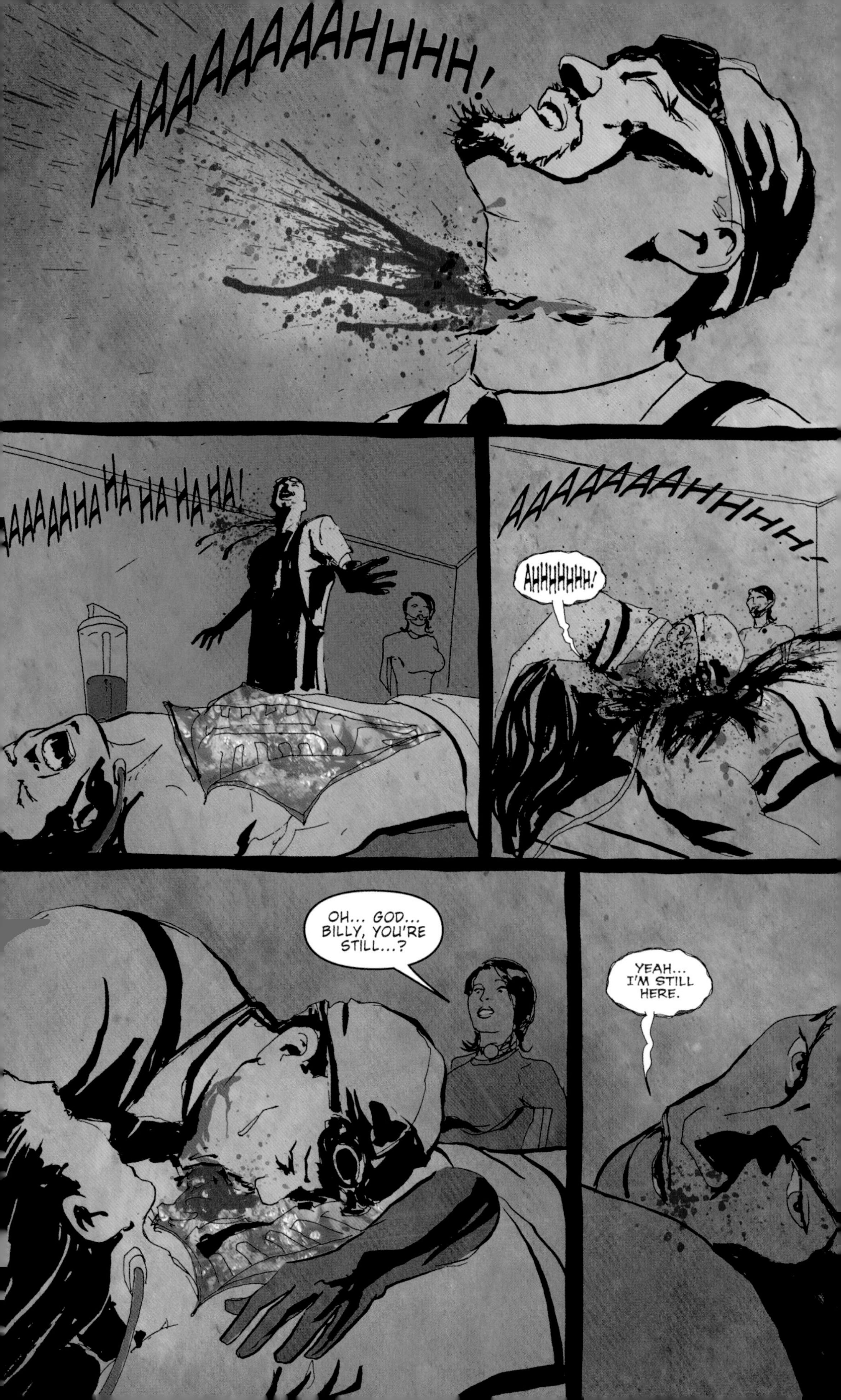
AAAAAAAAAAHHHH!
AAAAAAHAHA HA HA HA HA!
AAAAAAAAHHHHH!
AHHHHHHH!
OH... GOD... BILLY, YOU'RE STILL...?
YEAH... I'M STILL HERE.

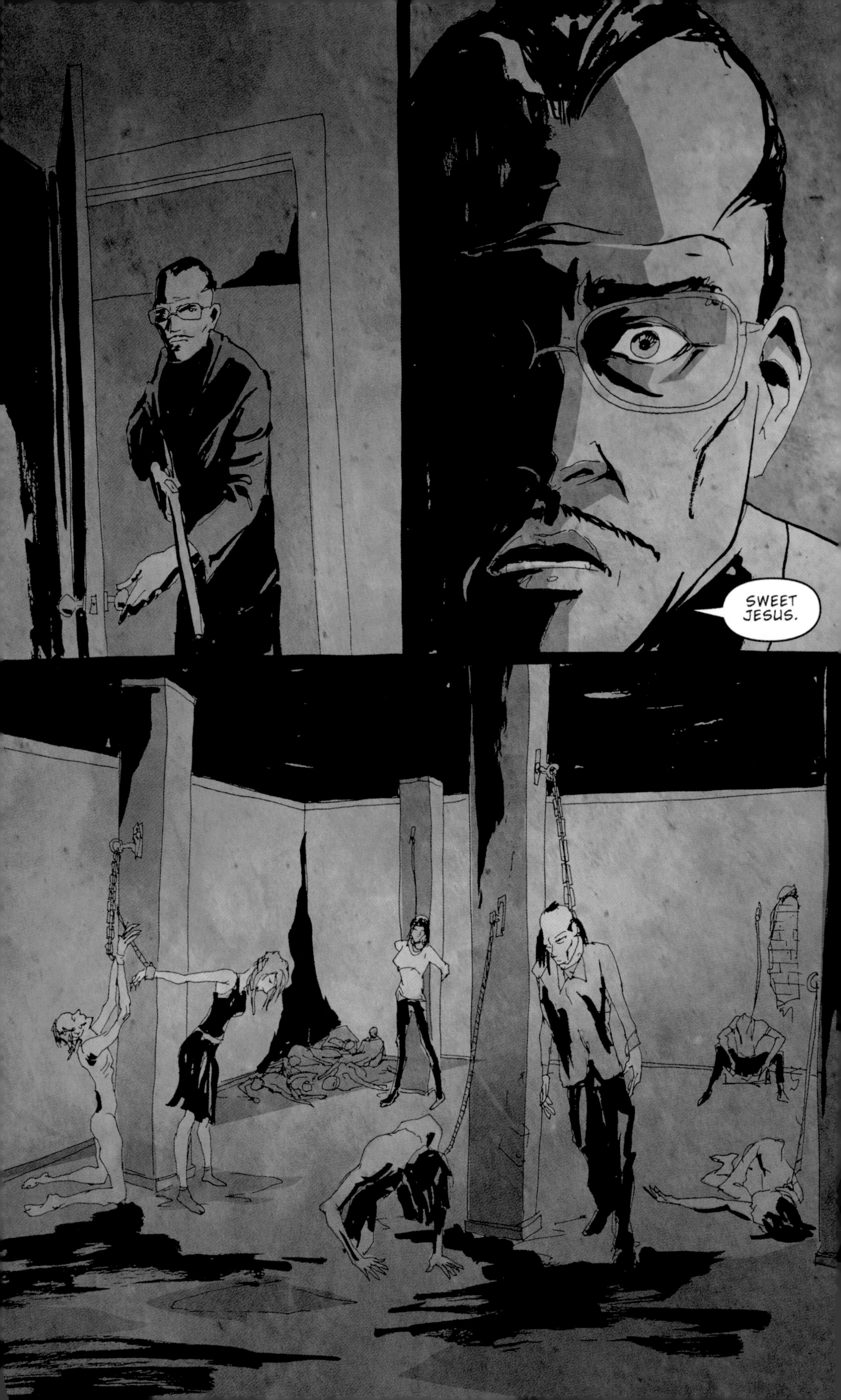
SWEET JESUS.

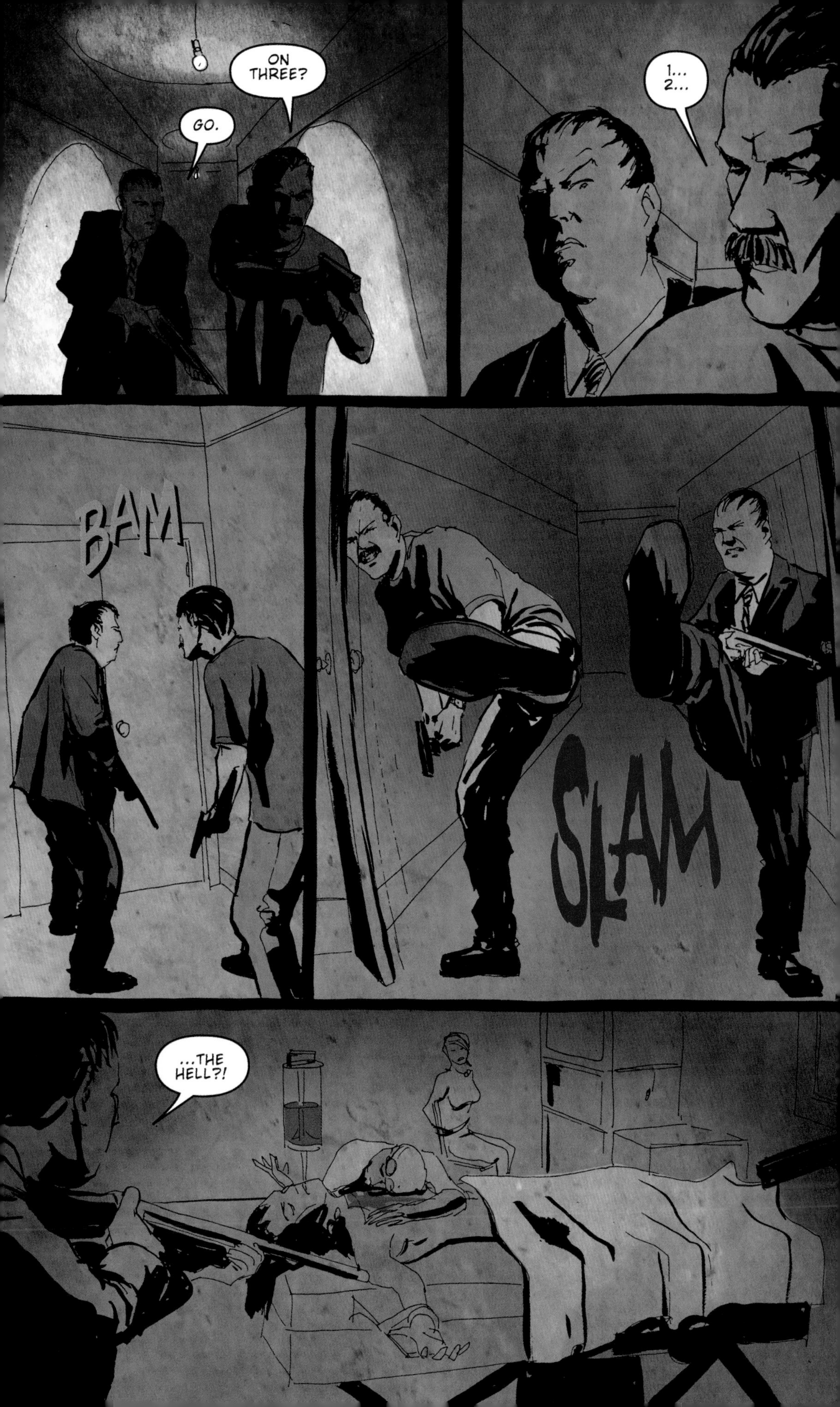
ON THREE?
GO.
1...
2...
BAM
SLAM
...THE HELL?!

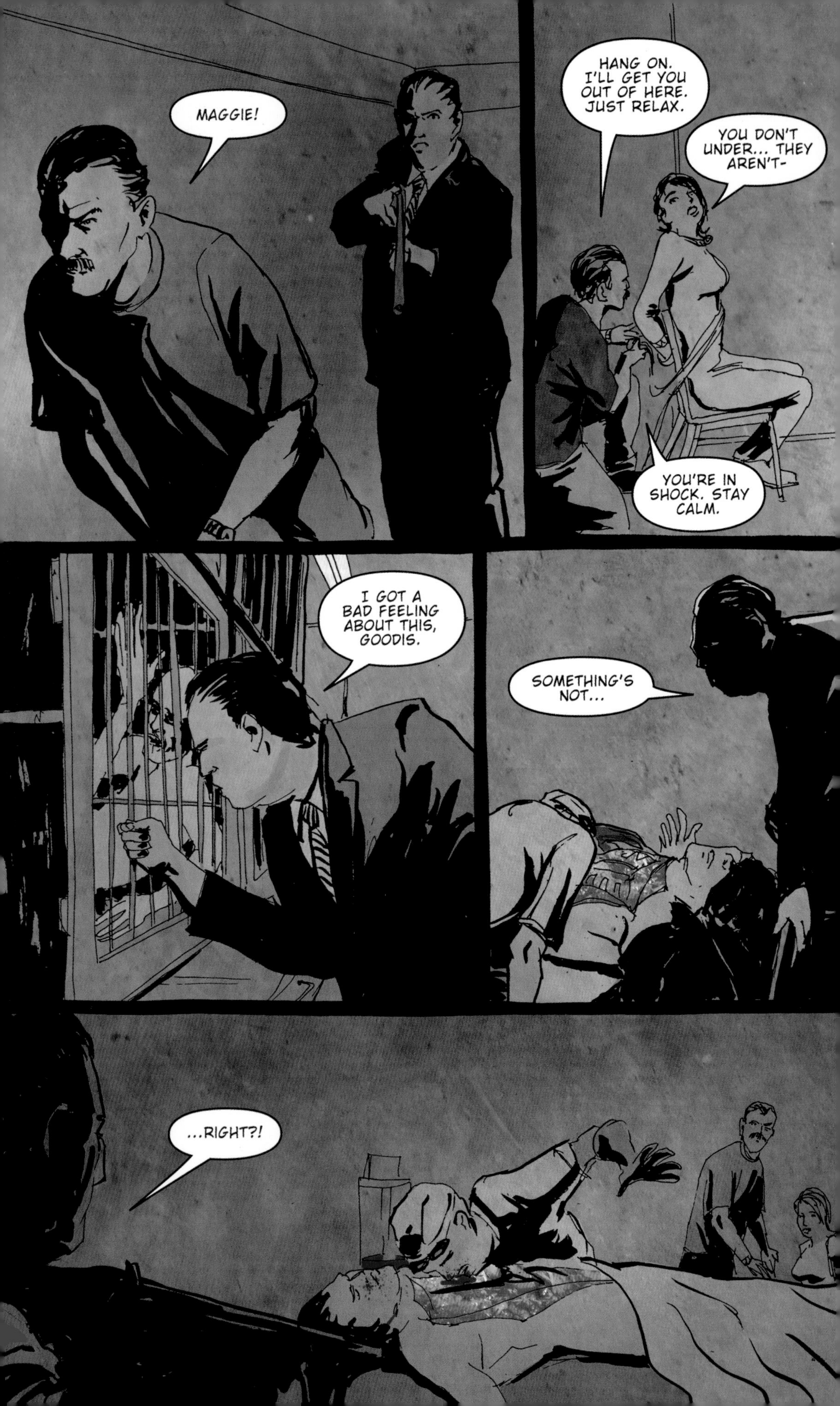
MAGGIE!
HANG ON. I'LL GET YOU OUT OF HERE. JUST RELAX.
YOU DON'T UNDER... THEY AREN'T-
YOU'RE IN SHOCK. STAY CALM.
I GOT A BAD FEELING ABOUT THIS, GOODIS.
SOMETHING'S NOT...
...RIGHT?!

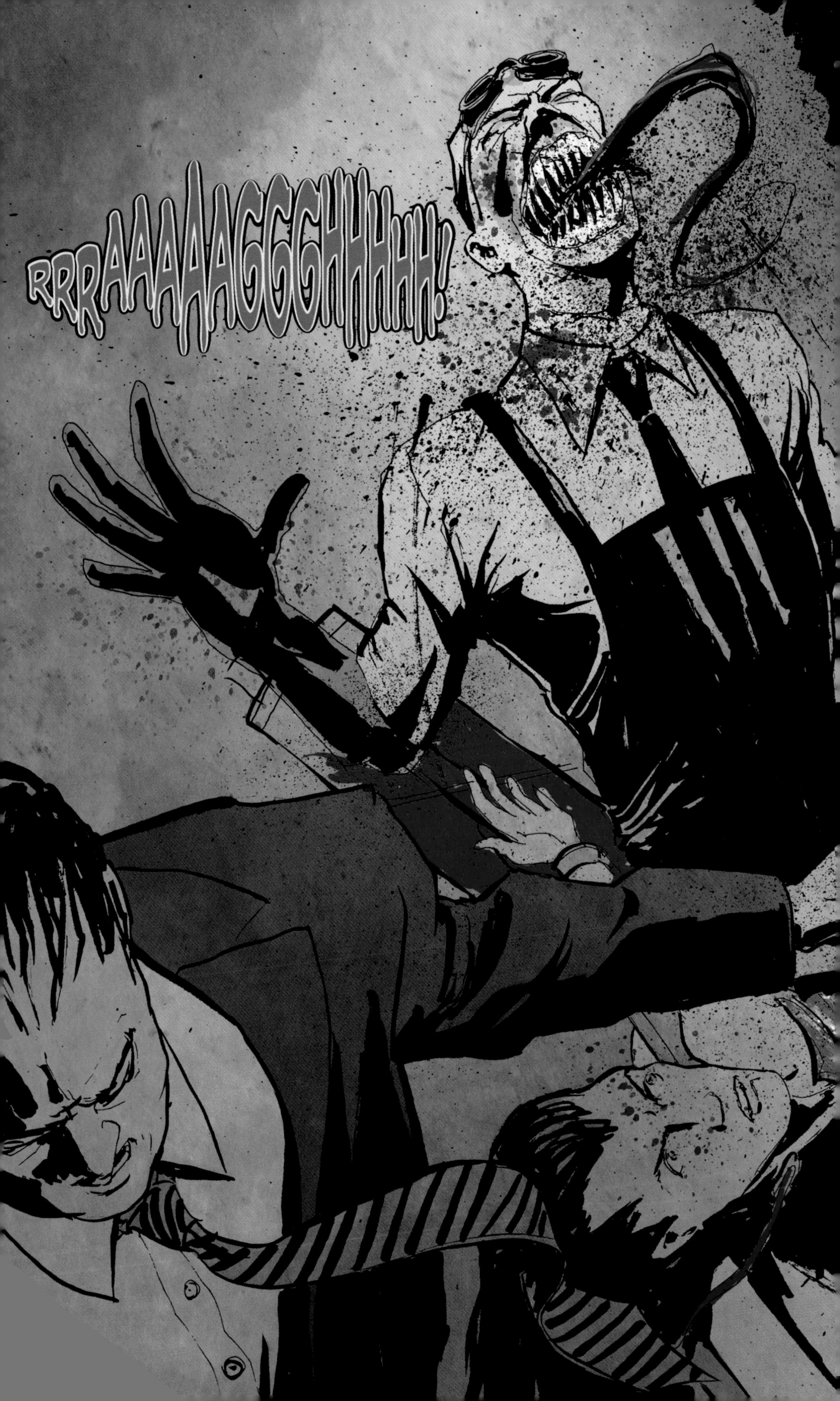
RRRAAAAAAGGGHHHHHH!

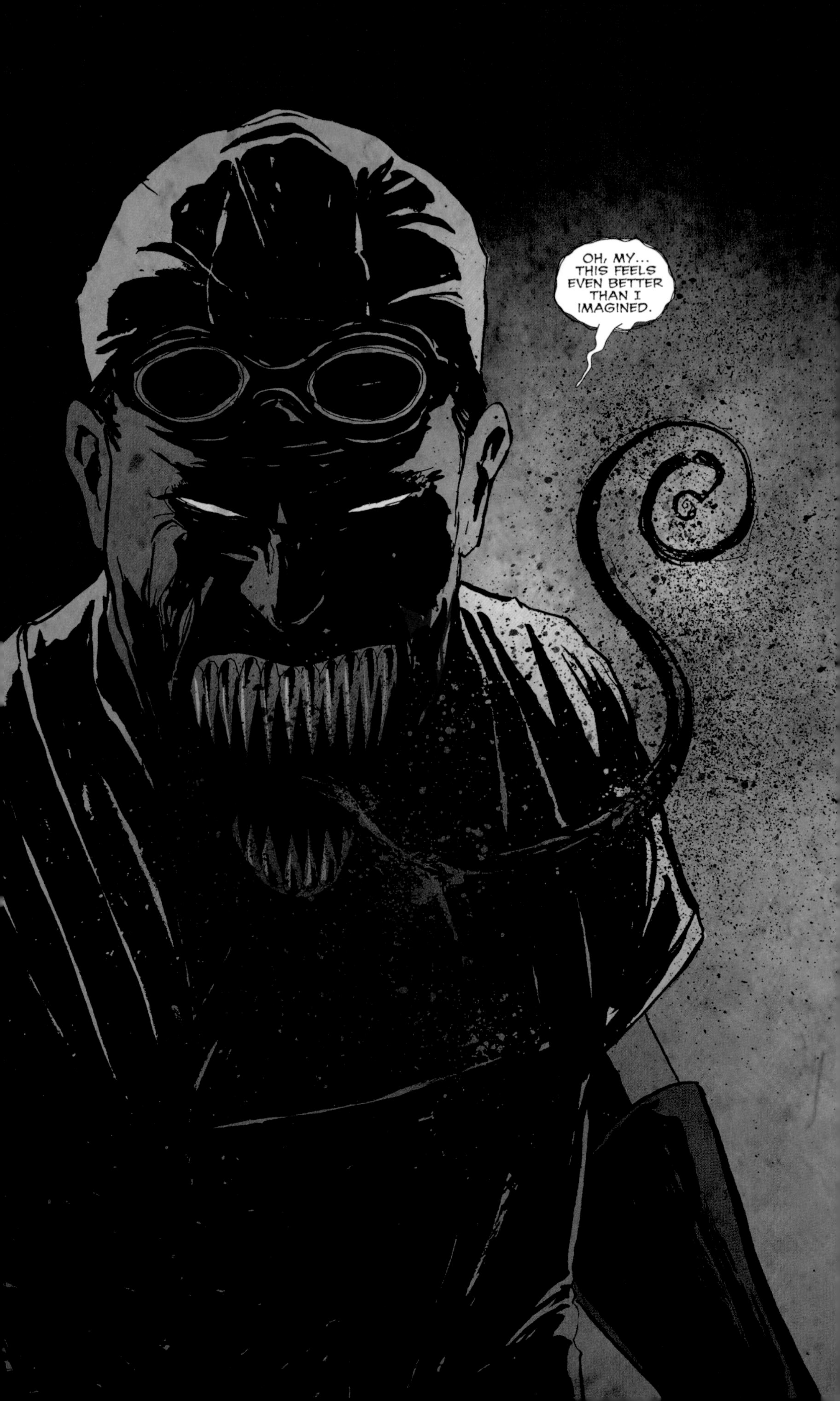
OH, MY... THIS FEELS EVEN BETTER THAN I IMAGINED.

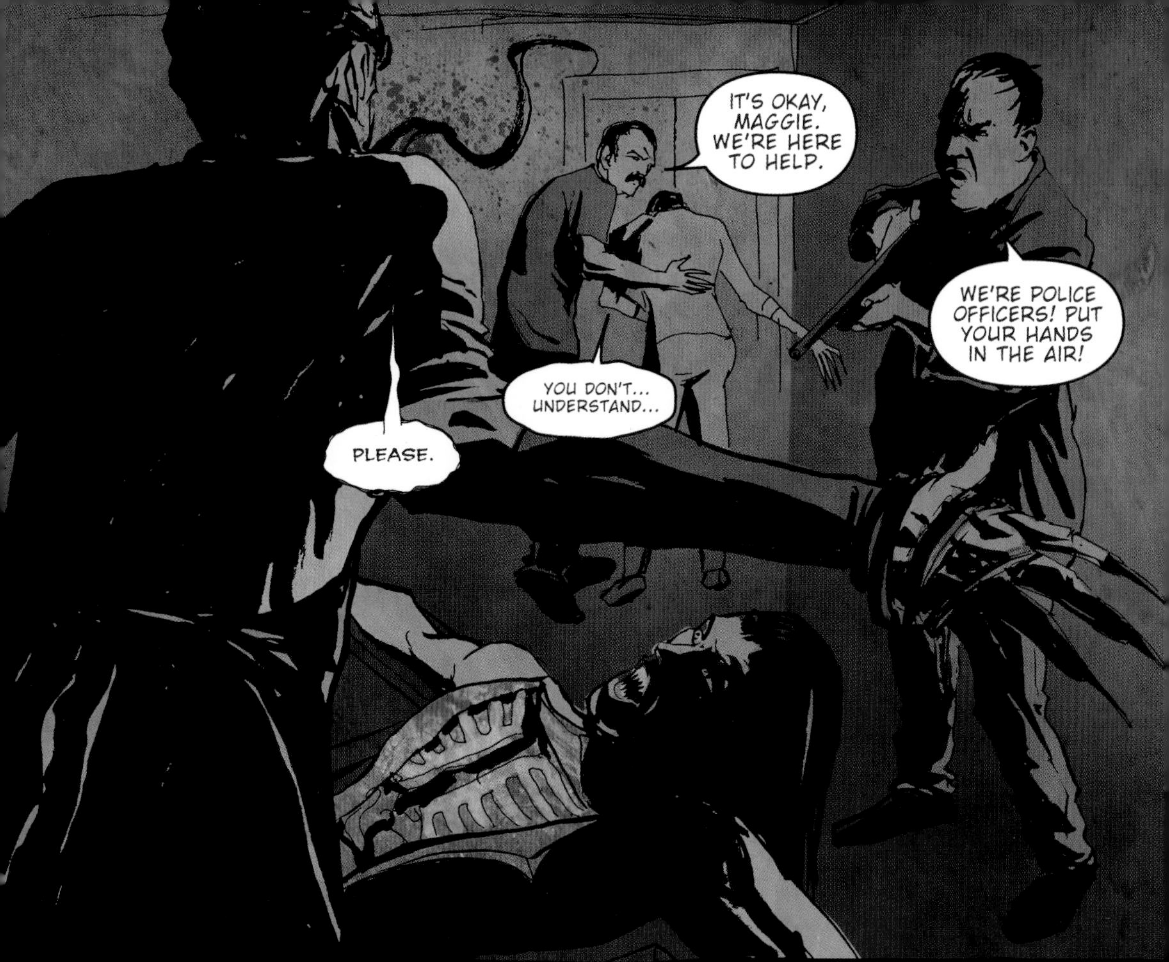
IT'S OKAY, MAGGIE. WE'RE HERE TO HELP.
WE'RE POLICE OFFICERS! PUT YOUR HANDS IN THE AIR!
YOU DON'T... UNDERSTAND...
PLEASE.

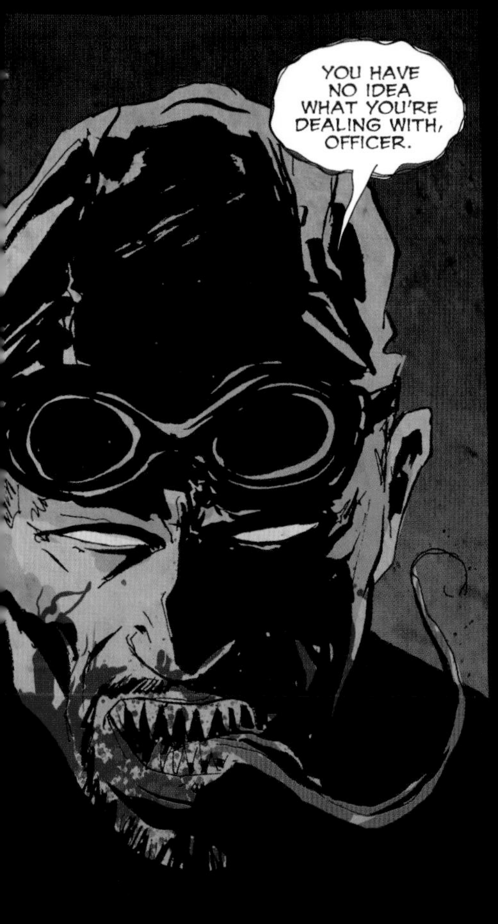
YOU HAVE NO IDEA WHAT YOU'RE DEALING WITH, OFFICER.

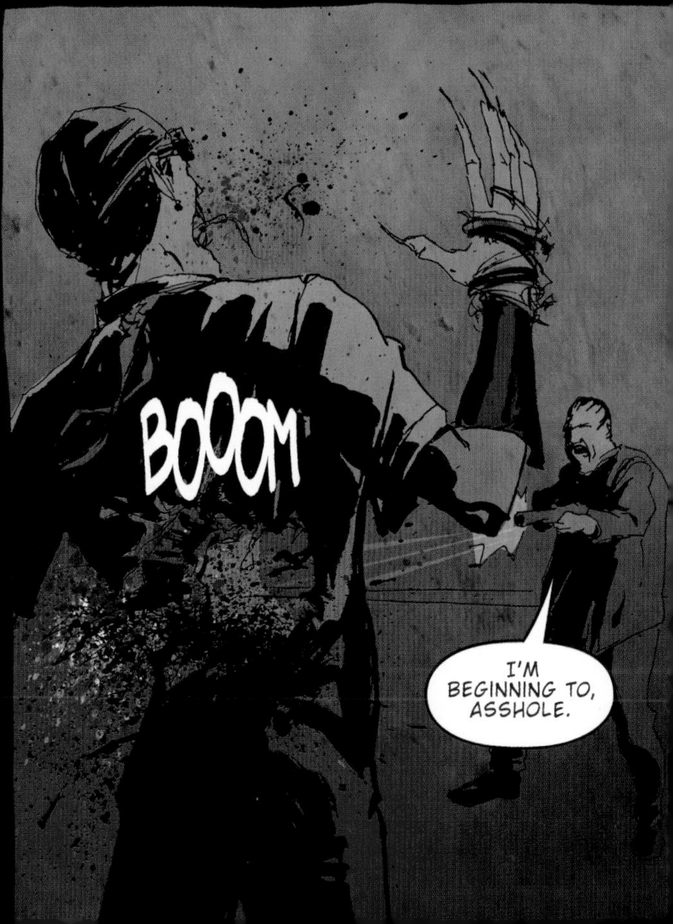
BOOOM
I'M BEGINNING TO, ASSHOLE.

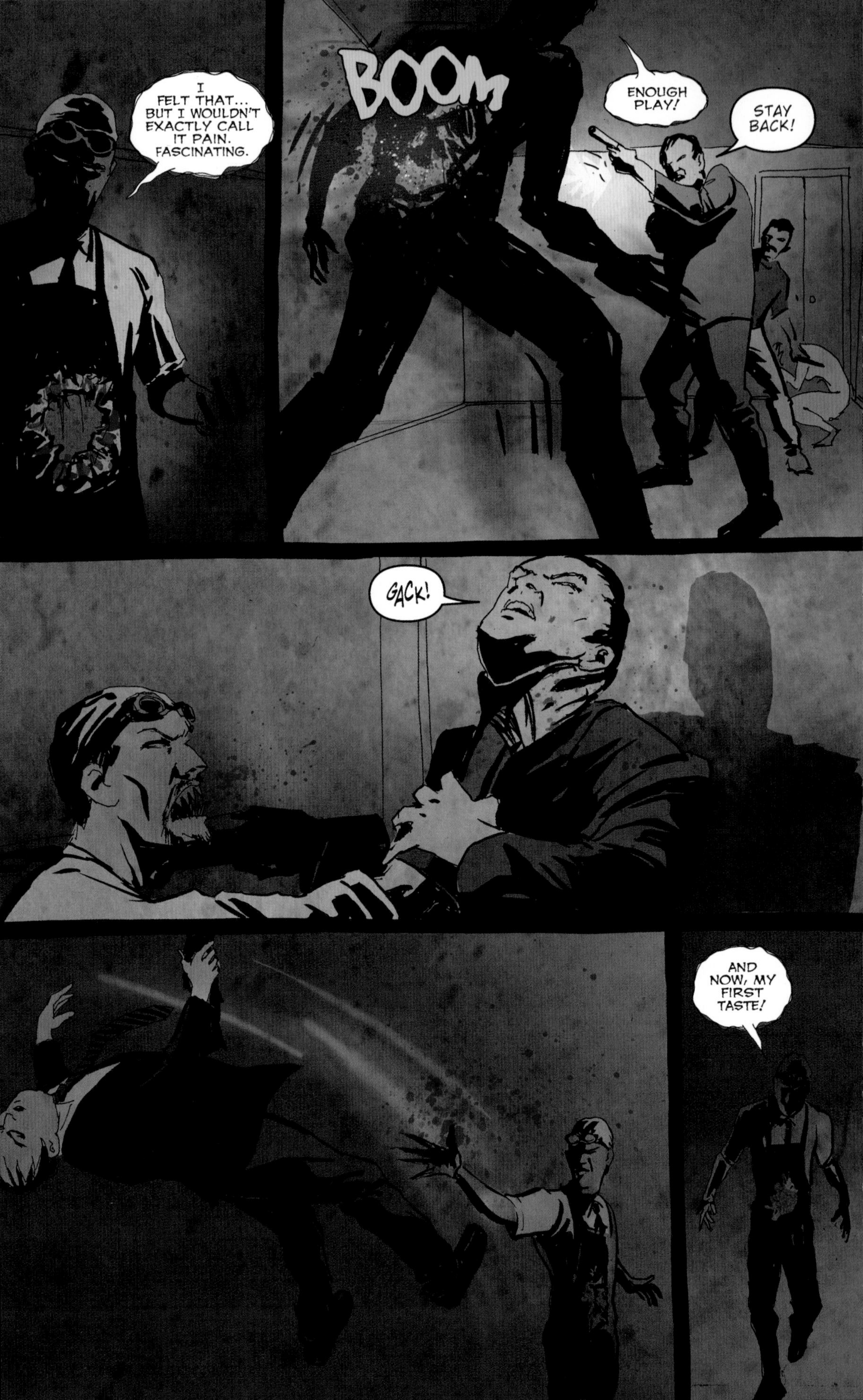
I FELT THAT... BUT I WOULDN'T EXACTLY CALL IT PAIN. FASCINATING.
BOOM
ENOUGH PLAY!
STAY BACK!
GACK!
AND NOW, MY FIRST TASTE!

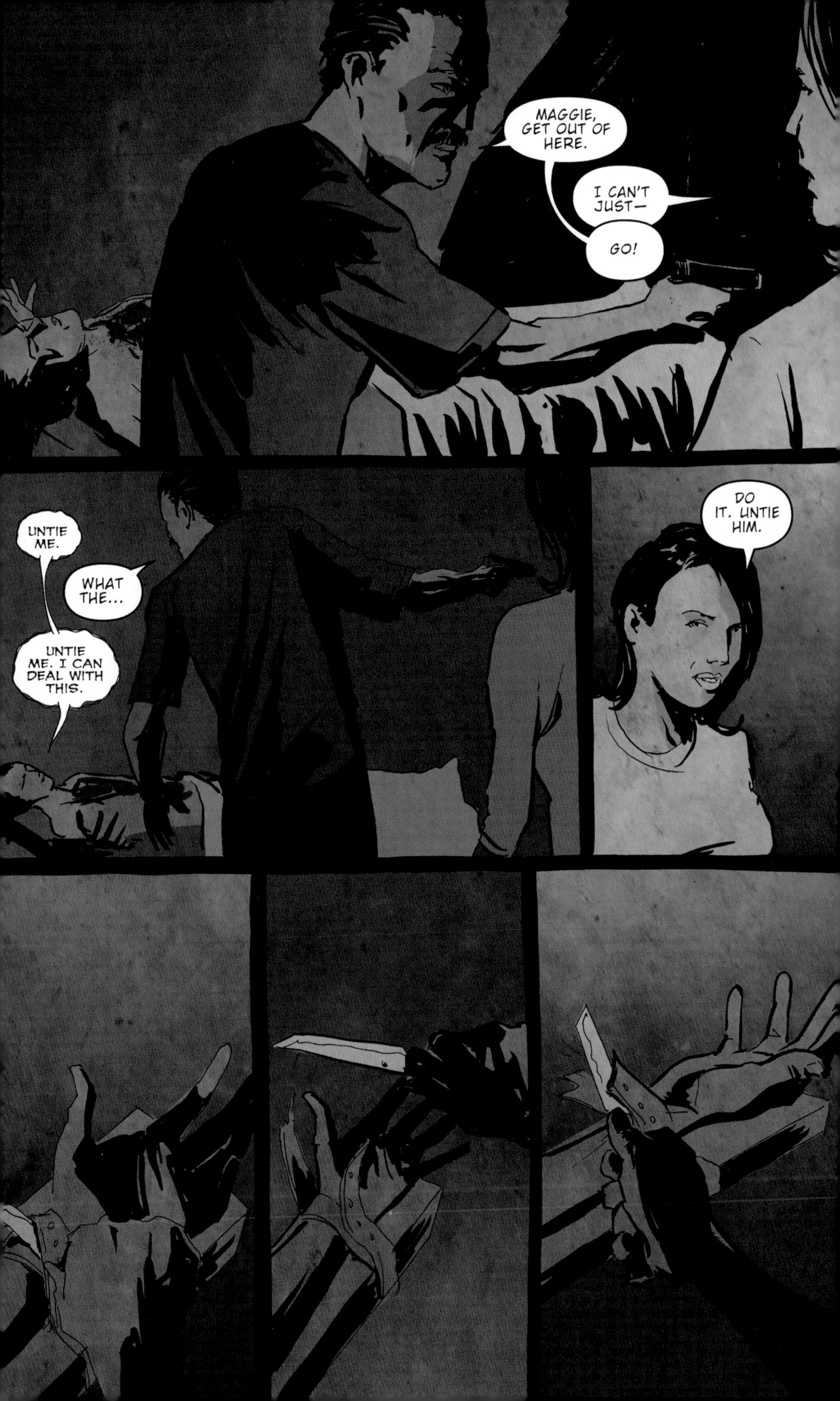
MAGGIE, GET OUT OF HERE.
I CAN'T JUST—
GO!
UNTIE ME.
WHAT THE...
UNTIE ME. I CAN DEAL WITH THIS.
DO IT. UNTIE HIM.

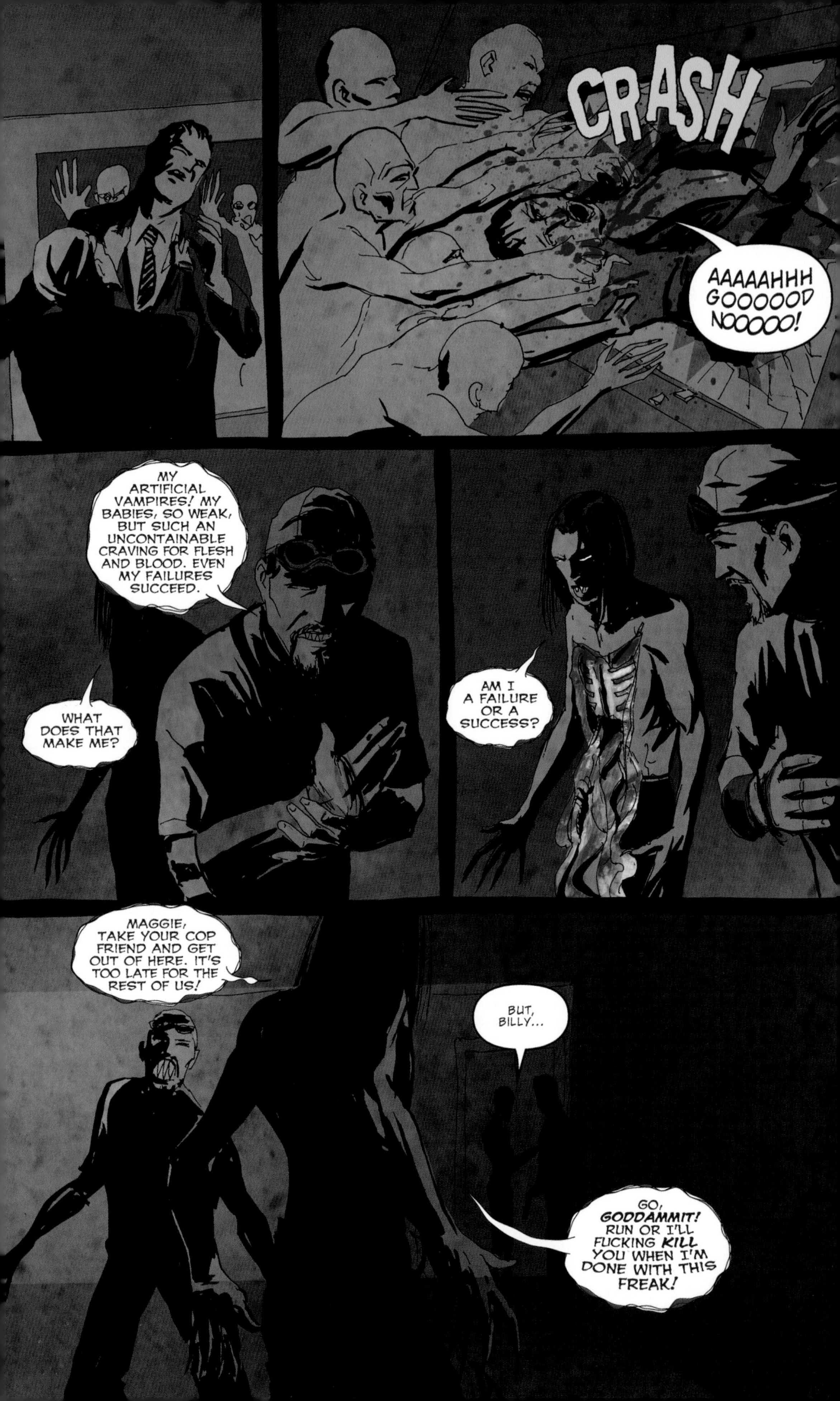
CRASH
AAAAAHHH GOOOOOD NOOOOO!
MY ARTIFICIAL VAMPIRES! MY BABIES, SO WEAK, BUT SUCH AN UNCONTAINABLE CRAVING FOR FLESH AND BLOOD. EVEN MY FAILURES SUCCEED.
WHAT DOES THAT MAKE ME?
AM I A FAILURE OR A SUCCESS?
MAGGIE, TAKE YOUR COP FRIEND AND GET OUT OF HERE. IT'S TOO LATE FOR THE REST OF US!
BUT, BILLY...
GO, GODDAMMIT! RUN OR I'LL FUCKING KILL YOU WHEN I'M DONE WITH THIS FREAK!

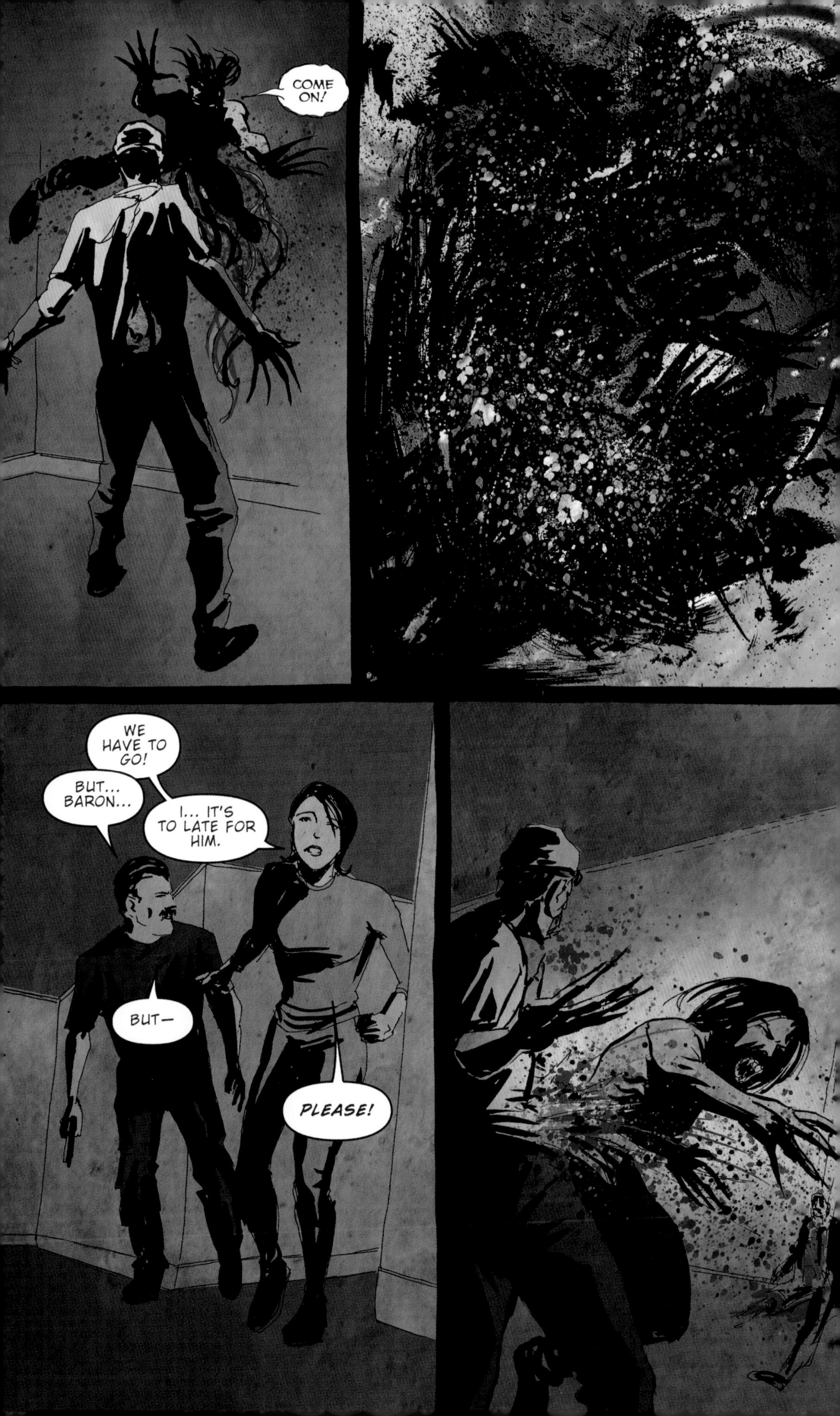
COME ON!
WE HAVE TO GO!
BUT... BARON...
I... IT'S TO LATE FOR HIM.
BUT—
PLEASE!

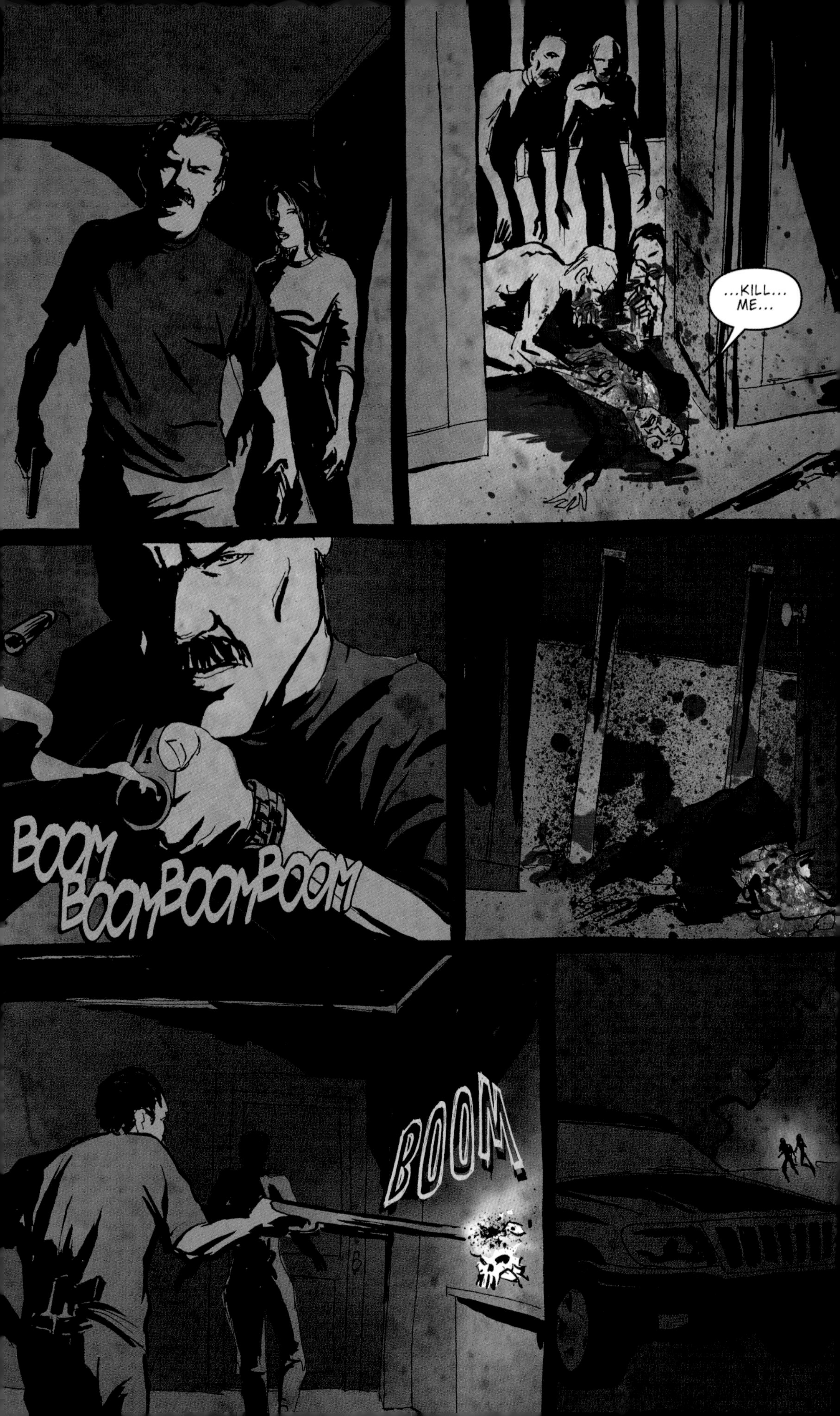
...KILL... ME...
BOOM
BOOMBOOMBOOM
BOOM

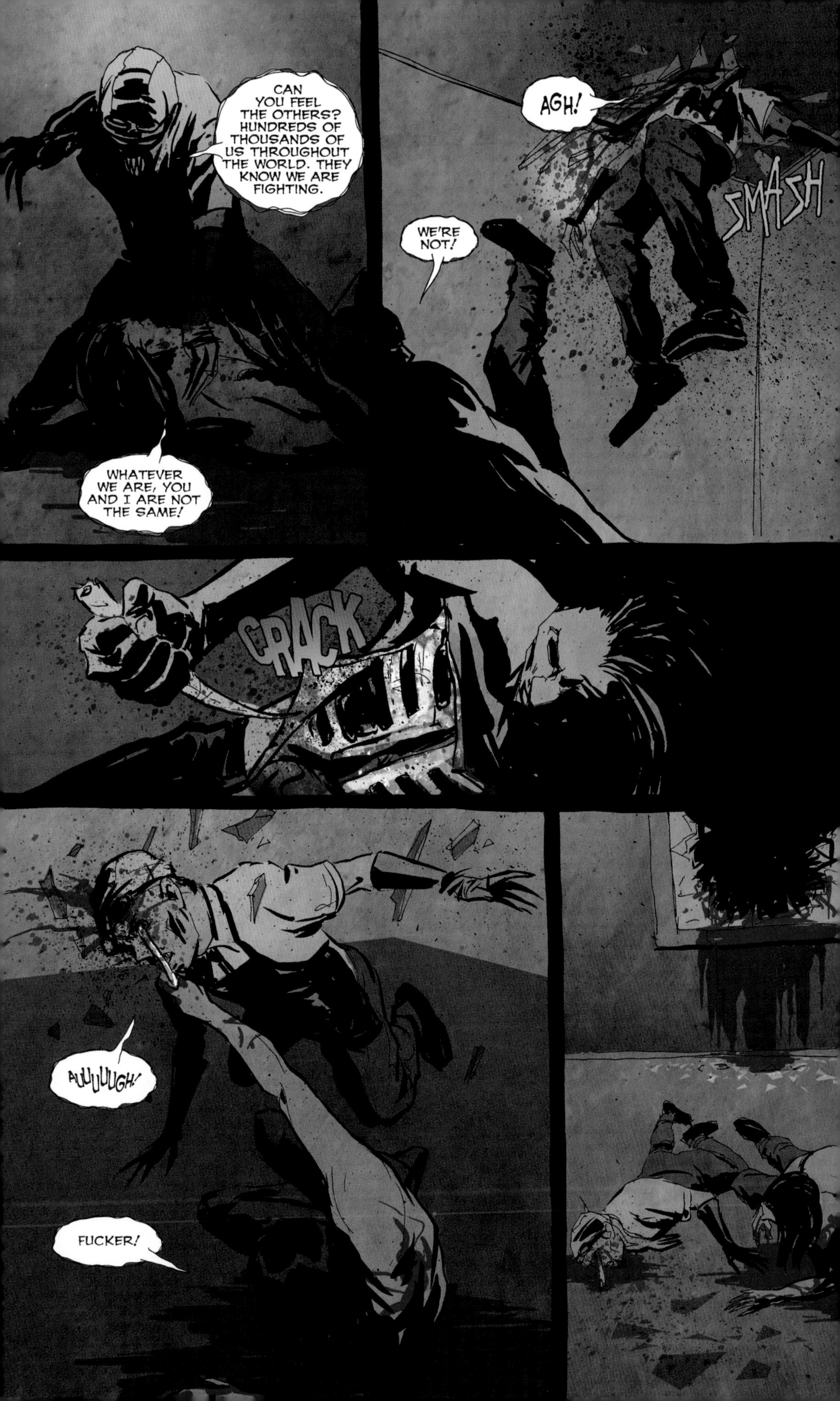
CAN YOU FEEL THE OTHERS? HUNDREDS OF THOUSANDS OF US THROUGHOUT THE WORLD. THEY KNOW WE ARE FIGHTING.
WHATEVER WE ARE, YOU AND I ARE NOT THE SAME!
WE'RE NOT!
AGH!
SMASH
CRACK
AUUUUUGH!
FUCKER!

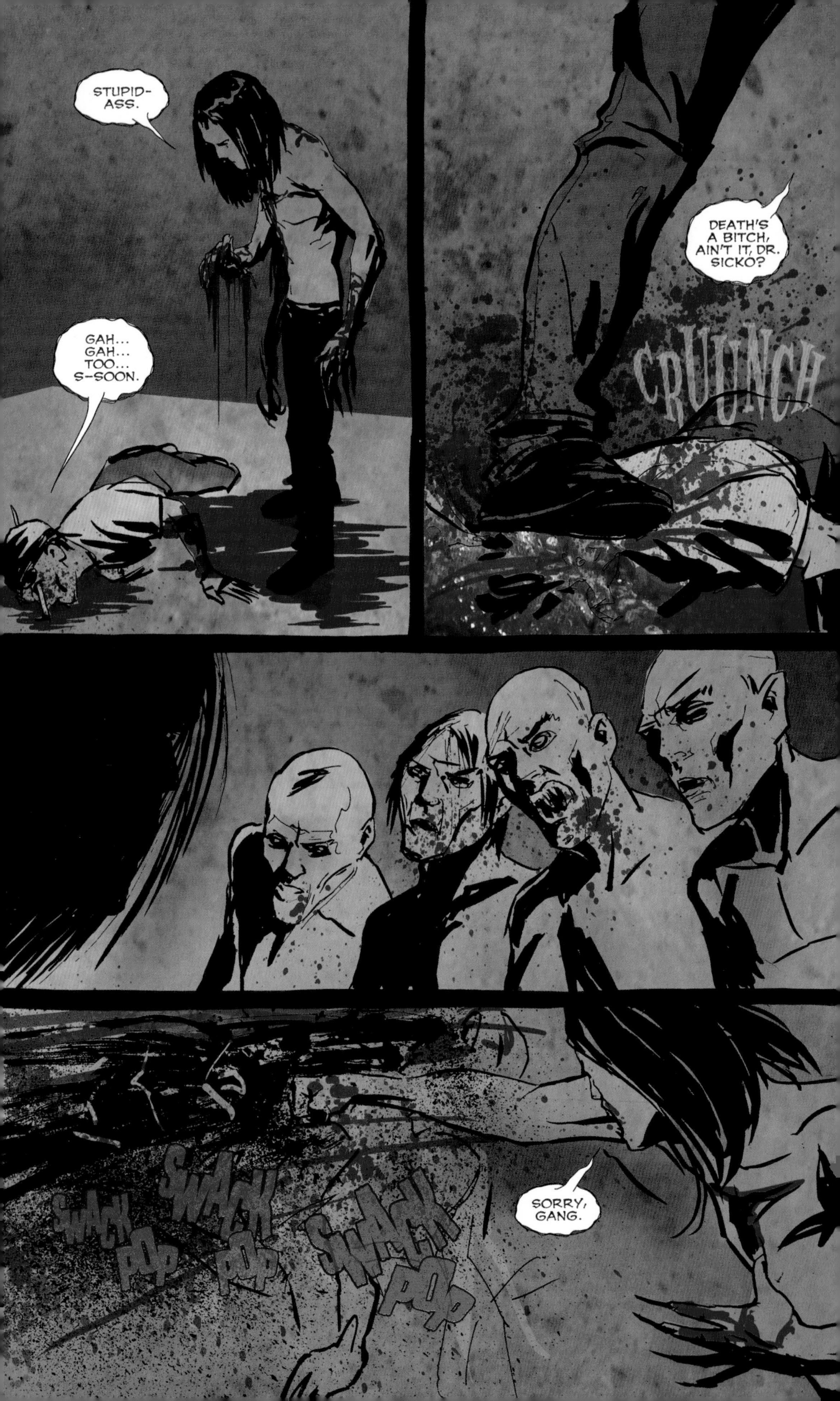

STUPID-ASS.
GAH... GAH... TOO... S-SOON.
DEATH'S A BITCH, AIN'T IT, DR. SICKO?
CRUUNCH
SWACK POP
SWACK POP
SWACK POP
SORRY, GANG.

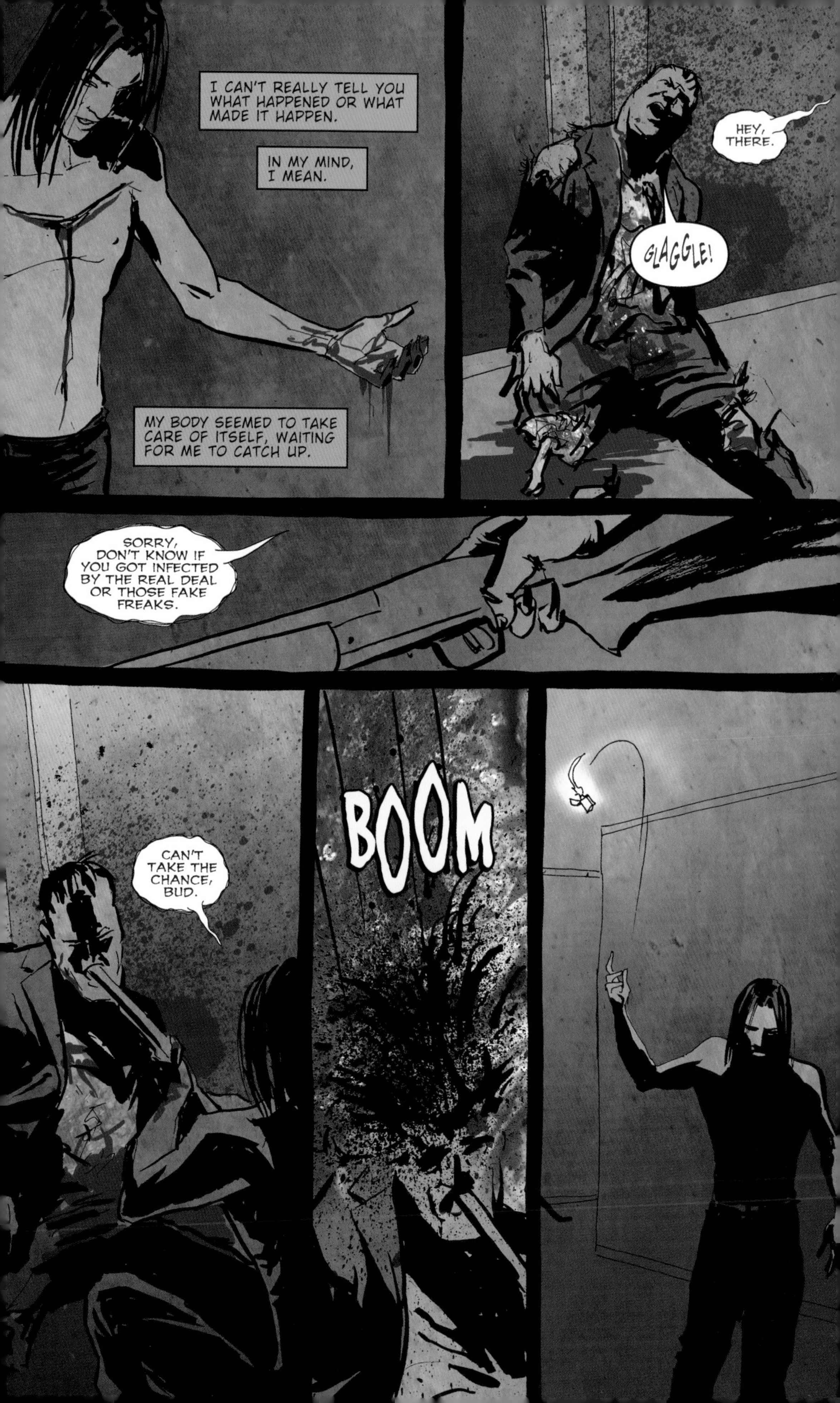
I CAN'T REALLY TELL YOU WHAT HAPPENED OR WHAT MADE IT HAPPEN.
IN MY MIND, I MEAN.
MY BODY SEEMED TO TAKE CARE OF ITSELF, WAITING FOR ME TO CATCH UP.
HEY, THERE.
GLAGGLE!
SORRY, DON'T KNOW IF YOU GOT INFECTED BY THE REAL DEAL OR THOSE FAKE FREAKS.
CAN'T TAKE THE CHANCE, BUD.
BOOM

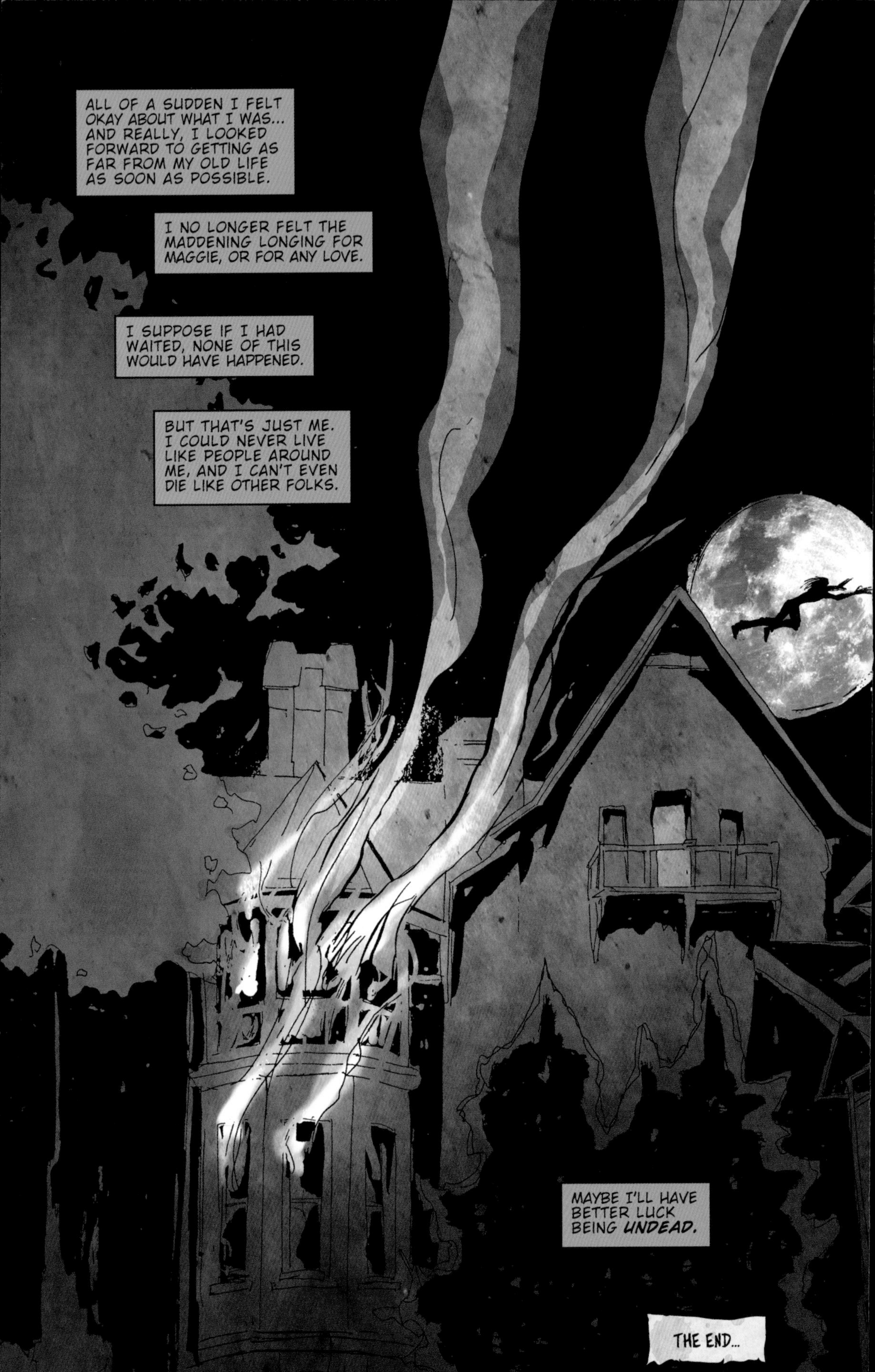
ALL OF A SUDDEN I FELT OKAY ABOUT WHAT I WAS... AND REALLY, I LOOKED FORWARD TO GETTING AS FAR FROM MY OLD LIFE AS SOON AS POSSIBLE.
I NO LONGER FELT THE MADDENING LONGING FOR MAGGIE, OR FOR ANY LOVE.
I SUPPOSE IF I HAD WAITED, NONE OF THIS WOULD HAVE HAPPENED.
BUT THAT'S JUST ME. I COULD NEVER LIVE LIKE PEOPLE AROUND ME, AND I CAN'T EVEN DIE LIKE OTHER FOLKS.
MAYBE I'LL HAVE BETTER LUCK BEING *UNDEAD.*
THE END...

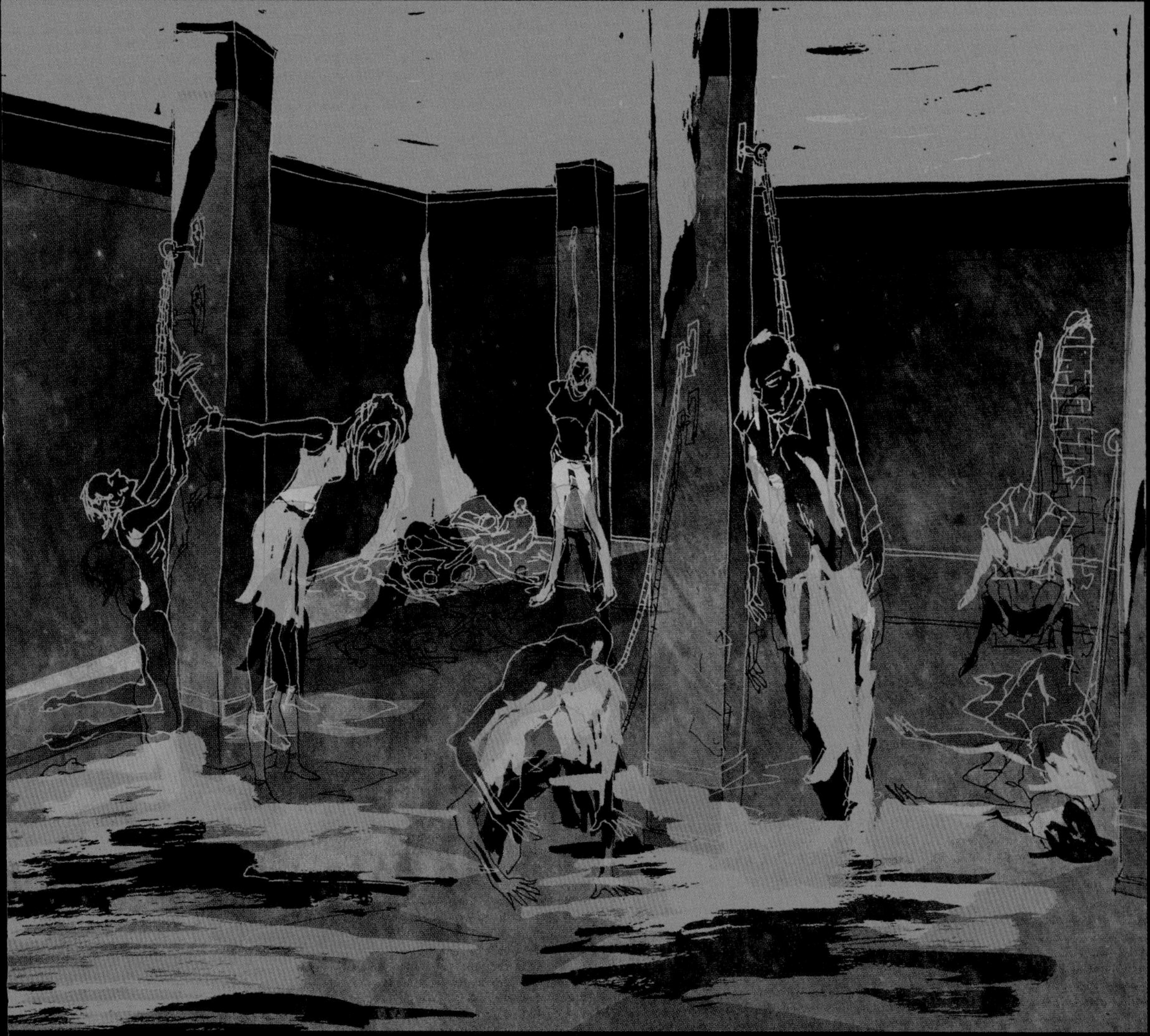

"JUAREZ
OR
LEX NOVA & THE CASE OF
THE 400 DEAD MEXICAN GIRLS"

STORY
MATT FRACTION

ART
BEN TEMPLESMITH

LETTERS
ROBBIE ROBBINS & TOM B. LONG

DESIGN
NEIL UYETAKE

EDITS
CHRIS RYALL

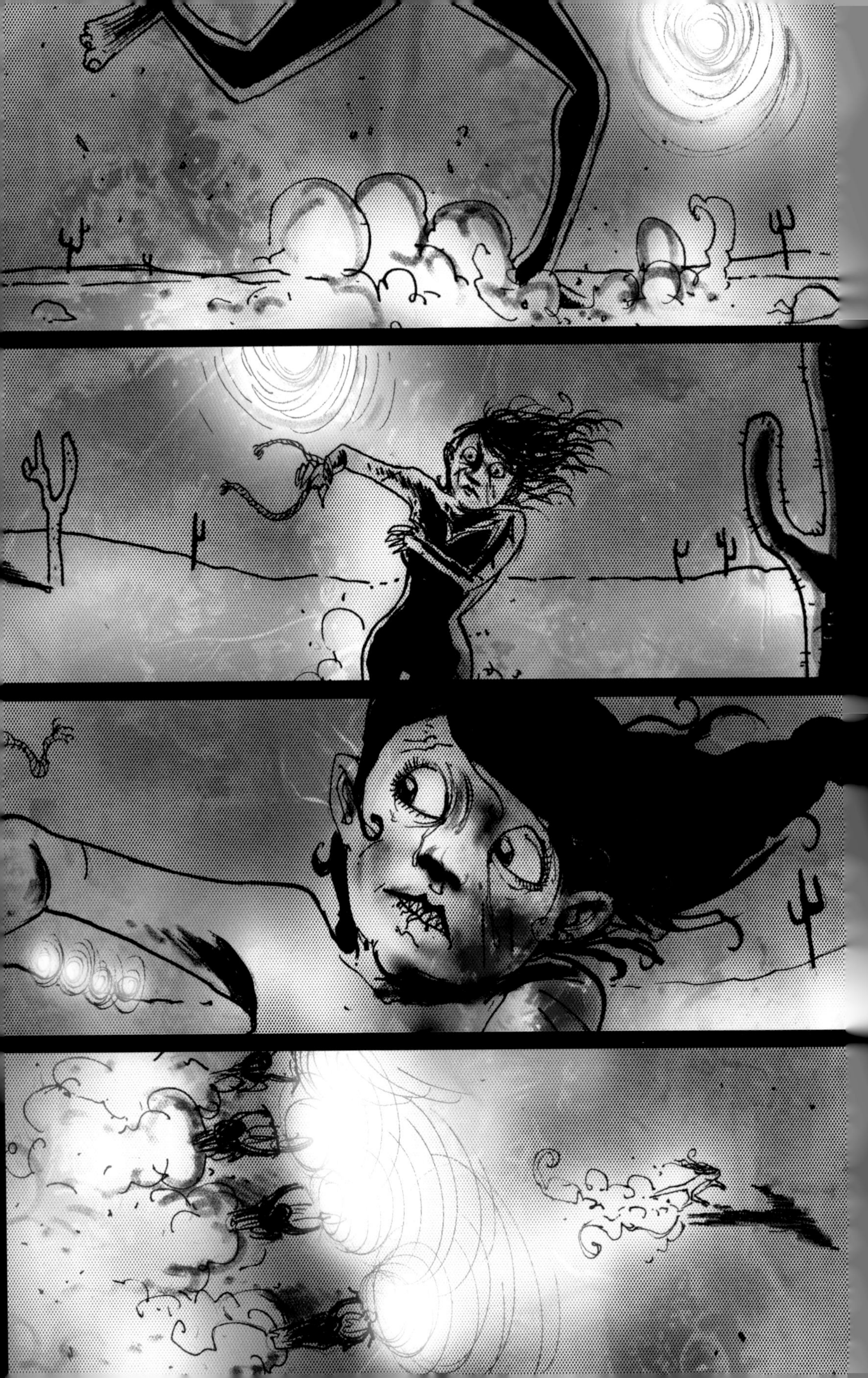

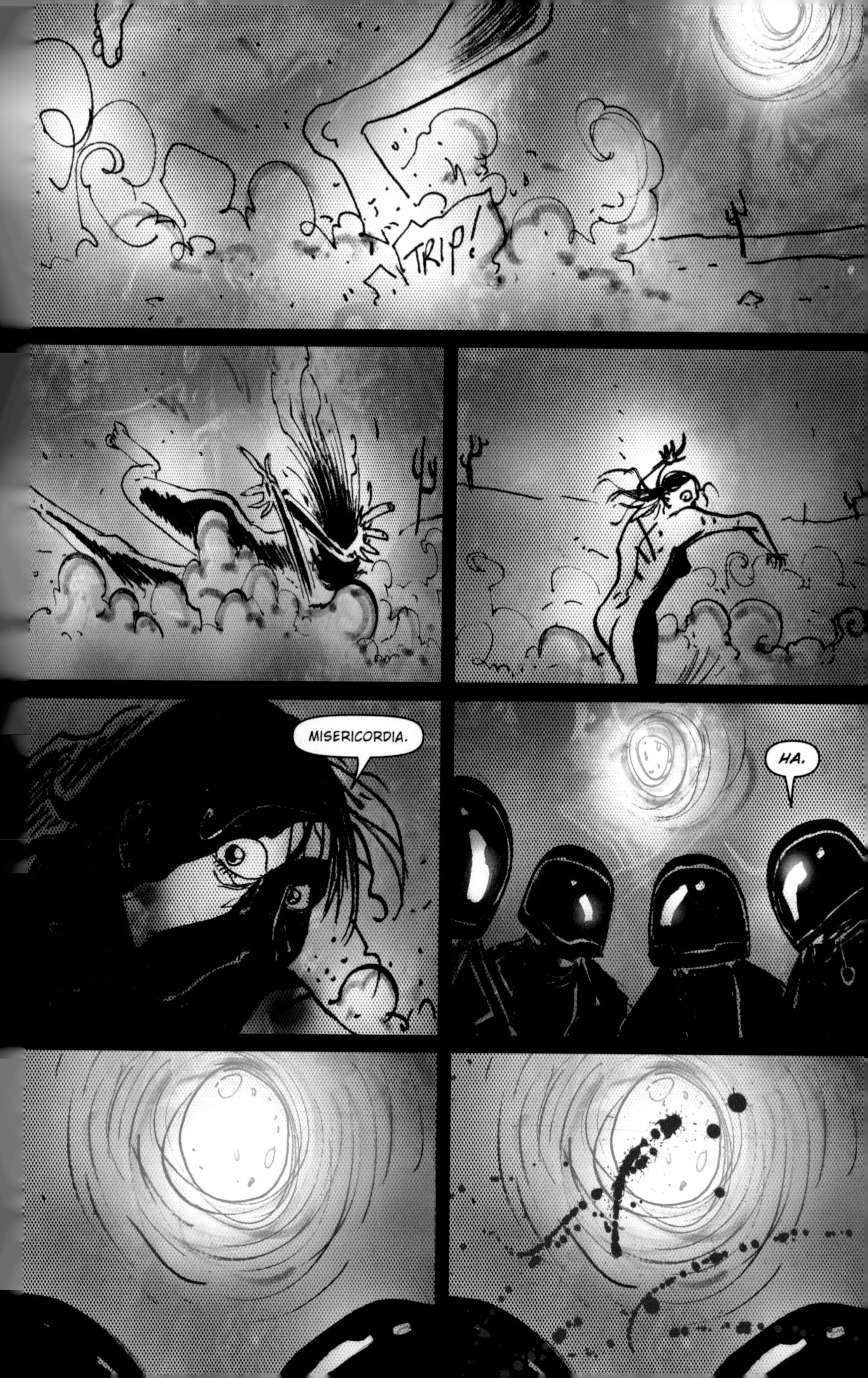
TRIP!
MISERICORDIA.
HA.

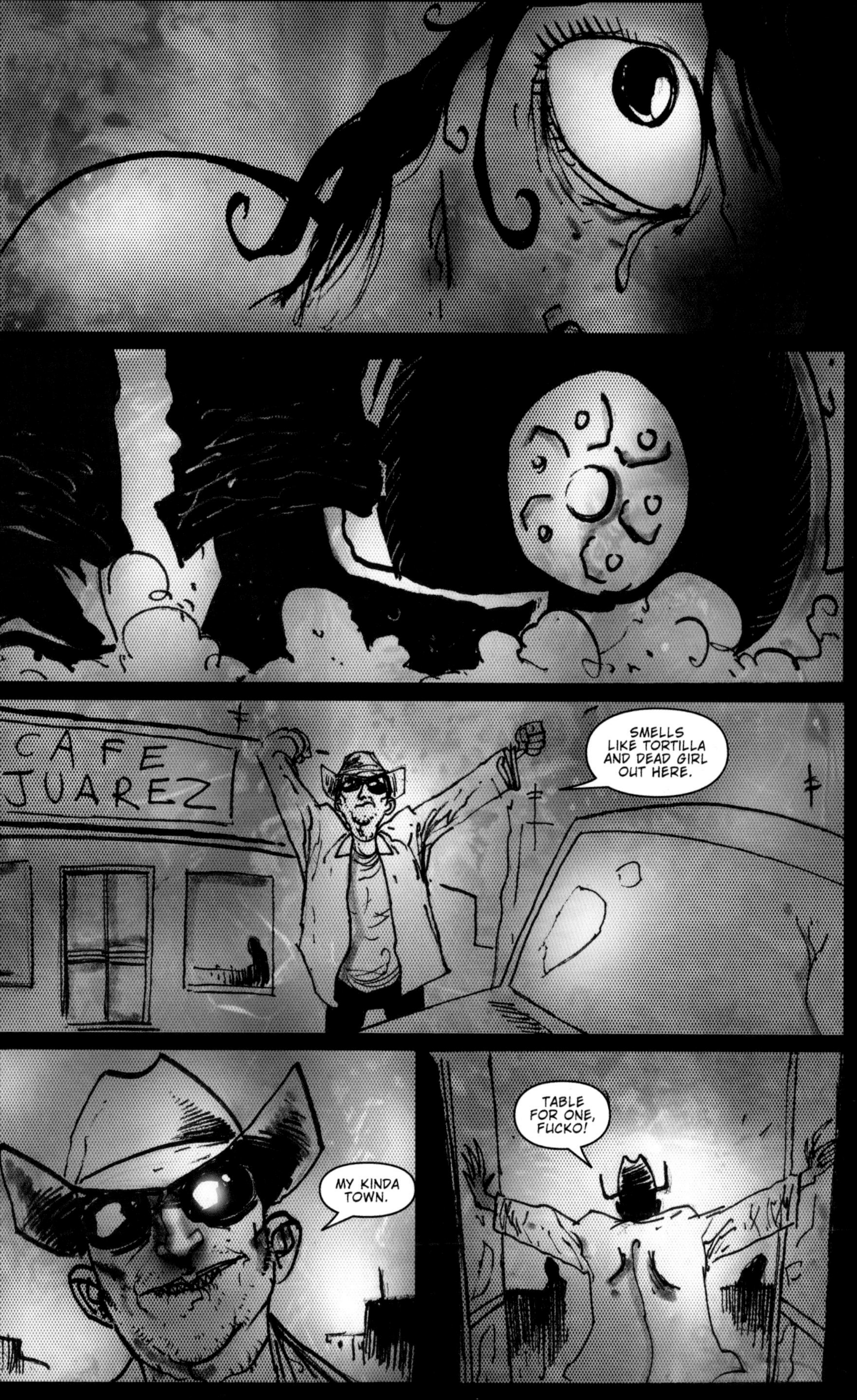
CAFE JUAREZ
SMELLS LIKE TORTILLA AND DEAD GIRL OUT HERE.
MY KINDA TOWN.
TABLE FOR ONE, FUCKO!

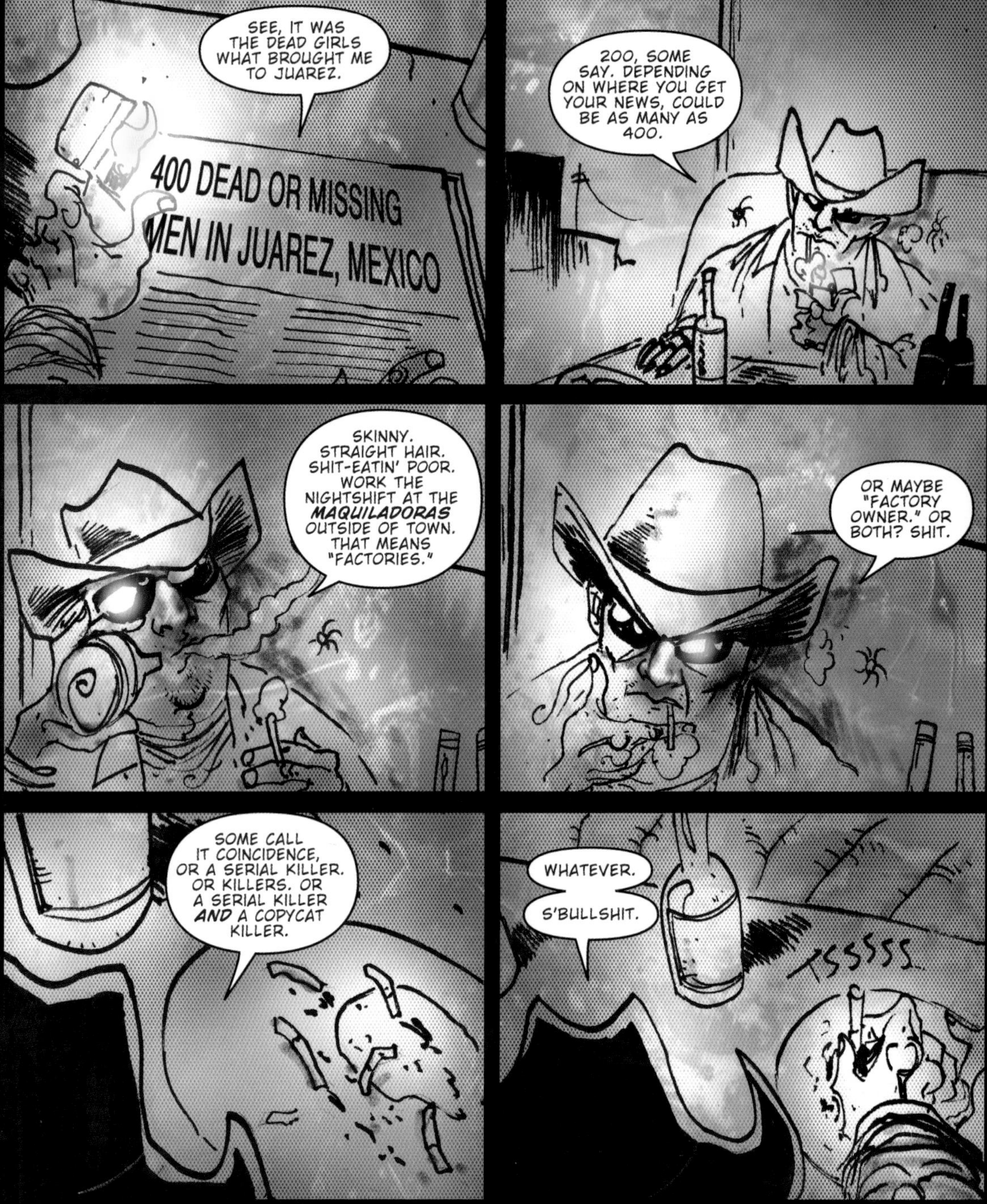
SEE, IT WAS THE DEAD GIRLS WHAT BROUGHT ME TO JUAREZ.
400 DEAD OR MISSING
MEN IN JUAREZ, MEXICO
200, SOME SAY. DEPENDING ON WHERE YOU GET YOUR NEWS, COULD BE AS MANY AS 400.
SKINNY. STRAIGHT HAIR. SHIT-EATIN' POOR. WORK THE NIGHTSHIFT AT THE ***MAQUILADORAS*** OUTSIDE OF TOWN. THAT MEANS "FACTORIES."
OR MAYBE "FACTORY OWNER." OR BOTH? SHIT.
SOME CALL IT COINCIDENCE, OR A SERIAL KILLER. OR KILLERS. OR A SERIAL KILLER ***AND*** A COPYCAT KILLER.
WHATEVER.
S'BULLSHIT.
TSSSSS.

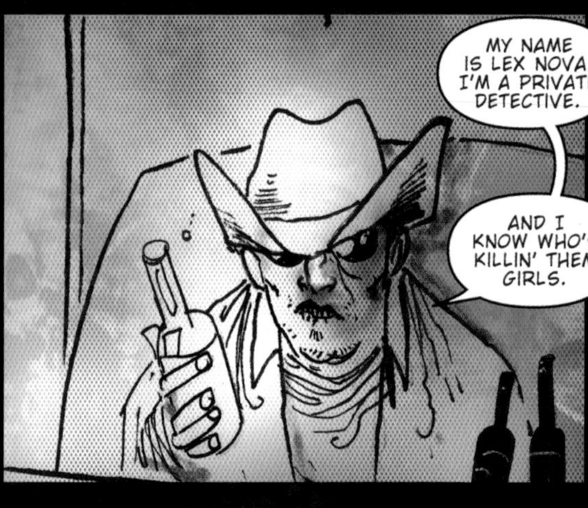
MY NAME IS LEX NOVA. I'M A PRIVATE DETECTIVE.
AND I KNOW WHO'S KILLIN' THEM GIRLS.

"JUAREZ

OR

LEX NOVA & THE CASE OF THE 400 DEAD MEXICAN GIRLS"

PART ONE: SENORA CERO

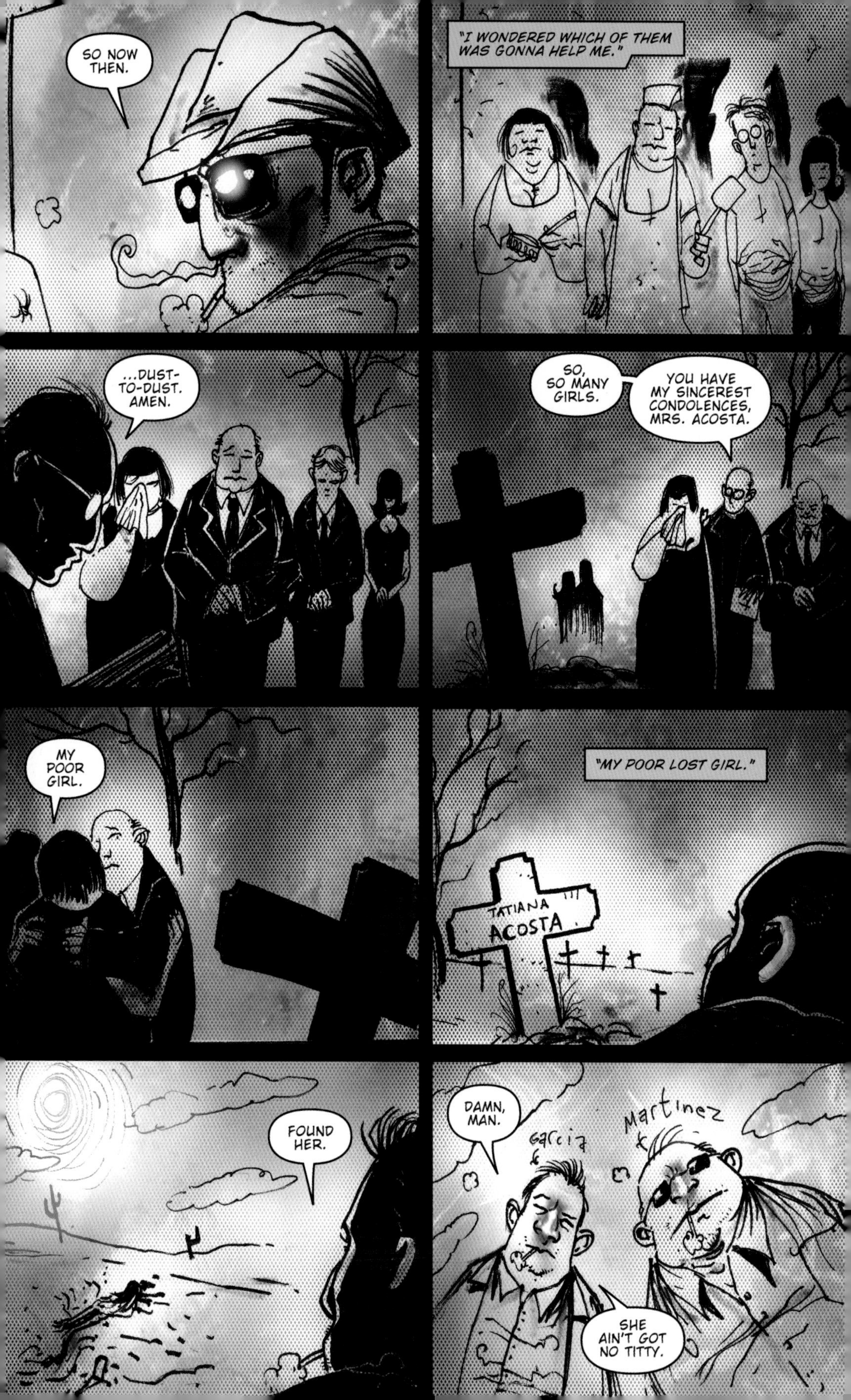
SO NOW THEN.
"I WONDERED WHICH OF THEM WAS GONNA HELP ME."
...DUST-TO-DUST. AMEN.
SO, SO MANY GIRLS.
YOU HAVE MY SINCEREST CONDOLENCES, MRS. ACOSTA.
MY POOR GIRL.
"MY POOR LOST GIRL."
TATIANA ACOSTA
FOUND HER.
DAMN, MAN.
Garcia
Martinez
SHE AIN'T GOT NO TITTY.

WE FOUND TATIANA, MA'AM.
WELL, MOST OF HER BODY, I GUESS.
"THIS IS HER, RIGHT?"
I MEAN, YOU CAN TELL AND ALL.
BECAUSE WE CAN'T.
MR. ACOSTA?
"MR. ACOSTA?"
SENORA CERO.

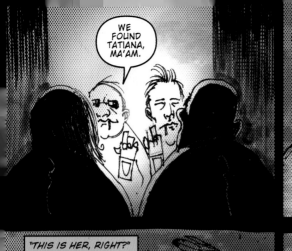

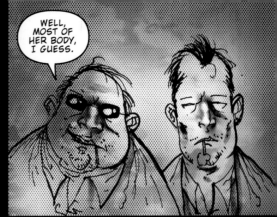

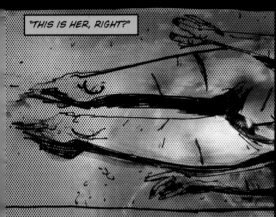

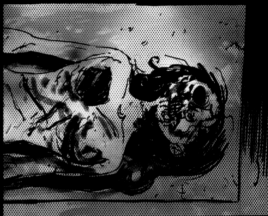

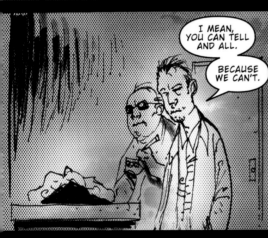

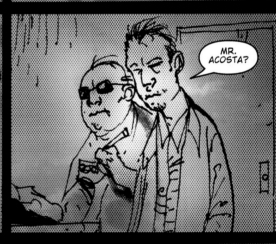

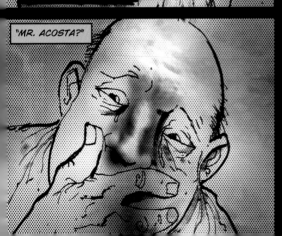

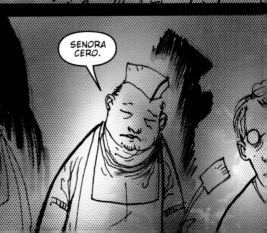

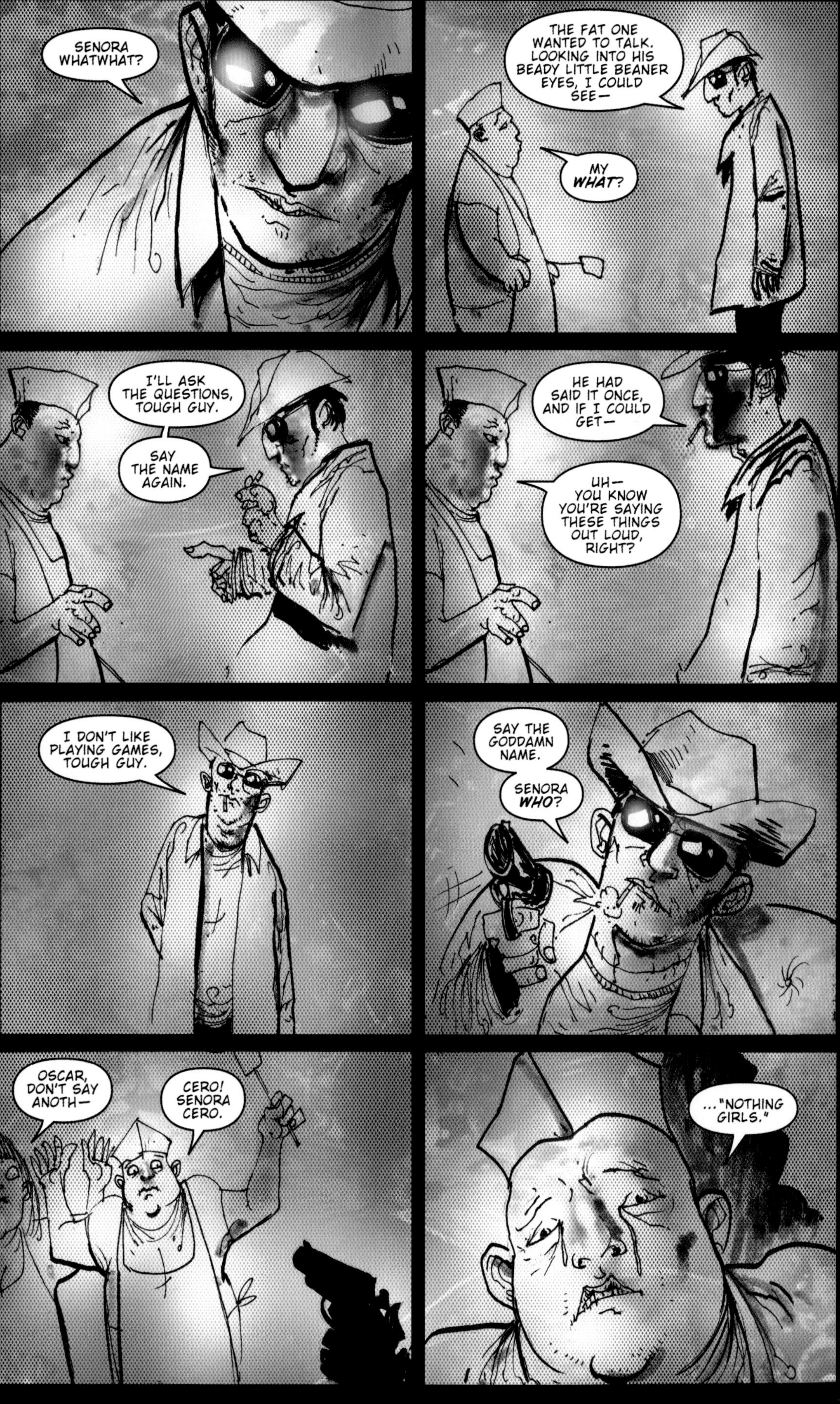
SENORA WHATWHAT?
THE FAT ONE WANTED TO TALK. LOOKING INTO HIS BEADY LITTLE BEANER EYES, I COULD SEE—
MY *WHAT*?
I'LL ASK THE QUESTIONS, TOUGH GUY.
SAY THE NAME AGAIN.
HE HAD SAID IT ONCE, AND IF I COULD GET—
UH— YOU KNOW YOU'RE SAYING THESE THINGS OUT LOUD, RIGHT?
I DON'T LIKE PLAYING GAMES, TOUGH GUY.
SAY THE GODDAMN NAME.
SENORA *WHO*?
OSCAR, DON'T SAY ANOTH—
CERO! SENORA CERO.
..."NOTHING GIRLS."

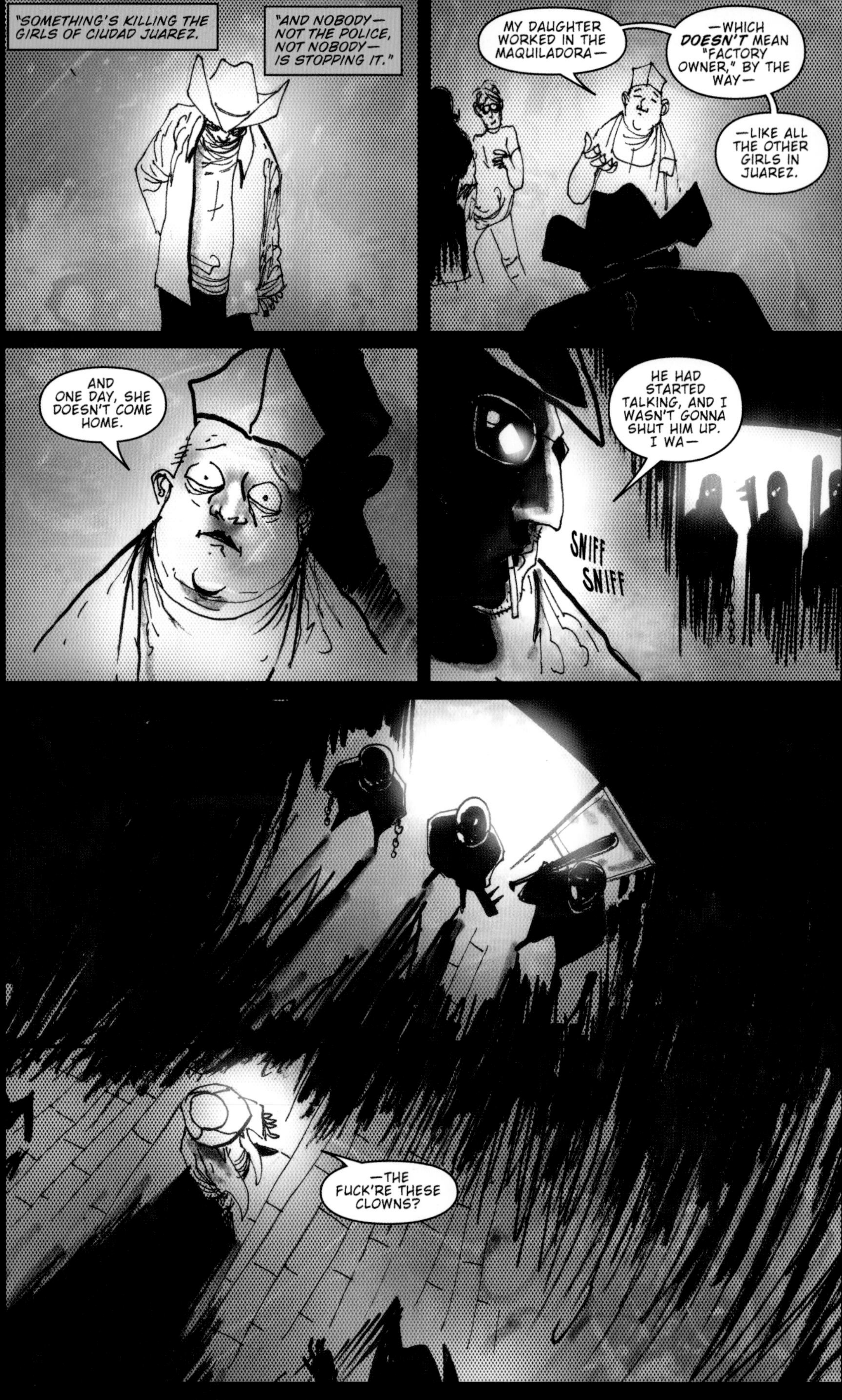
"SOMETHING'S KILLING THE GIRLS OF CIUDAD JUAREZ.
"AND NOBODY— NOT THE POLICE, NOT NOBODY— IS STOPPING IT."
MY DAUGHTER WORKED IN THE MAQUILADORA—
—WHICH **DOESN'T** MEAN "FACTORY OWNER," BY THE WAY—
—LIKE ALL THE OTHER GIRLS IN JUAREZ.
AND ONE DAY, SHE DOESN'T COME HOME.
HE HAD STARTED TALKING, AND I WASN'T GONNA SHUT HIM UP. I WA—
SNIFF
SNIFF
—THE FUCK'RE THESE CLOWNS?

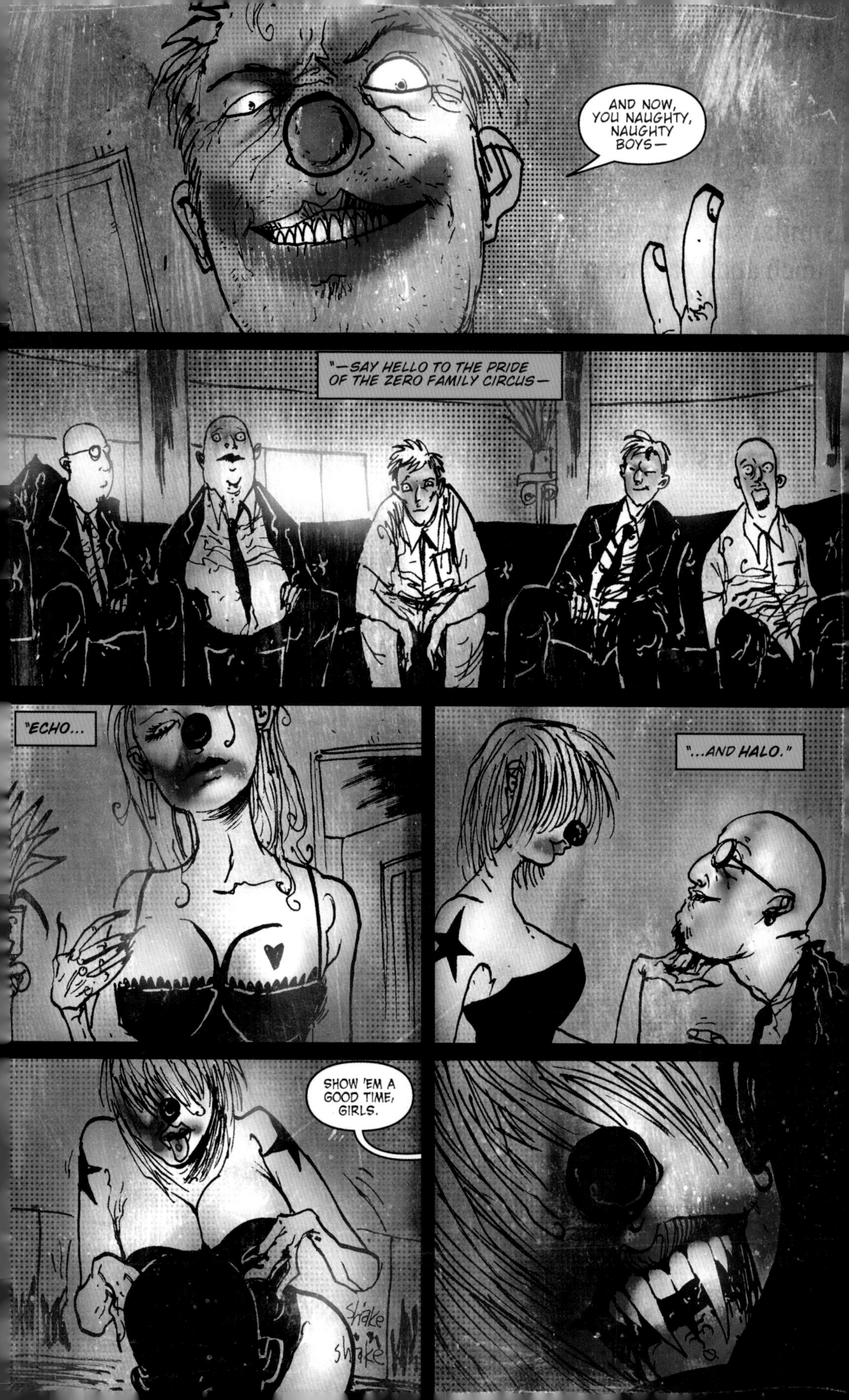
AND NOW, YOU NAUGHTY, NAUGHTY BOYS—
"—SAY HELLO TO THE PRIDE OF THE ZERO FAMILY CIRCUS—
"ECHO...
"...AND HALO."
SHOW 'EM A GOOD TIME, GIRLS.
shake
shake

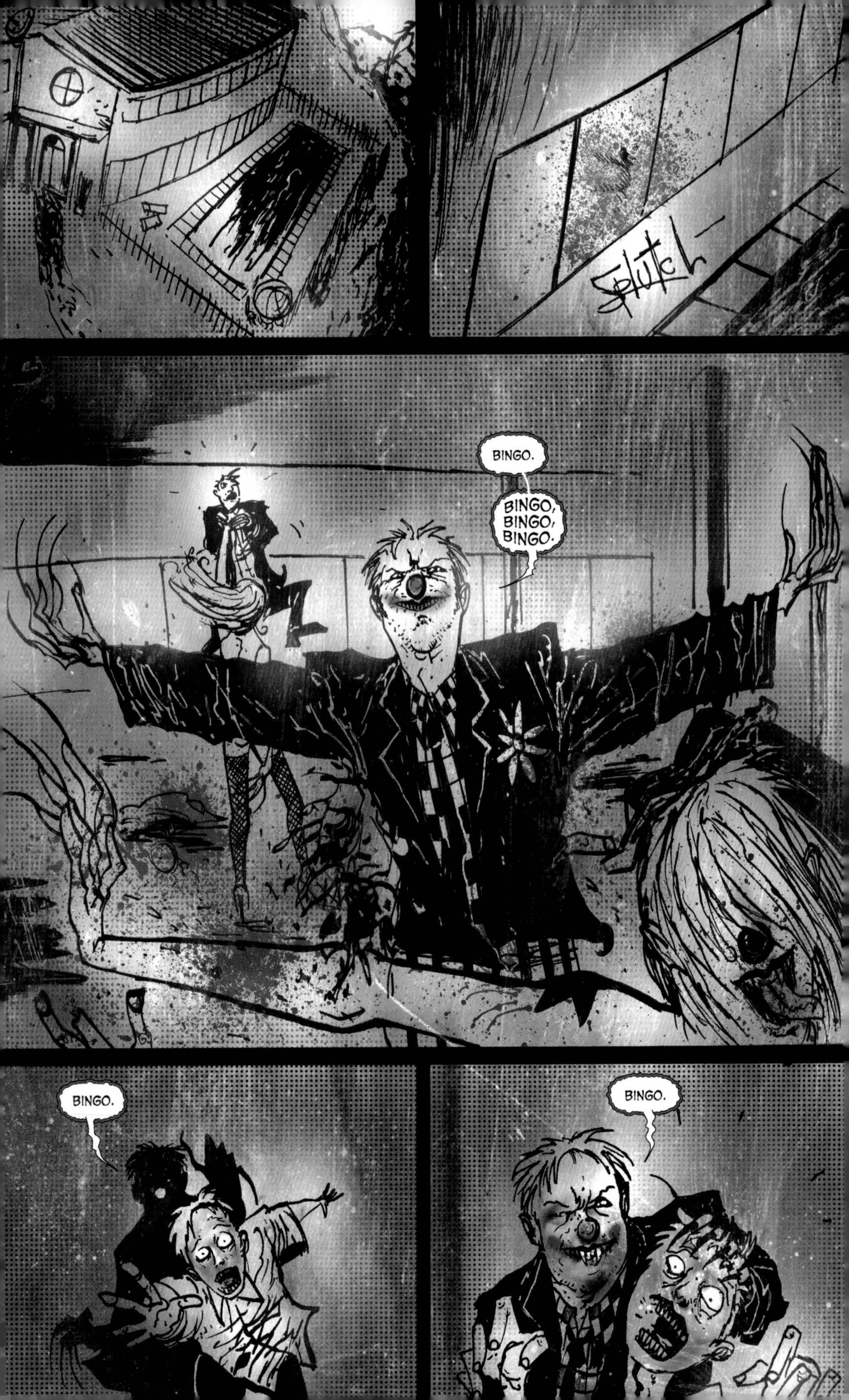
SPLUTCH
BINGO.
BINGO, BINGO, BINGO.
BINGO.
BINGO.

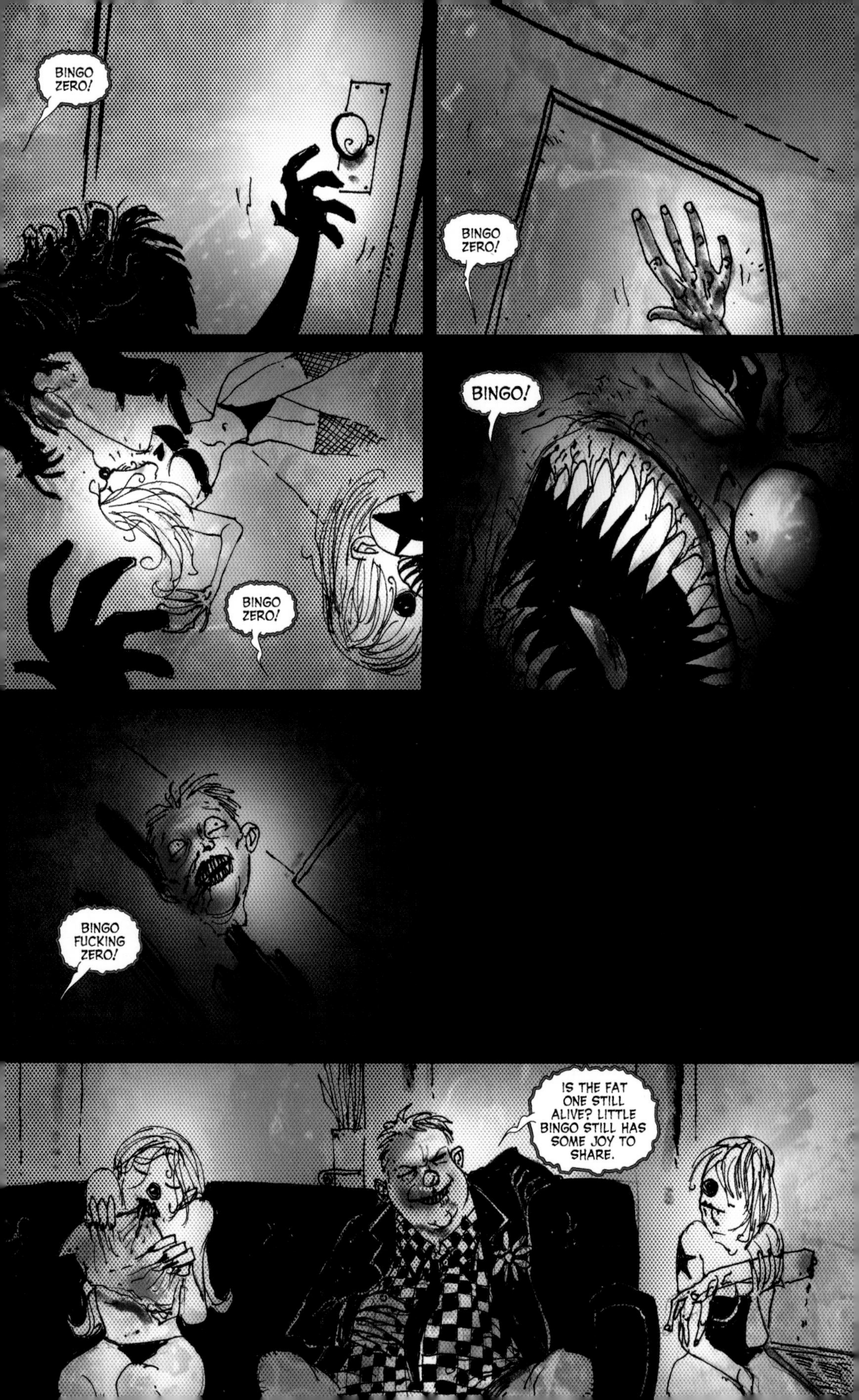
BINGO ZERO!
BINGO ZERO!
BINGO ZERO!
BINGO!
BINGO FUCKING ZERO!
IS THE FAT ONE STILL ALIVE? LITTLE BINGO STILL HAS SOME JOY TO SHARE.

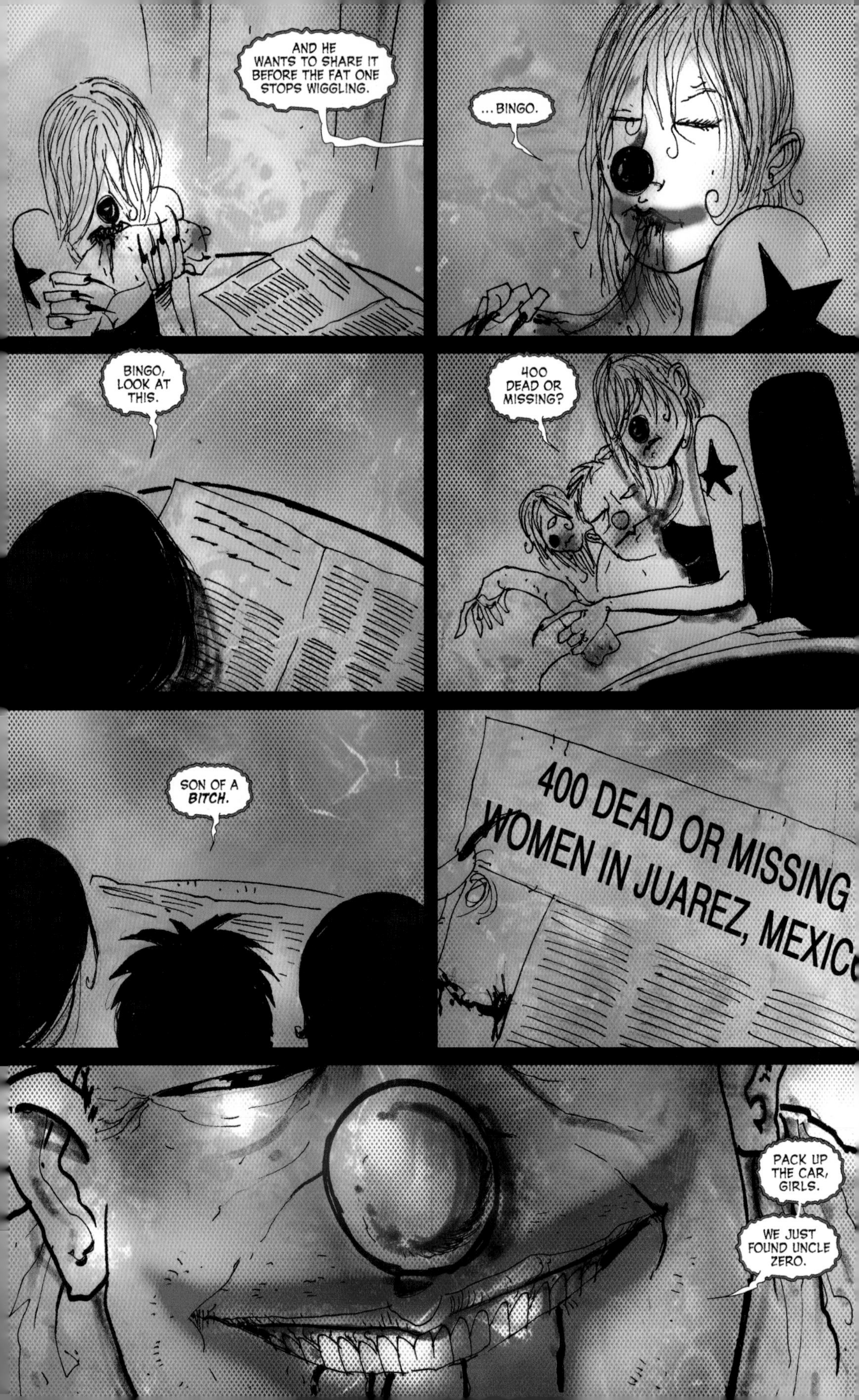
AND HE WANTS TO SHARE IT BEFORE THE FAT ONE STOPS WIGGLING.
...BINGO.
BINGO, LOOK AT THIS.
400 DEAD OR MISSING?
SON OF A BITCH.
400 DEAD OR MISSING
WOMEN IN JUAREZ, MEXICO
PACK UP THE CAR, GIRLS.
WE JUST FOUND UNCLE ZERO.

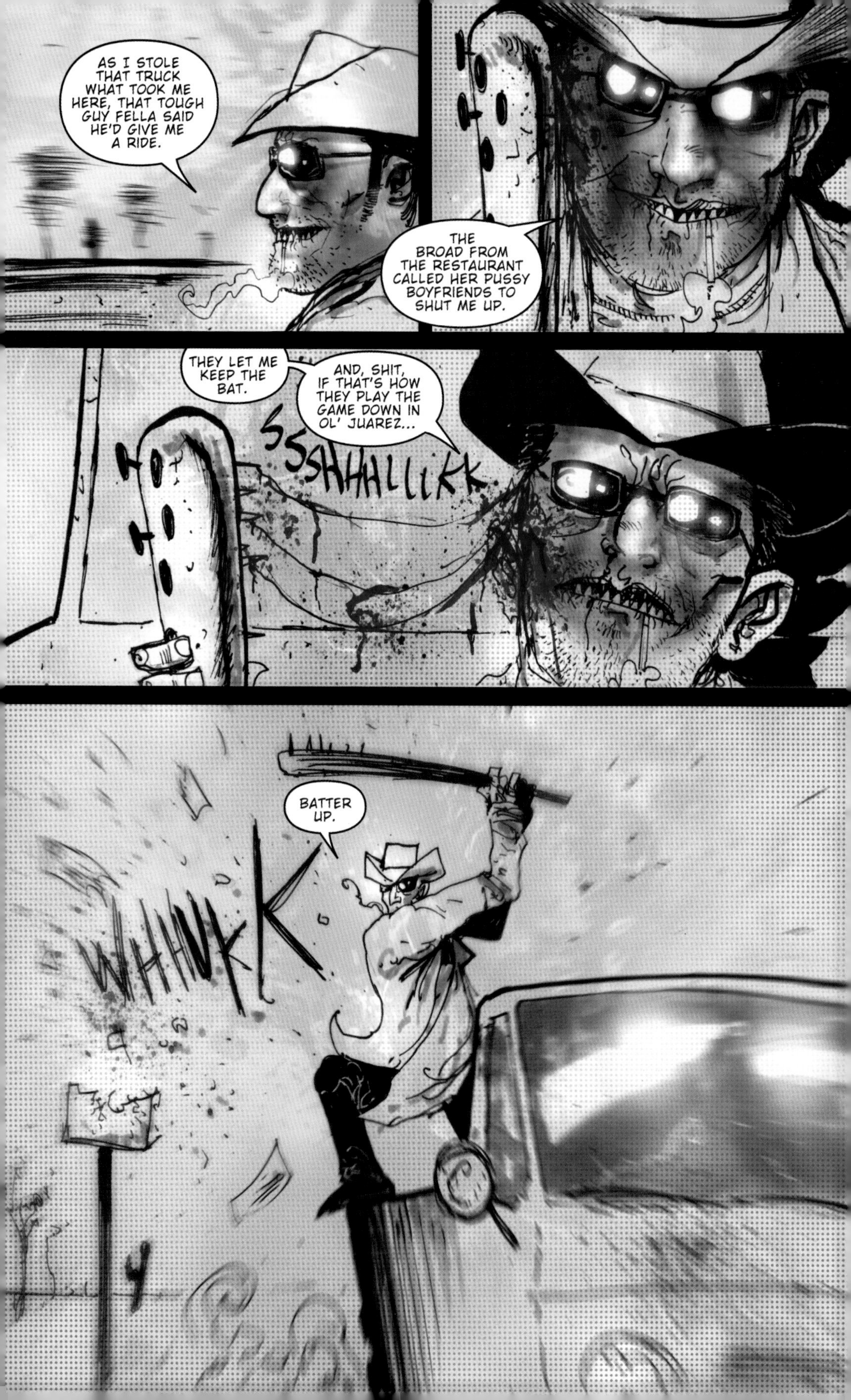
AS I STOLE THAT TRUCK WHAT TOOK ME HERE, THAT TOUGH GUY FELLA SAID HE'D GIVE ME A RIDE.
THE BROAD FROM THE RESTAURANT CALLED HER PUSSY BOYFRIENDS TO SHUT ME UP.
THEY LET ME KEEP THE BAT.
AND, SHIT, IF THAT'S HOW THEY PLAY THE GAME DOWN IN OL' JUAREZ...
SSSHHHLLIKK
BATTER UP.
WHHUK

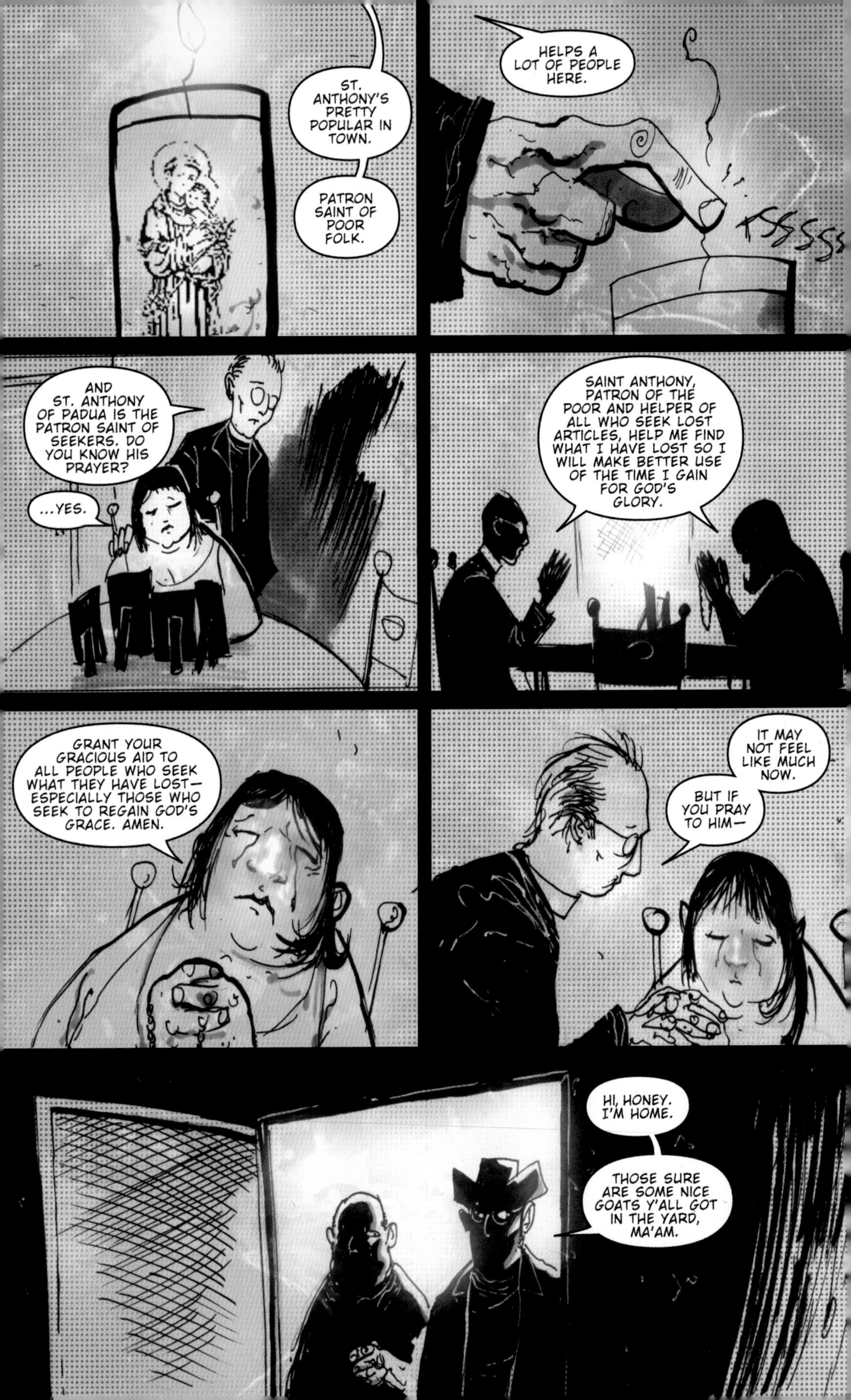
ST. ANTHONY'S PRETTY POPULAR IN TOWN.
PATRON SAINT OF POOR FOLK.
HELPS A LOT OF PEOPLE HERE.
TSSSSS
AND ST. ANTHONY OF PADUA IS THE PATRON SAINT OF SEEKERS. DO YOU KNOW HIS PRAYER?
...YES.
SAINT ANTHONY, PATRON OF THE POOR AND HELPER OF ALL WHO SEEK LOST ARTICLES, HELP ME FIND WHAT I HAVE LOST SO I WILL MAKE BETTER USE OF THE TIME I GAIN FOR GOD'S GLORY.
GRANT YOUR GRACIOUS AID TO ALL PEOPLE WHO SEEK WHAT THEY HAVE LOST—ESPECIALLY THOSE WHO SEEK TO REGAIN GOD'S GRACE. AMEN.
IT MAY NOT FEEL LIKE MUCH NOW.
BUT IF YOU PRAY TO HIM—
HI, HONEY. I'M HOME.
THOSE SURE ARE SOME NICE GOATS Y'ALL GOT IN THE YARD, MA'AM.

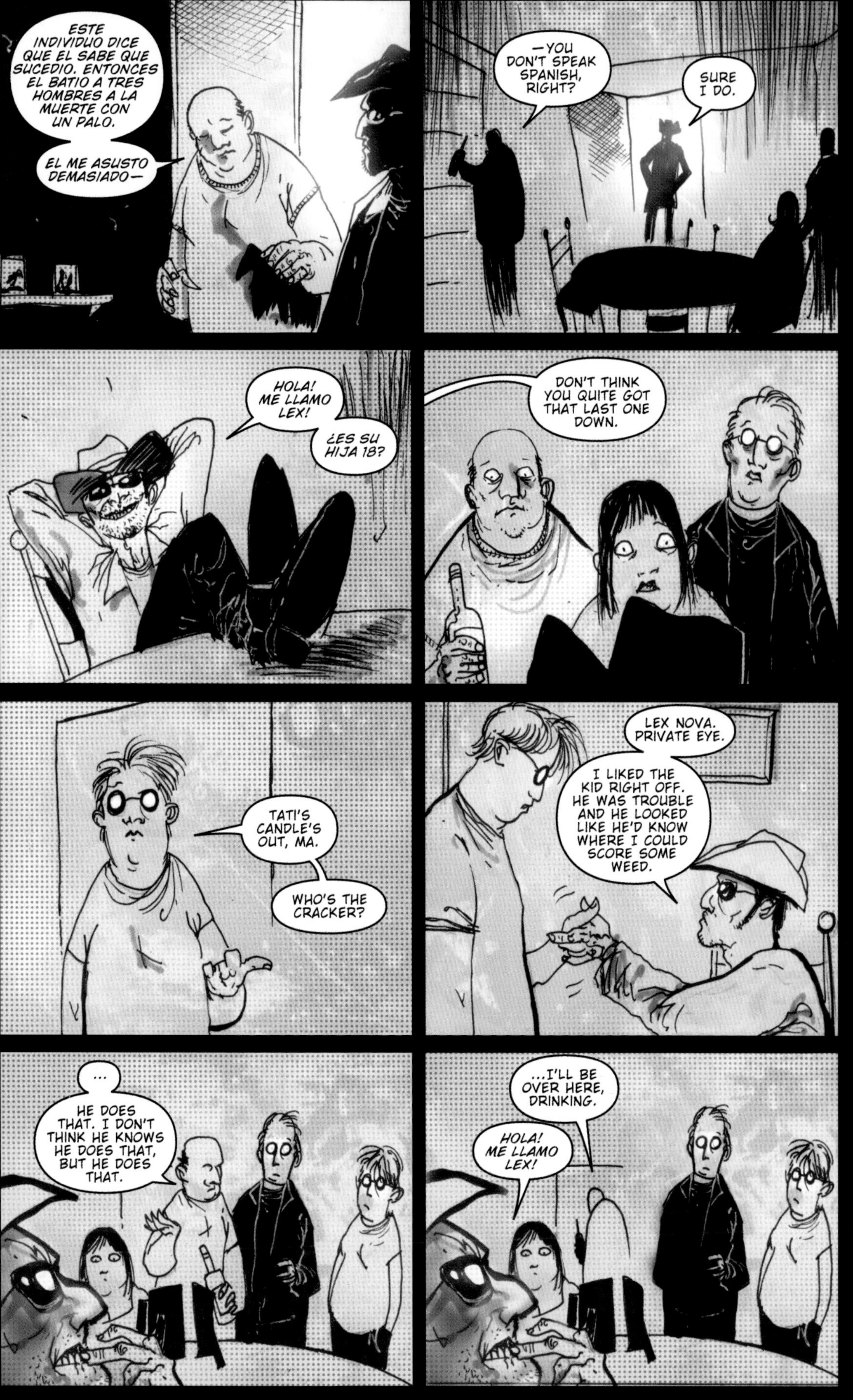

ESTE INDIVIDUO DICE QUE EL SABE QUE SUCEDIO. ENTONCES EL BATIO A TRES HOMBRES A LA MUERTE CON UN PALO.
EL ME ASUSTO DEMASIADO—
—YOU DON'T SPEAK SPANISH, RIGHT?
SURE I DO.
HOLA! ME LLAMO LEX!
¿ES SU HIJA 18?
DON'T THINK YOU QUITE GOT THAT LAST ONE DOWN.
TATI'S CANDLE'S OUT, MA.
WHO'S THE CRACKER?
LEX NOVA. PRIVATE EYE.
I LIKED THE KID RIGHT OFF. HE WAS TROUBLE AND HE LOOKED LIKE HE'D KNOW WHERE I COULD SCORE SOME WEED.
...
HE DOES THAT. I DON'T THINK HE KNOWS HE DOES THAT, BUT HE DOES THAT.
...I'LL BE OVER HERE, DRINKING.
HOLA! ME LLAMO LEX!

WHERE YOU FROM?

L.A.

EVER SEE ANYBODY FAMOUS?

NO. WAIT— PORNSTARS COUNT?

SURE.

THEN SURE.

WHAT, AHH... WHAT BRINGS YOU TO JUAREZ, MR. NOVA?

SENORA CERO. SENORITA EXTRAVIADA. LAS MUJERES PERDIDAS. THE LOST GIRLS'A JUAREZ. I KNOW WHO'S KILLING THEM.

NOT WHO. WHAT.

CHUPACABRA. I SAW IT ON THE INTERNE—

JOE, YOUR MOTHER NEEDS TO LIE DOWN.

TAKE HER?

OKAY.

AND I'D LIKE TO HAVE A WORD WITH MR. NOVA.

OKAY.

PLONK

SHALL WE?

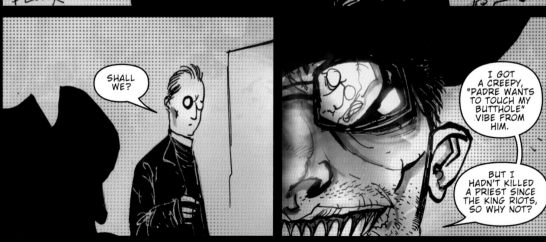

I GOT A CREEPY, "PADRE WANTS TO TOUCH MY BUTTHOLE" VIBE FROM HIM.

BUT I HADN'T KILLED A PRIEST SINCE THE KING RIOTS, SO WHY NOT?

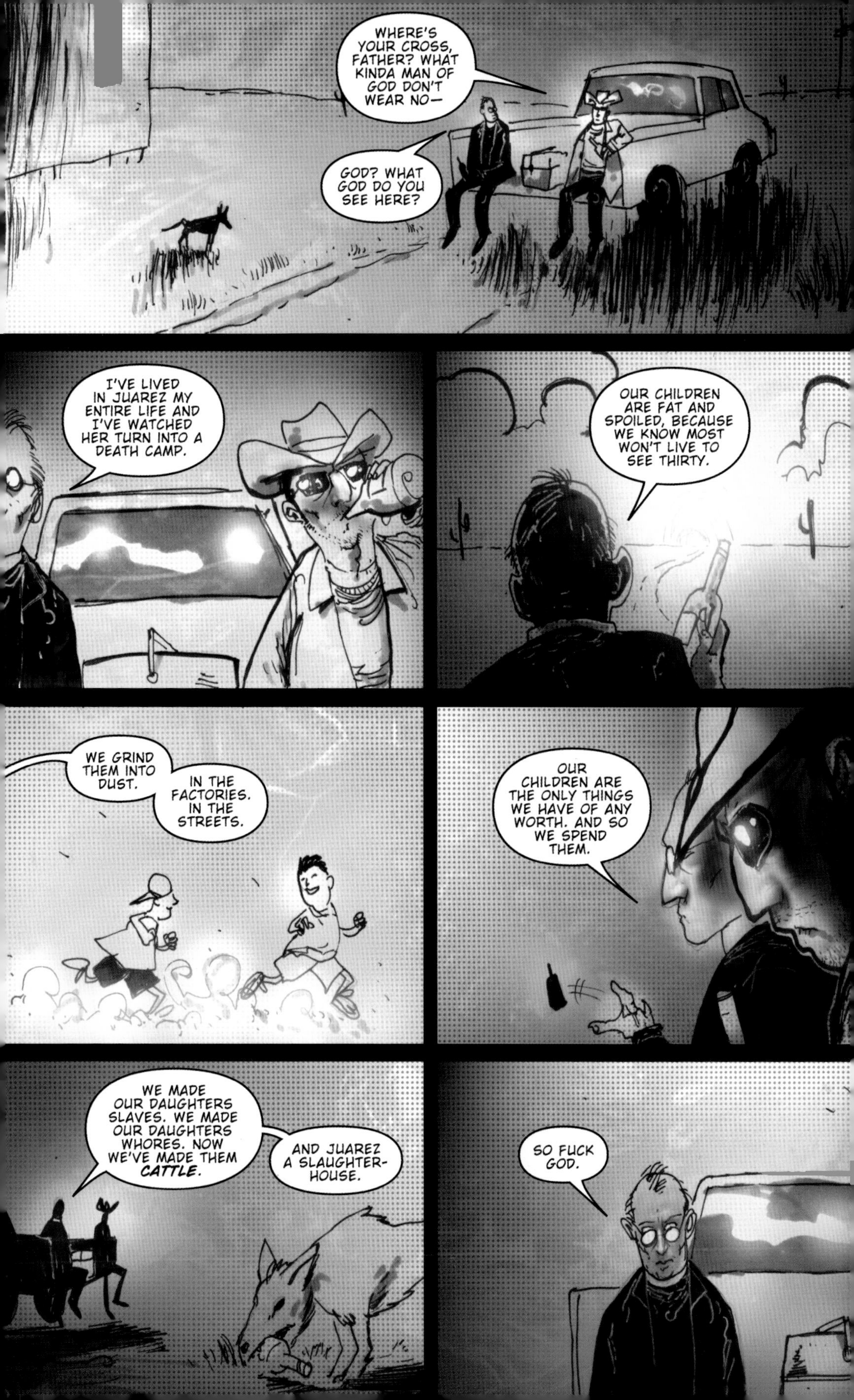
WHERE'S YOUR CROSS, FATHER? WHAT KINDA MAN OF GOD DON'T WEAR NO—
GOD? WHAT GOD DO YOU SEE HERE?
I'VE LIVED IN JUAREZ MY ENTIRE LIFE AND I'VE WATCHED HER TURN INTO A DEATH CAMP.
OUR CHILDREN ARE FAT AND SPOILED, BECAUSE WE KNOW MOST WON'T LIVE TO SEE THIRTY.
WE GRIND THEM INTO DUST.
IN THE FACTORIES. IN THE STREETS.
OUR CHILDREN ARE THE ONLY THINGS WE HAVE OF ANY WORTH. AND SO WE SPEND THEM.
WE MADE OUR DAUGHTERS SLAVES. WE MADE OUR DAUGHTERS WHORES. NOW WE'VE MADE THEM *CATTLE*.
AND JUAREZ A SLAUGHTER-HOUSE.
SO FUCK GOD.

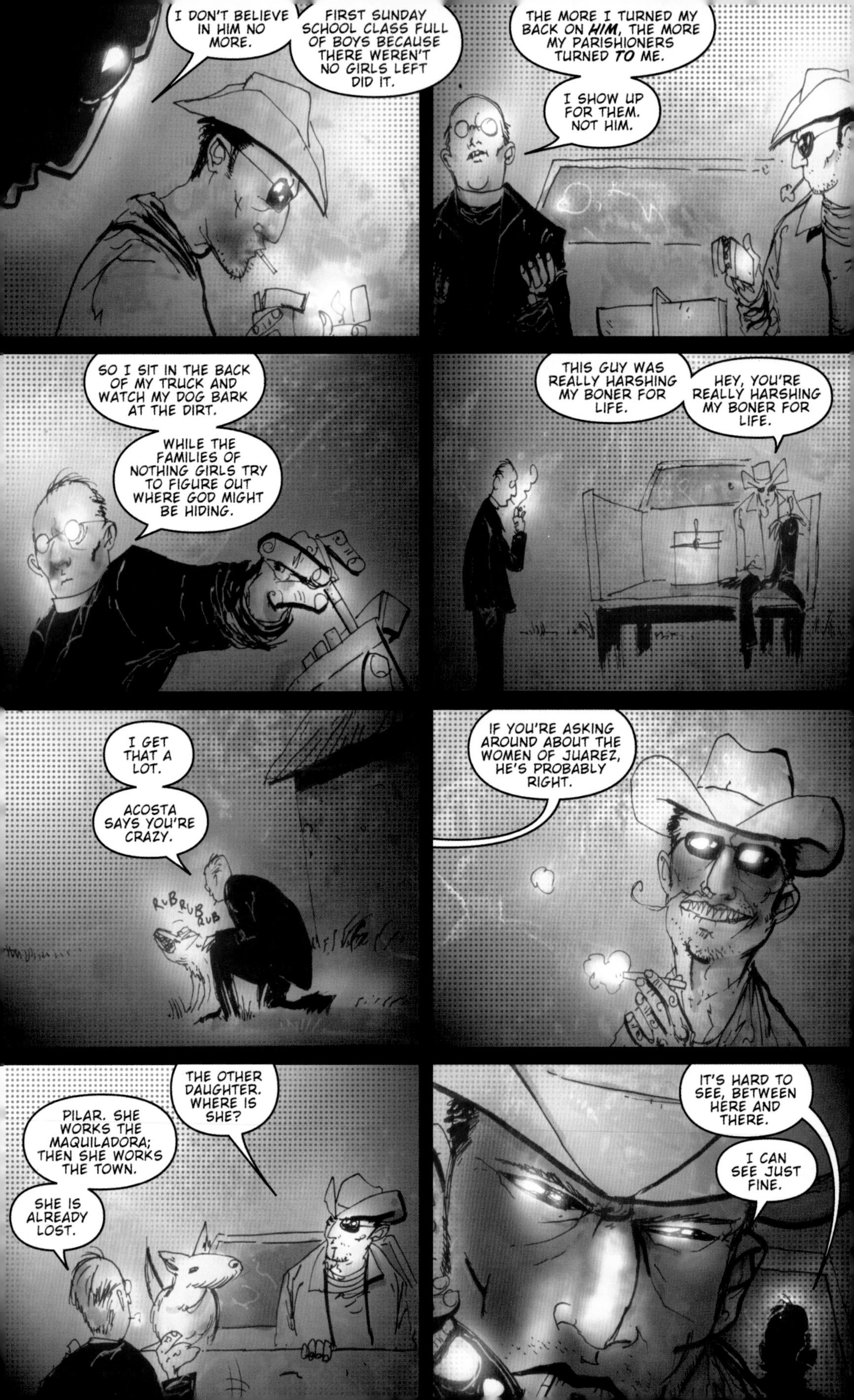
I DON'T BELIEVE IN HIM NO MORE.
FIRST SUNDAY SCHOOL CLASS FULL OF BOYS BECAUSE THERE WEREN'T NO GIRLS LEFT DID IT.
THE MORE I TURNED MY BACK ON *HIM*, THE MORE MY PARISHIONERS TURNED *TO* ME.
I SHOW UP FOR THEM. NOT HIM.
SO I SIT IN THE BACK OF MY TRUCK AND WATCH MY DOG BARK AT THE DIRT.
WHILE THE FAMILIES OF NOTHING GIRLS TRY TO FIGURE OUT WHERE GOD MIGHT BE HIDING.
THIS GUY WAS REALLY HARSHING MY BONER FOR LIFE.
HEY, YOU'RE REALLY HARSHING MY BONER FOR LIFE.
I GET THAT A LOT.
ACOSTA SAYS YOU'RE CRAZY.
RUB RUB RUB
IF YOU'RE ASKING AROUND ABOUT THE WOMEN OF JUAREZ, HE'S PROBABLY RIGHT.
THE OTHER DAUGHTER. WHERE IS SHE?
PILAR. SHE WORKS THE MAQUILADORA; THEN SHE WORKS THE TOWN.
SHE IS ALREADY LOST.
IT'S HARD TO SEE, BETWEEN HERE AND THERE.
I CAN SEE JUST FINE.

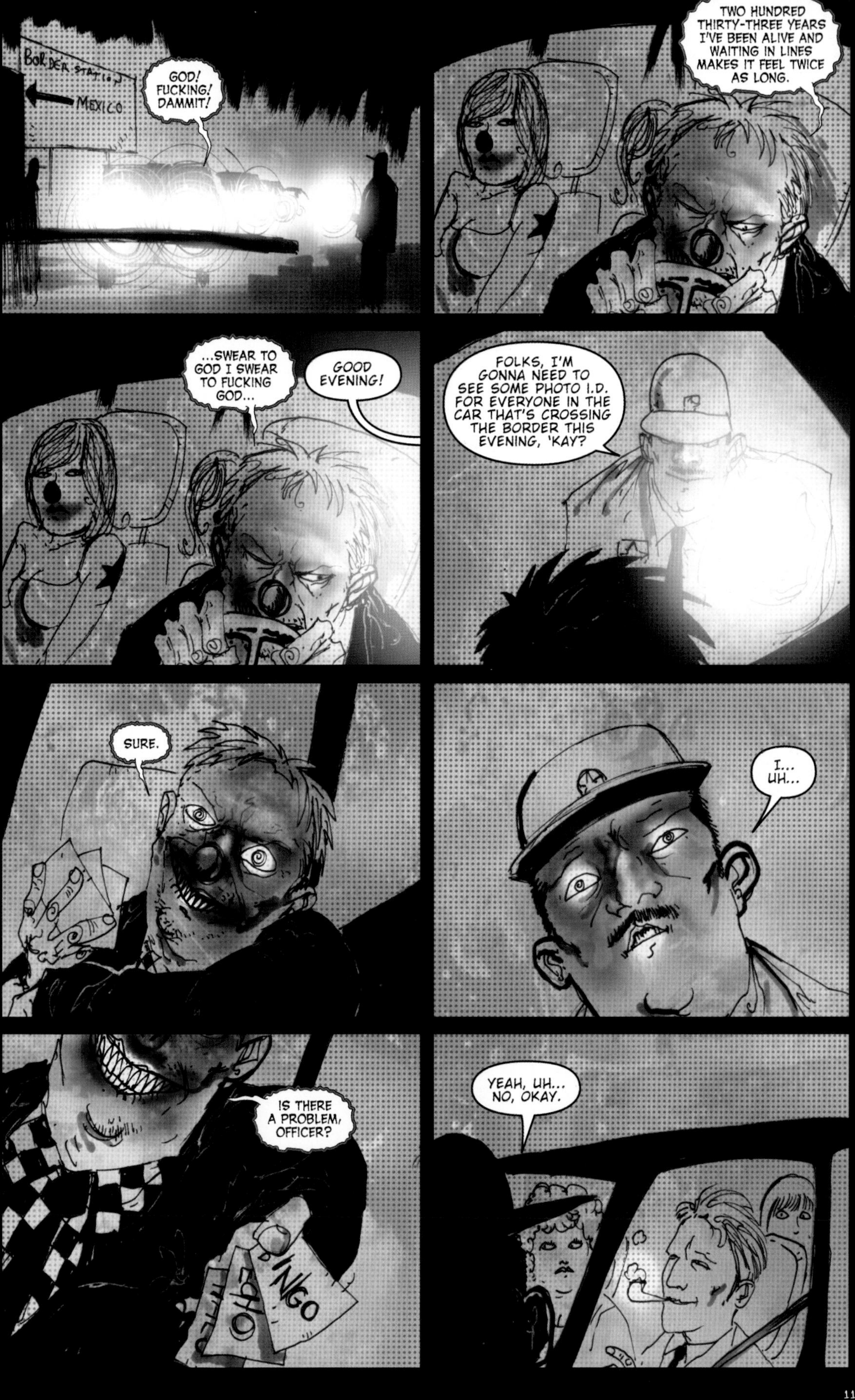
BORDER STATION
MEXICO
GOD! FUCKING! DAMMIT!
TWO HUNDRED THIRTY-THREE YEARS I'VE BEEN ALIVE AND WAITING IN LINES MAKES IT FEEL TWICE AS LONG.
...SWEAR TO GOD I SWEAR TO FUCKING GOD...
GOOD EVENING!
FOLKS, I'M GONNA NEED TO SEE SOME PHOTO I.D. FOR EVERYONE IN THE CAR THAT'S CROSSING THE BORDER THIS EVENING, 'KAY?
SURE.
I... UH...
IS THERE A PROBLEM, OFFICER?
BINGO
YEAH, UH... NO, OKAY.

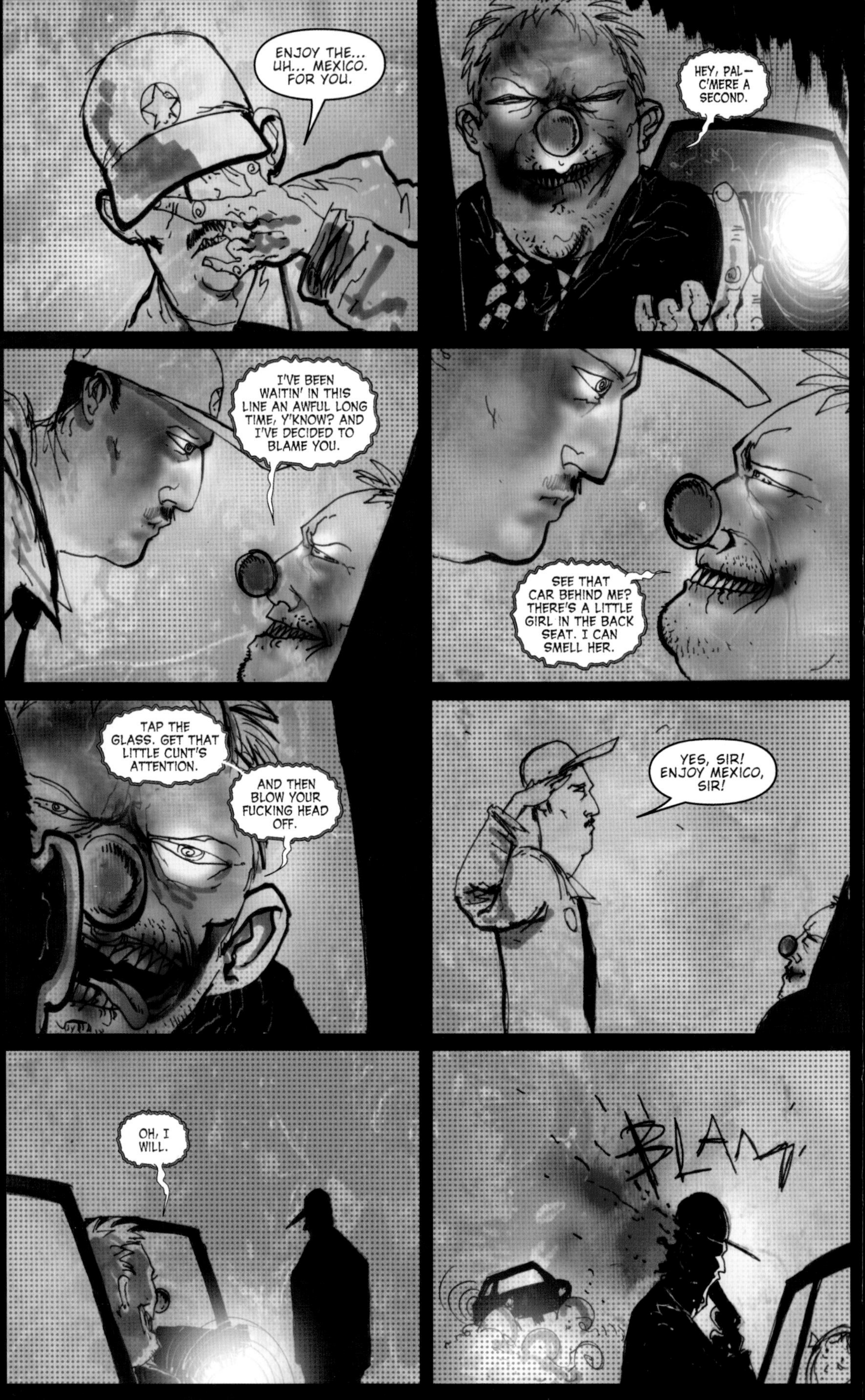
ENJOY THE... UH... MEXICO. FOR YOU.
HEY, PAL— C'MERE A SECOND.
I'VE BEEN WAITIN' IN THIS LINE AN AWFUL LONG TIME, Y'KNOW? AND I'VE DECIDED TO BLAME YOU.
SEE THAT CAR BEHIND ME? THERE'S A LITTLE GIRL IN THE BACK SEAT. I CAN SMELL HER.
TAP THE GLASS. GET THAT LITTLE CUNT'S ATTENTION.
AND THEN BLOW YOUR FUCKING HEAD OFF.
YES, SIR! ENJOY MEXICO, SIR!
OH, I WILL.
BLAM

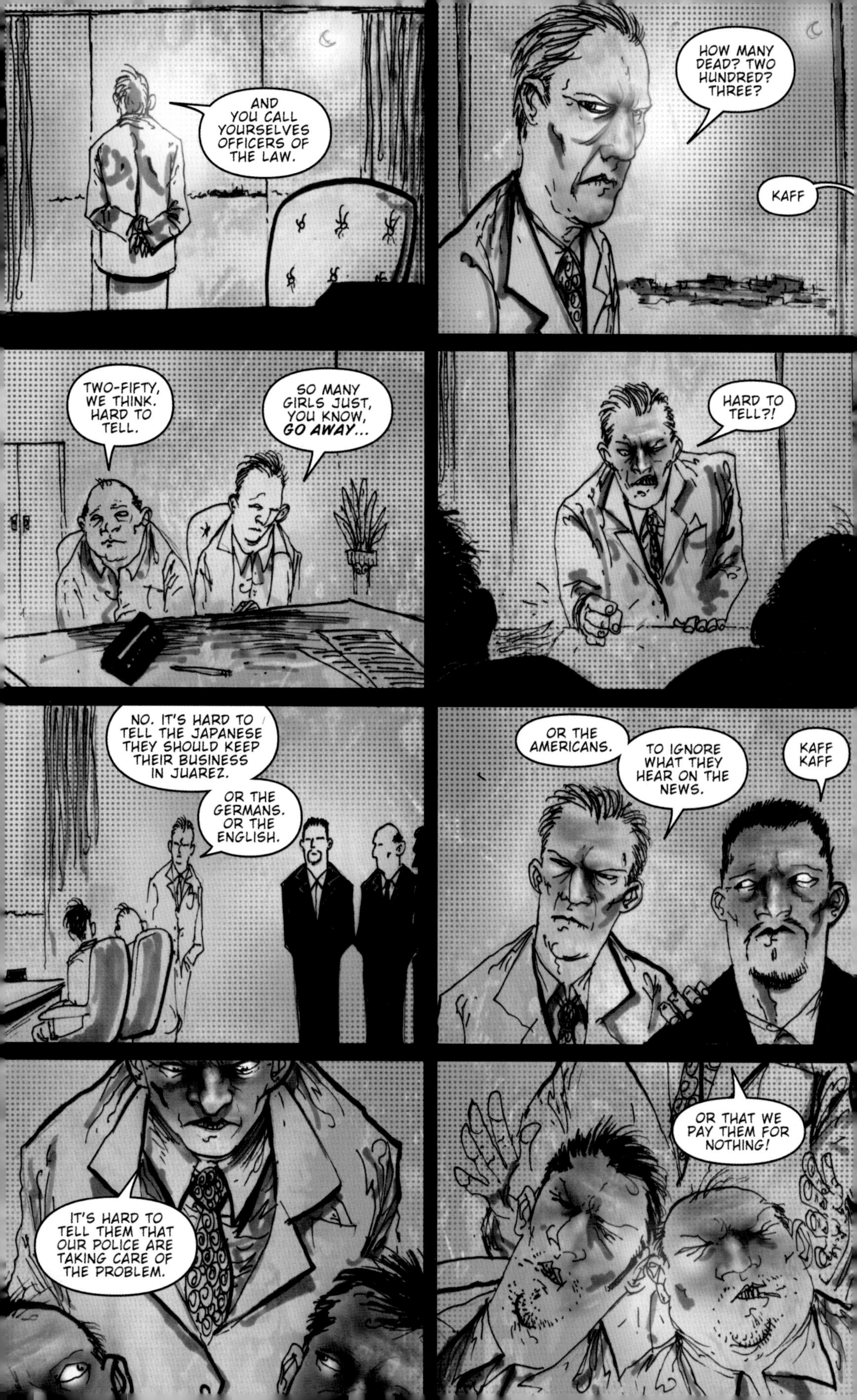
AND YOU CALL YOURSELVES OFFICERS OF THE LAW.
HOW MANY DEAD? TWO HUNDRED? THREE?
KAFF
TWO-FIFTY, WE THINK. HARD TO TELL.
SO MANY GIRLS JUST, YOU KNOW, GO AWAY...
HARD TO TELL?!
NO. IT'S HARD TO TELL THE JAPANESE THEY SHOULD KEEP THEIR BUSINESS IN JUAREZ.
OR THE GERMANS. OR THE ENGLISH.
OR THE AMERICANS.
TO IGNORE WHAT THEY HEAR ON THE NEWS.
KAFF KAFF
IT'S HARD TO TELL THEM THAT OUR POLICE ARE TAKING CARE OF THE PROBLEM.
OR THAT WE PAY THEM FOR NOTHING!

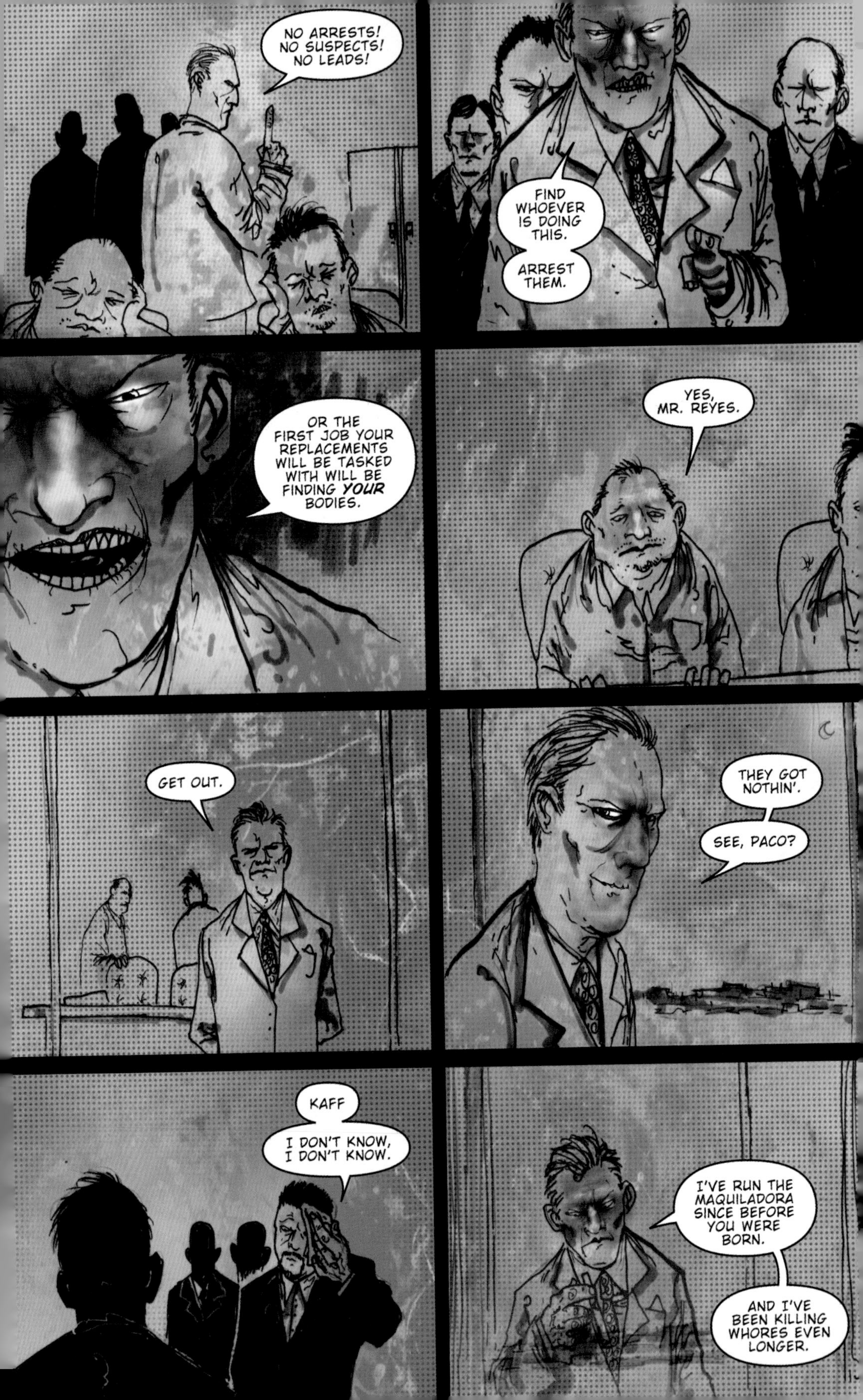
NO ARRESTS! NO SUSPECTS! NO LEADS!
FIND WHOEVER IS DOING THIS.
ARREST THEM.
OR THE FIRST JOB YOUR REPLACEMENTS WILL BE TASKED WITH WILL BE FINDING *YOUR* BODIES.
YES, MR. REYES.
GET OUT.
THEY GOT NOTHIN'.
SEE, PACO?
KAFF
I DON'T KNOW, I DON'T KNOW.
I'VE RUN THE MAQUILADORA SINCE BEFORE YOU WERE BORN.
AND I'VE BEEN KILLING WHORES EVEN LONGER.

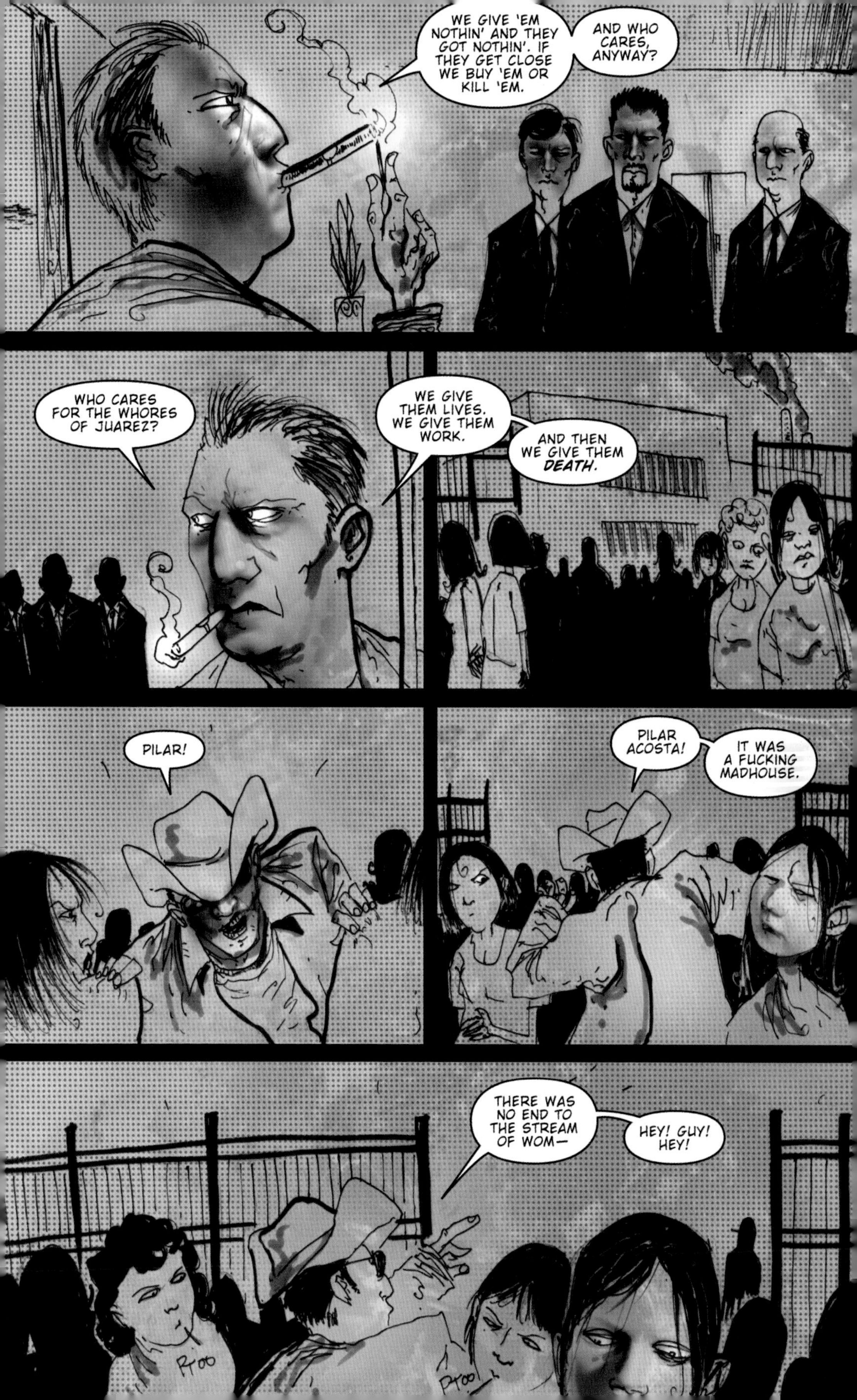
WE GIVE 'EM NOTHIN' AND THEY GOT NOTHIN'. IF THEY GET CLOSE WE BUY 'EM OR KILL 'EM.
AND WHO CARES, ANYWAY?
WHO CARES FOR THE WHORES OF JUAREZ?
WE GIVE THEM LIVES. WE GIVE THEM WORK.
AND THEN WE GIVE THEM *DEATH*.
PILAR!
PILAR ACOSTA!
IT WAS A FUCKING MADHOUSE.
THERE WAS NO END TO THE STREAM OF WOM—
HEY! GUY! HEY!

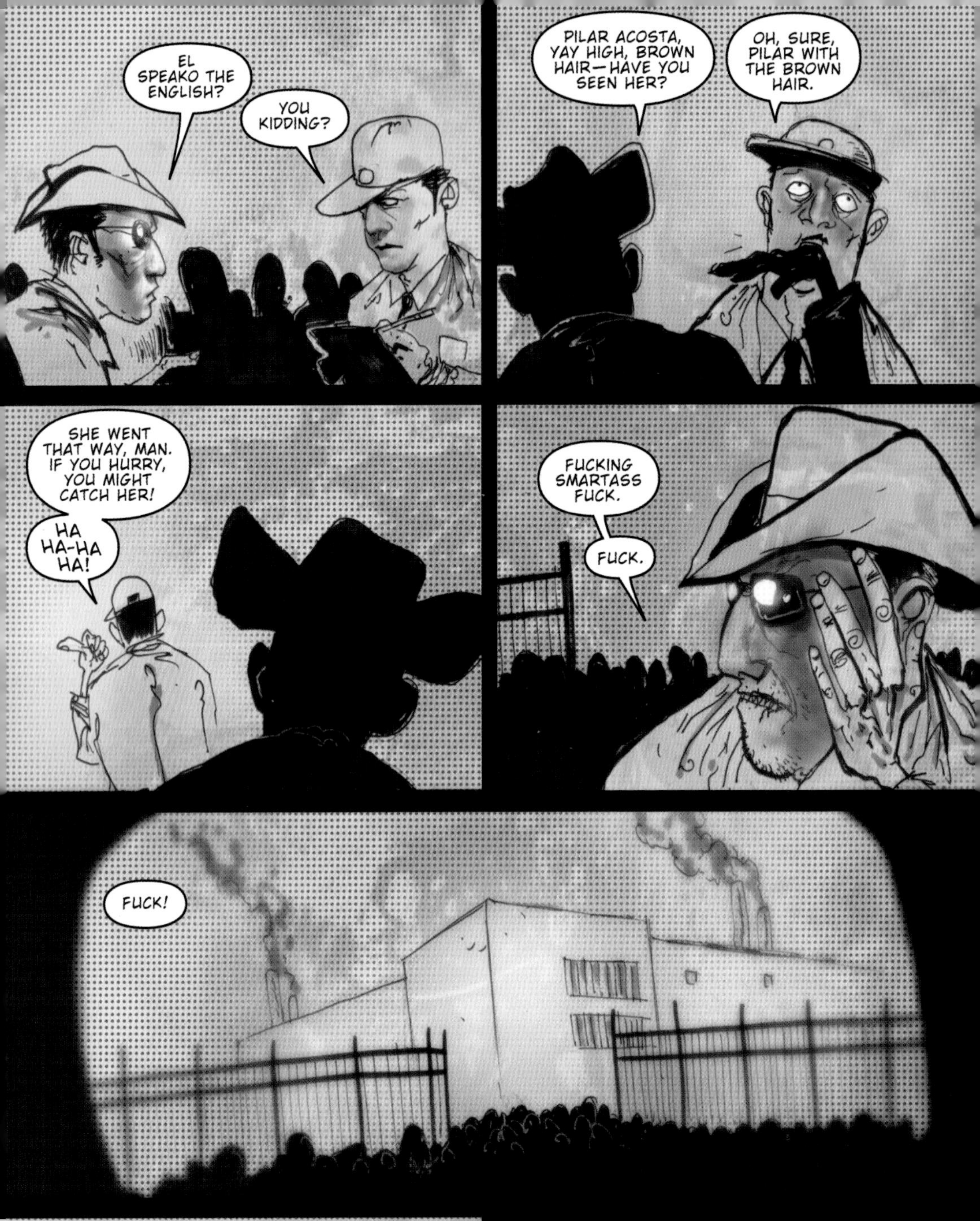
EL SPEAKO THE ENGLISH?
YOU KIDDING?
PILAR ACOSTA, YAY HIGH, BROWN HAIR—HAVE YOU SEEN HER?
OH, SURE, PILAR WITH THE BROWN HAIR.
SHE WENT THAT WAY, MAN. IF YOU HURRY, YOU MIGHT CATCH HER!
HA HA-HA HA!
FUCKING SMARTASS FUCK.
FUCK.
FUCK!

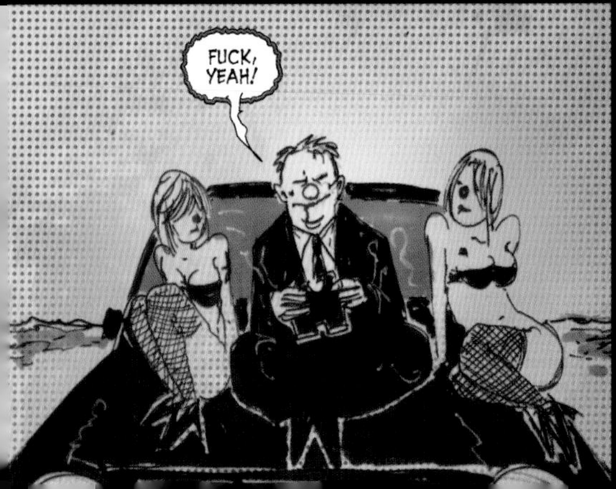
FUCK, YEAH!

"JUAREZ

OR

LEX NOVA & THE CASE OF THE 400 DEAD MEXICAN GIRLS"

END OF PART TWO:
GODS AND OTHER BOSSES

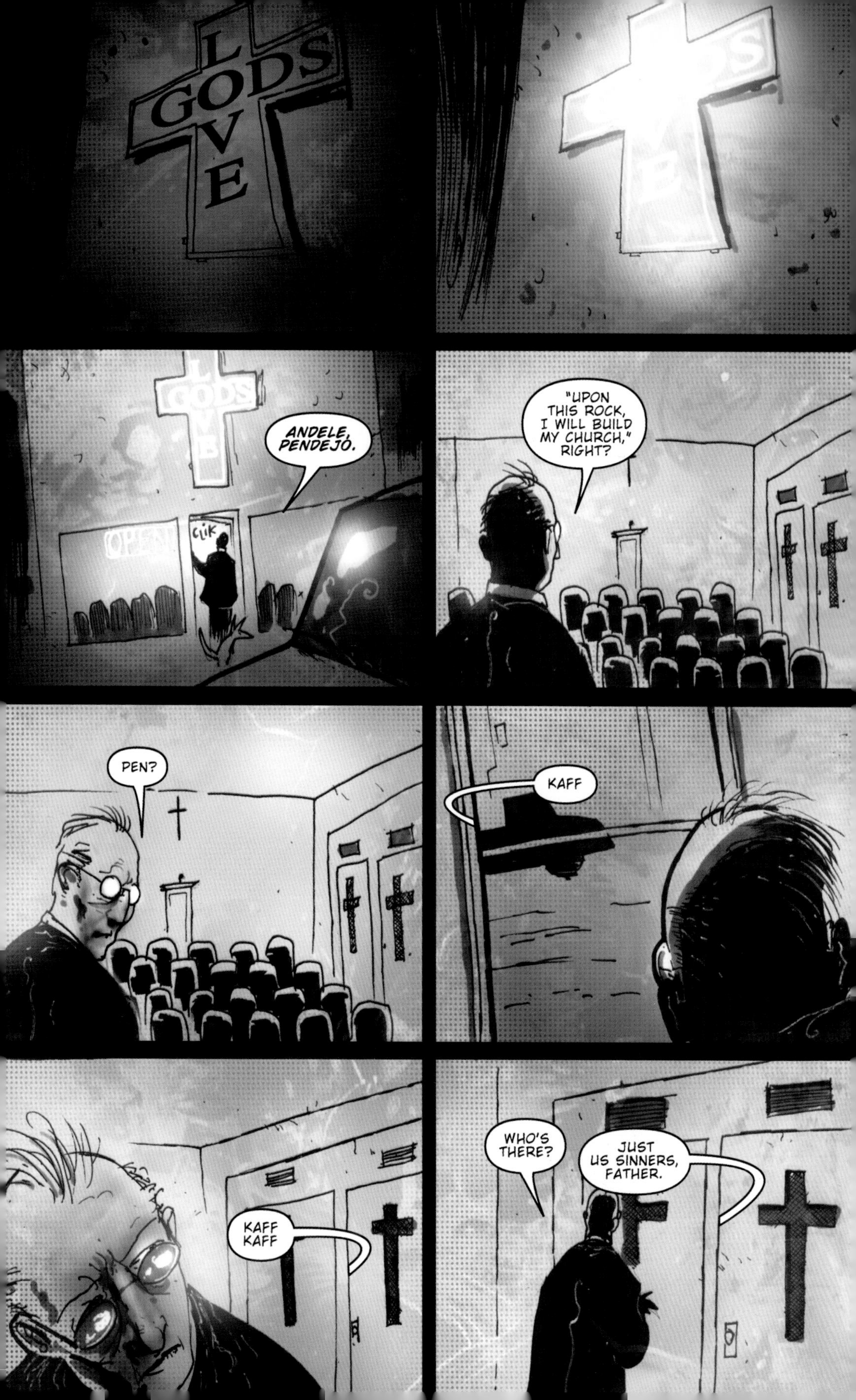

GODS
LOVE
OPEN
CLIK
ANDELE, PENDEJO.
"UPON THIS ROCK, I WILL BUILD MY CHURCH," RIGHT?
PEN?
KAFF
KAFF KAFF
WHO'S THERE?
JUST US SINNERS, FATHER.

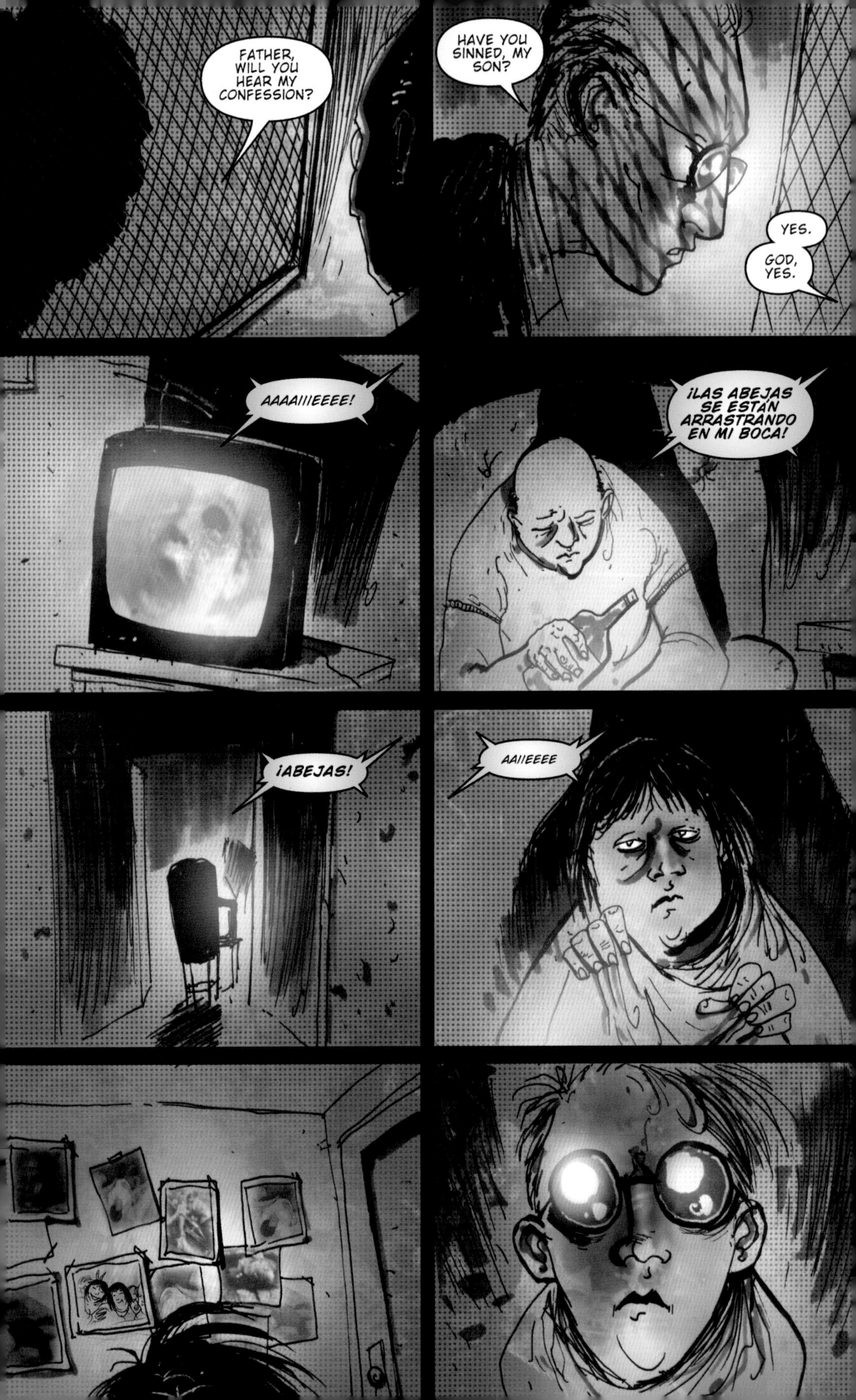
FATHER, WILL YOU HEAR MY CONFESSION?
HAVE YOU SINNED, MY SON?
YES.
GOD, YES.
AAAAIIIEEEE!
¡LAS ABEJAS SE ESTÁN ARRASTRANDO EN MI BOCA!
¡ABEJAS!
AAIIEEEE

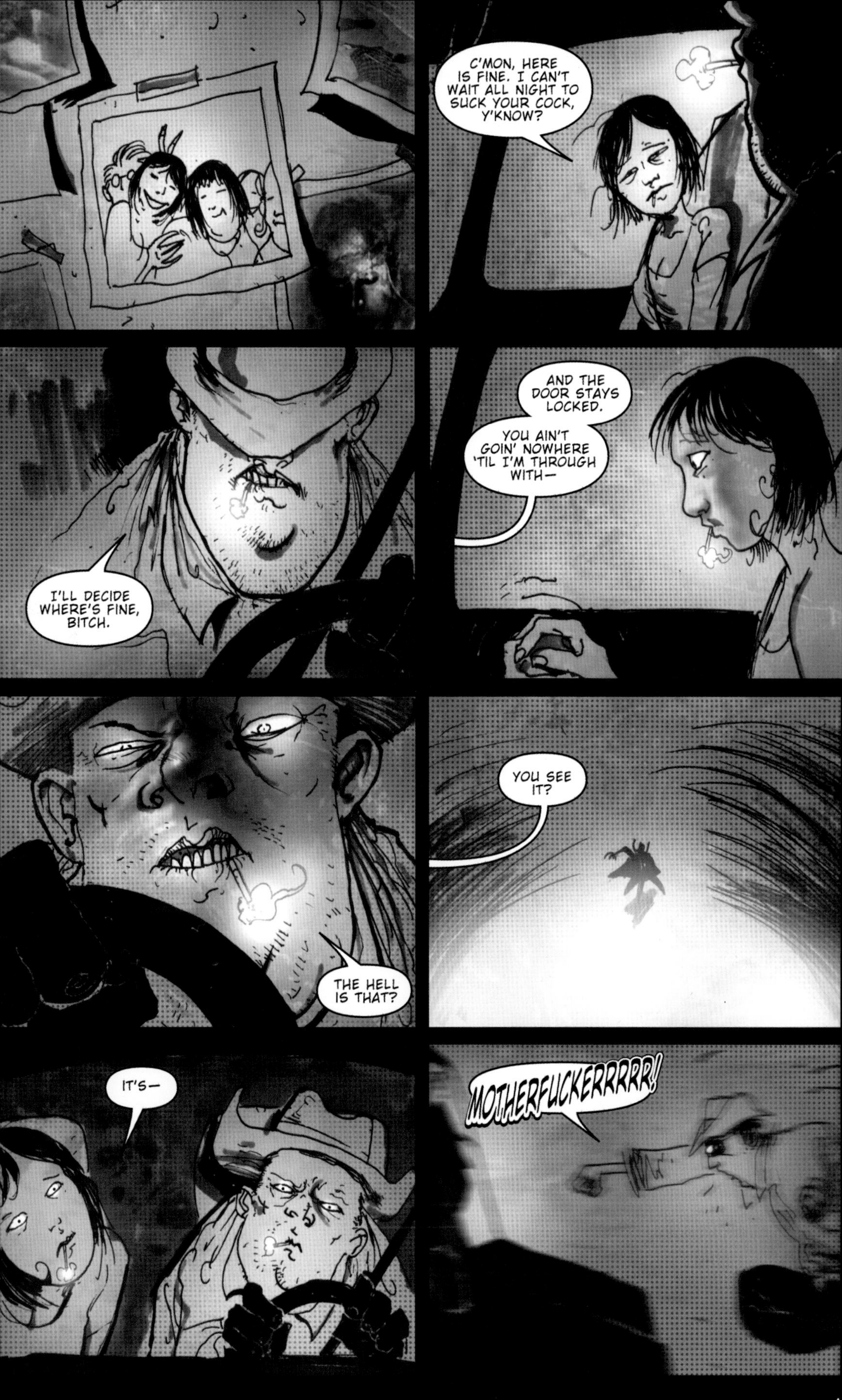

C'MON, HERE IS FINE. I CAN'T WAIT ALL NIGHT TO SUCK YOUR COCK, Y'KNOW?
I'LL DECIDE WHERE'S FINE, BITCH.
AND THE DOOR STAYS LOCKED.
YOU AIN'T GOIN' NOWHERE 'TIL I'M THROUGH WITH—
THE HELL IS THAT?
YOU SEE IT?
IT'S—
MOTHERFUCKERRRRR!

...REYES AND THE REST, IT'S THEM, ALL OF THEM—

—US, I MEAN. ALL OF US.

MARIA AND CONSUELA AND MARIA AGAIN, AND MARTINA AND ROSARIO, TWO OR THREE OR FOUR THAT NEVER HAD NAMES TO LEARN...

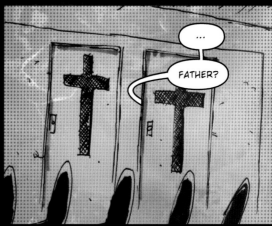

...

FATHER?

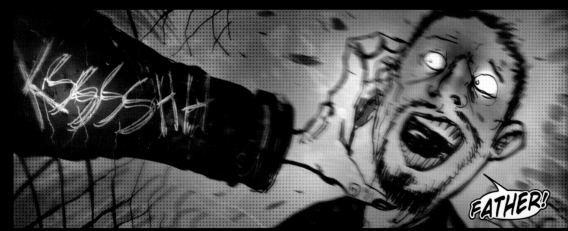

FATHER!

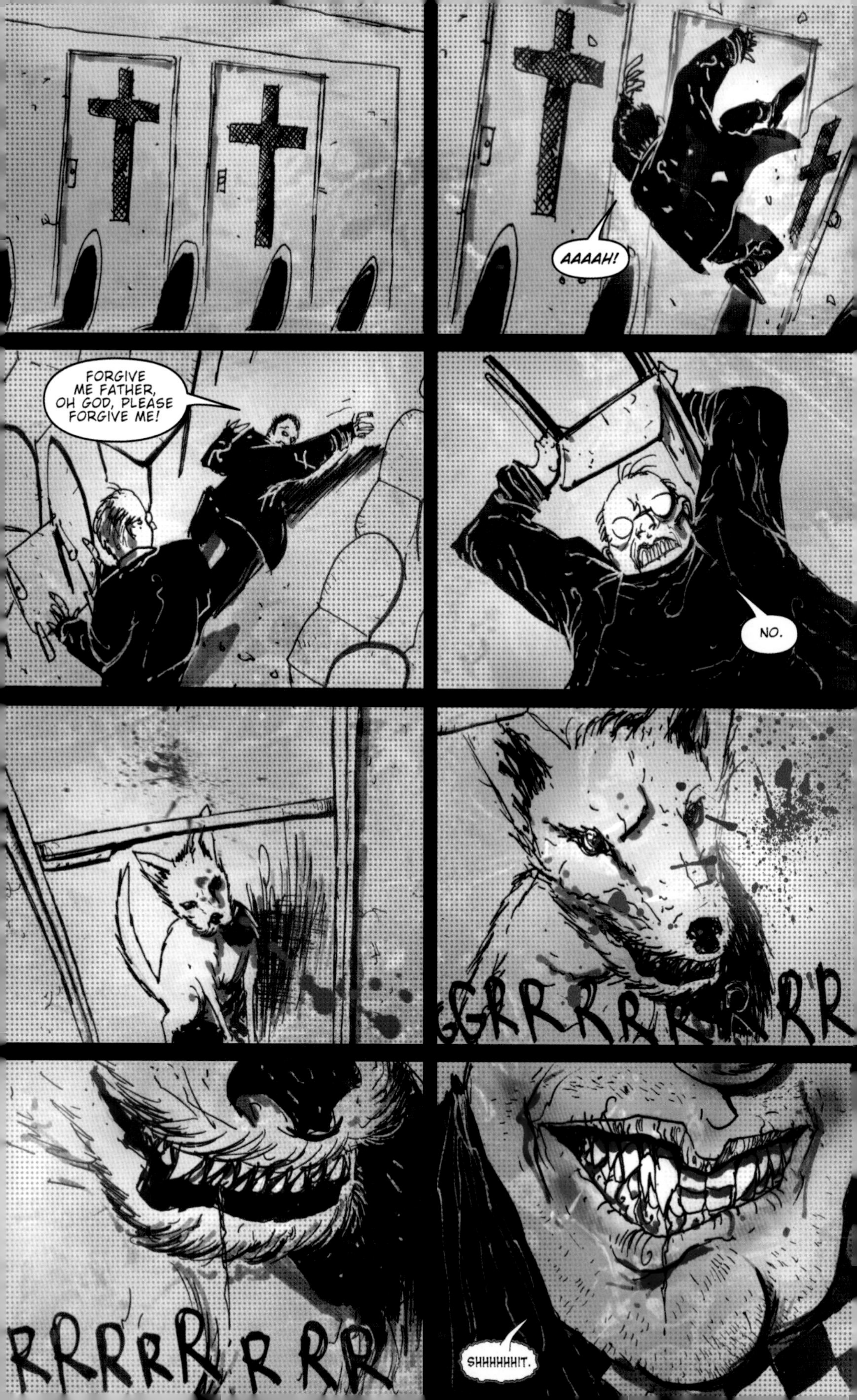
AAAAH!
FORGIVE ME FATHER, OH GOD, PLEASE FORGIVE ME!
NO.
GRRRRRRRR
RRRRRRRR
SHHHHHHIT.

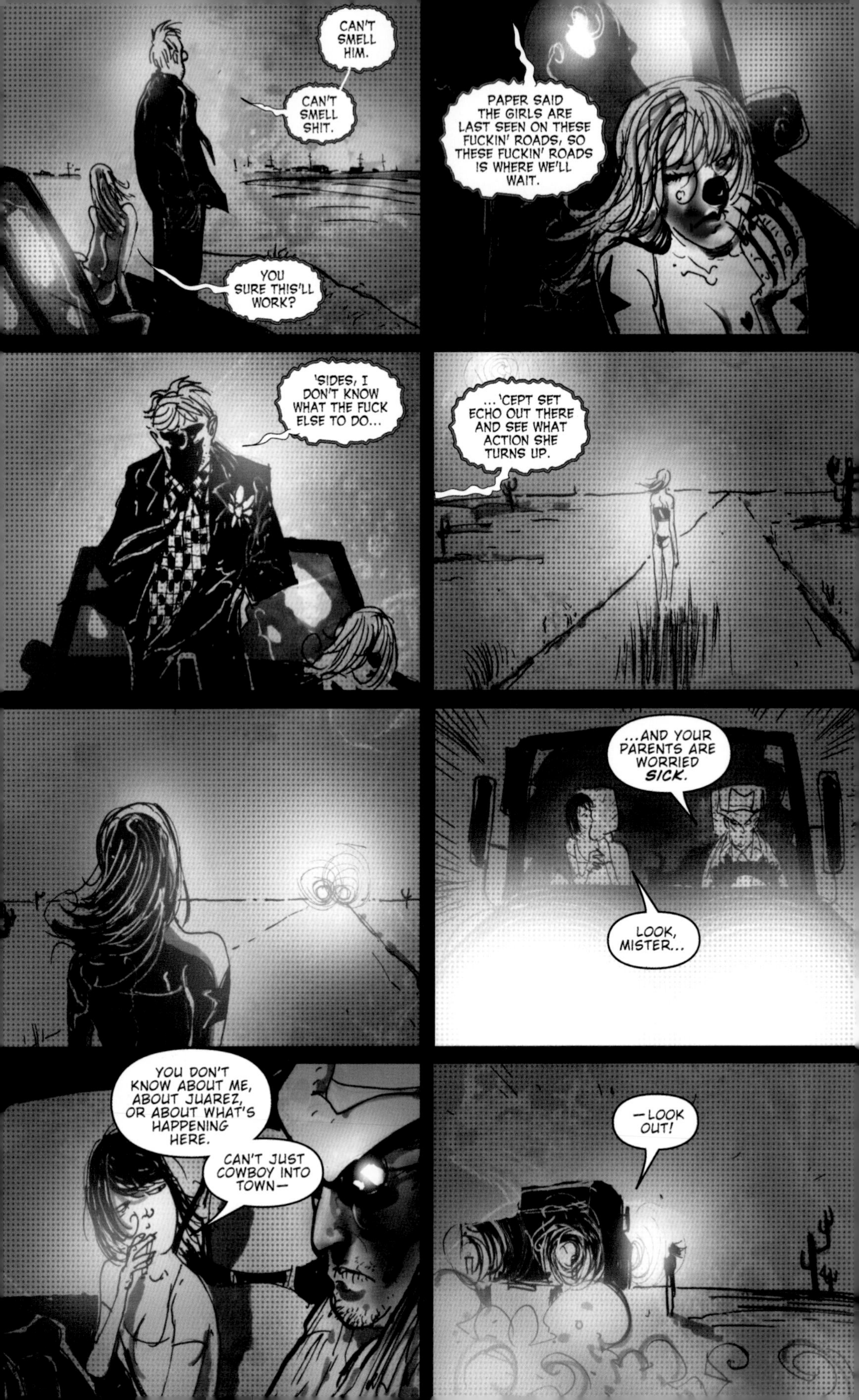
CAN'T SMELL HIM.
CAN'T SMELL SHIT.
YOU SURE THIS'LL WORK?
PAPER SAID THE GIRLS ARE LAST SEEN ON THESE FUCKIN' ROADS, SO THESE FUCKIN' ROADS IS WHERE WE'LL WAIT.
'SIDES, I DON'T KNOW WHAT THE FUCK ELSE TO DO...
...'CEPT SET ECHO OUT THERE AND SEE WHAT ACTION SHE TURNS UP.
...AND YOUR PARENTS ARE WORRIED SICK.
LOOK, MISTER...
YOU DON'T KNOW ABOUT ME, ABOUT JUAREZ, OR ABOUT WHAT'S HAPPENING HERE.
CAN'T JUST COWBOY INTO TOWN—
—LOOK OUT!

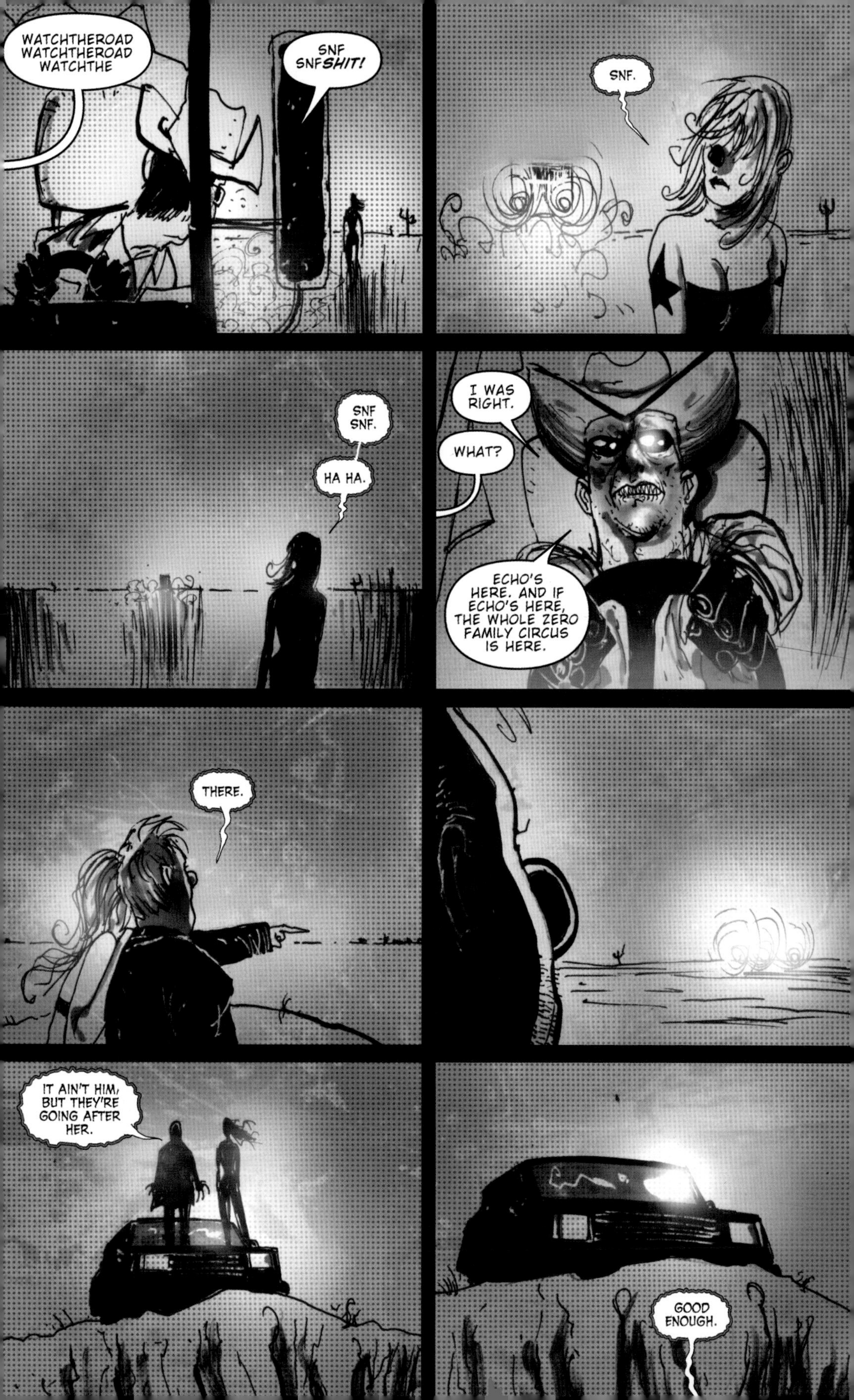
WATCHTHEROAD WATCHTHEROAD WATCHTHE
SNF SNF*SHIT!*
SNF.
SNF SNF.
HA HA.
I WAS RIGHT.
WHAT?
ECHO'S HERE. AND IF ECHO'S HERE, THE WHOLE ZERO FAMILY CIRCUS IS HERE.
THERE.
IT AIN'T HIM, BUT THEY'RE GOING AFTER HER.
GOOD ENOUGH.

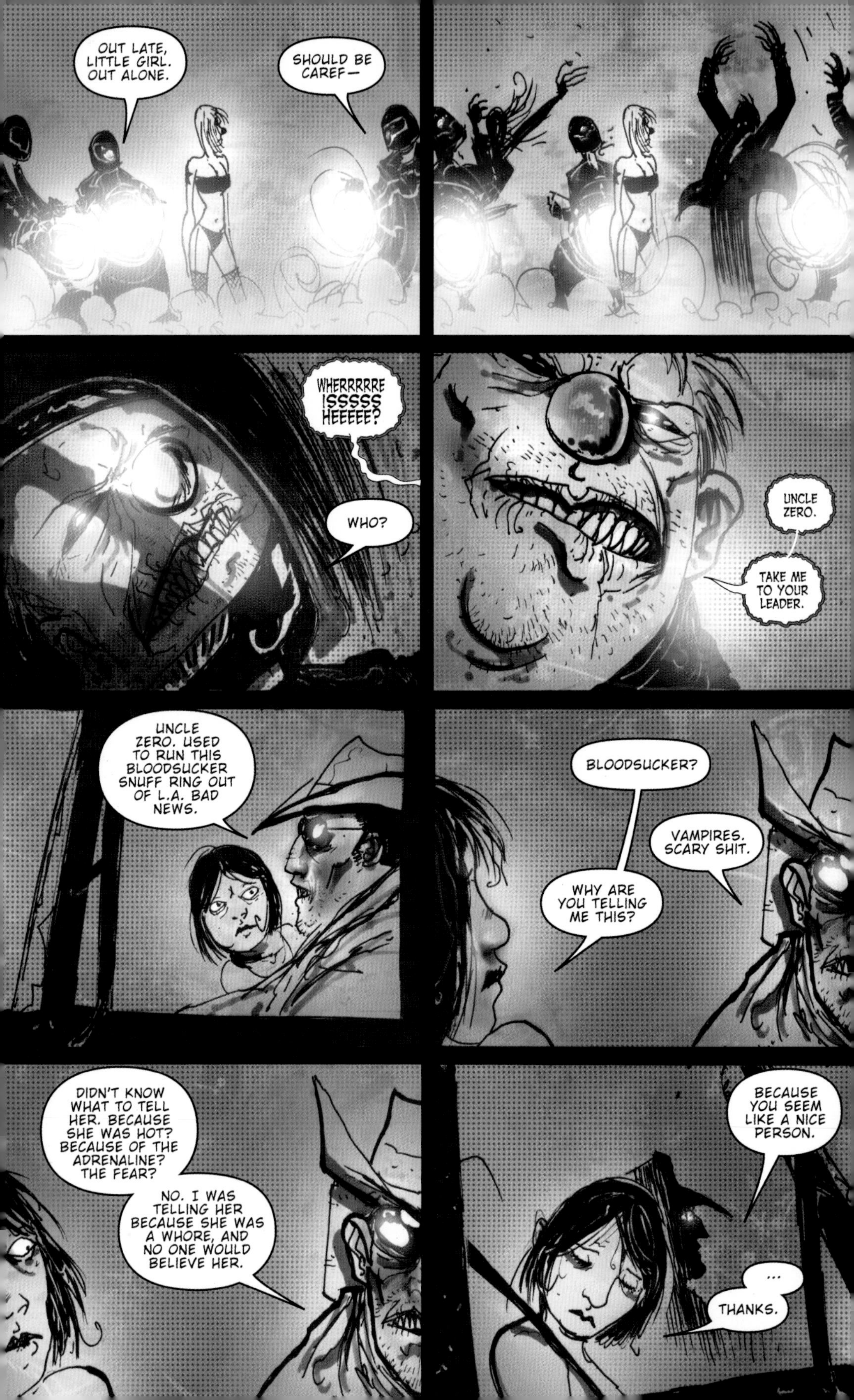
OUT LATE, LITTLE GIRL. OUT ALONE.
SHOULD BE CAREF—
WHERRRRRE ISSSSS HEEEEE?
WHO?
UNCLE ZERO.
TAKE ME TO YOUR LEADER.
UNCLE ZERO. USED TO RUN THIS BLOODSUCKER SNUFF RING OUT OF L.A. BAD NEWS.
BLOODSUCKER?
VAMPIRES. SCARY SHIT.
WHY ARE YOU TELLING ME THIS?
DIDN'T KNOW WHAT TO TELL HER. BECAUSE SHE WAS HOT? BECAUSE OF THE ADRENALINE? THE FEAR?
NO. I WAS TELLING HER BECAUSE SHE WAS A WHORE, AND NO ONE WOULD BELIEVE HER.
BECAUSE YOU SEEM LIKE A NICE PERSON.
...
THANKS.

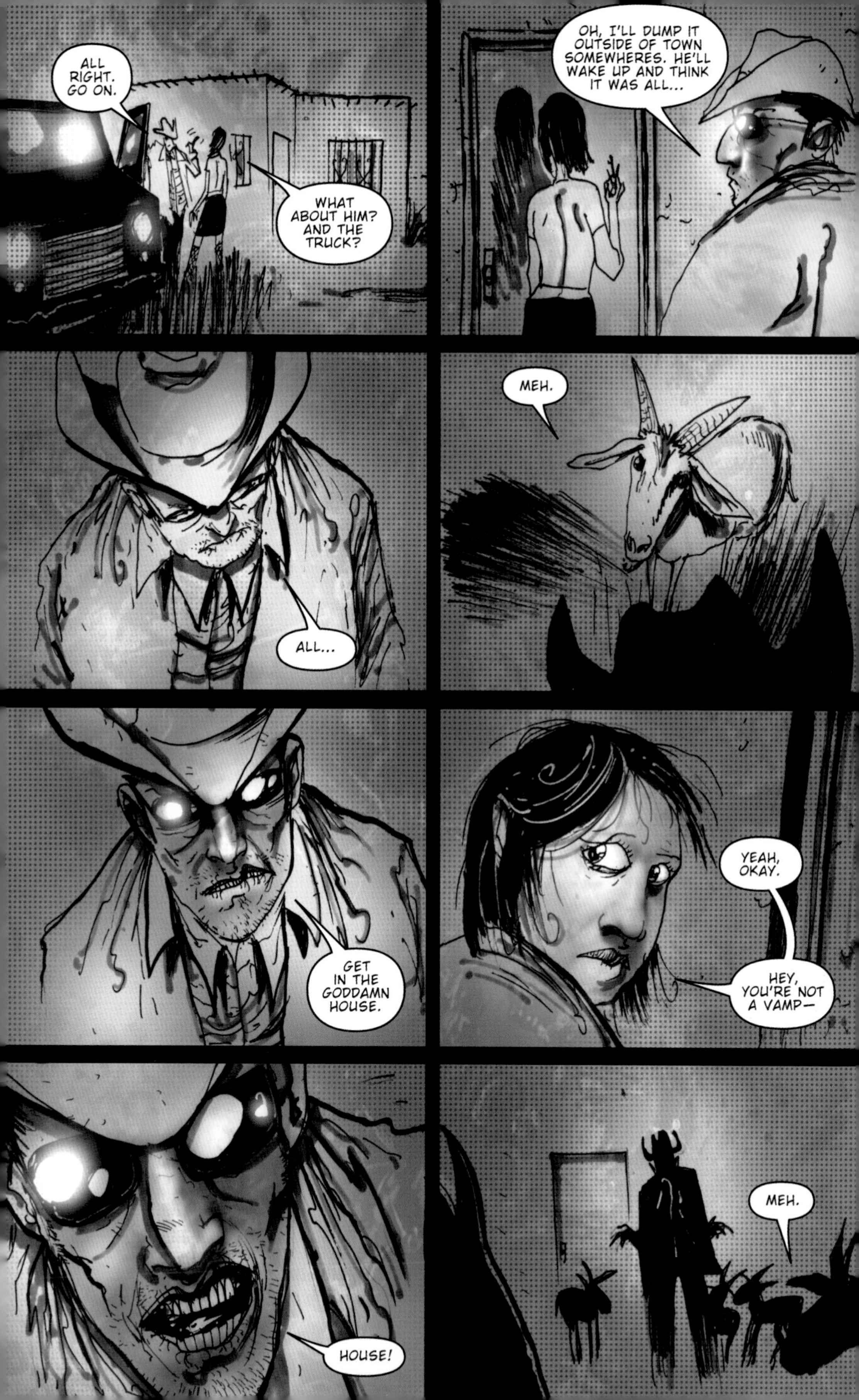
ALL RIGHT. GO ON.
WHAT ABOUT HIM? AND THE TRUCK?
OH, I'LL DUMP IT OUTSIDE OF TOWN SOMEWHERES. HE'LL WAKE UP AND THINK IT WAS ALL...
ALL...
MEH.
GET IN THE GODDAMN HOUSE.
YEAH, OKAY.
HEY, YOU'RE NOT A VAMP—
HOUSE!
MEH.

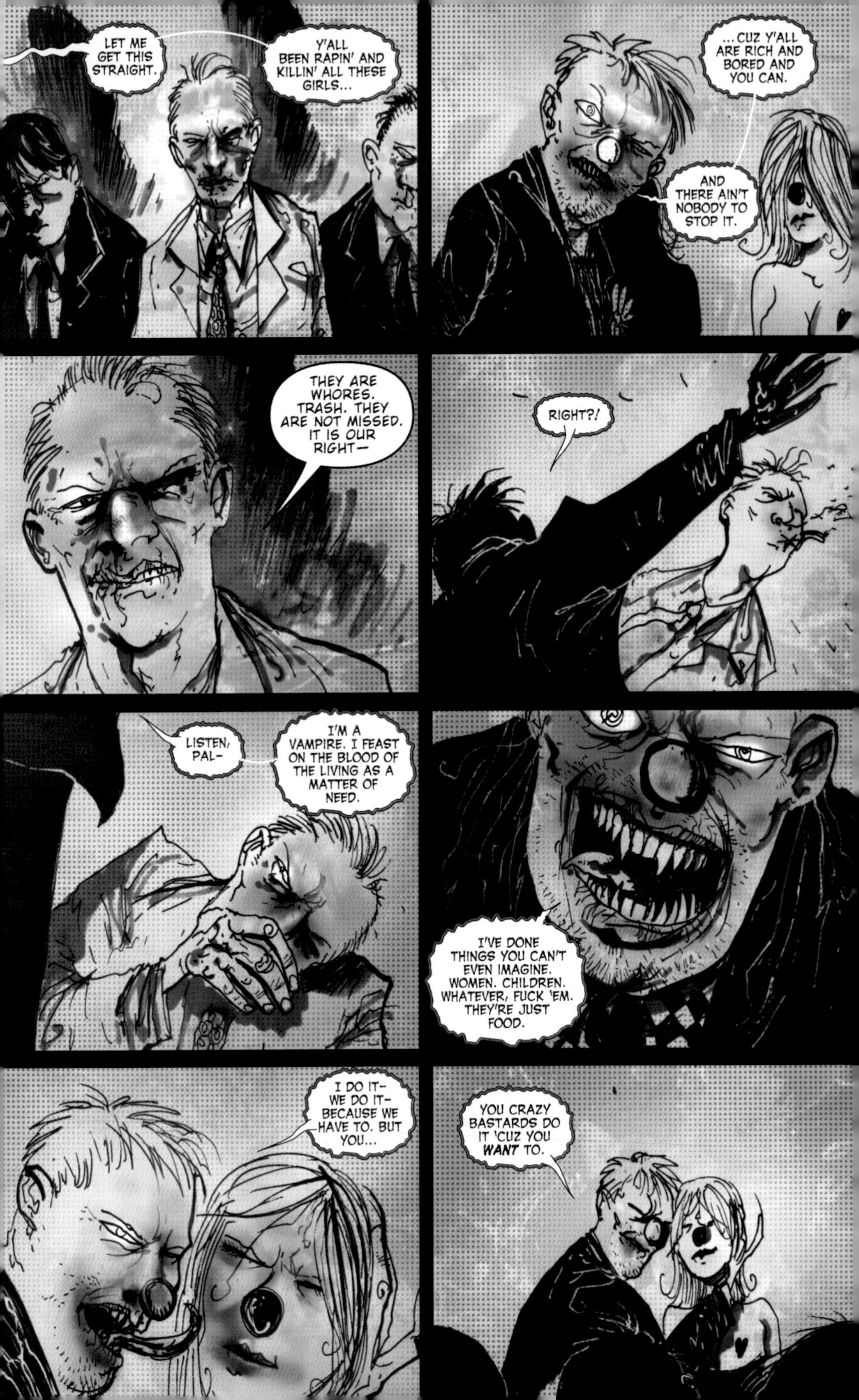
LET ME GET THIS STRAIGHT.
Y'ALL BEEN RAPIN' AND KILLIN' ALL THESE GIRLS...
...CUZ Y'ALL ARE RICH AND BORED AND YOU CAN.
AND THERE AIN'T NOBODY TO STOP IT.
THEY ARE WHORES. TRASH. THEY ARE NOT MISSED. IT IS OUR RIGHT—
RIGHT?!
LISTEN, PAL-
I'M A VAMPIRE. I FEAST ON THE BLOOD OF THE LIVING AS A MATTER OF NEED.
I'VE DONE THINGS YOU CAN'T EVEN IMAGINE. WOMEN. CHILDREN. WHATEVER, FUCK 'EM. THEY'RE JUST FOOD.
I DO IT- WE DO IT- BECAUSE WE HAVE TO. BUT YOU...
YOU CRAZY BASTARDS DO IT 'CUZ YOU WANT TO.

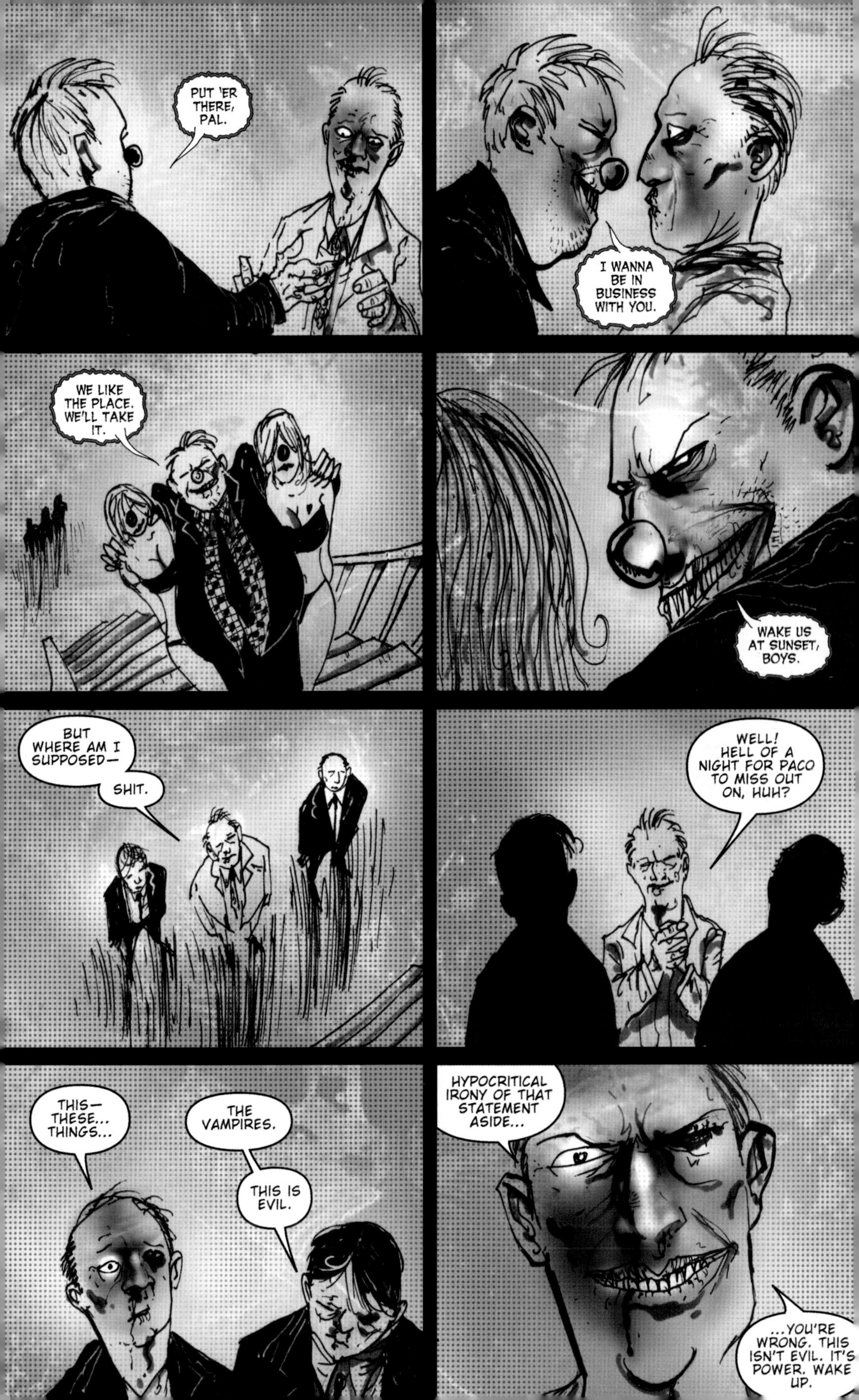
PUT 'ER THERE, PAL.
I WANNA BE IN BUSINESS WITH YOU.
WE LIKE THE PLACE. WE'LL TAKE IT.
WAKE US AT SUNSET, BOYS.
BUT WHERE AM I SUPPOSED—
SHIT.
WELL! HELL OF A NIGHT FOR PACO TO MISS OUT ON, HUH?
THIS— THESE... THINGS...
THE VAMPIRES.
THIS IS EVIL.
HYPOCRITICAL IRONY OF THAT STATEMENT ASIDE...
...YOU'RE WRONG. THIS ISN'T EVIL. IT'S POWER. WAKE UP.

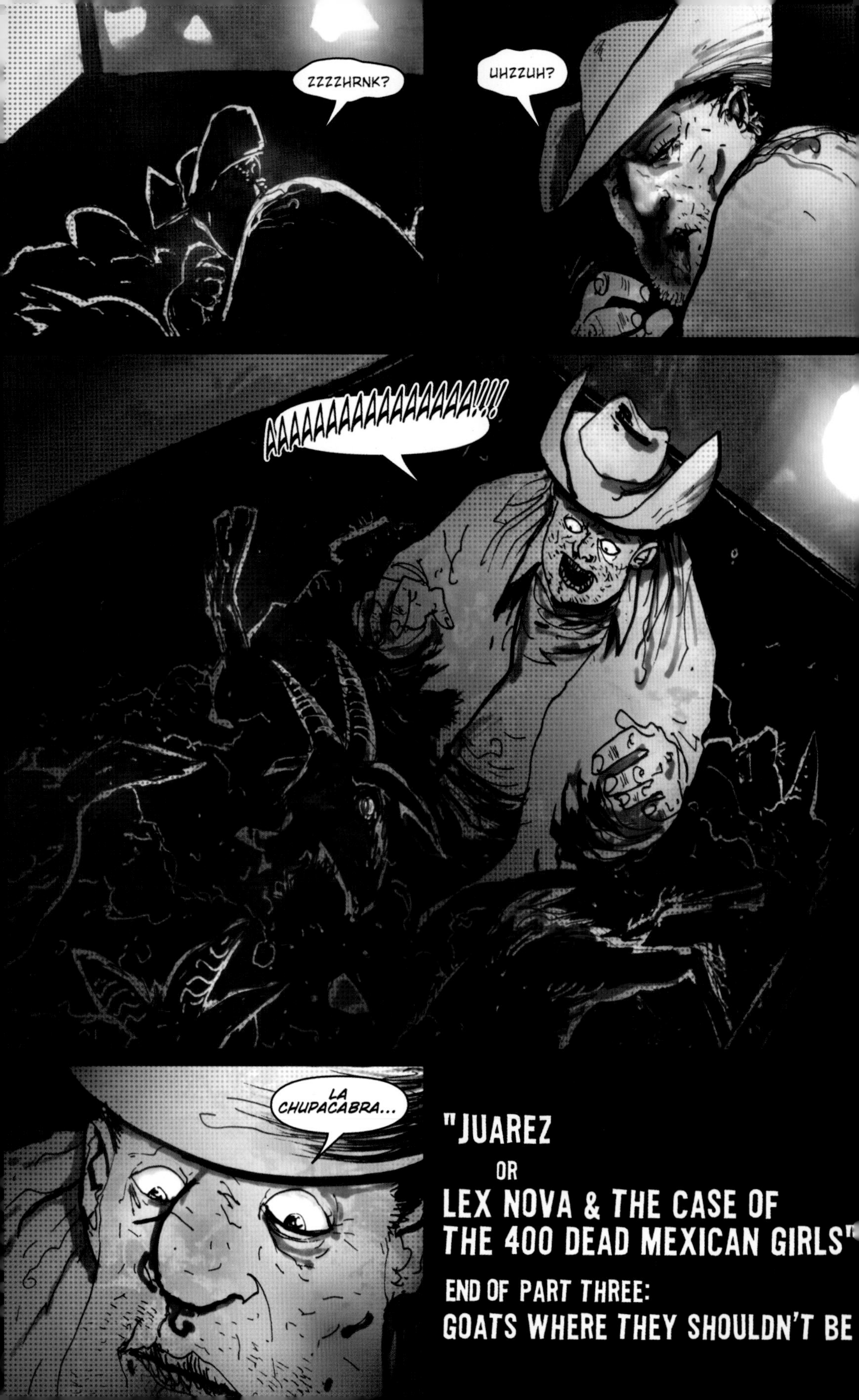
ZZZZHRNK?
UHZZUH?
AAAAAAAAAAAAAAAA!!!
LA CHUPACABRA...
"JUAREZ
OR
LEX NOVA & THE CASE OF
THE 400 DEAD MEXICAN GIRLS"
END OF PART THREE:
GOATS WHERE THEY SHOULDN'T BE

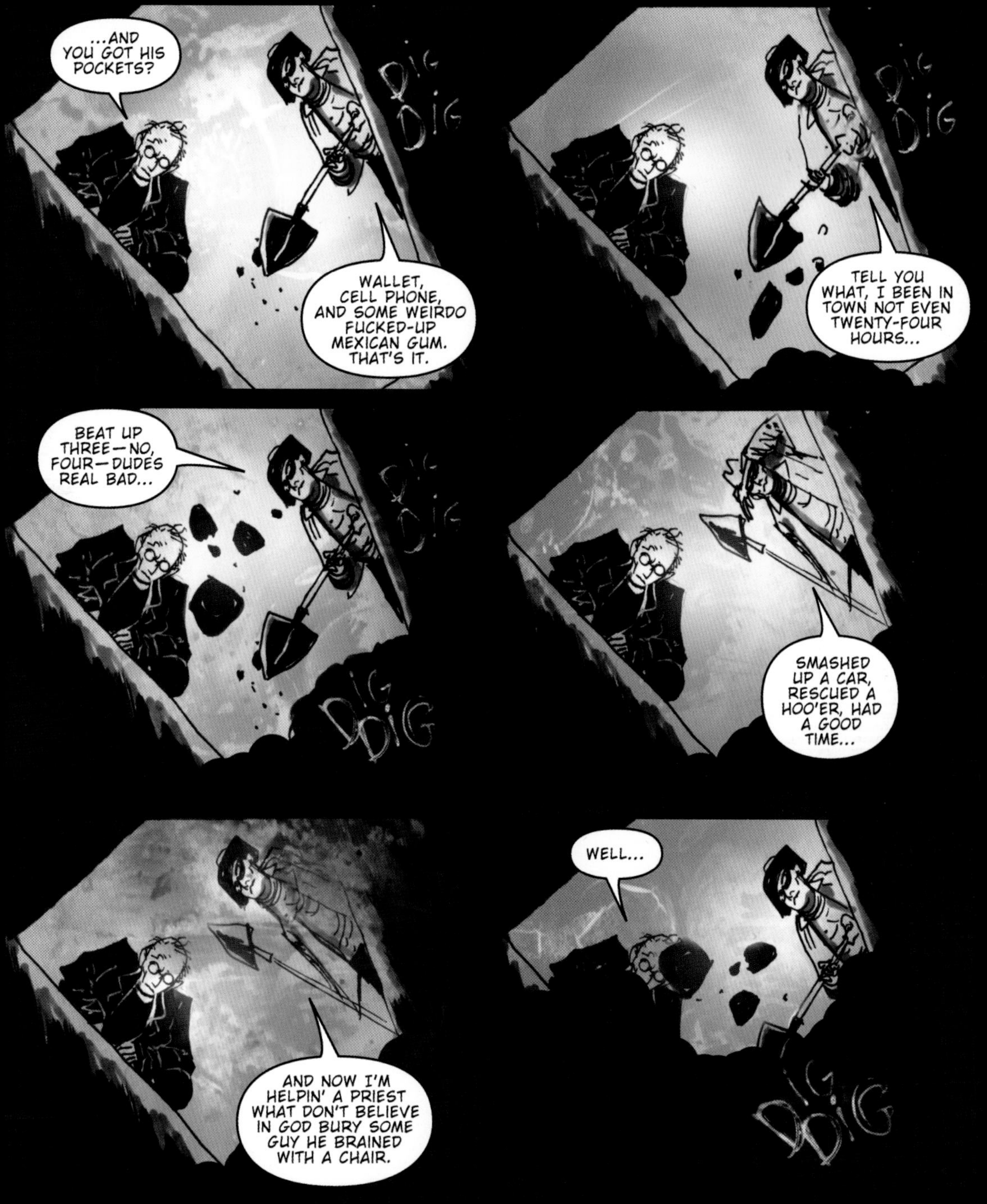
...AND YOU GOT HIS POCKETS?
DIG DIG
WALLET, CELL PHONE, AND SOME WEIRDO FUCKED-UP MEXICAN GUM. THAT'S IT.
DIG DIG
TELL YOU WHAT, I BEEN IN TOWN NOT EVEN TWENTY-FOUR HOURS...
BEAT UP THREE—NO, FOUR—DUDES REAL BAD...
DIG DIG
DIG DIG
SMASHED UP A CAR, RESCUED A HOO'ER, HAD A GOOD TIME...
AND NOW I'M HELPIN' A PRIEST WHAT DON'T BELIEVE IN GOD BURY SOME GUY HE BRAINED WITH A CHAIR.
WELL...
DIG DIG

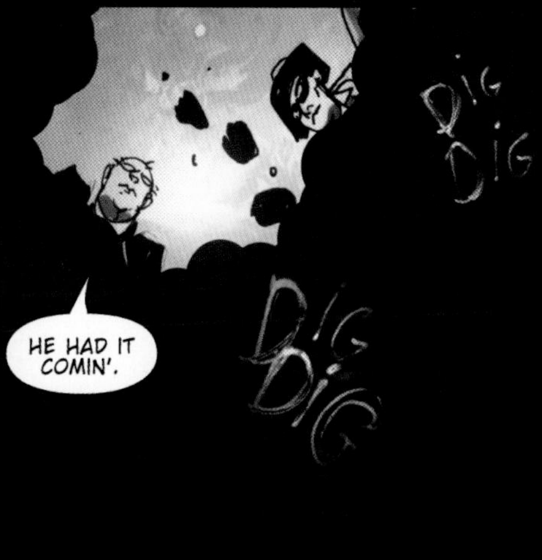
DIG DIG
DIG DIG
HE HAD IT COMIN'.

"JUAREZ
OR
LEX NOVA & THE CASE OF THE 400 DEAD MEXICAN GIRLS"

PART FOUR:
PLOTS

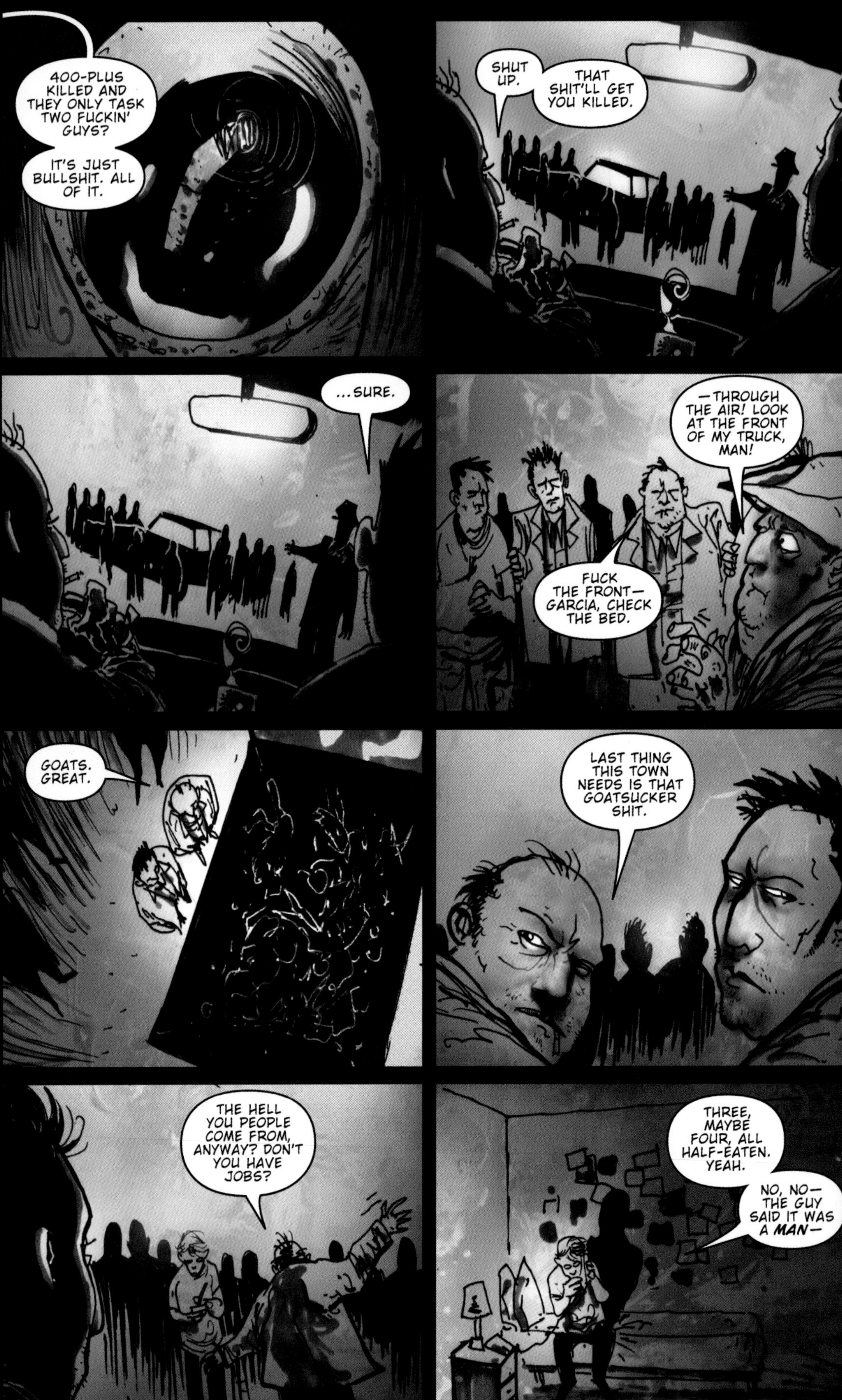
400-PLUS KILLED AND THEY ONLY TASK TWO FUCKIN' GUYS?
IT'S JUST BULLSHIT. ALL OF IT.
SHUT UP.
THAT SHIT'LL GET YOU KILLED.
...SURE.
—THROUGH THE AIR! LOOK AT THE FRONT OF MY TRUCK, MAN!
FUCK THE FRONT— GARCIA, CHECK THE BED.
GOATS. GREAT.
LAST THING THIS TOWN NEEDS IS THAT GOATSUCKER SHIT.
THE HELL YOU PEOPLE COME FROM, ANYWAY? DON'T YOU HAVE JOBS?
THREE, MAYBE FOUR, ALL HALF-EATEN. YEAH.
NO, NO— THE GUY SAID IT WAS A MAN—

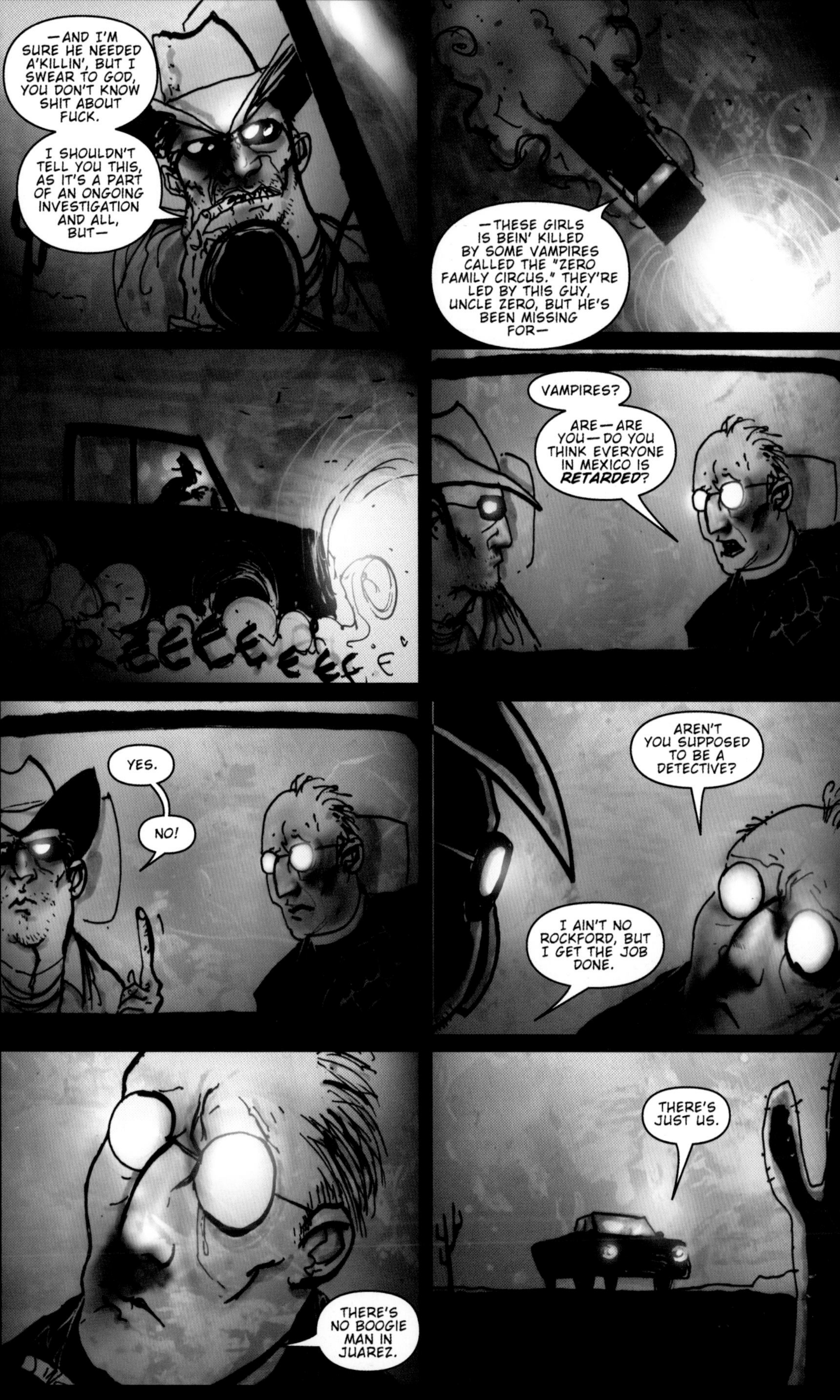
—AND I'M SURE HE NEEDED A'KILLIN', BUT I SWEAR TO GOD, YOU DON'T KNOW SHIT ABOUT FUCK.
I SHOULDN'T TELL YOU THIS, AS IT'S A PART OF AN ONGOING INVESTIGATION AND ALL, BUT—
—THESE GIRLS IS BEIN' KILLED BY SOME VAMPIRES CALLED THE "ZERO FAMILY CIRCUS." THEY'RE LED BY THIS GUY, UNCLE ZERO, BUT HE'S BEEN MISSING FOR—
VAMPIRES?
ARE—ARE YOU—DO YOU THINK EVERYONE IN MEXICO IS *RETARDED*?
YES.
NO!
AREN'T YOU SUPPOSED TO BE A DETECTIVE?
I AIN'T NO ROCKFORD, BUT I GET THE JOB DONE.
THERE'S NO BOOGIE MAN IN JUAREZ.
THERE'S JUST US.

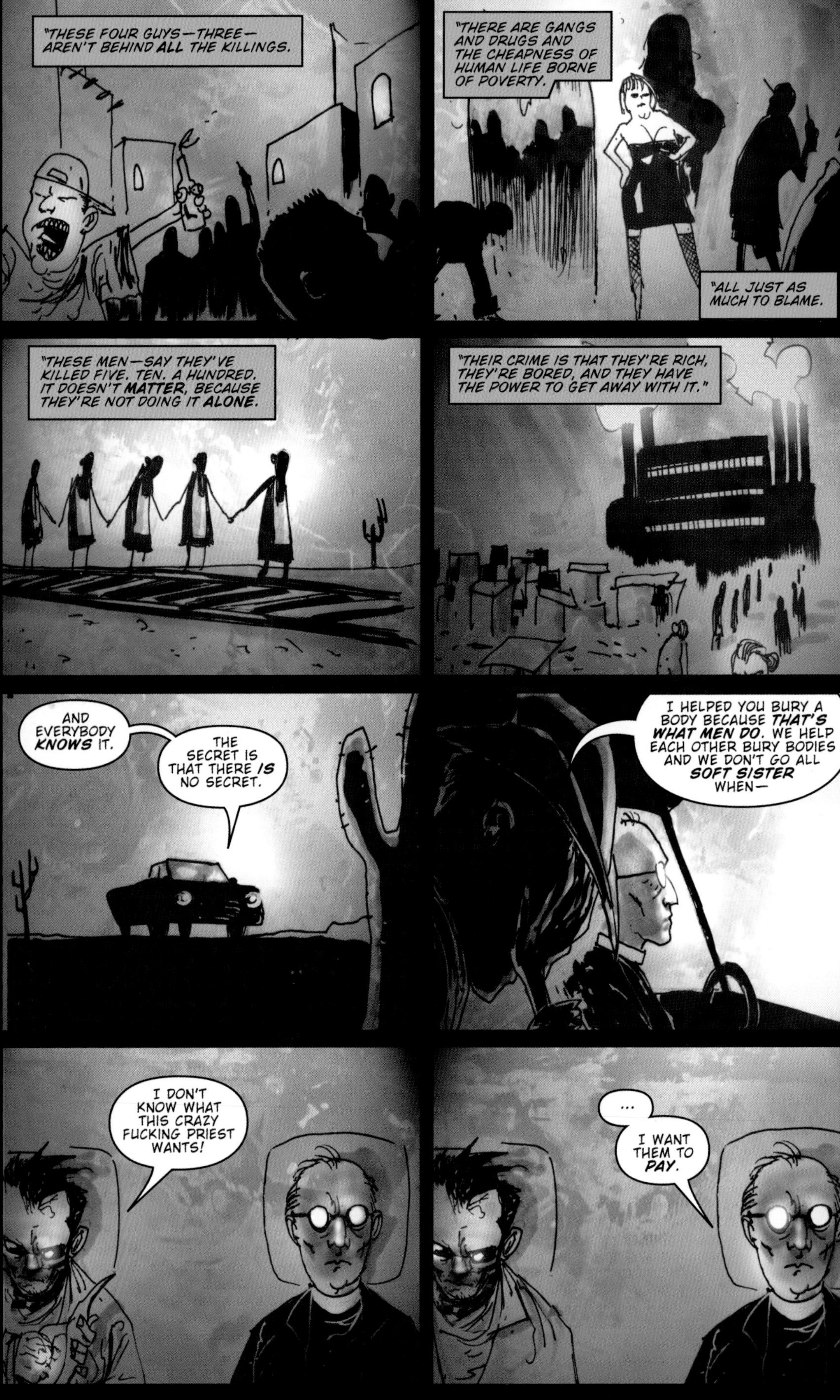
"THESE FOUR GUYS—THREE—AREN'T BEHIND ALL THE KILLINGS.
"THERE ARE GANGS AND DRUGS AND THE CHEAPNESS OF HUMAN LIFE BORNE OF POVERTY.
"ALL JUST AS MUCH TO BLAME.
"THESE MEN—SAY THEY'VE KILLED FIVE. TEN. A HUNDRED. IT DOESN'T MATTER, BECAUSE THEY'RE NOT DOING IT ALONE.
"THEIR CRIME IS THAT THEY'RE RICH, THEY'RE BORED, AND THEY HAVE THE POWER TO GET AWAY WITH IT."
AND EVERYBODY KNOWS IT.
THE SECRET IS THAT THERE IS NO SECRET.
I HELPED YOU BURY A BODY BECAUSE THAT'S WHAT MEN DO. WE HELP EACH OTHER BURY BODIES AND WE DON'T GO ALL SOFT SISTER WHEN—
I DON'T KNOW WHAT THIS CRAZY FUCKING PRIEST WANTS!
...
I WANT THEM TO PAY.

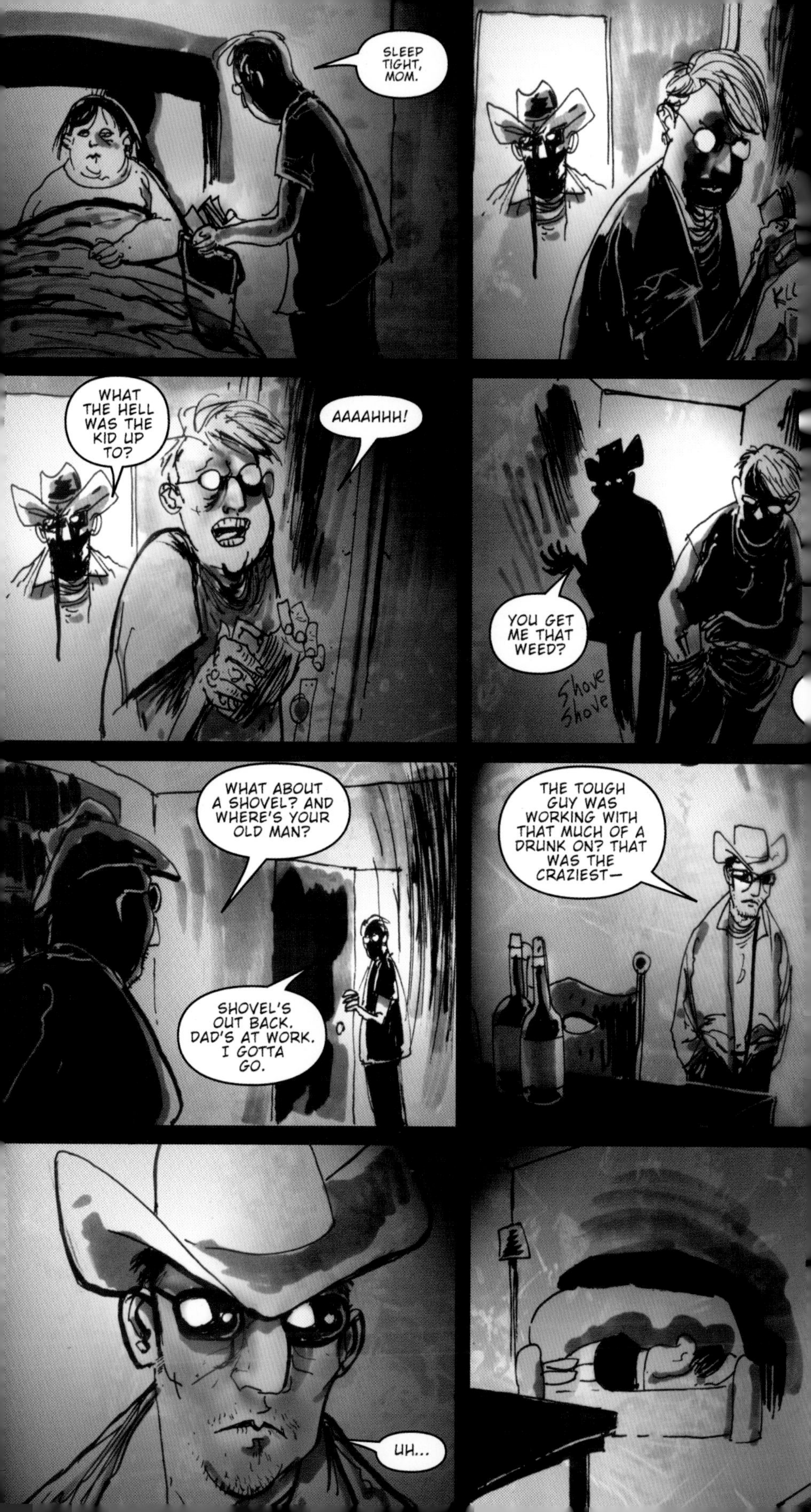

SLEEP TIGHT, MOM.
WHAT THE HELL WAS THE KID UP TO?
AAAAHHH!
YOU GET ME THAT WEED?
Shove Shove
WHAT ABOUT A SHOVEL? AND WHERE'S YOUR OLD MAN?
SHOVEL'S OUT BACK. DAD'S AT WORK. I GOTTA GO.
THE TOUGH GUY WAS WORKING WITH THAT MUCH OF A DRUNK ON? THAT WAS THE CRAZIEST—
UH...

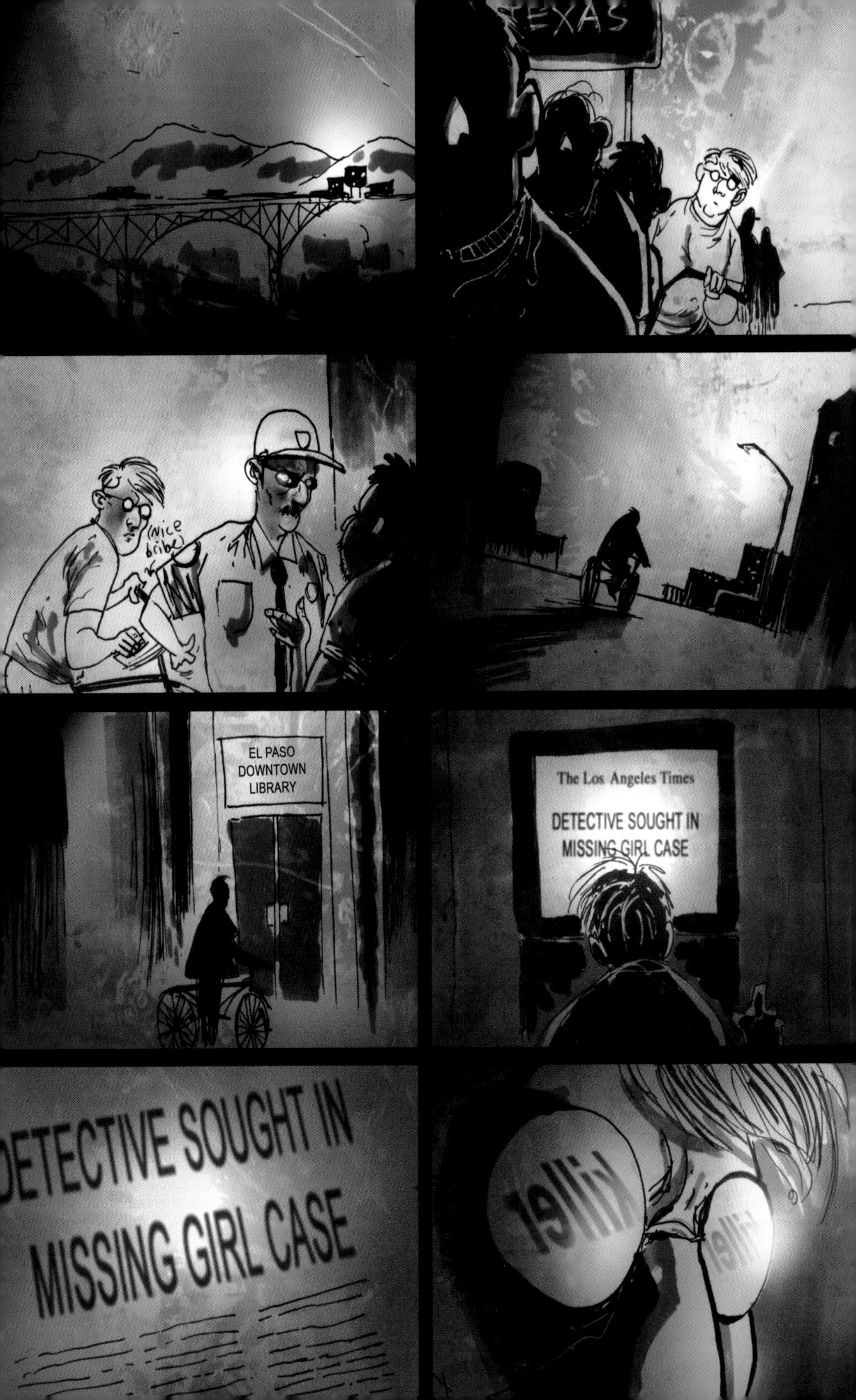
TEXAS
(nice bribe)
EL PASO
DOWNTOWN
LIBRARY
The Los Angeles Times
DETECTIVE SOUGHT IN
MISSING GIRL CASE
ETECTIVE SOUGHT IN
MISSING GIRL CASE

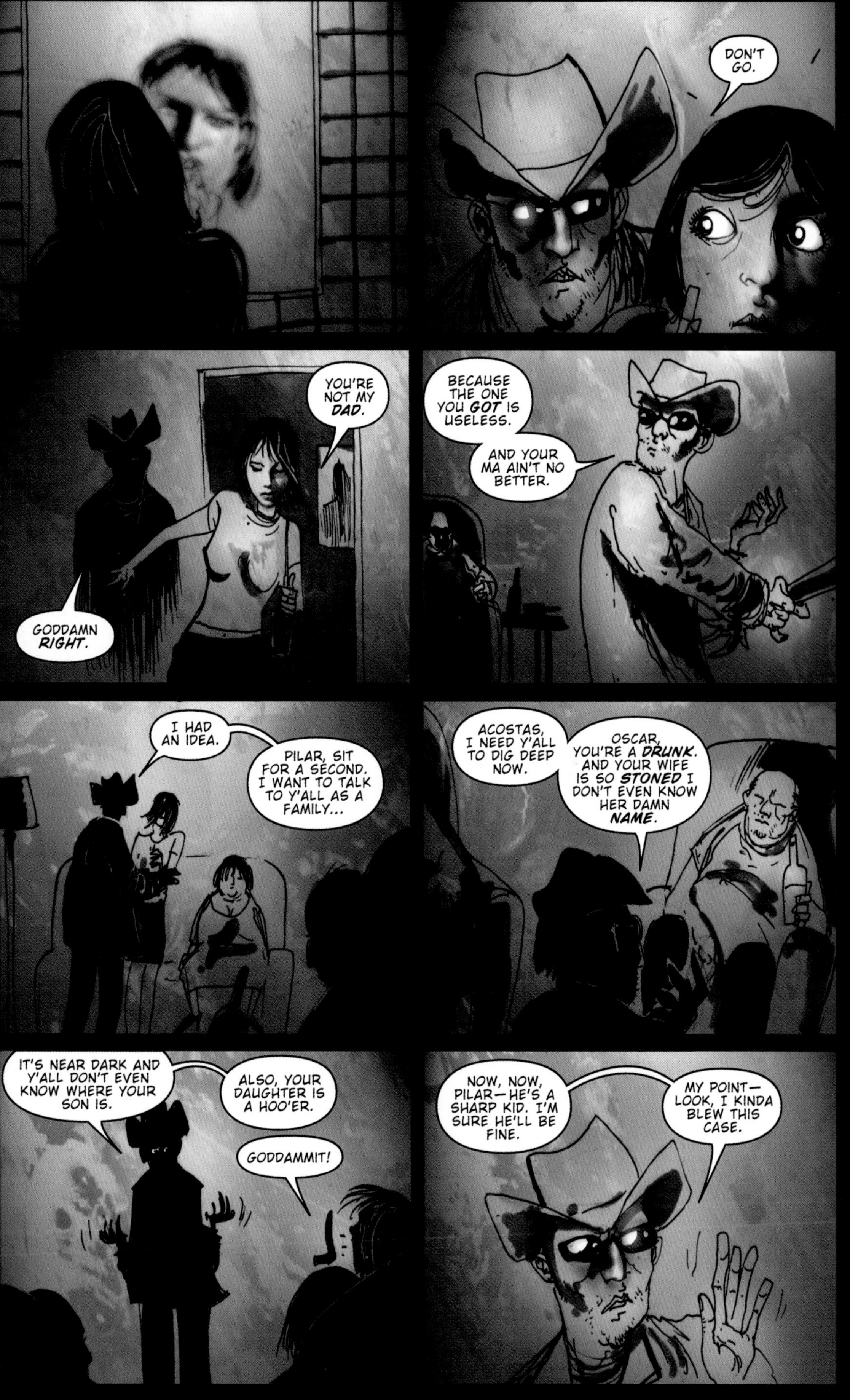
DON'T GO.
YOU'RE NOT MY DAD.
GODDAMN RIGHT.
BECAUSE THE ONE YOU GOT IS USELESS.
AND YOUR MA AIN'T NO BETTER.
I HAD AN IDEA.
PILAR, SIT FOR A SECOND. I WANT TO TALK TO Y'ALL AS A FAMILY...
ACOSTAS, I NEED Y'ALL TO DIG DEEP NOW.
OSCAR, YOU'RE A DRUNK. AND YOUR WIFE IS SO STONED I DON'T EVEN KNOW HER DAMN NAME.
IT'S NEAR DARK AND Y'ALL DON'T EVEN KNOW WHERE YOUR SON IS.
ALSO, YOUR DAUGHTER IS A HOO'ER.
GODDAMMIT!
NOW, NOW, PILAR—HE'S A SHARP KID. I'M SURE HE'LL BE FINE.
MY POINT—LOOK, I KINDA BLEW THIS CASE.

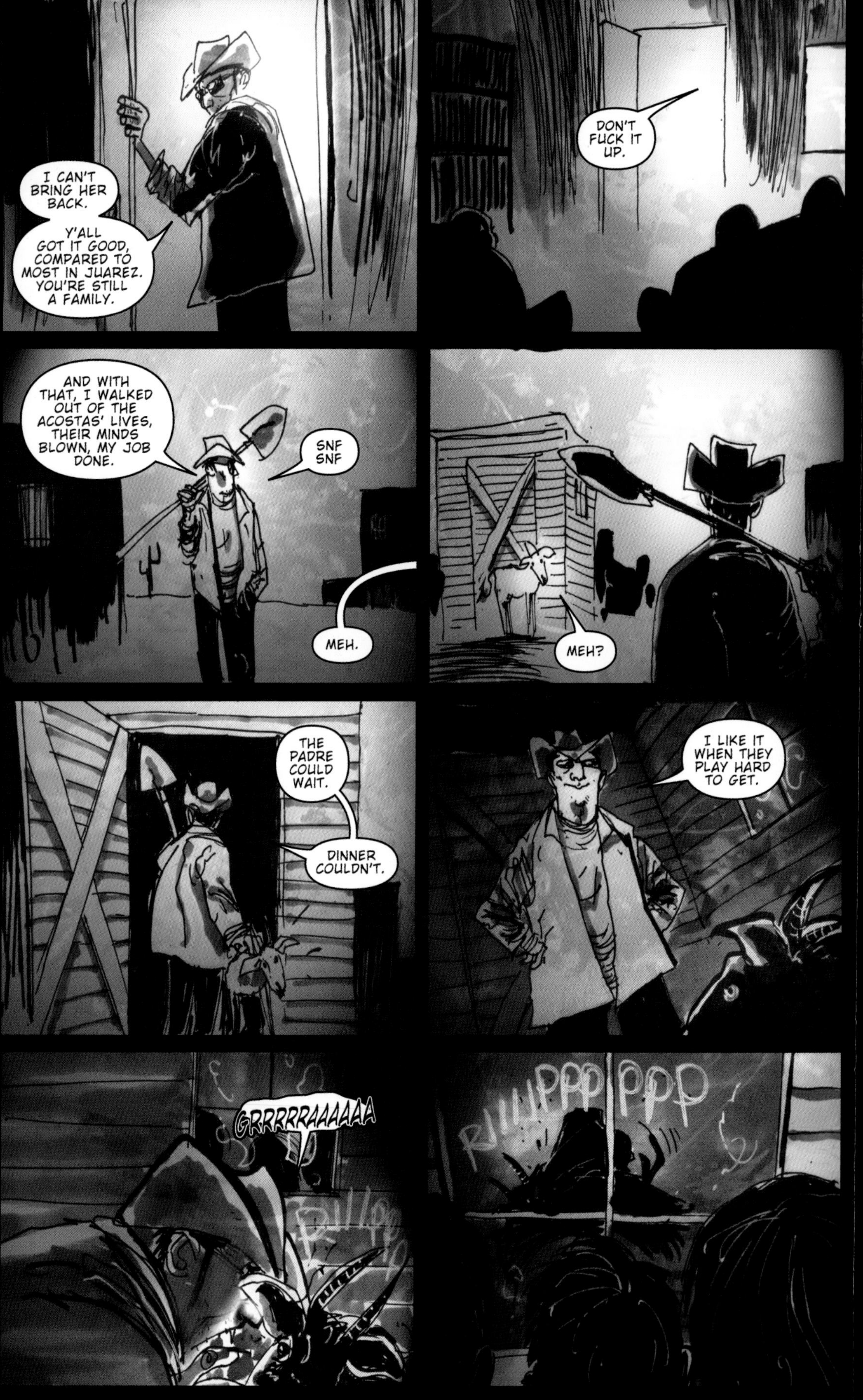
I CAN'T BRING HER BACK.
Y'ALL GOT IT GOOD, COMPARED TO MOST IN JUAREZ. YOU'RE STILL A FAMILY.
DON'T FUCK IT UP.
AND WITH THAT, I WALKED OUT OF THE ACOSTAS' LIVES, THEIR MINDS BLOWN, MY JOB DONE.
SNF SNF
MEH.
MEH?
THE PADRE COULD WAIT.
DINNER COULDN'T.
I LIKE IT WHEN THEY PLAY HARD TO GET.
GRRRRRAAAAAA
RIIIPPP PPP

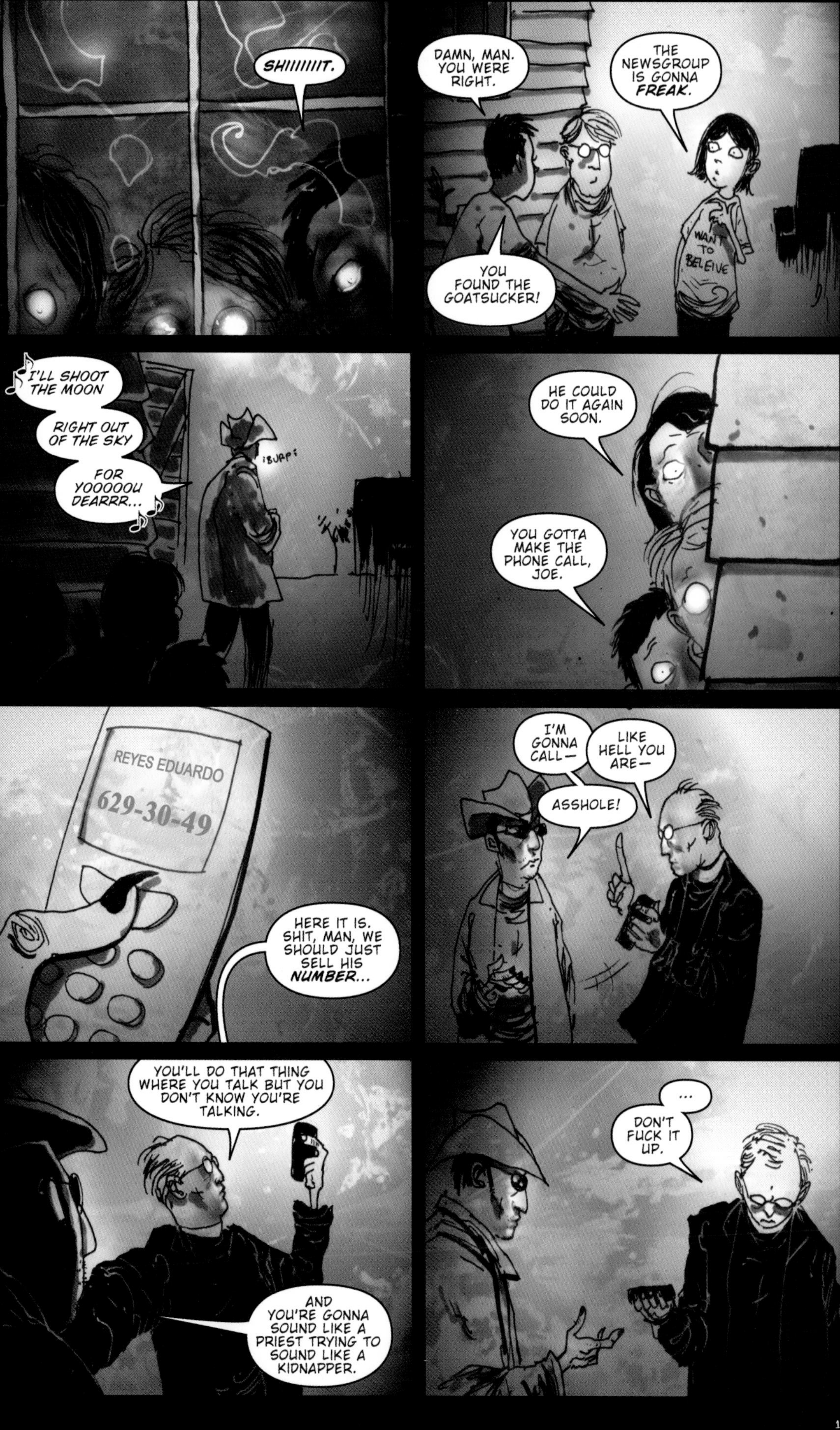
SHIIIIIIIT.
DAMN, MAN. YOU WERE RIGHT.
THE NEWSGROUP IS GONNA FREAK.
YOU FOUND THE GOATSUCKER!
WANT TO BELEIVE
I'LL SHOOT THE MOON
RIGHT OUT OF THE SKY
FOR YOOOOOU DEARRR...
¡BURP!
HE COULD DO IT AGAIN SOON.
YOU GOTTA MAKE THE PHONE CALL, JOE.
REYES EDUARDO
629-30-49
HERE IT IS. SHIT, MAN, WE SHOULD JUST SELL HIS NUMBER...
I'M GONNA CALL—
LIKE HELL YOU ARE—
ASSHOLE!
YOU'LL DO THAT THING WHERE YOU TALK BUT YOU DON'T KNOW YOU'RE TALKING.
AND YOU'RE GONNA SOUND LIKE A PRIEST TRYING TO SOUND LIKE A KIDNAPPER.
...
DON'T FUCK IT UP.

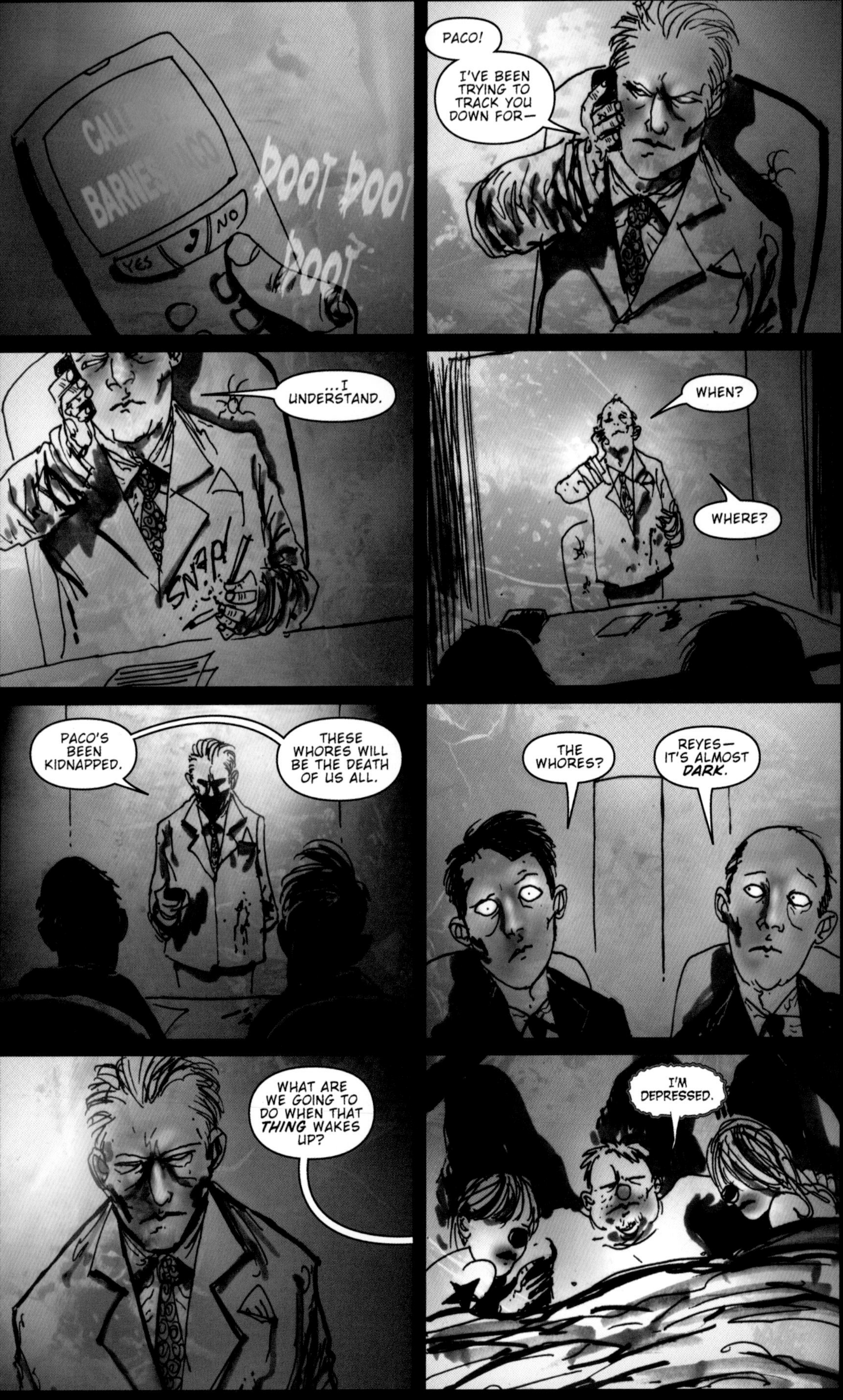
YES
NO
DOOT DOOT
DOOT
PACO!
I'VE BEEN TRYING TO TRACK YOU DOWN FOR—
...I UNDERSTAND.
SNAP
WHEN?
WHERE?
PACO'S BEEN KIDNAPPED.
THESE WHORES WILL BE THE DEATH OF US ALL.
THE WHORES?
REYES— IT'S ALMOST *DARK*.
WHAT ARE WE GOING TO DO WHEN THAT *THING* WAKES UP?
I'M DEPRESSED.

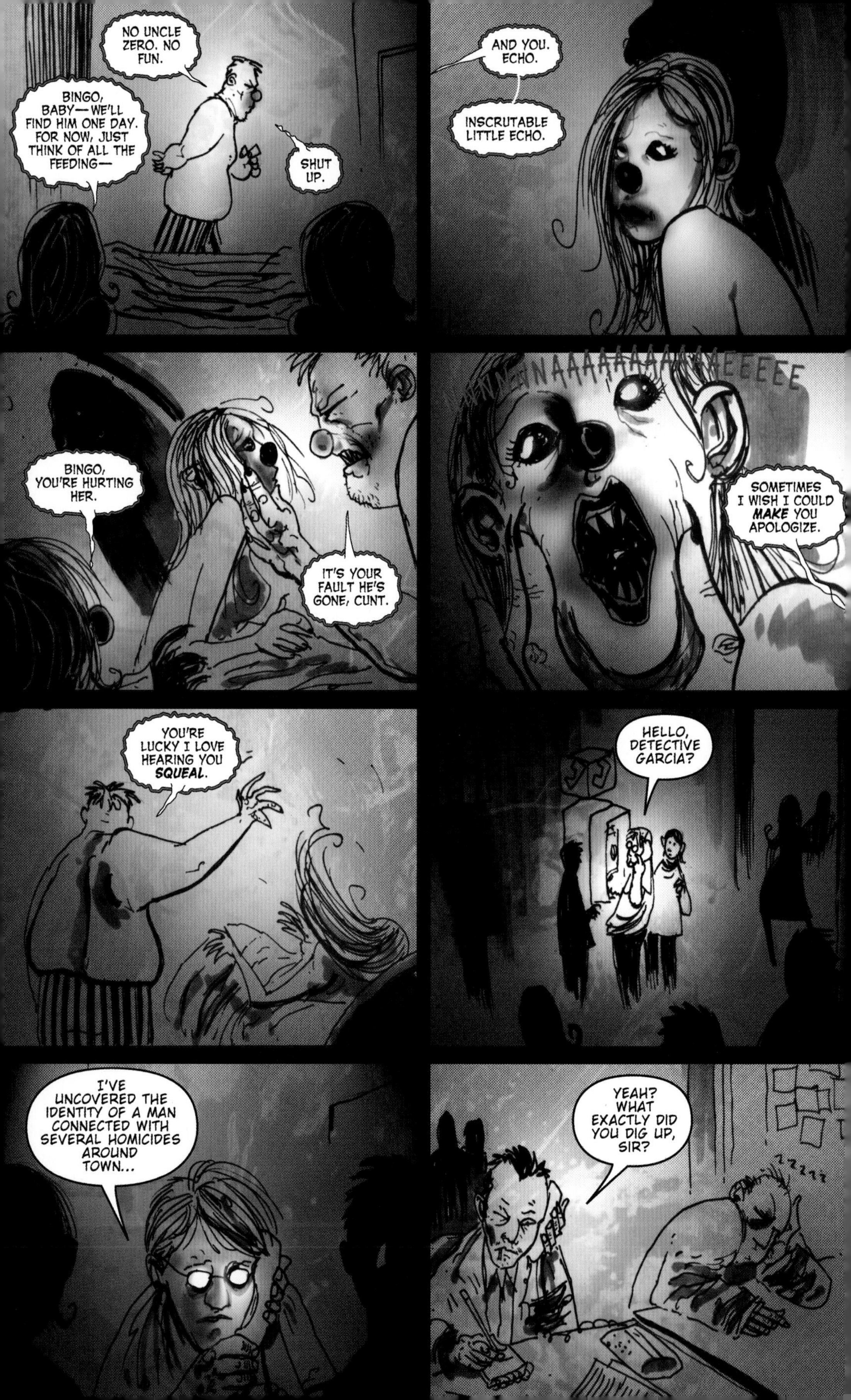

NO UNCLE ZERO. NO FUN.
BINGO, BABY—WE'LL FIND HIM ONE DAY. FOR NOW, JUST THINK OF ALL THE FEEDING—
SHUT UP.
AND YOU. ECHO.
INSCRUTABLE LITTLE ECHO.
BINGO, YOU'RE HURTING HER.
IT'S YOUR FAULT HE'S GONE, CUNT.
SOMETIMES I WISH I COULD **MAKE** YOU APOLOGIZE.
YOU'RE LUCKY I LOVE HEARING YOU **SQUEAL**.
HELLO, DETECTIVE GARCIA?
I'VE UNCOVERED THE IDENTITY OF A MAN CONNECTED WITH SEVERAL HOMICIDES AROUND TOWN...
YEAH? WHAT EXACTLY DID YOU DIG UP, SIR?

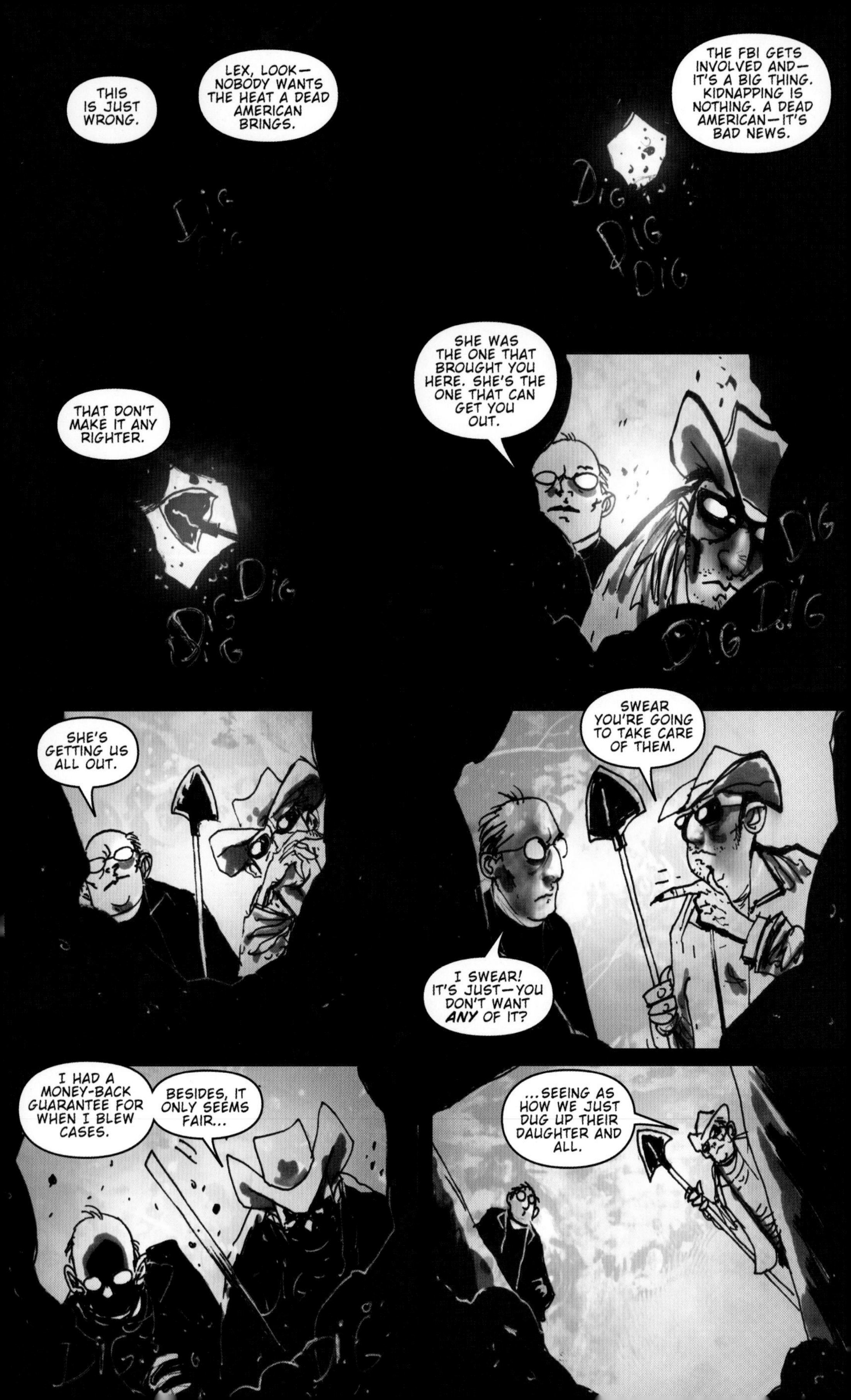

THIS IS JUST WRONG.
LEX, LOOK—NOBODY WANTS THE HEAT A DEAD AMERICAN BRINGS.
DIG DIG
THE FBI GETS INVOLVED AND—IT'S A BIG THING. KIDNAPPING IS NOTHING. A DEAD AMERICAN—IT'S BAD NEWS.
DIG DIG DIG
THAT DON'T MAKE IT ANY RIGHTER.
DIG DIG DIG
SHE WAS THE ONE THAT BROUGHT YOU HERE. SHE'S THE ONE THAT CAN GET YOU OUT.
DIG DIG DIG
SHE'S GETTING US ALL OUT.
SWEAR YOU'RE GOING TO TAKE CARE OF THEM.
I SWEAR! IT'S JUST—YOU DON'T WANT *ANY* OF IT?
I HAD A MONEY-BACK GUARANTEE FOR WHEN I BLEW CASES.
BESIDES, IT ONLY SEEMS FAIR...
...SEEING AS HOW WE JUST DUG UP THEIR DAUGHTER AND ALL.

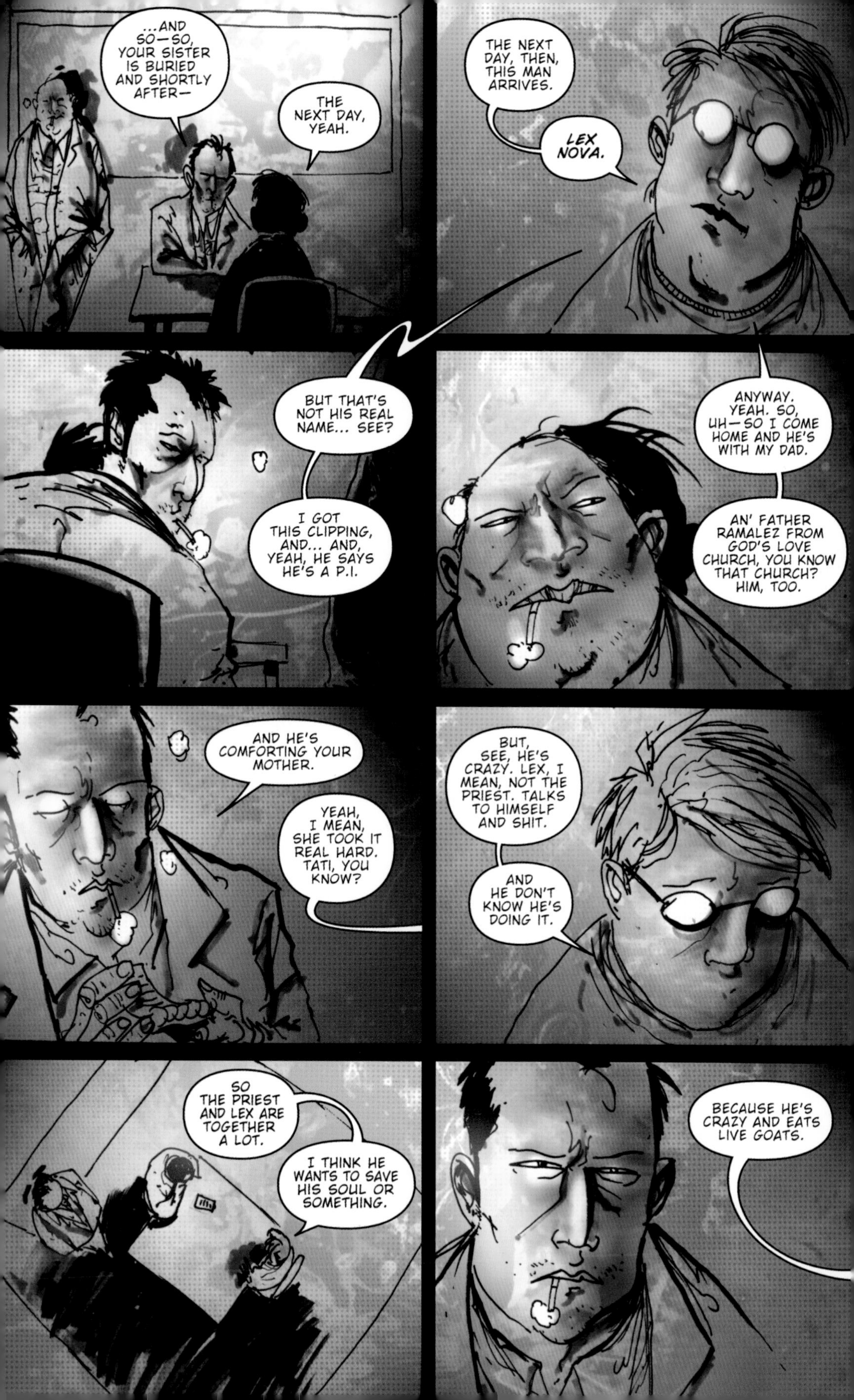
...AND SO—SO, YOUR SISTER IS BURIED AND SHORTLY AFTER—
THE NEXT DAY, YEAH.
THE NEXT DAY, THEN, THIS MAN ARRIVES.
LEX NOVA.
BUT THAT'S NOT HIS REAL NAME... SEE?
I GOT THIS CLIPPING, AND... AND, YEAH, HE SAYS HE'S A P.I.
ANYWAY. YEAH. SO, UH—SO I COME HOME AND HE'S WITH MY DAD.
AN' FATHER RAMALEZ FROM GOD'S LOVE CHURCH, YOU KNOW THAT CHURCH? HIM, TOO.
AND HE'S COMFORTING YOUR MOTHER.
YEAH, I MEAN, SHE TOOK IT REAL HARD. TATI, YOU KNOW?
BUT, SEE, HE'S CRAZY. LEX, I MEAN, NOT THE PRIEST. TALKS TO HIMSELF AND SHIT.
AND HE DON'T KNOW HE'S DOING IT.
SO THE PRIEST AND LEX ARE TOGETHER A LOT.
I THINK HE WANTS TO SAVE HIS SOUL OR SOMETHING.
BECAUSE HE'S CRAZY AND EATS LIVE GOATS.

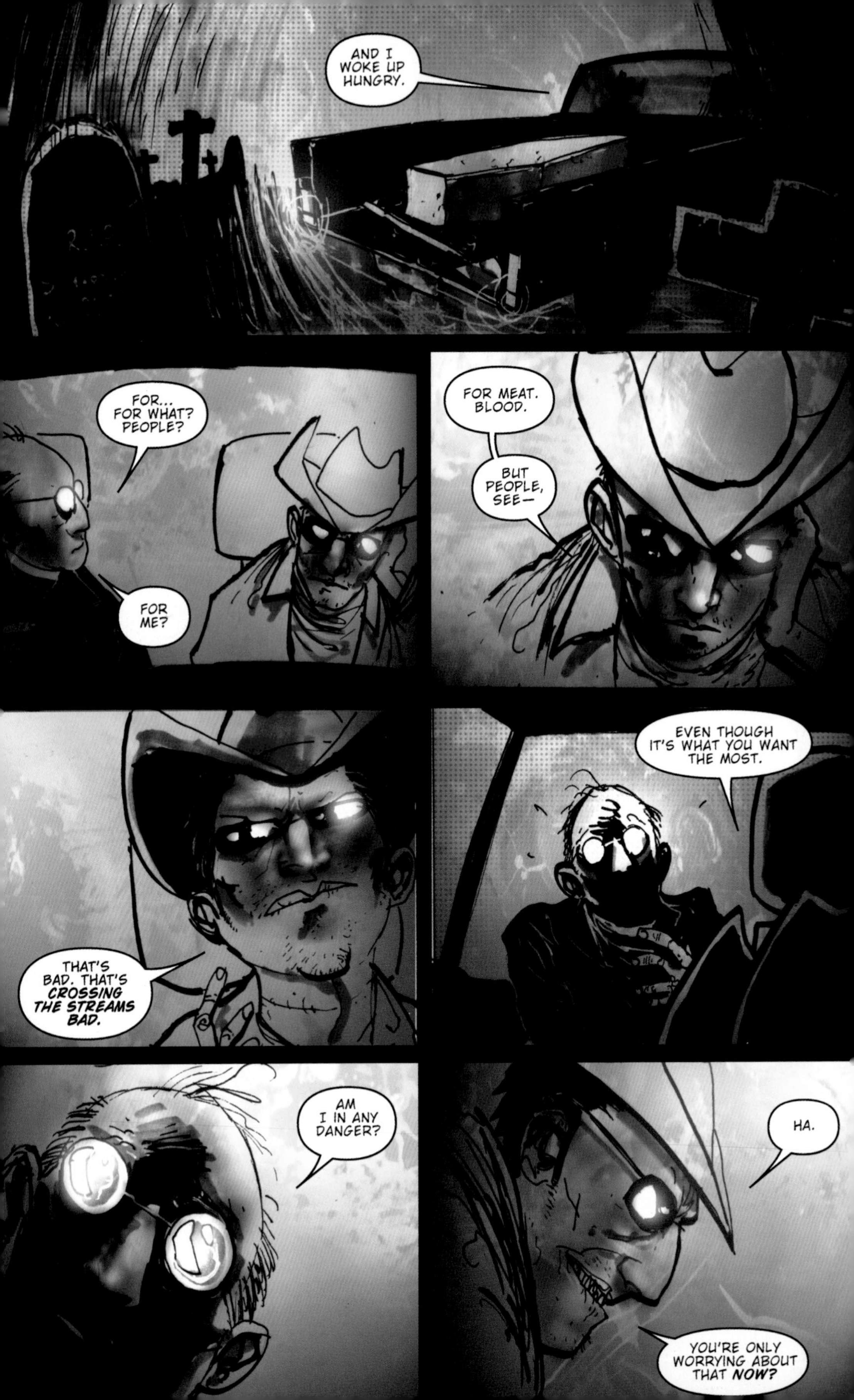
AND I WOKE UP HUNGRY.
FOR... FOR WHAT? PEOPLE?
FOR ME?
FOR MEAT. BLOOD.
BUT PEOPLE, SEE—
THAT'S BAD. THAT'S ***CROSSING THE STREAMS BAD.***
EVEN THOUGH IT'S WHAT YOU WANT THE MOST.
AM I IN ANY DANGER?
HA.
YOU'RE ONLY WORRYING ABOUT THAT ***NOW?***

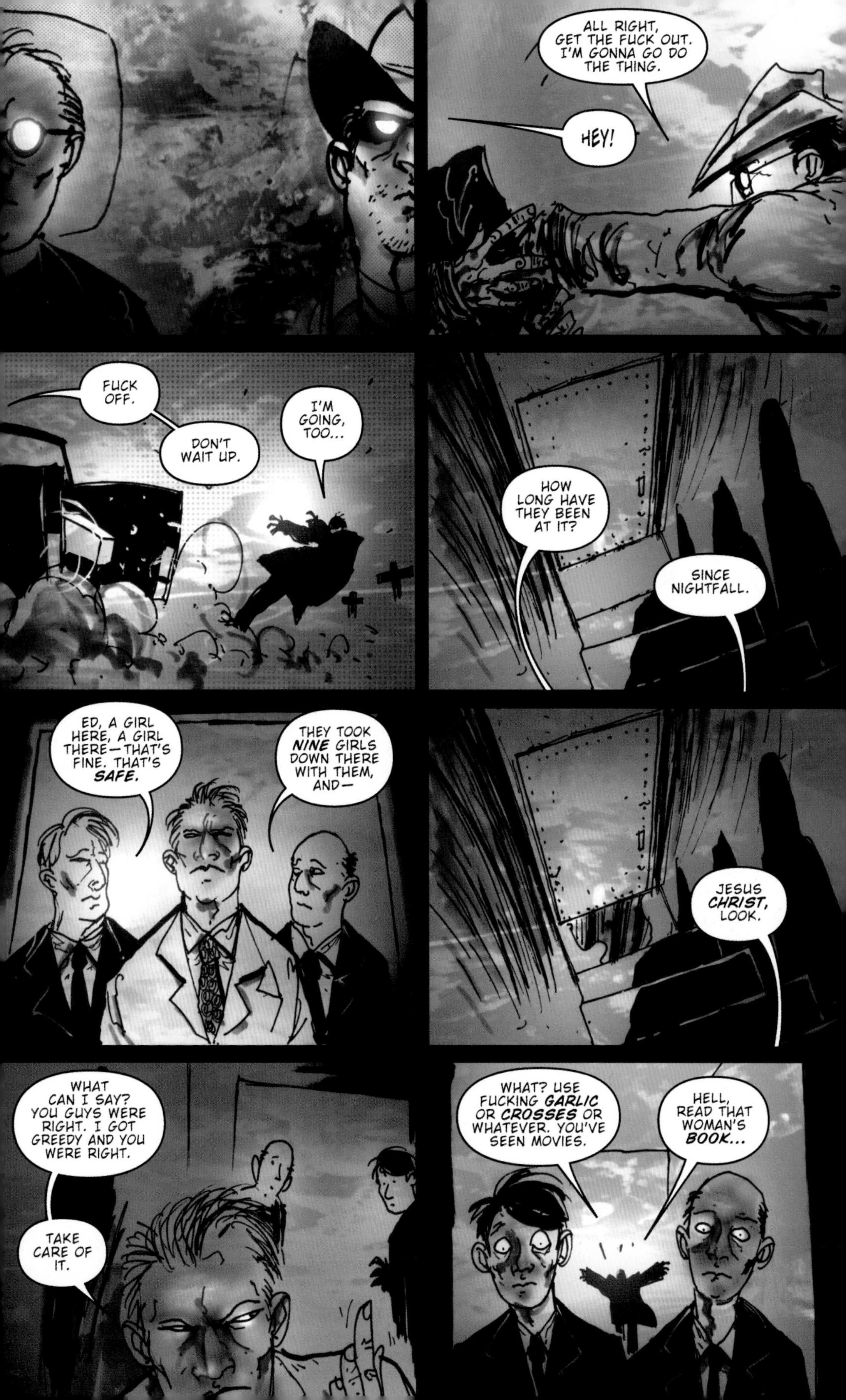
ALL RIGHT, GET THE FUCK OUT. I'M GONNA GO DO THE THING.
HEY!
FUCK OFF.
DON'T WAIT UP.
I'M GOING, TOO...
HOW LONG HAVE THEY BEEN AT IT?
SINCE NIGHTFALL.
ED, A GIRL HERE, A GIRL THERE—THAT'S FINE. THAT'S **SAFE.**
THEY TOOK **NINE** GIRLS DOWN THERE WITH THEM, AND—
JESUS **CHRIST,** LOOK.
WHAT CAN I SAY? YOU GUYS WERE RIGHT. I GOT GREEDY AND YOU WERE RIGHT.
TAKE CARE OF IT.
WHAT? USE FUCKING **GARLIC** OR **CROSSES** OR WHATEVER. YOU'VE SEEN MOVIES.
HELL, READ THAT WOMAN'S **BOOK...**

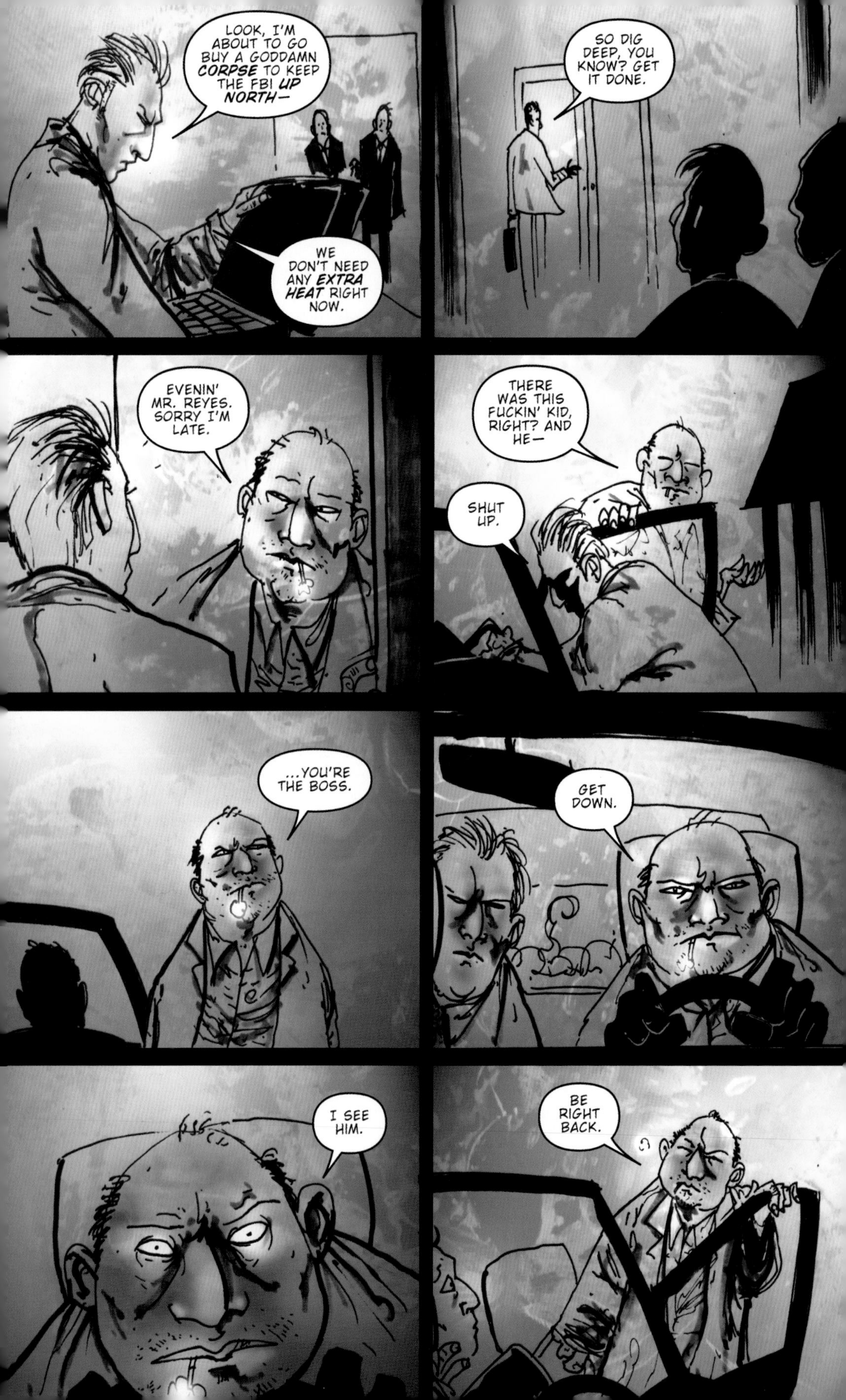
LOOK, I'M ABOUT TO GO BUY A GODDAMN CORPSE TO KEEP THE FBI UP NORTH—
WE DON'T NEED ANY EXTRA HEAT RIGHT NOW.
SO DIG DEEP, YOU KNOW? GET IT DONE.
EVENIN' MR. REYES. SORRY I'M LATE.
THERE WAS THIS FUCKIN' KID, RIGHT? AND HE—
SHUT UP.
...YOU'RE THE BOSS.
GET DOWN.
I SEE HIM.
BE RIGHT BACK.

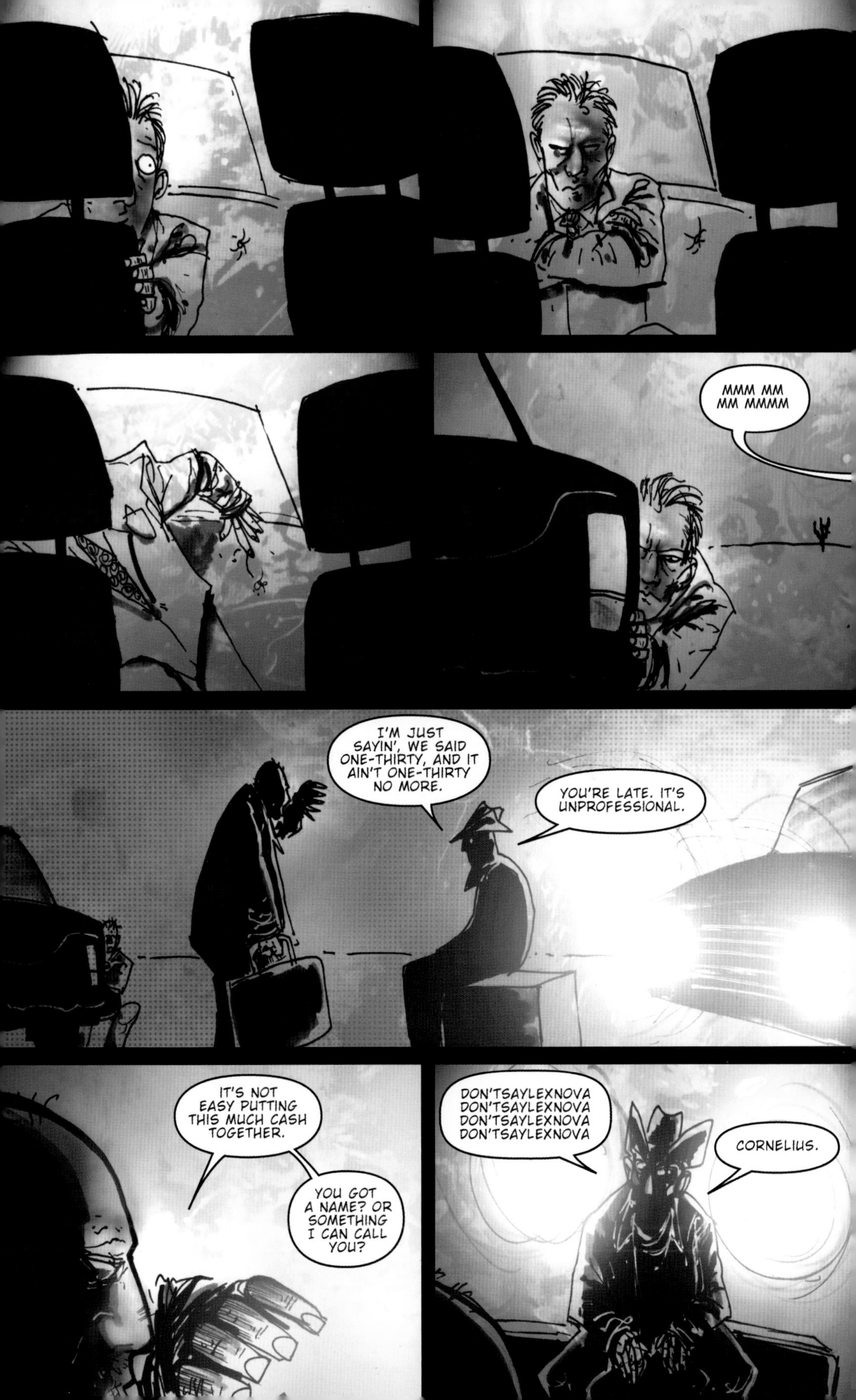
MMM MM
MM MMMM
I'M JUST SAYIN', WE SAID ONE-THIRTY, AND IT AIN'T ONE-THIRTY NO MORE.
YOU'RE LATE. IT'S UNPROFESSIONAL.
IT'S NOT EASY PUTTING THIS MUCH CASH TOGETHER.
YOU GOT A NAME? OR SOMETHING I CAN CALL YOU?
DON'TSAYLEXNOVA DON'TSAYLEXNOVA DON'TSAYLEXNOVA DON'TSAYLEXNOVA
CORNELIUS.

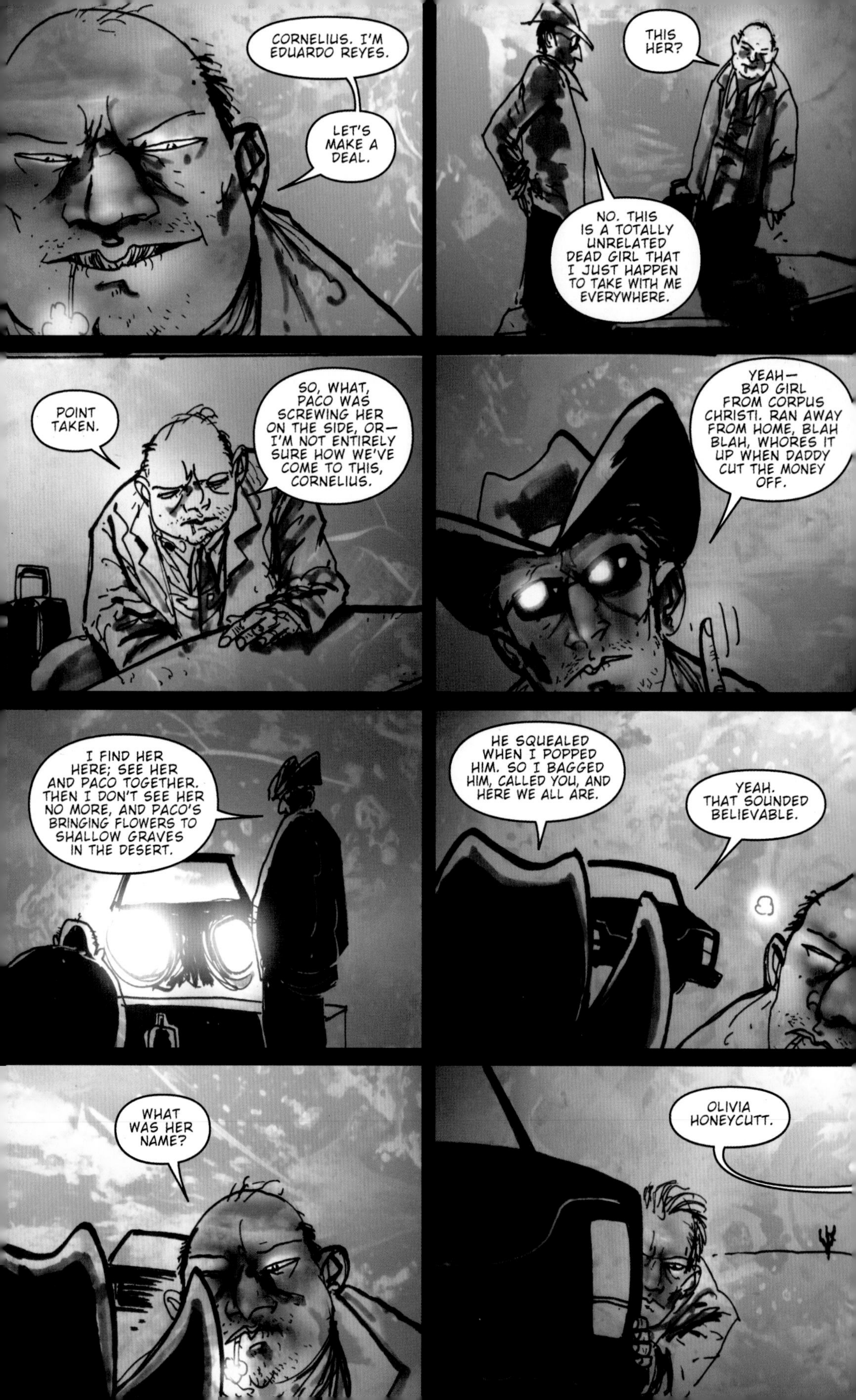
CORNELIUS. I'M EDUARDO REYES.
LET'S MAKE A DEAL.
THIS HER?
NO. THIS IS A TOTALLY UNRELATED DEAD GIRL THAT I JUST HAPPEN TO TAKE WITH ME EVERYWHERE.
POINT TAKEN.
SO, WHAT, PACO WAS SCREWING HER ON THE SIDE, OR— I'M NOT ENTIRELY SURE HOW WE'VE COME TO THIS, CORNELIUS.
YEAH— BAD GIRL FROM CORPUS CHRISTI. RAN AWAY FROM HOME, BLAH BLAH, WHORES IT UP WHEN DADDY CUT THE MONEY OFF.
I FIND HER HERE; SEE HER AND PACO TOGETHER. THEN I DON'T SEE HER NO MORE, AND PACO'S BRINGING FLOWERS TO SHALLOW GRAVES IN THE DESERT.
HE SQUEALED WHEN I POPPED HIM. SO I BAGGED HIM, CALLED YOU, AND HERE WE ALL ARE.
YEAH. THAT SOUNDED BELIEVABLE.
WHAT WAS HER NAME?
OLIVIA HONEYCUTT.

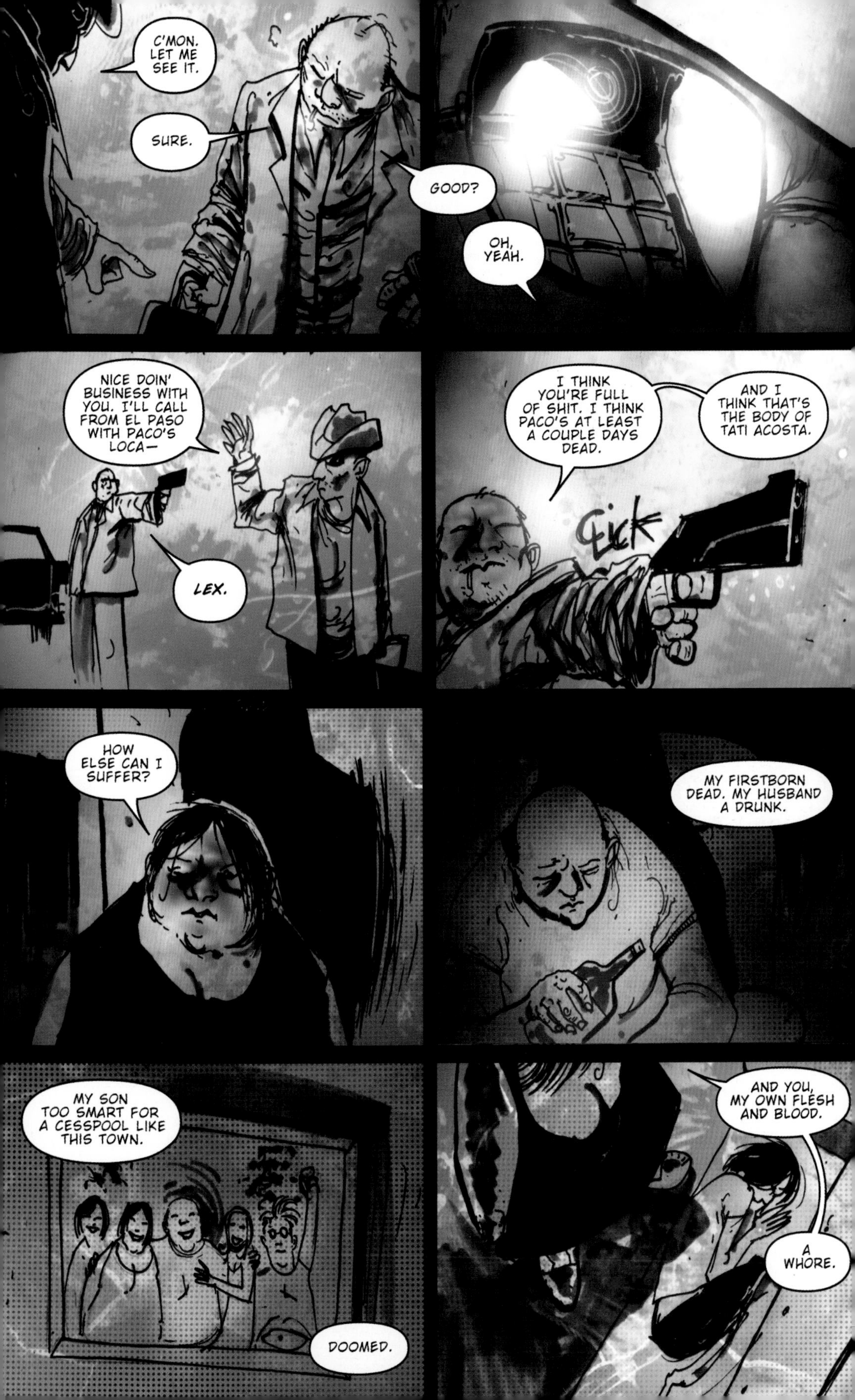
C'MON. LET ME SEE IT.
SURE.
GOOD?
OH, YEAH.
NICE DOIN' BUSINESS WITH YOU. I'LL CALL FROM EL PASO WITH PACO'S LOCA—
LEX.
I THINK YOU'RE FULL OF SHIT. I THINK PACO'S AT LEAST A COUPLE DAYS DEAD.
AND I THINK THAT'S THE BODY OF TATI ACOSTA.
CLICK
HOW ELSE CAN I SUFFER?
MY FIRSTBORN DEAD. MY HUSBAND A DRUNK.
MY SON TOO SMART FOR A CESSPOOL LIKE THIS TOWN.
DOOMED.
AND YOU, MY OWN FLESH AND BLOOD.
A WHORE.

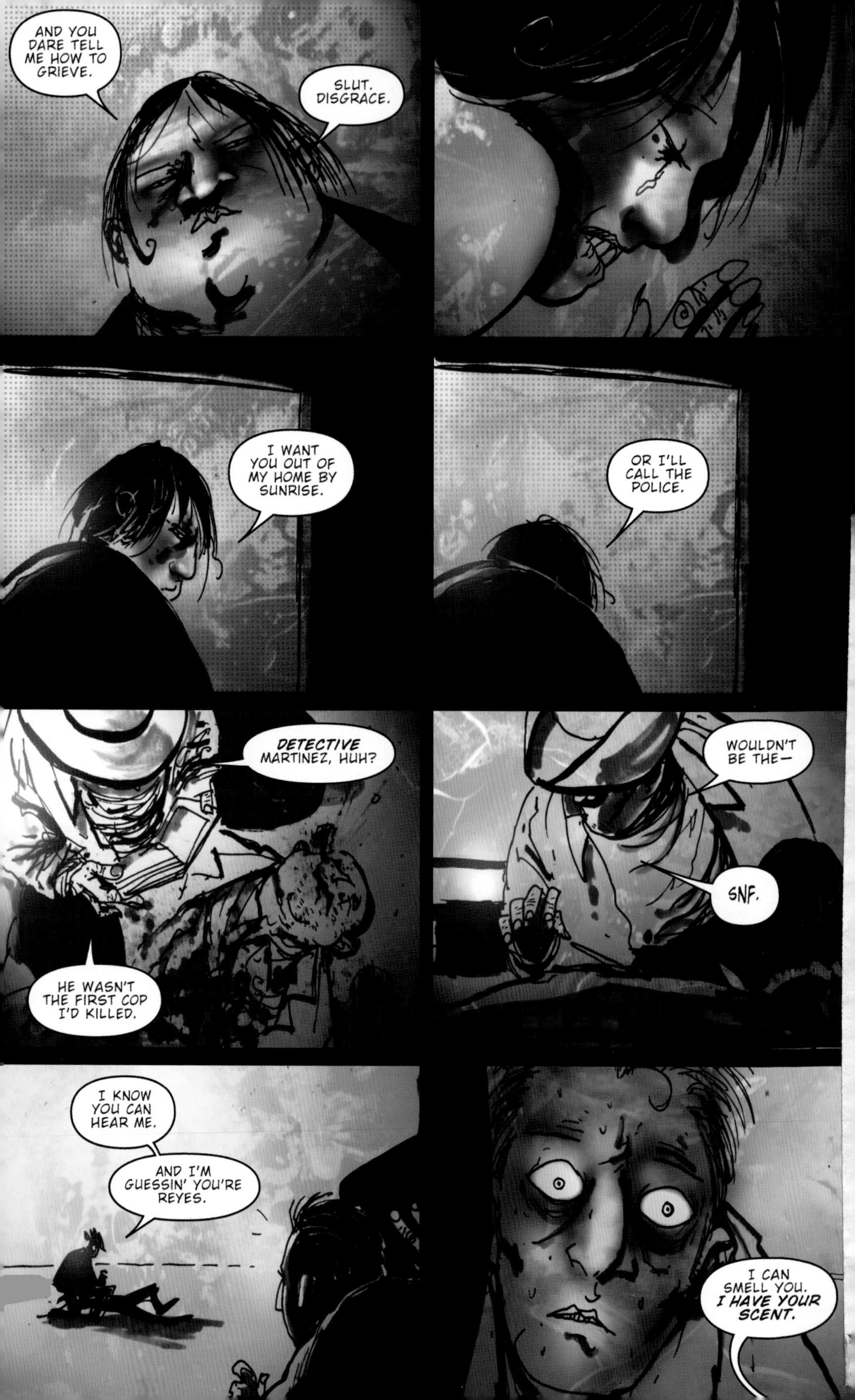
AND YOU DARE TELL ME HOW TO GRIEVE.
SLUT. DISGRACE.
I WANT YOU OUT OF MY HOME BY SUNRISE.
OR I'LL CALL THE POLICE.
DETECTIVE MARTINEZ, HUH?
HE WASN'T THE FIRST COP I'D KILLED.
WOULDN'T BE THE—
SNF.
I KNOW YOU CAN HEAR ME.
AND I'M GUESSIN' YOU'RE REYES.
I CAN SMELL YOU. ***I HAVE YOUR SCENT.***

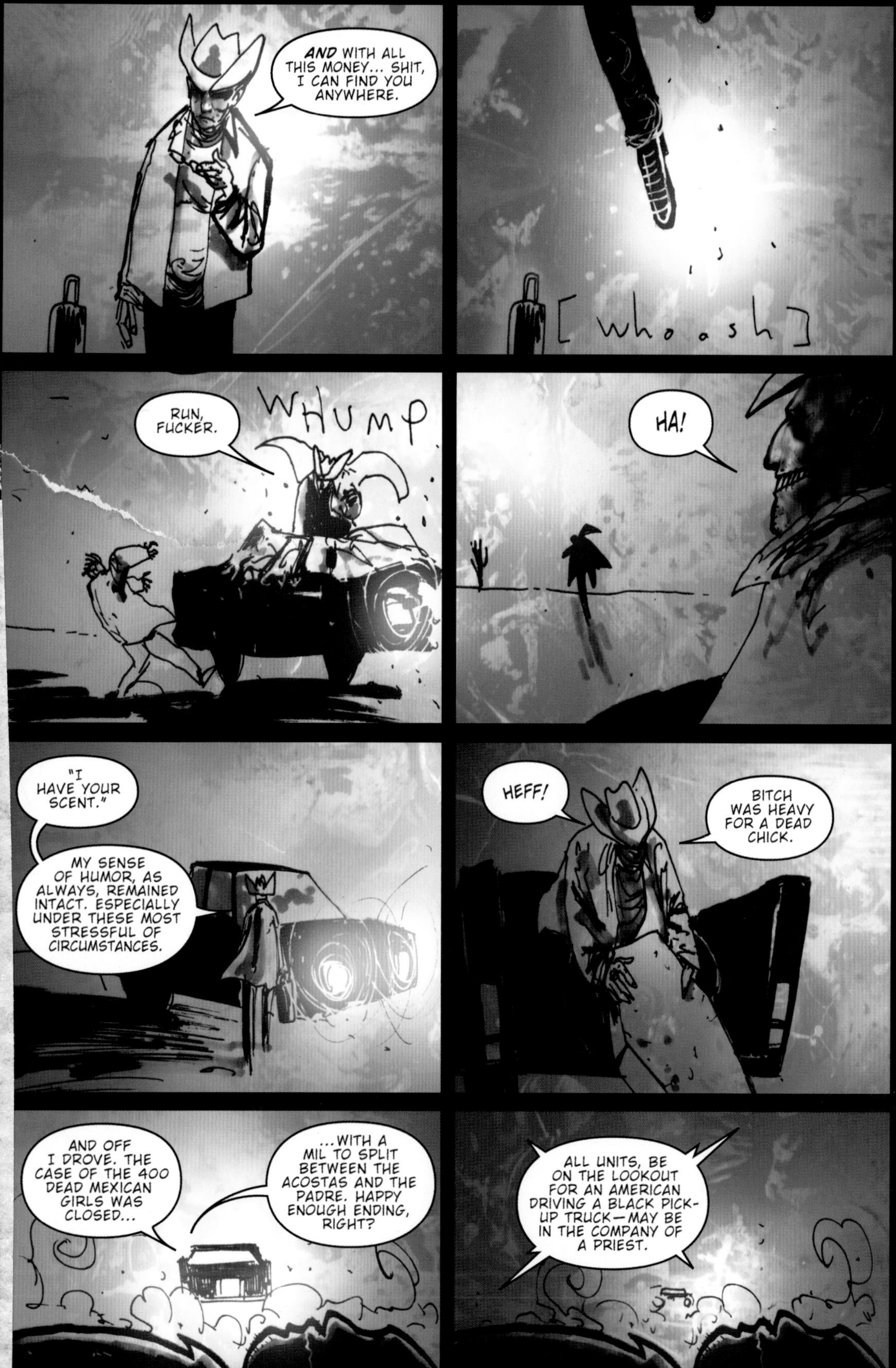
AND WITH ALL THIS MONEY... SHIT, I CAN FIND YOU ANYWHERE.
[whoosh]
RUN, FUCKER.
WHUMP
HA!
"I HAVE YOUR SCENT."
MY SENSE OF HUMOR, AS ALWAYS, REMAINED INTACT. ESPECIALLY UNDER THESE MOST STRESSFUL OF CIRCUMSTANCES.
HEFF!
BITCH WAS HEAVY FOR A DEAD CHICK.
AND OFF I DROVE. THE CASE OF THE 400 DEAD MEXICAN GIRLS WAS CLOSED...
...WITH A MIL TO SPLIT BETWEEN THE ACOSTAS AND THE PADRE. HAPPY ENOUGH ENDING, RIGHT?
ALL UNITS, BE ON THE LOOKOUT FOR AN AMERICAN DRIVING A BLACK PICK-UP TRUCK—MAY BE IN THE COMPANY OF A PRIEST.

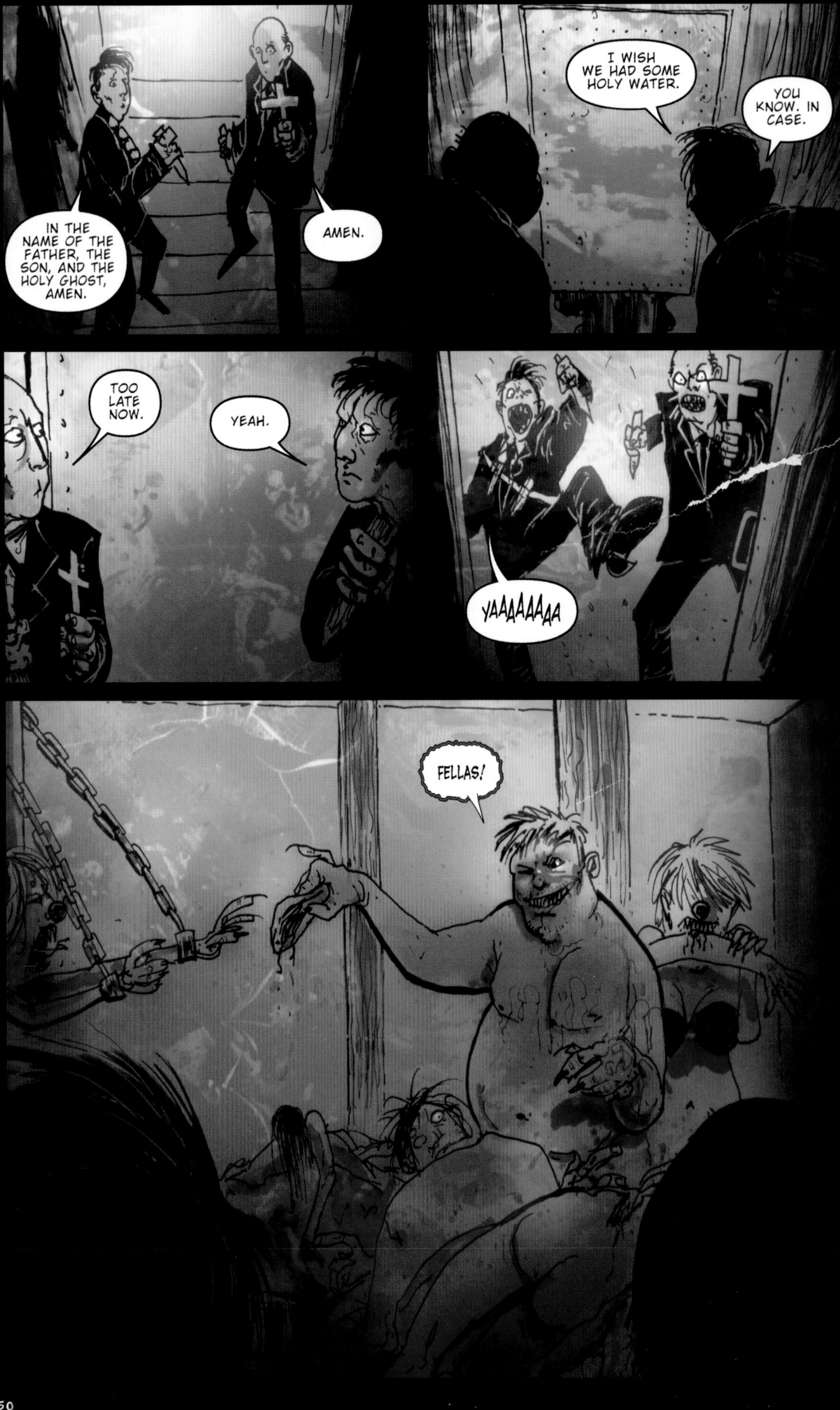
IN THE NAME OF THE FATHER, THE SON, AND THE HOLY GHOST, AMEN.
AMEN.
I WISH WE HAD SOME HOLY WATER.
YOU KNOW. IN CASE.
TOO LATE NOW.
YEAH.
YAAAAAAAA
FELLAS!

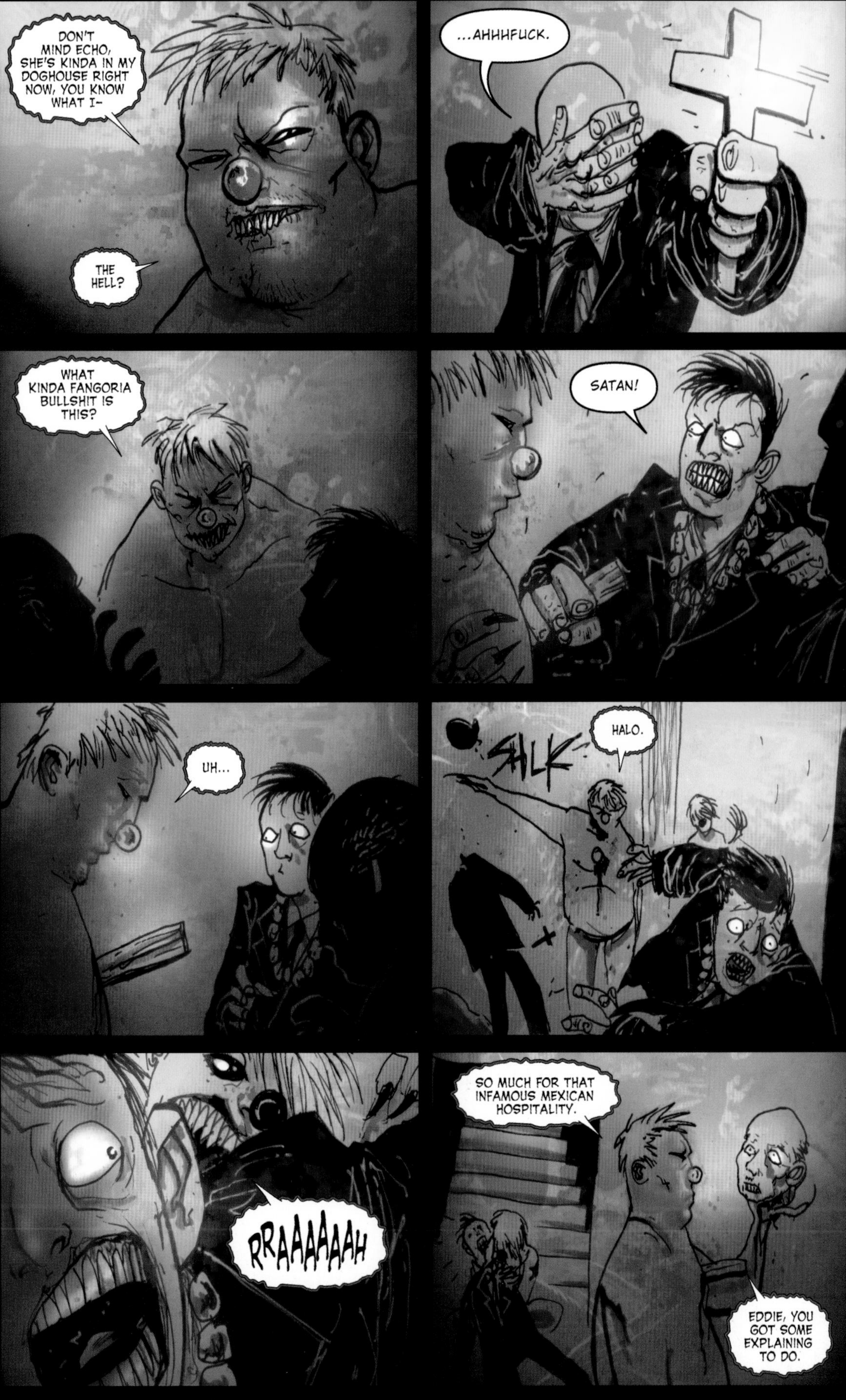
DON'T MIND ECHO, SHE'S KINDA IN MY DOGHOUSE RIGHT NOW, YOU KNOW WHAT I-
THE HELL?
...AHHHFUCK.
WHAT KINDA FANGORIA BULLSHIT IS THIS?
SATAN!
UH...
SHLK
HALO.
RRAAAAAAH
SO MUCH FOR THAT INFAMOUS MEXICAN HOSPITALITY.
EDDIE, YOU GOT SOME EXPLAINING TO DO.

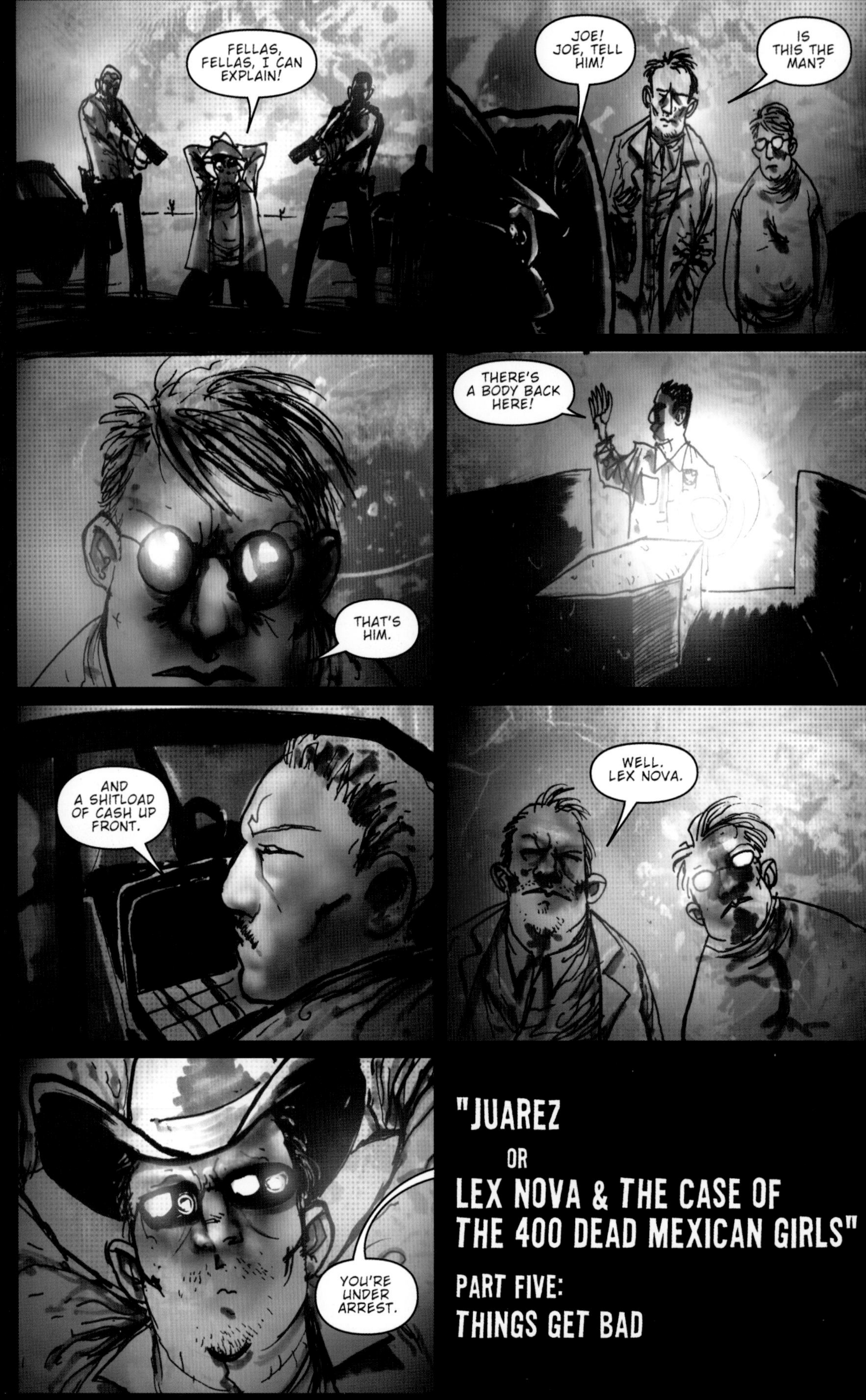
FELLAS, FELLAS, I CAN EXPLAIN!
JOE! JOE, TELL HIM!
IS THIS THE MAN?
THAT'S HIM.
THERE'S A BODY BACK HERE!
AND A SHITLOAD OF CASH UP FRONT.
WELL. LEX NOVA.
YOU'RE UNDER ARREST.
"JUAREZ
OR
LEX NOVA & THE CASE OF THE 400 DEAD MEXICAN GIRLS"
PART FIVE:
THINGS GET BAD

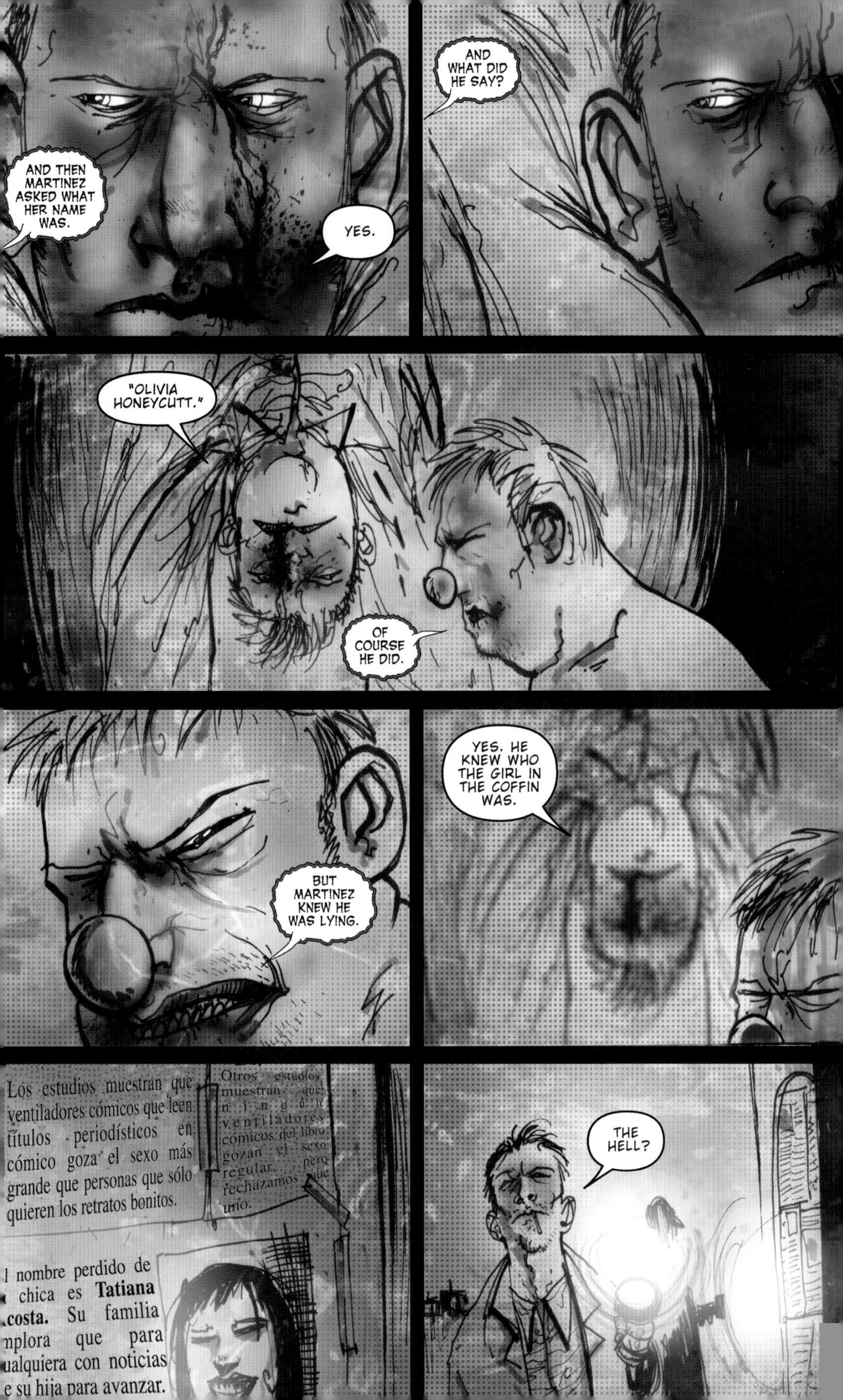
AND THEN MARTINEZ ASKED WHAT HER NAME WAS.
YES.
AND WHAT DID HE SAY?
"OLIVIA HONEYCUTT."
OF COURSE HE DID.
BUT MARTINEZ KNEW HE WAS LYING.
YES. HE KNEW WHO THE GIRL IN THE COFFIN WAS.
Los estudios muestran que ventiladores cómicos que leen títulos periodísticos en cómico goza el sexo más grande que personas que sólo quieren los retratos bonitos.
Otros estudios muestran que n i n g ú n ventiladores cómicos del libro gozan el sexo regular, pero rechazamos que unió.
l nombre perdido de chica es Tatiana costa. Su familia nplora que para ualquiera con noticias e su hija para avanzar.
THE HELL?

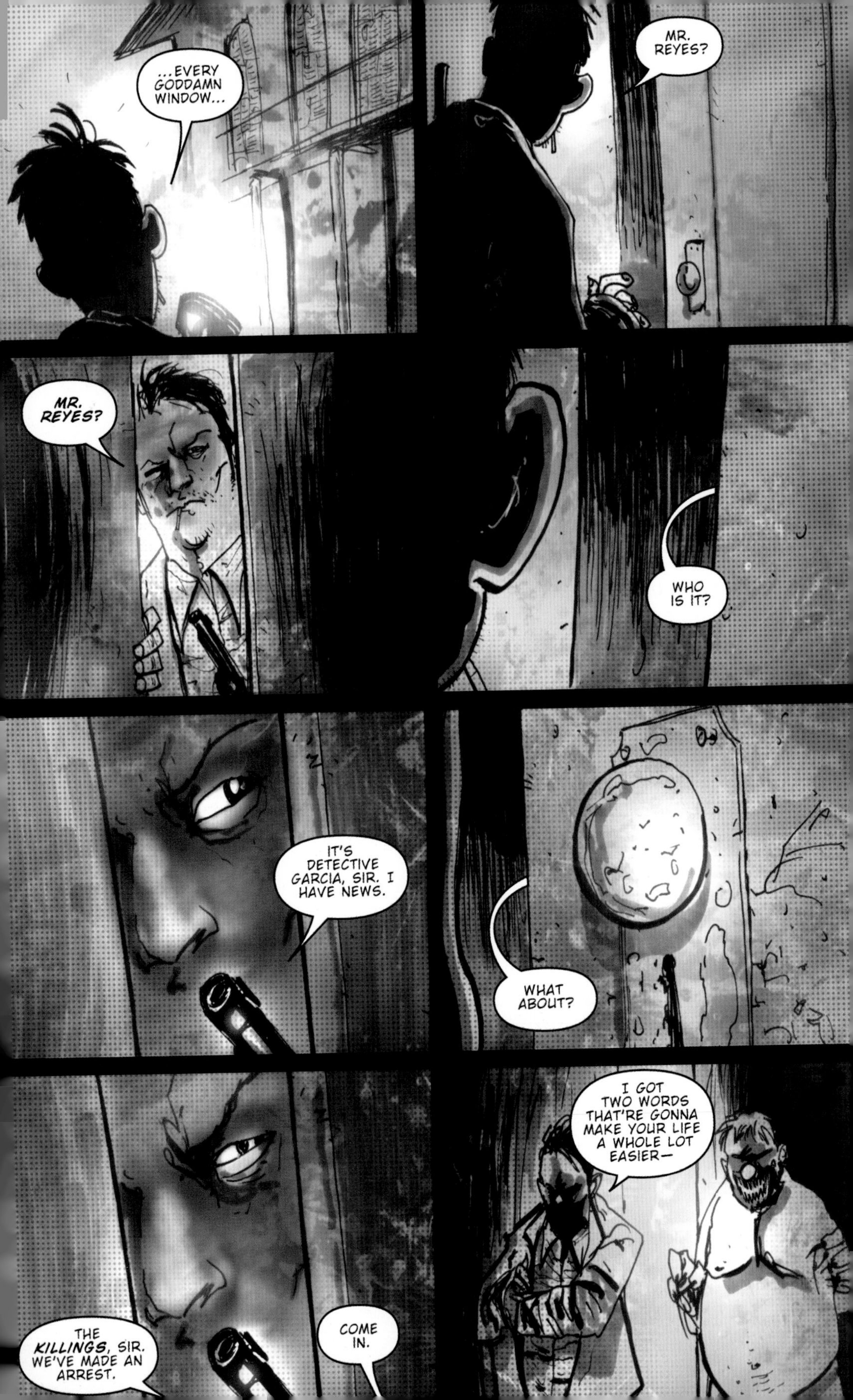
...EVERY GODDAMN WINDOW...
MR. REYES?
MR. REYES?
WHO IS IT?
IT'S DETECTIVE GARCIA, SIR. I HAVE NEWS.
WHAT ABOUT?
THE *KILLINGS*, SIR. WE'VE MADE AN ARREST.
COME IN.
I GOT TWO WORDS THAT'RE GONNA MAKE YOUR LIFE A WHOLE LOT EASIER—

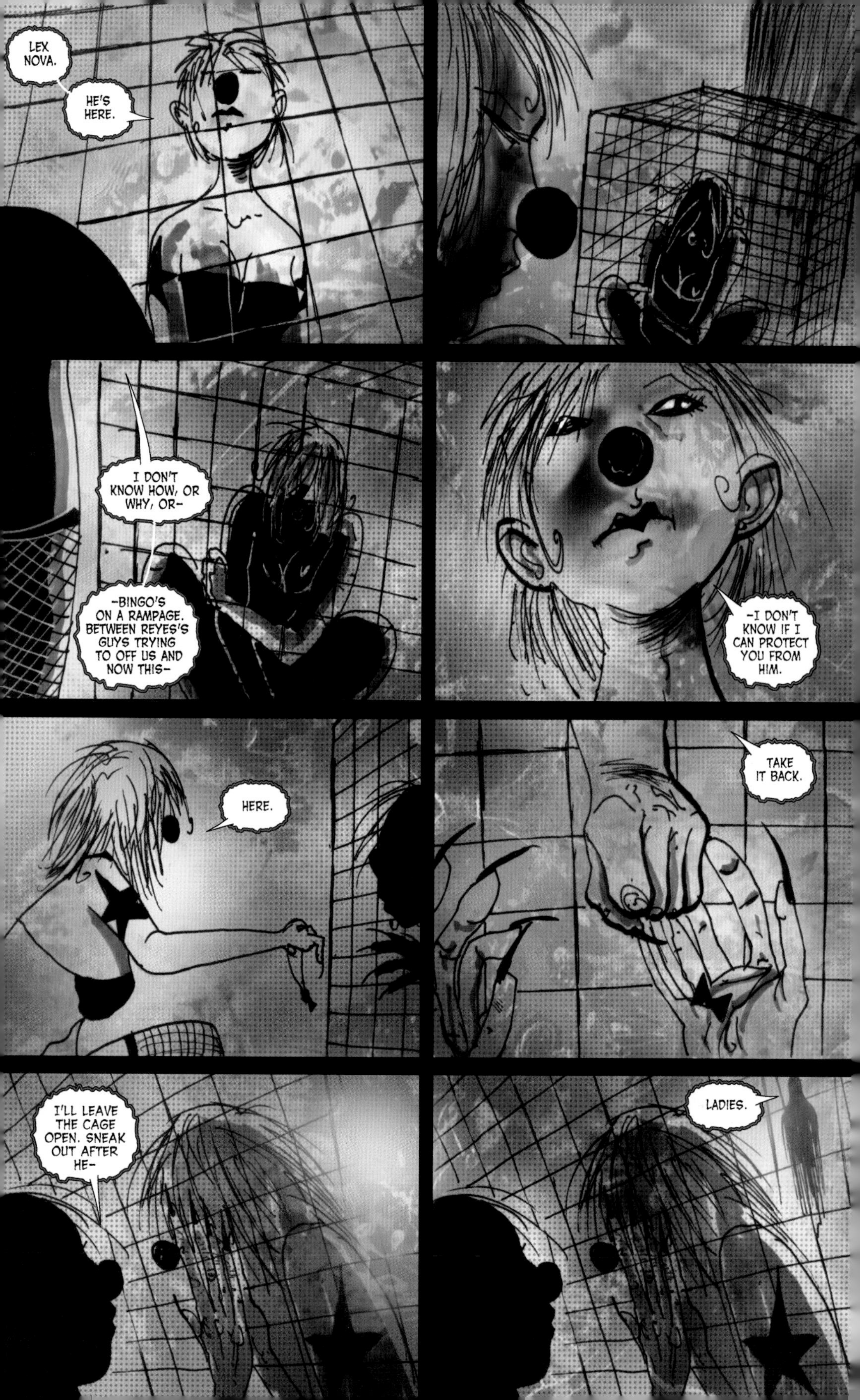
LEX NOVA.
HE'S HERE.
I DON'T KNOW HOW, OR WHY, OR-
-BINGO'S ON A RAMPAGE. BETWEEN REYES'S GUYS TRYING TO OFF US AND NOW THIS-
-I DON'T KNOW IF I CAN PROTECT YOU FROM HIM.
HERE.
TAKE IT BACK.
I'LL LEAVE THE CAGE OPEN. SNEAK OUT AFTER HE-
LADIES.

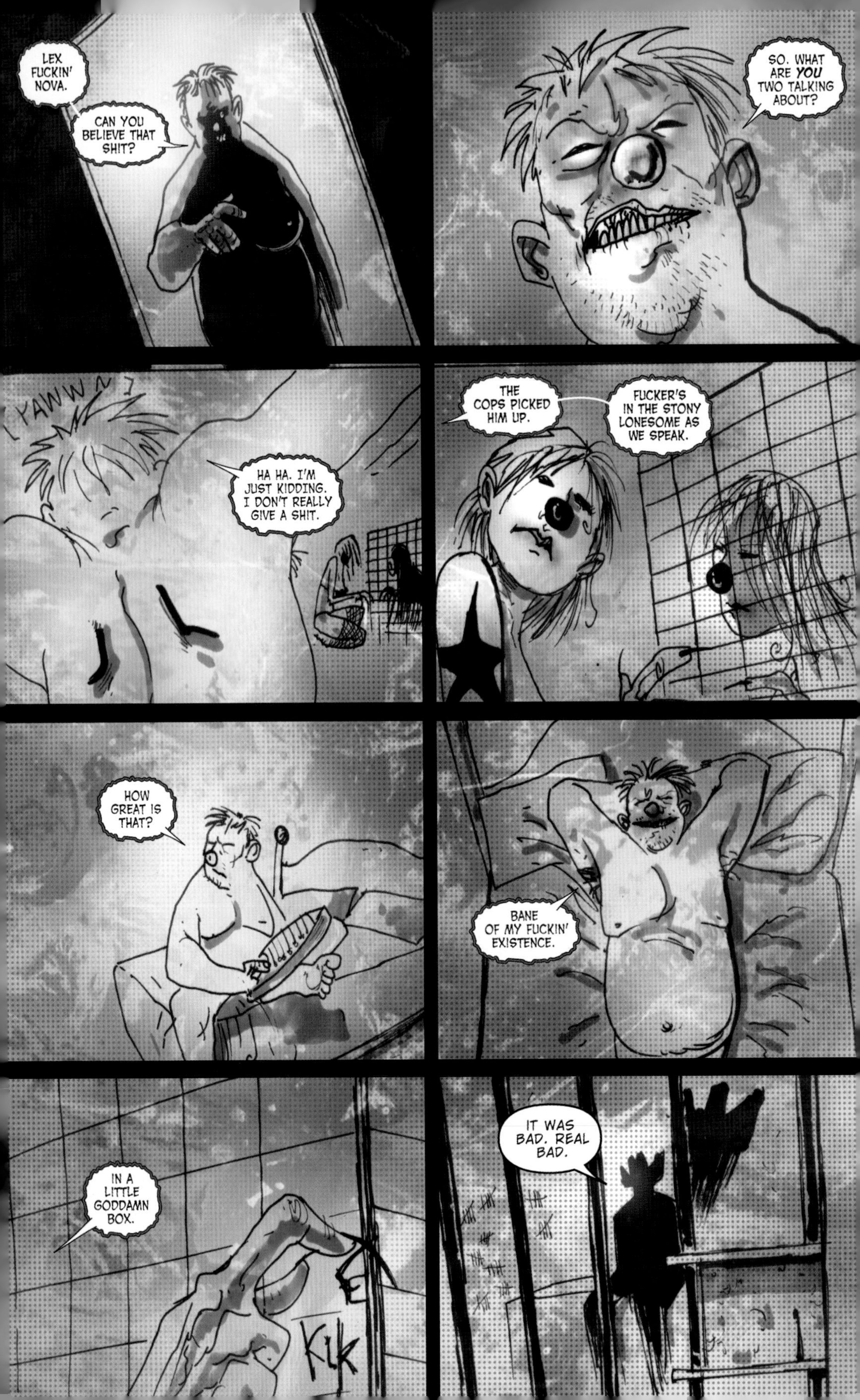
LEX FUCKIN' NOVA.
CAN YOU BELIEVE THAT SHIT?
SO. WHAT ARE *YOU* TWO TALKING ABOUT?
YAWWN
HA HA. I'M JUST KIDDING. I DON'T REALLY GIVE A SHIT.
THE COPS PICKED HIM UP.
FUCKER'S IN THE STONY LONESOME AS WE SPEAK.
HOW GREAT IS THAT?
BANE OF MY FUCKIN' EXISTENCE.
IN A LITTLE GODDAMN BOX.
KLIK
IT WAS BAD. REAL BAD.

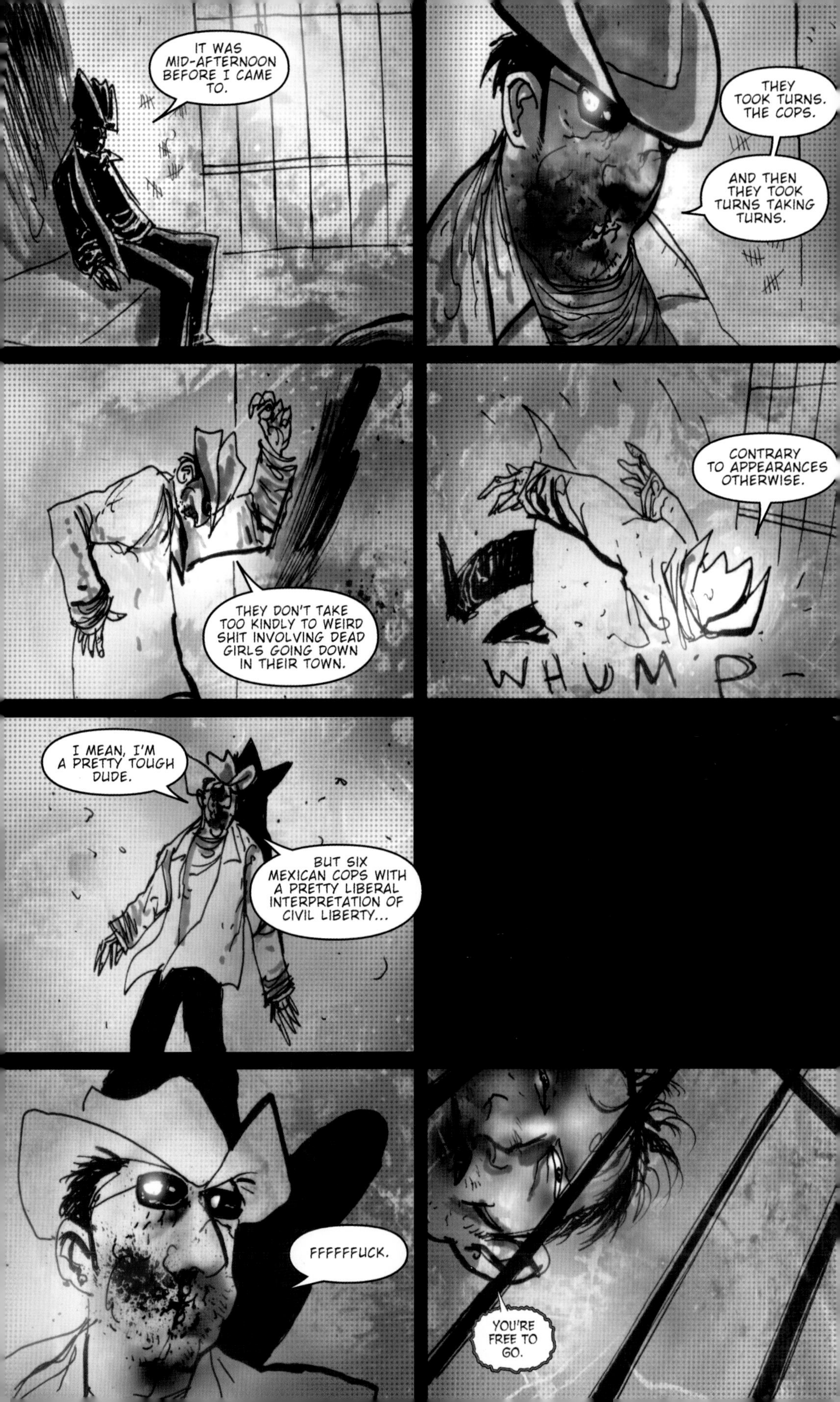
IT WAS MID-AFTERNOON BEFORE I CAME TO.
THEY TOOK TURNS. THE COPS.
AND THEN THEY TOOK TURNS TAKING TURNS.
THEY DON'T TAKE TOO KINDLY TO WEIRD SHIT INVOLVING DEAD GIRLS GOING DOWN IN THEIR TOWN.
CONTRARY TO APPEARANCES OTHERWISE.
WHUMP
I MEAN, I'M A PRETTY TOUGH DUDE.
BUT SIX MEXICAN COPS WITH A PRETTY LIBERAL INTERPRETATION OF CIVIL LIBERTY...
FFFFFFUCK.
YOU'RE FREE TO GO.

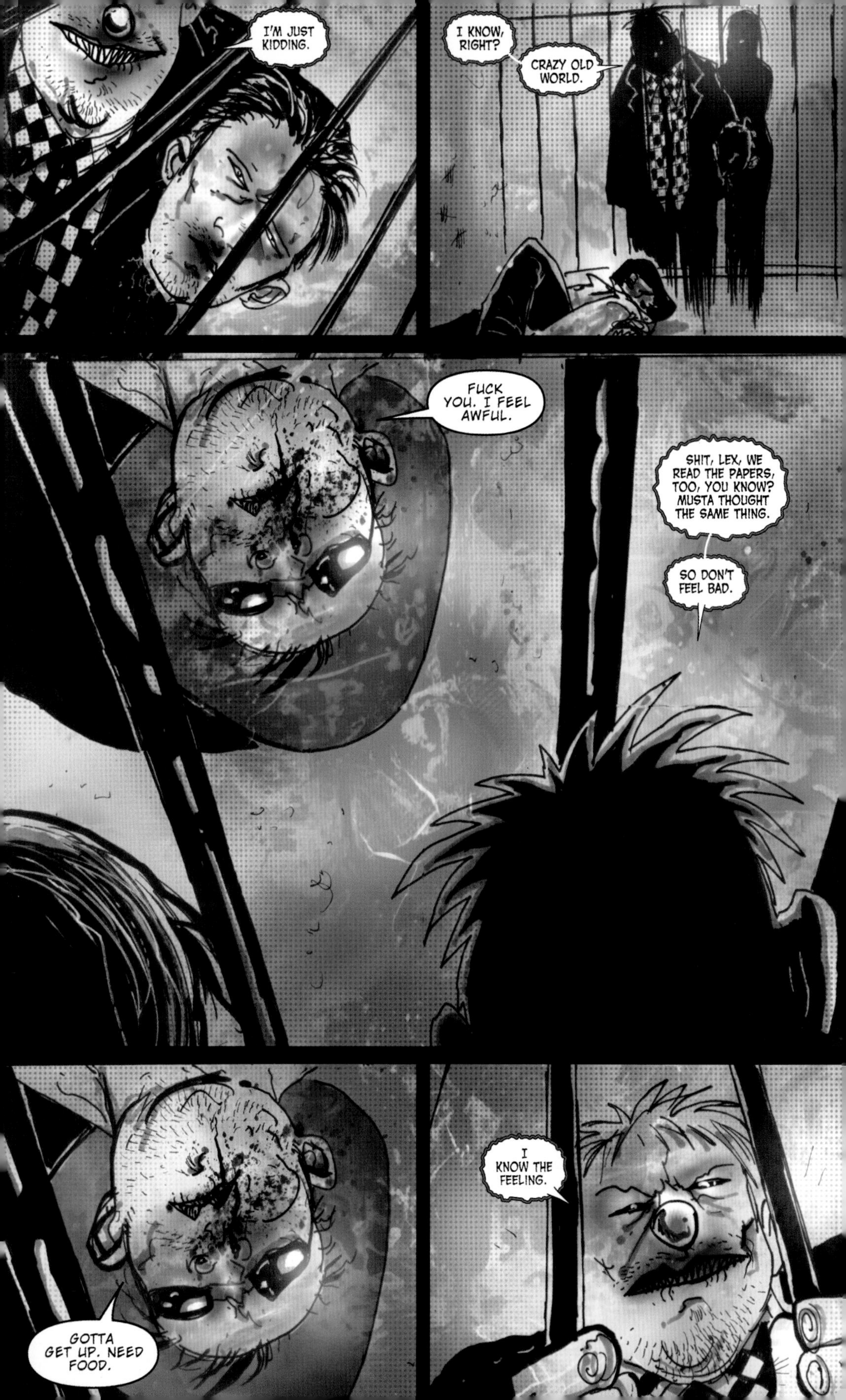
I'M JUST KIDDING.
I KNOW, RIGHT?
CRAZY OLD WORLD.
FUCK YOU. I FEEL AWFUL.
SHIT, LEX, WE READ THE PAPERS, TOO, YOU KNOW? MUSTA THOUGHT THE SAME THING.
SO DON'T FEEL BAD.
GOTTA GET UP. NEED FOOD.
I KNOW THE FEELING.

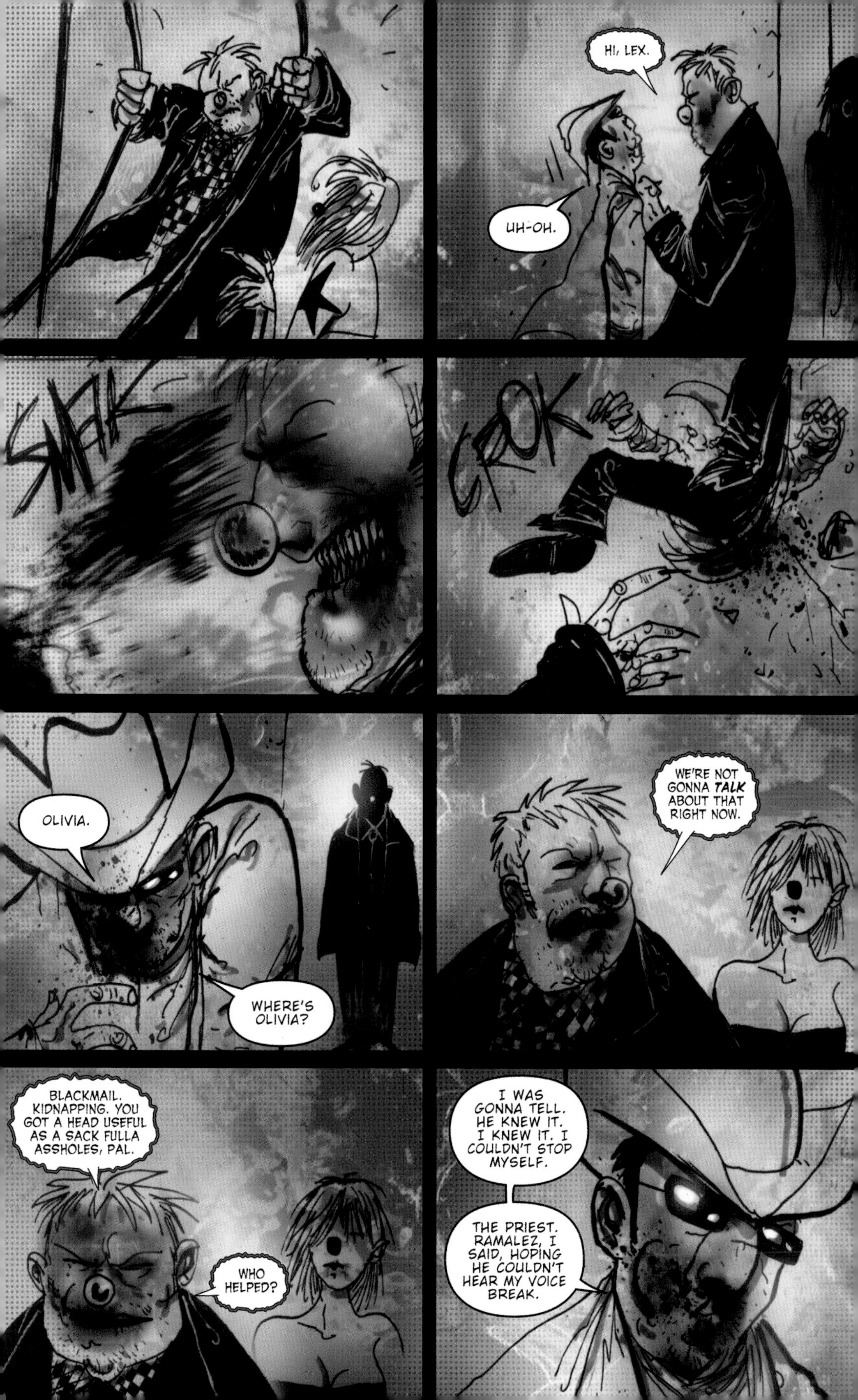
HI, LEX.
UH-OH.
SMAK
CROK
OLIVIA.
WHERE'S OLIVIA?
WE'RE NOT GONNA TALK ABOUT THAT RIGHT NOW.
BLACKMAIL. KIDNAPPING. YOU GOT A HEAD USEFUL AS A SACK FULLA ASSHOLES, PAL.
WHO HELPED?
I WAS GONNA TELL. HE KNEW IT. I KNEW IT. I COULDN'T STOP MYSELF.
THE PRIEST. RAMALEZ, I SAID, HOPING HE COULDN'T HEAR MY VOICE BREAK.

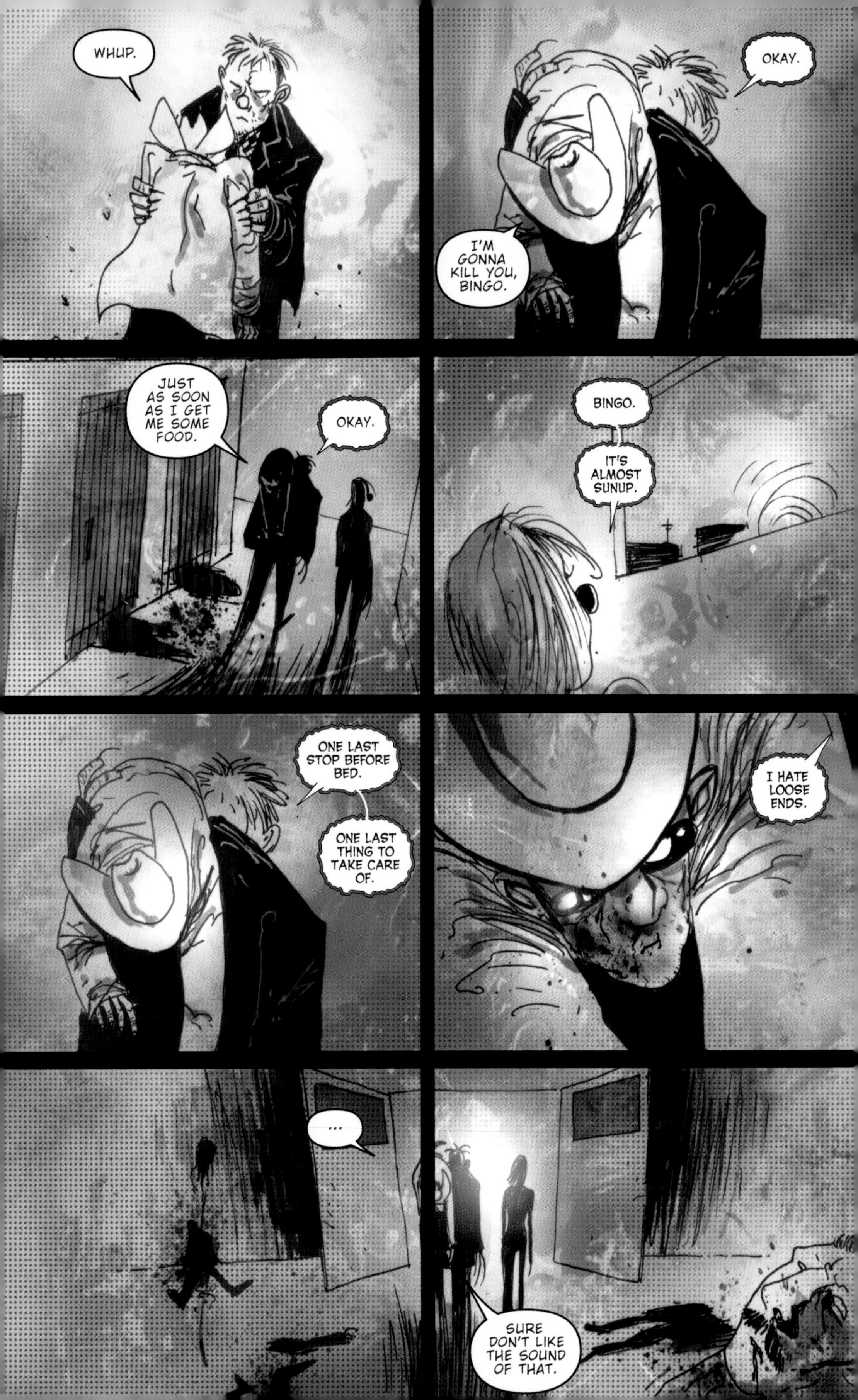
WHUP.
OKAY.
I'M GONNA KILL YOU, BINGO.
JUST AS SOON AS I GET ME SOME FOOD.
OKAY.
BINGO.
IT'S ALMOST SUNUP.
ONE LAST STOP BEFORE BED.
ONE LAST THING TO TAKE CARE OF.
I HATE LOOSE ENDS.
...
SURE DON'T LIKE THE SOUND OF THAT.

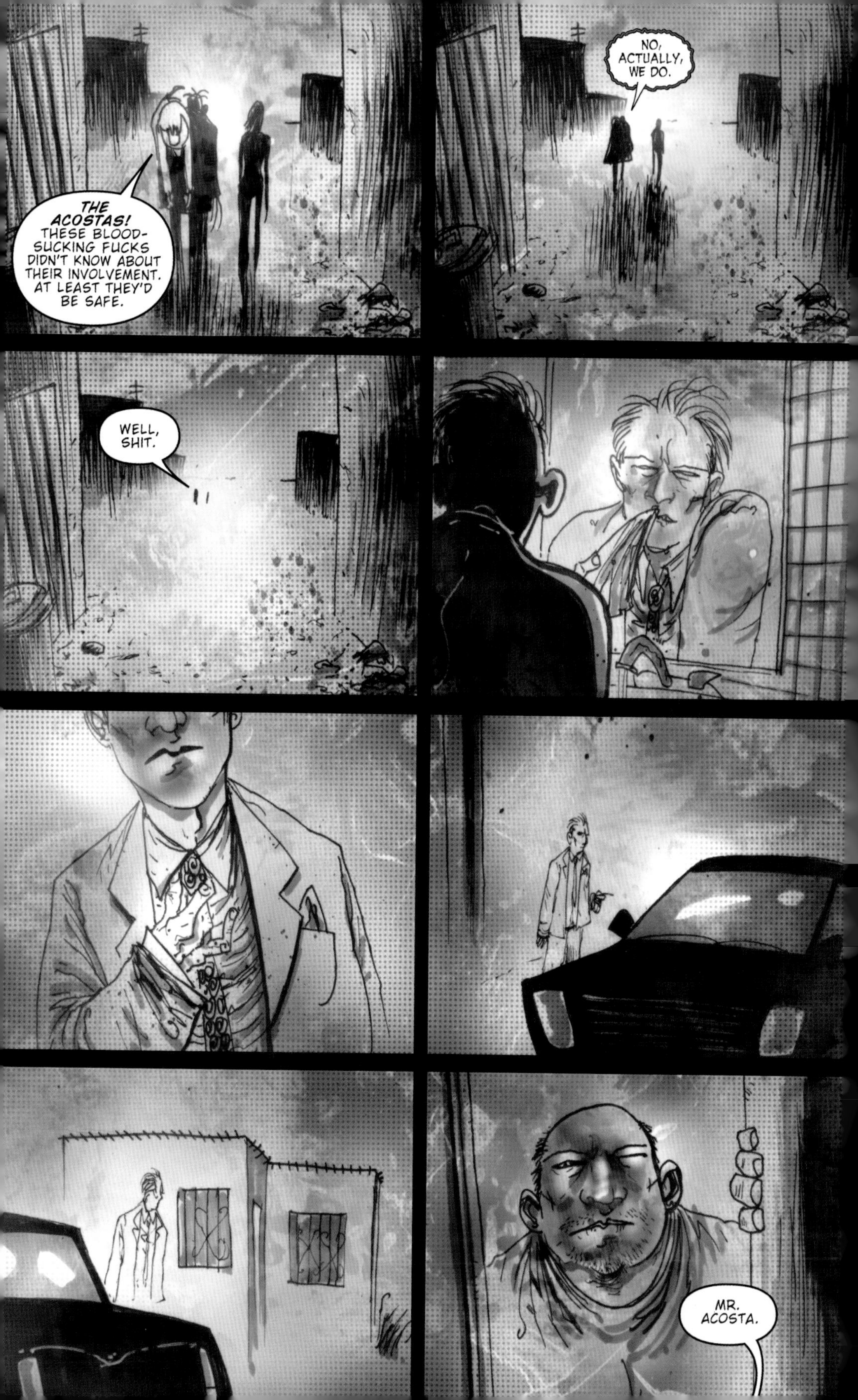
THE ACOSTAS! THESE BLOOD-SUCKING FUCKS DIDN'T KNOW ABOUT THEIR INVOLVEMENT. AT LEAST THEY'D BE SAFE.
NO, ACTUALLY, WE DO.
WELL, SHIT.
MR. ACOSTA.

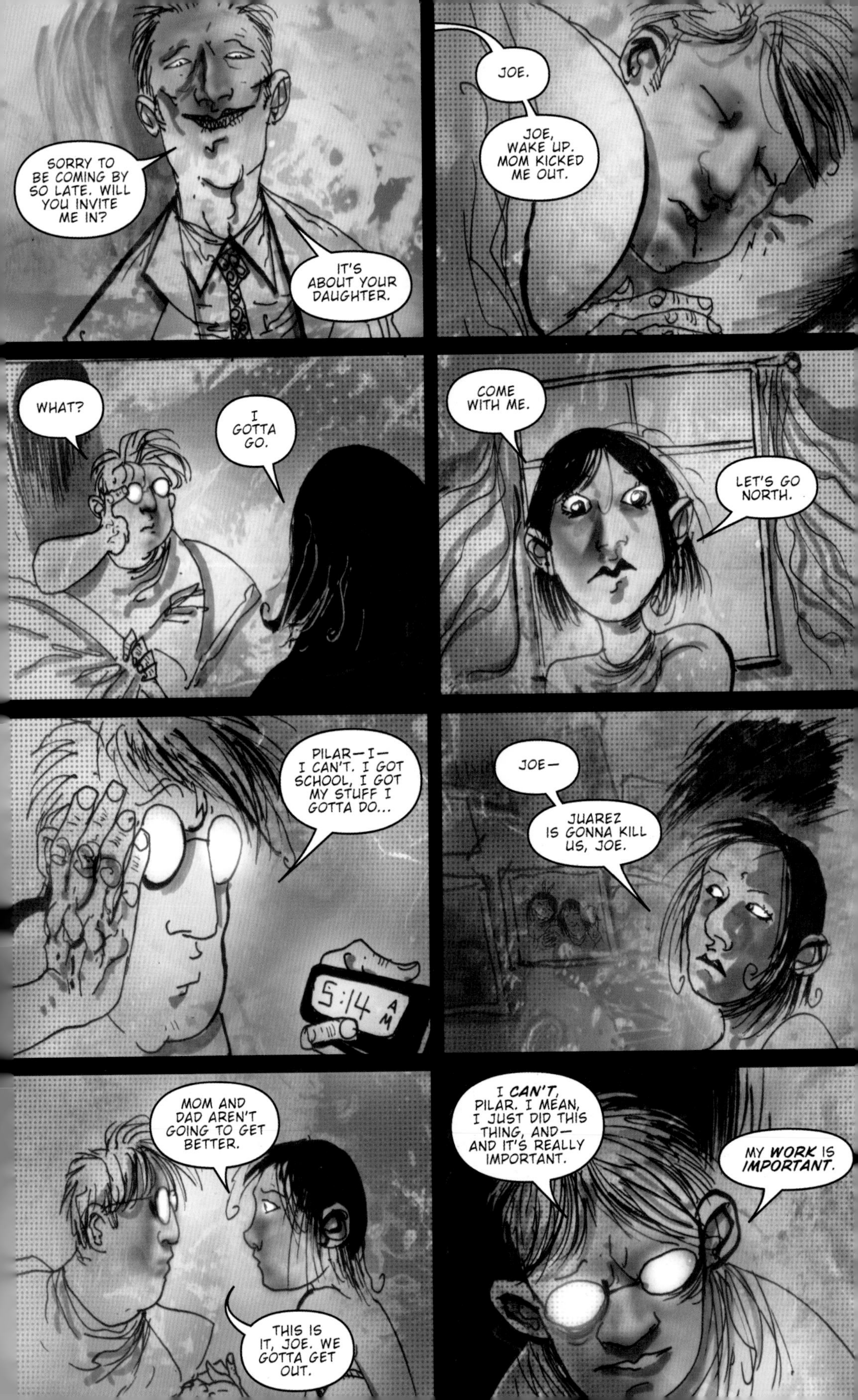
SORRY TO BE COMING BY SO LATE. WILL YOU INVITE ME IN?
IT'S ABOUT YOUR DAUGHTER.
JOE.
JOE, WAKE UP. MOM KICKED ME OUT.
WHAT?
I GOTTA GO.
COME WITH ME.
LET'S GO NORTH.
PILAR—I—I CAN'T. I GOT SCHOOL, I GOT MY STUFF I GOTTA DO...
5:14 AM
JOE—
JUAREZ IS GONNA KILL US, JOE.
MOM AND DAD AREN'T GOING TO GET BETTER.
THIS IS IT, JOE. WE GOTTA GET OUT.
I ***CAN'T***, PILAR. I MEAN, I JUST DID THIS THING, AND—AND IT'S REALLY IMPORTANT.
MY ***WORK*** IS ***IMPORTANT***.

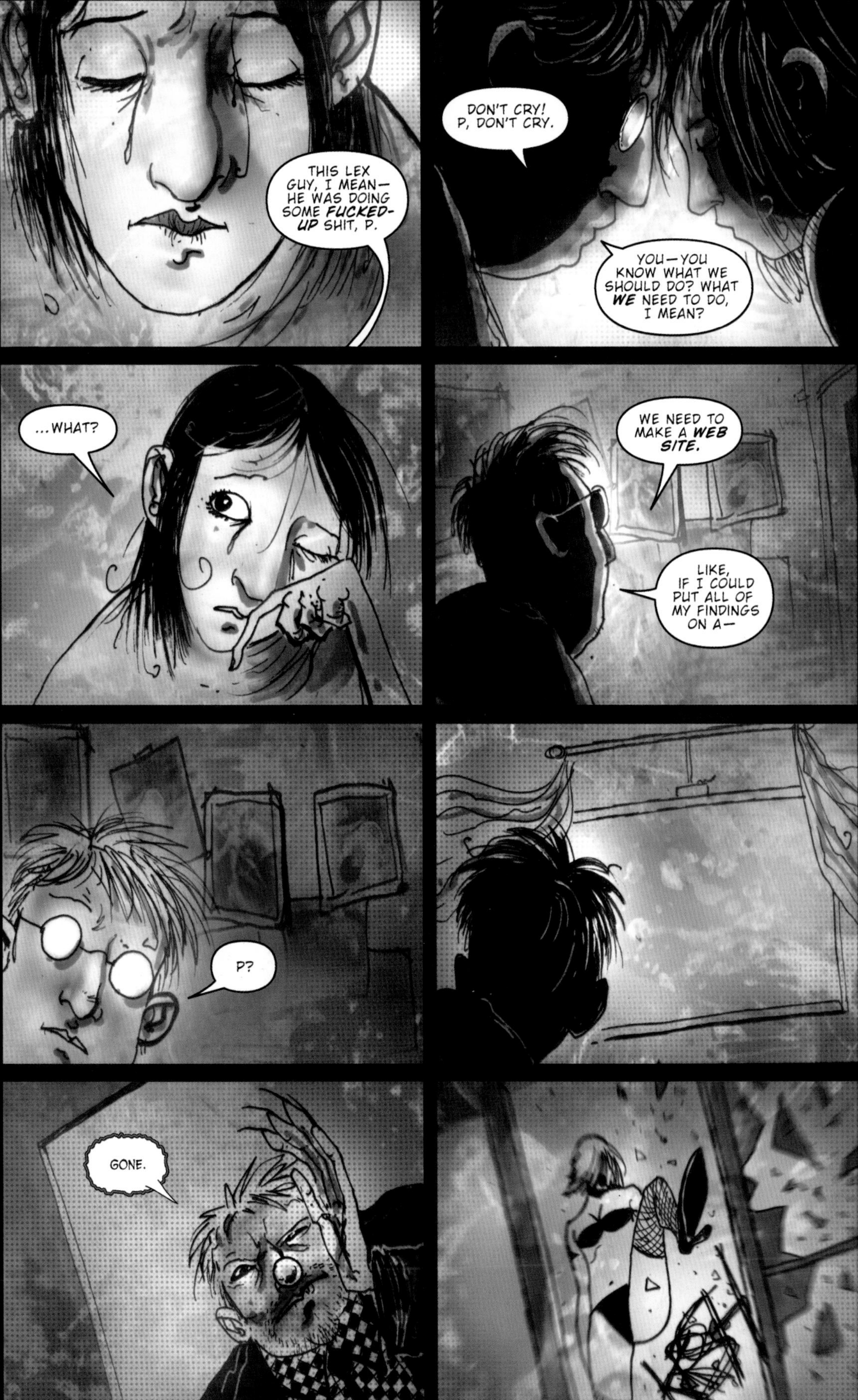
THIS LEX GUY, I MEAN— HE WAS DOING SOME FUCKED-UP SHIT, P.
DON'T CRY! P, DON'T CRY.
YOU—YOU KNOW WHAT WE SHOULD DO? WHAT WE NEED TO DO, I MEAN?
...WHAT?
WE NEED TO MAKE A WEB SITE.
LIKE, IF I COULD PUT ALL OF MY FINDINGS ON A—
P?
GONE.

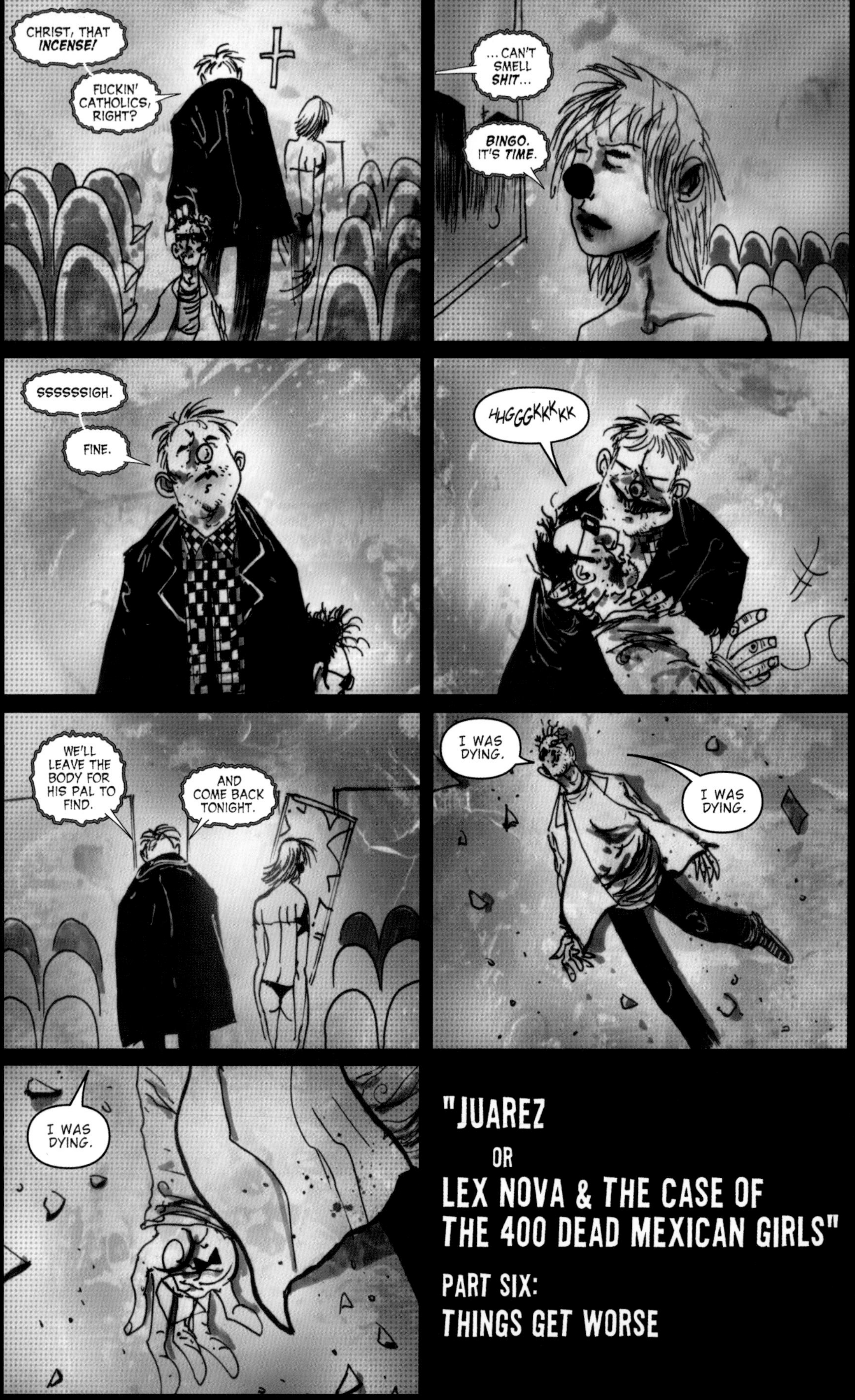
CHRIST, THAT INCENSE!
FUCKIN' CATHOLICS, RIGHT?
...CAN'T SMELL SHIT...
BINGO. IT'S TIME.
SSSSSSIGH.
FINE.
HHGGKKKKK
WE'LL LEAVE THE BODY FOR HIS PAL TO FIND.
AND COME BACK TONIGHT.
I WAS DYING.
I WAS DYING.
I WAS DYING.
"JUAREZ
OR
LEX NOVA & THE CASE OF THE 400 DEAD MEXICAN GIRLS"
PART SIX:
THINGS GET WORSE

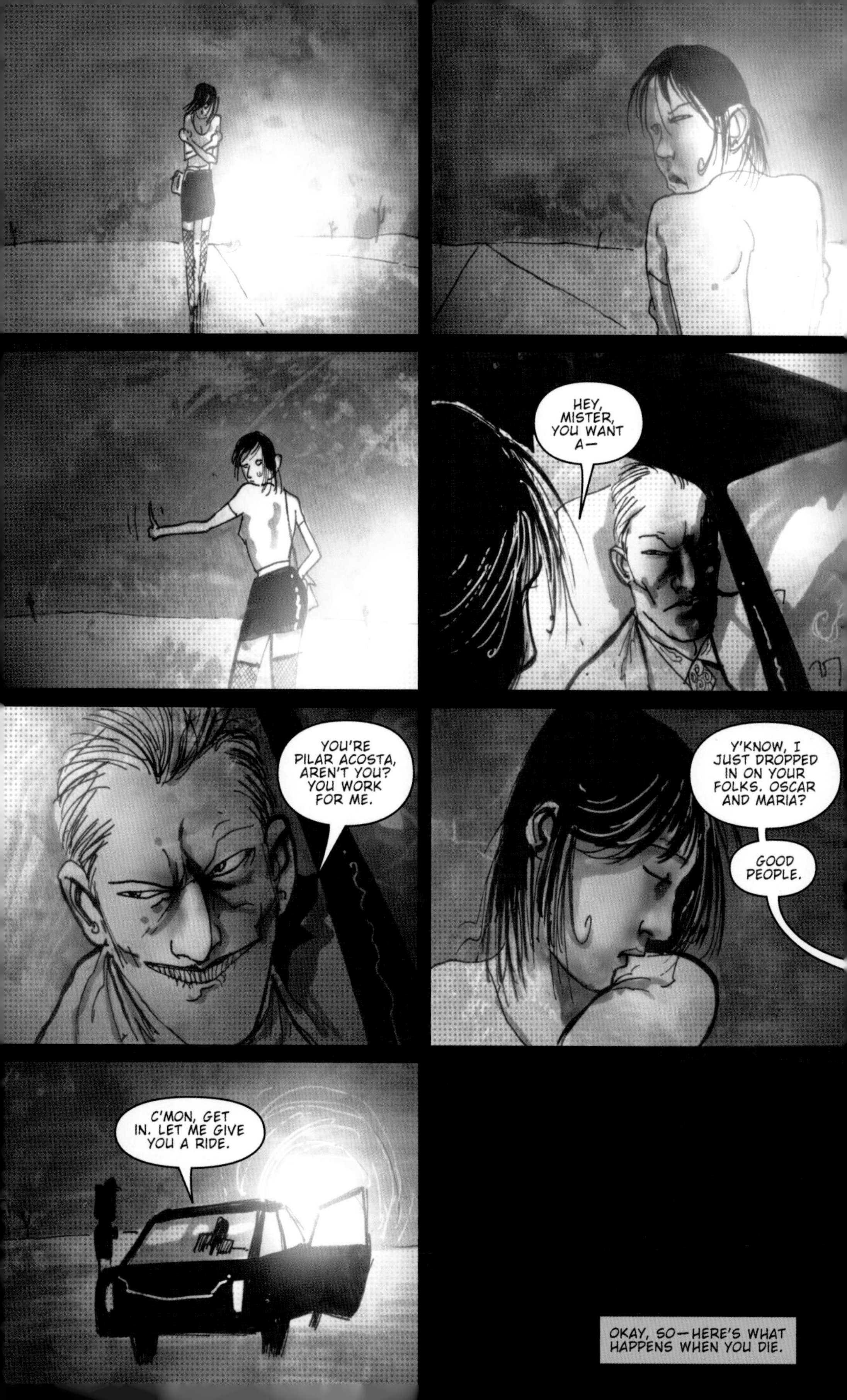
HEY, MISTER, YOU WANT A—
YOU'RE PILAR ACOSTA, AREN'T YOU? YOU WORK FOR ME.
Y'KNOW, I JUST DROPPED IN ON YOUR FOLKS. OSCAR AND MARIA?
GOOD PEOPLE.
C'MON, GET IN. LET ME GIVE YOU A RIDE.
OKAY, SO—HERE'S WHAT HAPPENS WHEN YOU DIE.

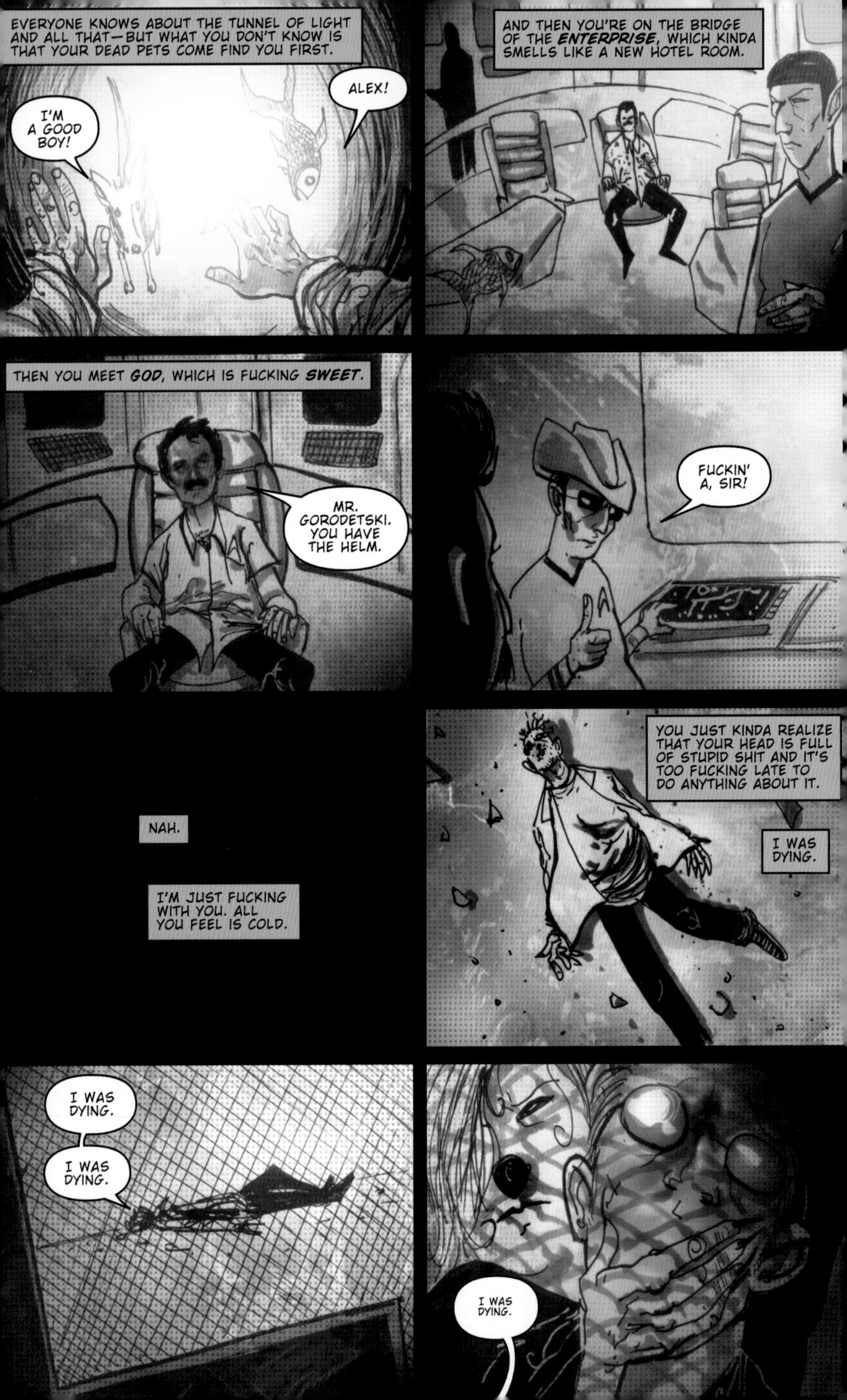
EVERYONE KNOWS ABOUT THE TUNNEL OF LIGHT AND ALL THAT—BUT WHAT YOU DON'T KNOW IS THAT YOUR DEAD PETS COME FIND YOU FIRST.
I'M A GOOD BOY!
ALEX!
AND THEN YOU'RE ON THE BRIDGE OF THE ENTERPRISE, WHICH KINDA SMELLS LIKE A NEW HOTEL ROOM.
THEN YOU MEET GOD, WHICH IS FUCKING SWEET.
MR. GORODETSKI. YOU HAVE THE HELM.
FUCKIN' A, SIR!
NAH.
I'M JUST FUCKING WITH YOU. ALL YOU FEEL IS COLD.
YOU JUST KINDA REALIZE THAT YOUR HEAD IS FULL OF STUPID SHIT AND IT'S TOO FUCKING LATE TO DO ANYTHING ABOUT IT.
I WAS DYING.
I WAS DYING.
I WAS DYING.
I WAS DYING.

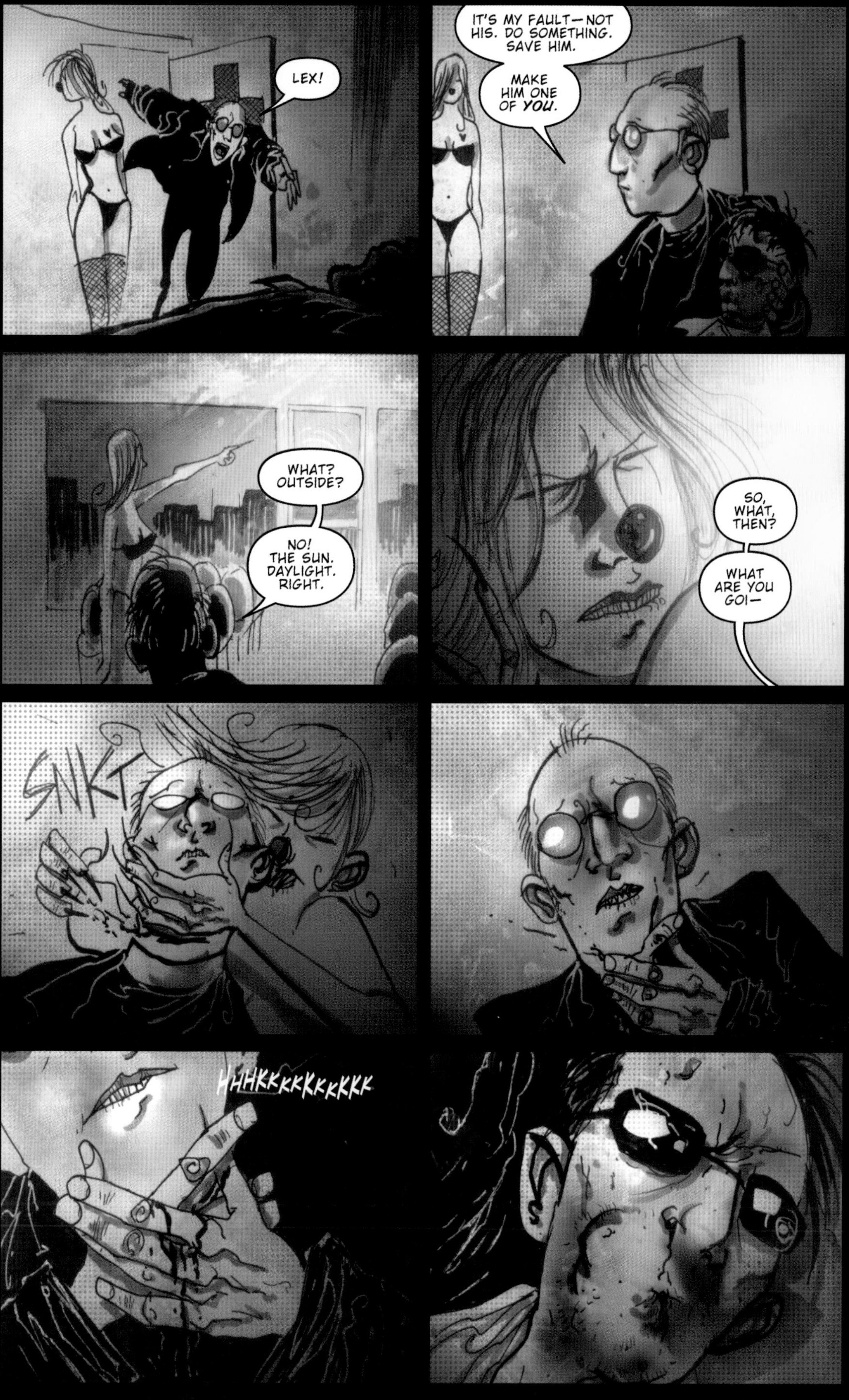

LEX!
IT'S MY FAULT—NOT HIS. DO SOMETHING. SAVE HIM.
MAKE HIM ONE OF *YOU*.
WHAT? OUTSIDE?
NO! THE SUN. DAYLIGHT. RIGHT.
SO, WHAT, THEN?
WHAT ARE YOU GOI—
SNKT
HHHKKKKKKKKK

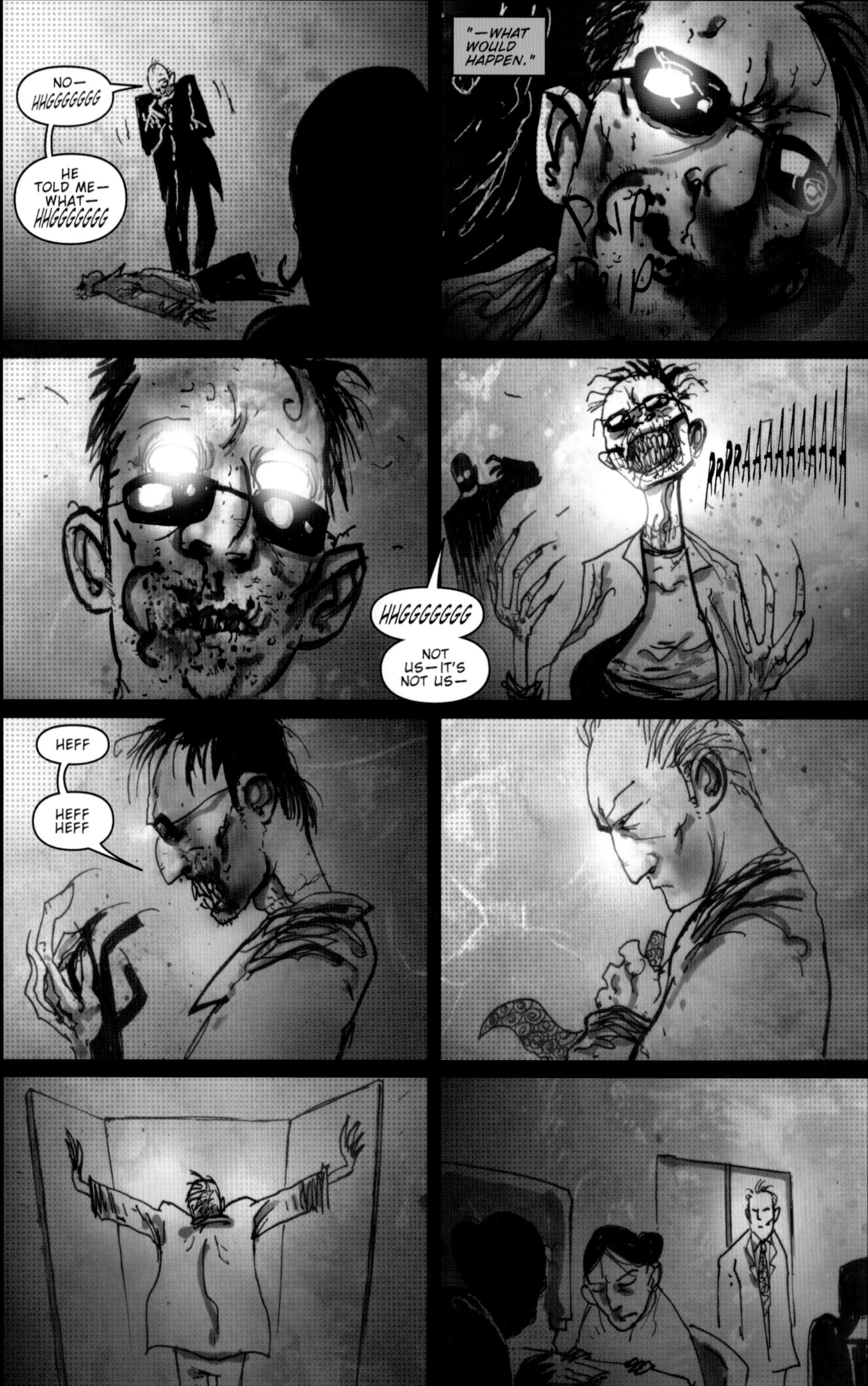
NO—HHGGGGGGG
HE TOLD ME—WHAT—HHGGGGGGG
"—WHAT WOULD HAPPEN."
DRIP
DRIP
RRRRAAAAAAAAAA
HHGGGGGGG
NOT US—IT'S NOT US—
HEFF
HEFF HEFF

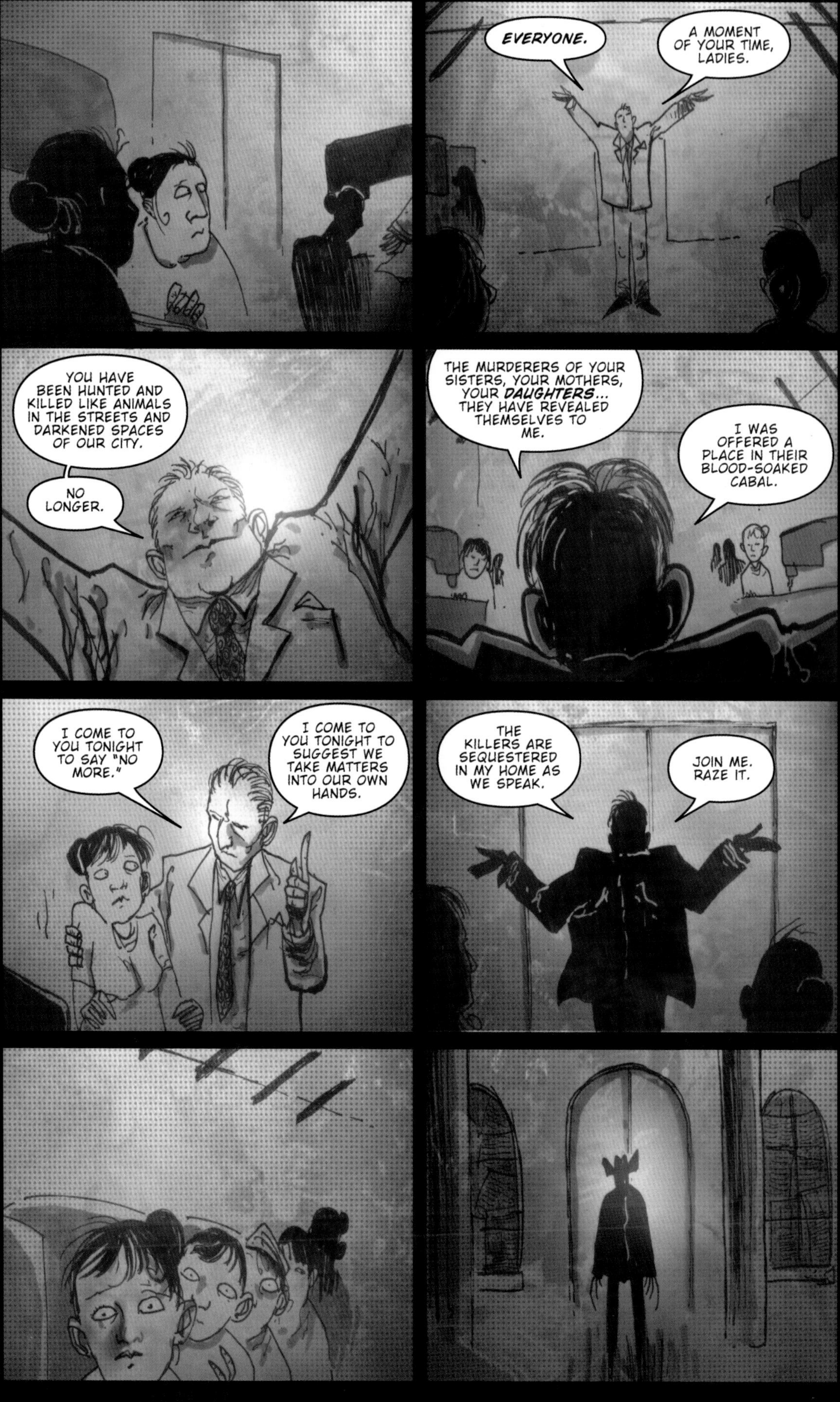
EVERYONE.
A MOMENT OF YOUR TIME, LADIES.
YOU HAVE BEEN HUNTED AND KILLED LIKE ANIMALS IN THE STREETS AND DARKENED SPACES OF OUR CITY.
NO LONGER.
THE MURDERERS OF YOUR SISTERS, YOUR MOTHERS, YOUR *DAUGHTERS*... THEY HAVE REVEALED THEMSELVES TO ME.
I WAS OFFERED A PLACE IN THEIR BLOOD-SOAKED CABAL.
I COME TO YOU TONIGHT TO SAY "NO MORE."
I COME TO YOU TONIGHT TO SUGGEST WE TAKE MATTERS INTO OUR OWN HANDS.
THE KILLERS ARE SEQUESTERED IN MY HOME AS WE SPEAK.
JOIN ME. RAZE IT.

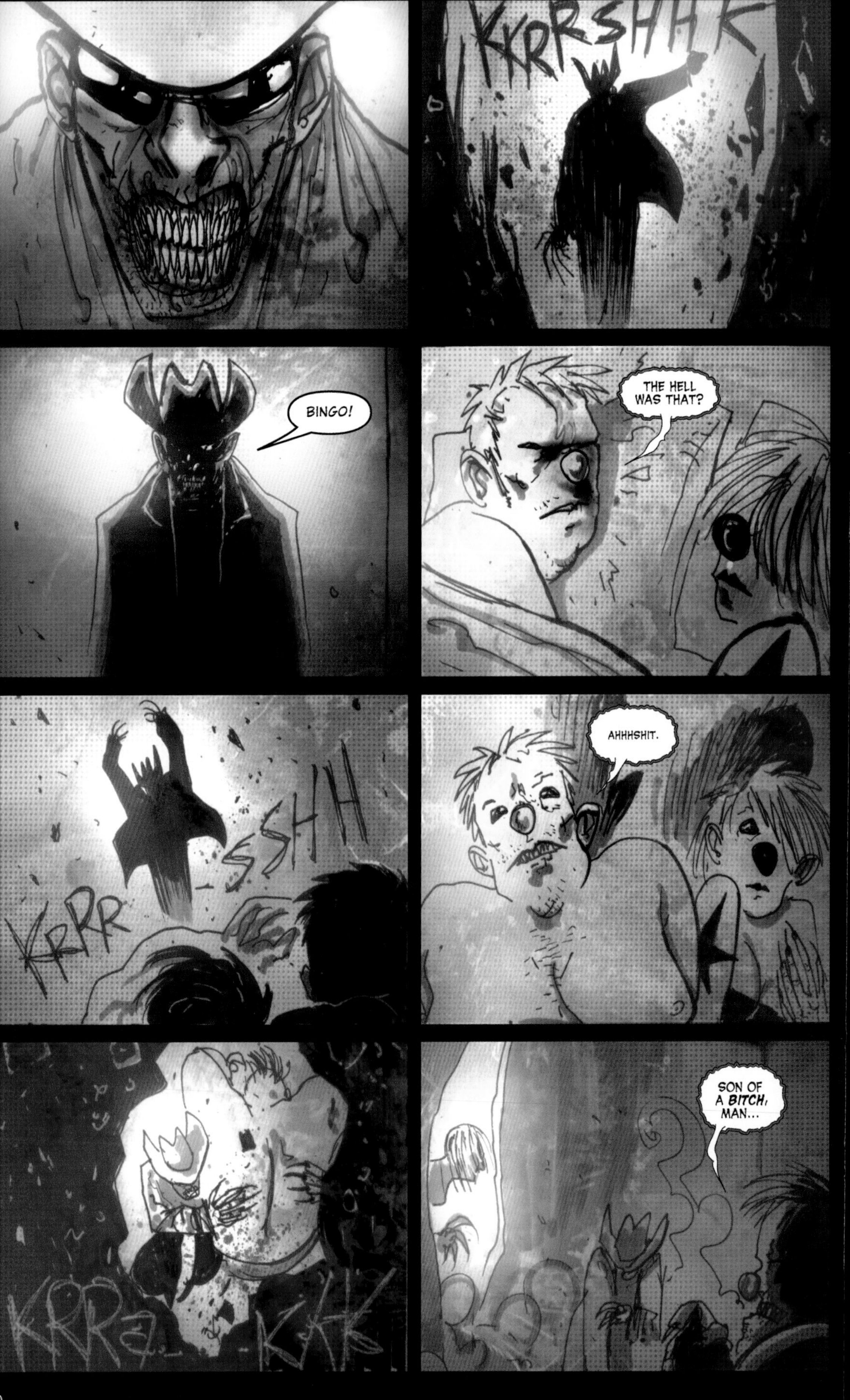
KKRSHHK
BINGO!
THE HELL WAS THAT?
KRRR
SSHH
AHHHSHIT.
SON OF A BITCH, MAN...

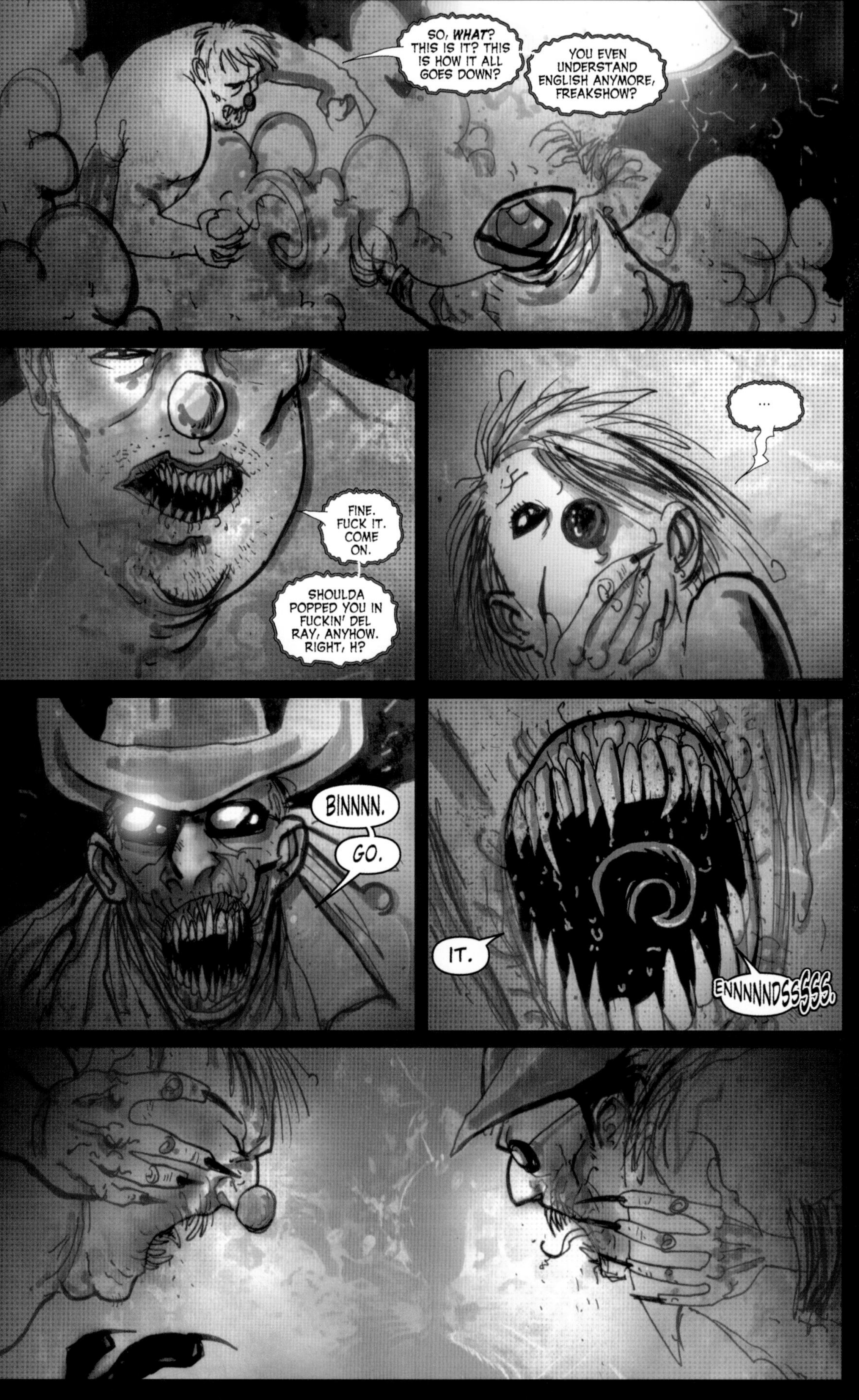
SO, WHAT? THIS IS IT? THIS IS HOW IT ALL GOES DOWN?
YOU EVEN UNDERSTAND ENGLISH ANYMORE, FREAKSHOW?
FINE. FUCK IT. COME ON.
SHOULDA POPPED YOU IN FUCKIN' DEL RAY, ANYHOW. RIGHT, H?
...
BINNNN.
GO.
IT.
ENNNNNDSSSSS.

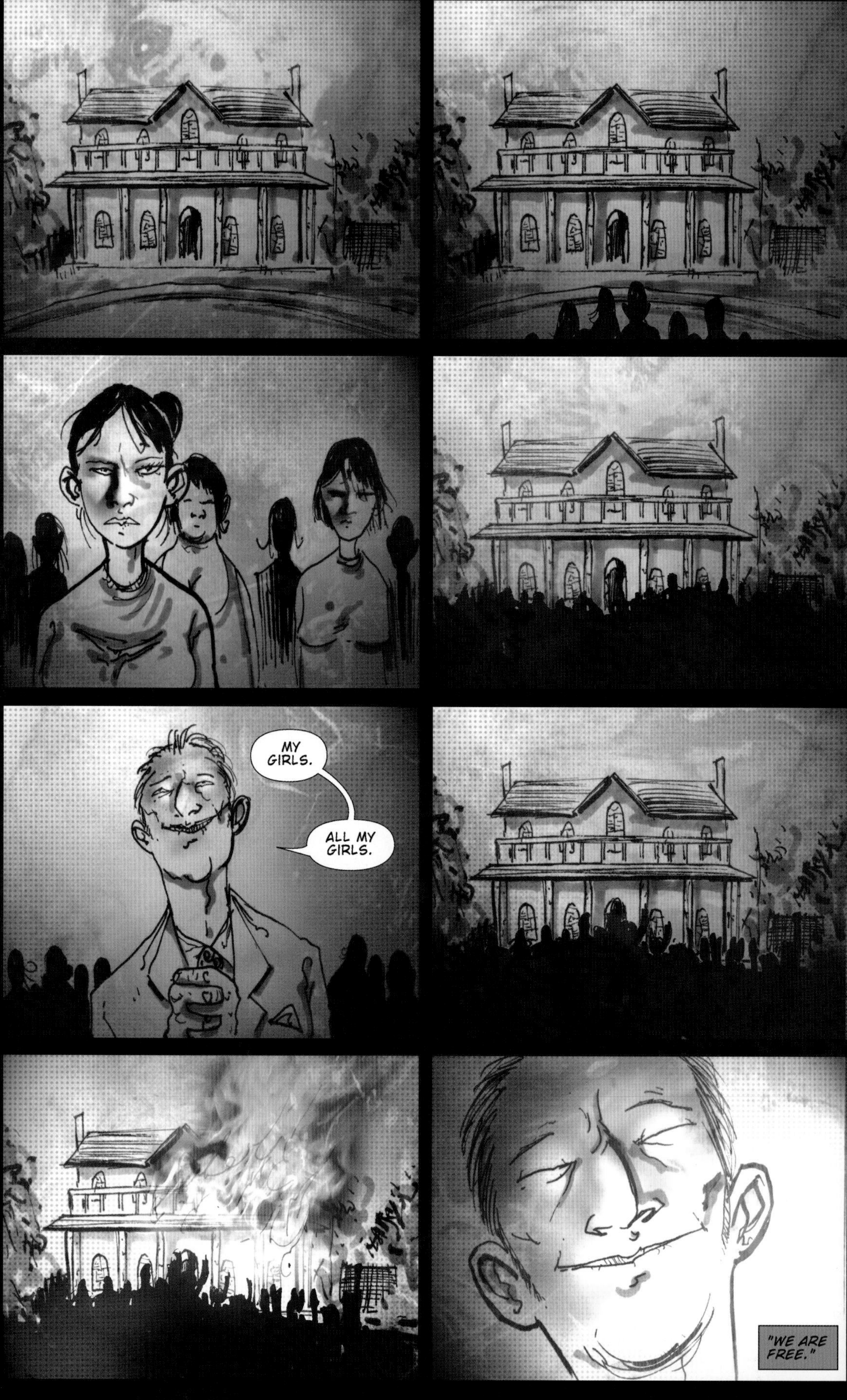
MY GIRLS.
ALL MY GIRLS.
"WE ARE FREE."

FREE FROM FEAR, FREE FROM TYRANNY, FREE FROM TERROR. JUAREZ IS REBORN, PURIFIED BY FIRE.

IN THE YEAR SINCE MY HOME, AND THE JUAREZ KILLERS, BURNED...

MERCIFUL AND GOOD *GODDAMN* JESUS CHRIST ON A CRUTCH FOR CHRISTMAS *FUCK.*

I KNOW, RIGHT?

MARTINEZ IS GOD KNOWS— FAT FUCK AIN'T ANSWERIN'. THINK GARCIA'S ON DUTY, THOUGH...

DETECTIVE GARCIA, THIS—

DETECTIVE GARCIA, THIS—

FUCK.

FUCK.

THE POLICE—THEIR BEST, FALLEN, AND THEIR WORST, FALLEN FARTHER STILL...

"...ARE REBORN. WITH FINANCING I PROVIDED, OUR POLICE ARE NOW STRONG, PROUD, AND READY AT LAST TO PROTECT AND SERVE.

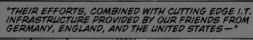

"THEIR EFFORTS, COMBINED WITH CUTTING EDGE I.T. INFRASTRUCTURE PROVIDED BY OUR FRIENDS FROM GERMANY, ENGLAND, AND THE UNITED STATES—"

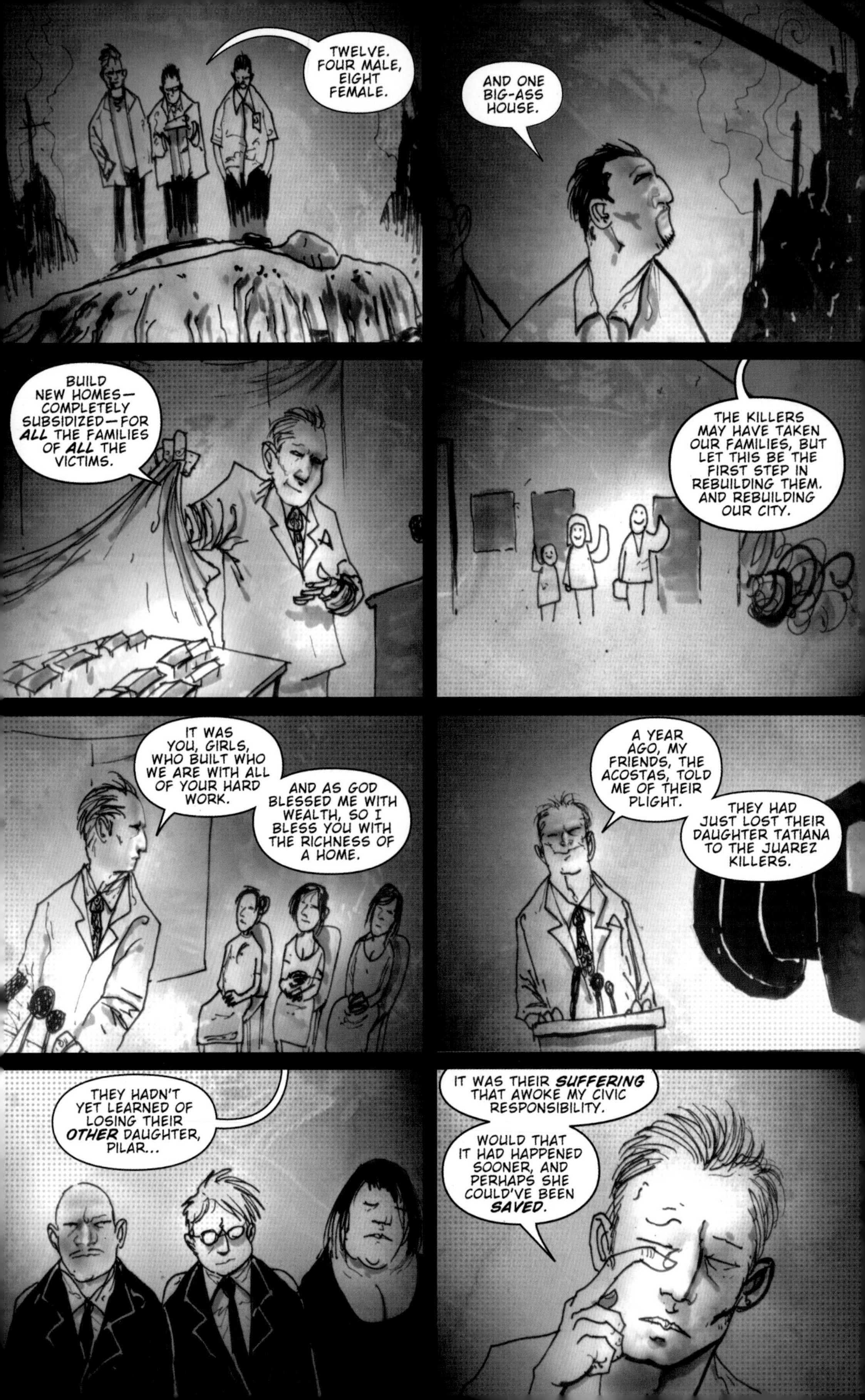
TWELVE. FOUR MALE, EIGHT FEMALE.
AND ONE BIG-ASS HOUSE.
BUILD NEW HOMES—COMPLETELY SUBSIDIZED—FOR ALL THE FAMILIES OF ALL THE VICTIMS.
THE KILLERS MAY HAVE TAKEN OUR FAMILIES, BUT LET THIS BE THE FIRST STEP IN REBUILDING THEM. AND REBUILDING OUR CITY.
IT WAS YOU, GIRLS, WHO BUILT WHO WE ARE WITH ALL OF YOUR HARD WORK.
AND AS GOD BLESSED ME WITH WEALTH, SO I BLESS YOU WITH THE RICHNESS OF A HOME.
A YEAR AGO, MY FRIENDS, THE ACOSTAS, TOLD ME OF THEIR PLIGHT.
THEY HAD JUST LOST THEIR DAUGHTER TATIANA TO THE JUAREZ KILLERS.
THEY HADN'T YET LEARNED OF LOSING THEIR OTHER DAUGHTER, PILAR...
IT WAS THEIR SUFFERING THAT AWOKE MY CIVIC RESPONSIBILITY.
WOULD THAT IT HAD HAPPENED SOONER, AND PERHAPS SHE COULD'VE BEEN SAVED.

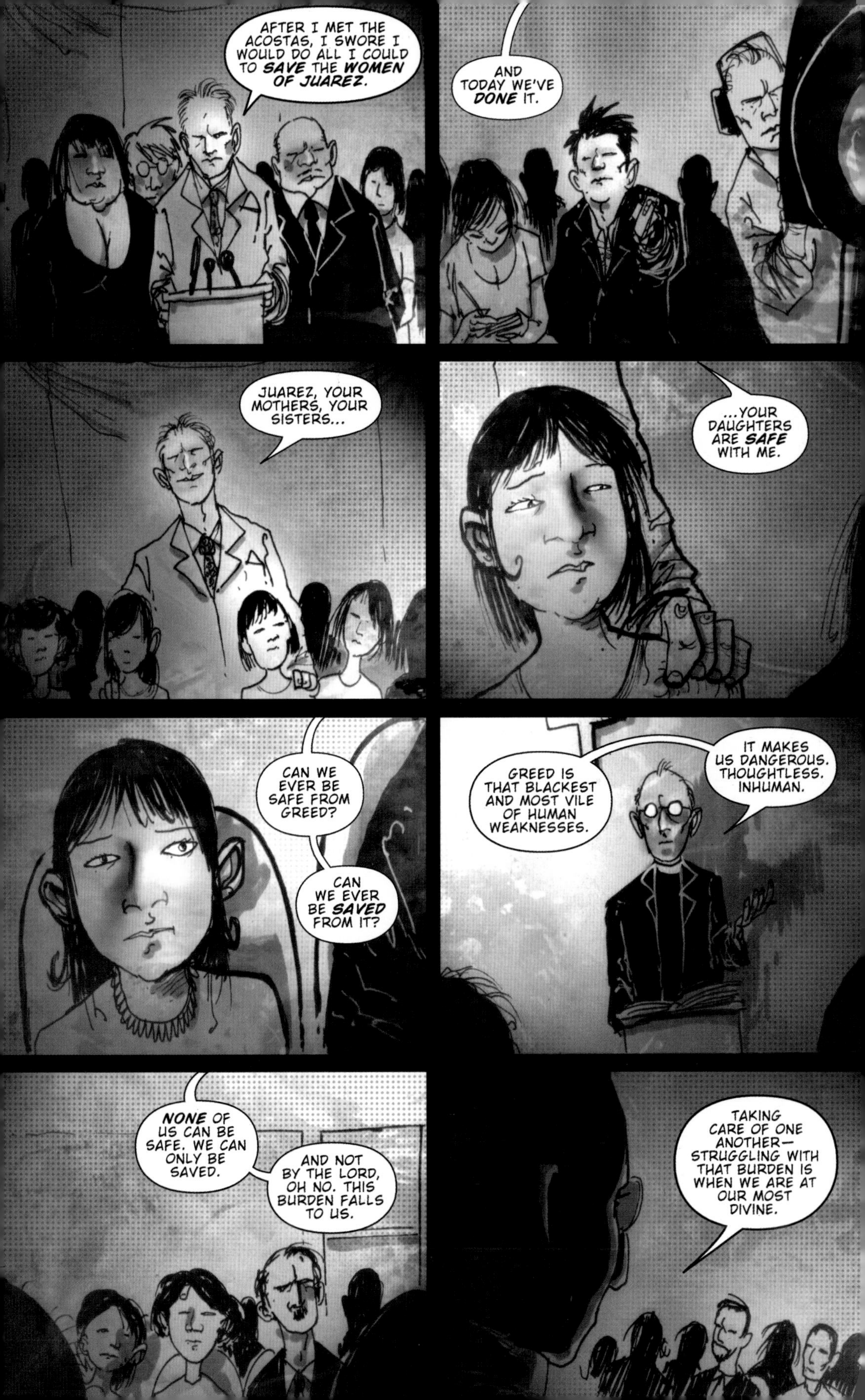
AFTER I MET THE ACOSTAS, I SWORE I WOULD DO ALL I COULD TO SAVE THE WOMEN OF JUAREZ.
AND TODAY WE'VE DONE IT.
JUAREZ, YOUR MOTHERS, YOUR SISTERS...
...YOUR DAUGHTERS ARE SAFE WITH ME.
CAN WE EVER BE SAFE FROM GREED?
CAN WE EVER BE SAVED FROM IT?
GREED IS THAT BLACKEST AND MOST VILE OF HUMAN WEAKNESSES.
IT MAKES US DANGEROUS. THOUGHTLESS. INHUMAN.
NONE OF US CAN BE SAFE. WE CAN ONLY BE SAVED.
AND NOT BY THE LORD, OH NO. THIS BURDEN FALLS TO US.
TAKING CARE OF ONE ANOTHER— STRUGGLING WITH THAT BURDEN IS WHEN WE ARE AT OUR MOST DIVINE.

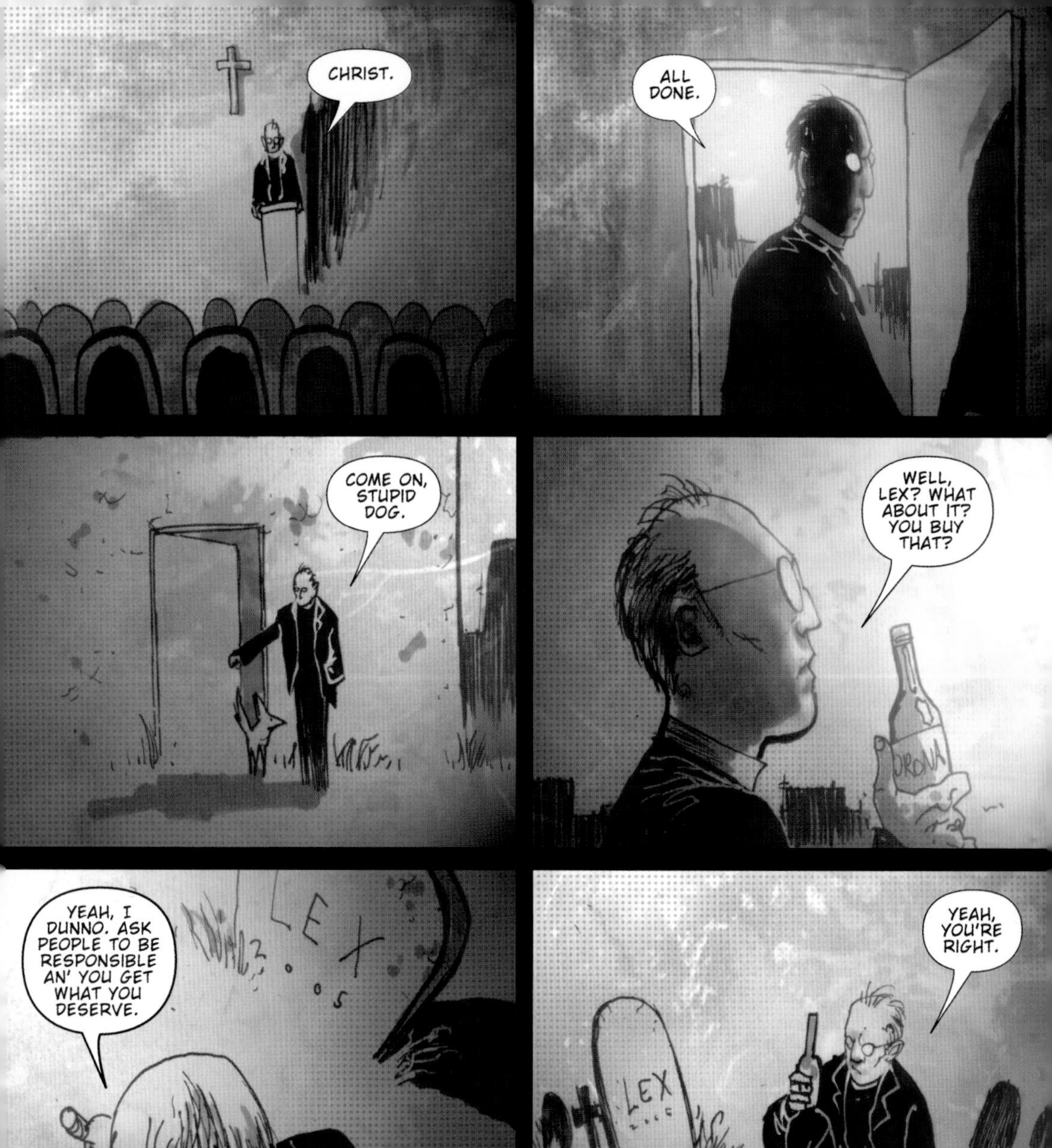
CHRIST.
ALL DONE.
COME ON, STUPID DOG.
WELL, LEX? WHAT ABOUT IT? YOU BUY THAT?
YEAH, I DUNNO. ASK PEOPLE TO BE RESPONSIBLE AN' YOU GET WHAT YOU DESERVE.
YEAH, YOU'RE RIGHT.

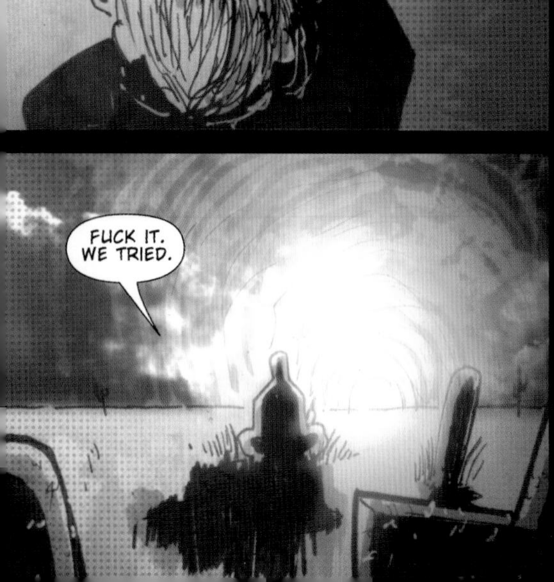
FUCK IT. WE TRIED.

"JUAREZ

OR

LEX NOVA & THE CASE OF THE 400 DEAD MEXICAN GIRLS"

END OF PART SEVEN:

THE END

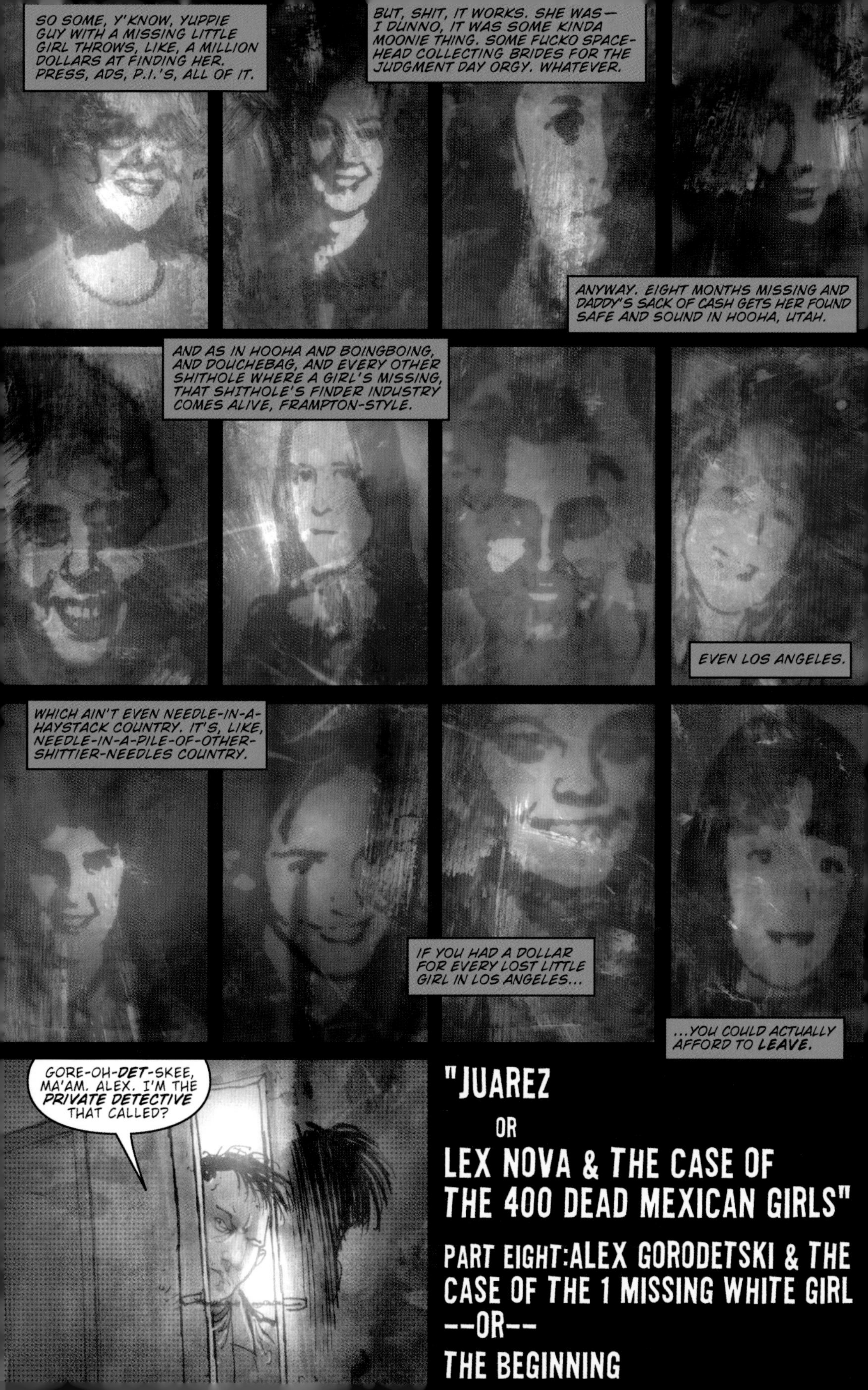
SO SOME, Y'KNOW, YUPPIE GUY WITH A MISSING LITTLE GIRL THROWS, LIKE, A MILLION DOLLARS AT FINDING HER. PRESS, ADS, P.I.'S, ALL OF IT.
BUT, SHIT, IT WORKS. SHE WAS— I DUNNO, IT WAS SOME KINDA MOONIE THING. SOME FUCKO SPACE-HEAD COLLECTING BRIDES FOR THE JUDGMENT DAY ORGY. WHATEVER.
ANYWAY. EIGHT MONTHS MISSING AND DADDY'S SACK OF CASH GETS HER FOUND SAFE AND SOUND IN HOOHA, UTAH.
AND AS IN HOOHA AND BOINGBOING, AND DOUCHEBAG, AND EVERY OTHER SHITHOLE WHERE A GIRL'S MISSING, THAT SHITHOLE'S FINDER INDUSTRY COMES ALIVE, FRAMPTON-STYLE.
EVEN LOS ANGELES.
WHICH AIN'T EVEN NEEDLE-IN-A-HAYSTACK COUNTRY. IT'S, LIKE, NEEDLE-IN-A-PILE-OF-OTHER-SHITTIER-NEEDLES COUNTRY.
IF YOU HAD A DOLLAR FOR EVERY LOST LITTLE GIRL IN LOS ANGELES...
...YOU COULD ACTUALLY AFFORD TO LEAVE.
GORE-OH-DET-SKEE, MA'AM. ALEX. I'M THE PRIVATE DETECTIVE THAT CALLED?
"JUAREZ
OR
LEX NOVA & THE CASE OF THE 400 DEAD MEXICAN GIRLS"
PART EIGHT: ALEX GORODETSKI & THE CASE OF THE 1 MISSING WHITE GIRL
--OR--
THE BEGINNING

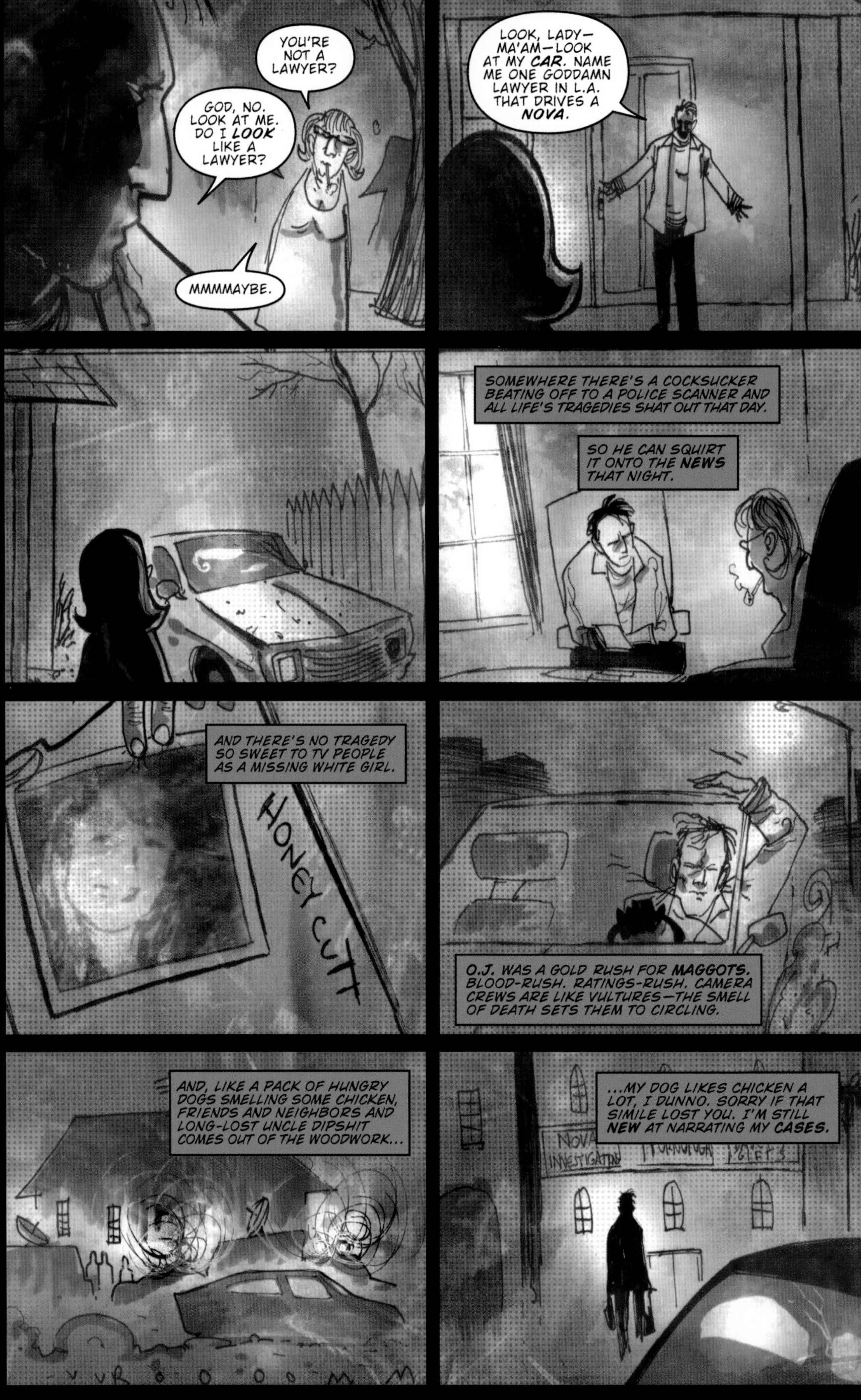
YOU'RE NOT A LAWYER?
GOD, NO. LOOK AT ME. DO I LOOK LIKE A LAWYER?
MMMMAYBE.
LOOK, LADY— MA'AM—LOOK AT MY CAR. NAME ME ONE GODDAMN LAWYER IN L.A. THAT DRIVES A NOVA.
SOMEWHERE THERE'S A COCKSUCKER BEATING OFF TO A POLICE SCANNER AND ALL LIFE'S TRAGEDIES SHAT OUT THAT DAY.
SO HE CAN SQUIRT IT ONTO THE NEWS THAT NIGHT.
AND THERE'S NO TRAGEDY SO SWEET TO TV PEOPLE AS A MISSING WHITE GIRL.
HONEY CUTT
O.J. WAS A GOLD RUSH FOR MAGGOTS. BLOOD-RUSH. RATINGS-RUSH. CAMERA CREWS ARE LIKE VULTURES—THE SMELL OF DEATH SETS THEM TO CIRCLING.
AND, LIKE A PACK OF HUNGRY DOGS SMELLING SOME CHICKEN, FRIENDS AND NEIGHBORS AND LONG-LOST UNCLE DIPSHIT COMES OUT OF THE WOODWORK...
...MY DOG LIKES CHICKEN A LOT, I DUNNO. SORRY IF THAT SIMILE LOST YOU. I'M STILL NEW AT NARRATING MY CASES.

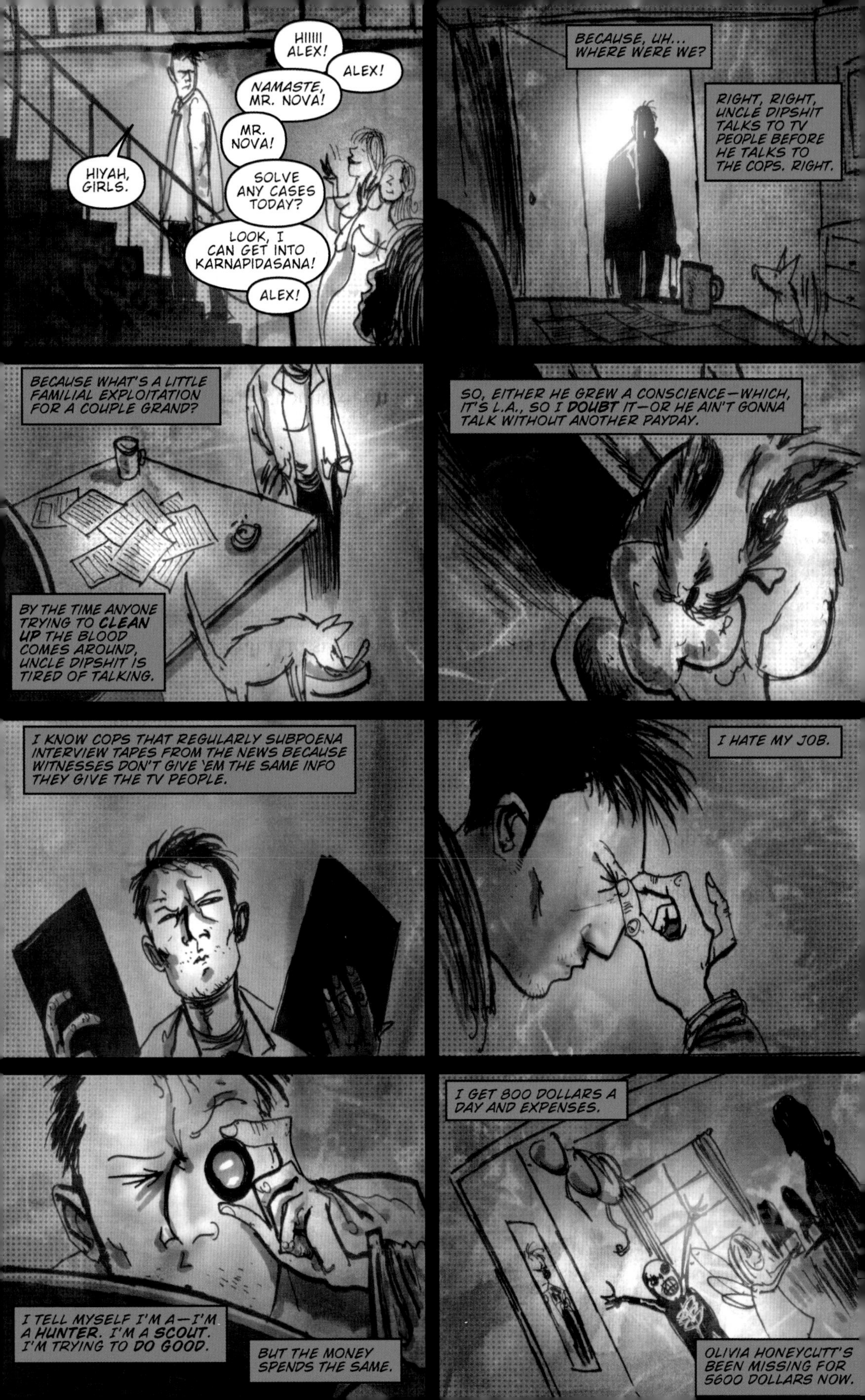
HI!!!!
ALEX!
ALEX!
NAMASTE, MR. NOVA!
MR. NOVA!
HIYAH, GIRLS.
SOLVE ANY CASES TODAY?
LOOK, I CAN GET INTO KARNAPIDASANA!
ALEX!
BECAUSE, UH... WHERE WERE WE?
RIGHT, RIGHT, UNCLE DIPSHIT TALKS TO TV PEOPLE BEFORE HE TALKS TO THE COPS. RIGHT.
BECAUSE WHAT'S A LITTLE FAMILIAL EXPLOITATION FOR A COUPLE GRAND?
BY THE TIME ANYONE TRYING TO CLEAN UP THE BLOOD COMES AROUND, UNCLE DIPSHIT IS TIRED OF TALKING.
SO, EITHER HE GREW A CONSCIENCE—WHICH, IT'S L.A., SO I DOUBT IT—OR HE AIN'T GONNA TALK WITHOUT ANOTHER PAYDAY.
I KNOW COPS THAT REGULARLY SUBPOENA INTERVIEW TAPES FROM THE NEWS BECAUSE WITNESSES DON'T GIVE 'EM THE SAME INFO THEY GIVE THE TV PEOPLE.
I HATE MY JOB.
I TELL MYSELF I'M A—I'M A HUNTER. I'M A SCOUT. I'M TRYING TO DO GOOD.
BUT THE MONEY SPENDS THE SAME.
I GET 800 DOLLARS A DAY AND EXPENSES.
OLIVIA HONEYCUTT'S BEEN MISSING FOR 5600 DOLLARS NOW.

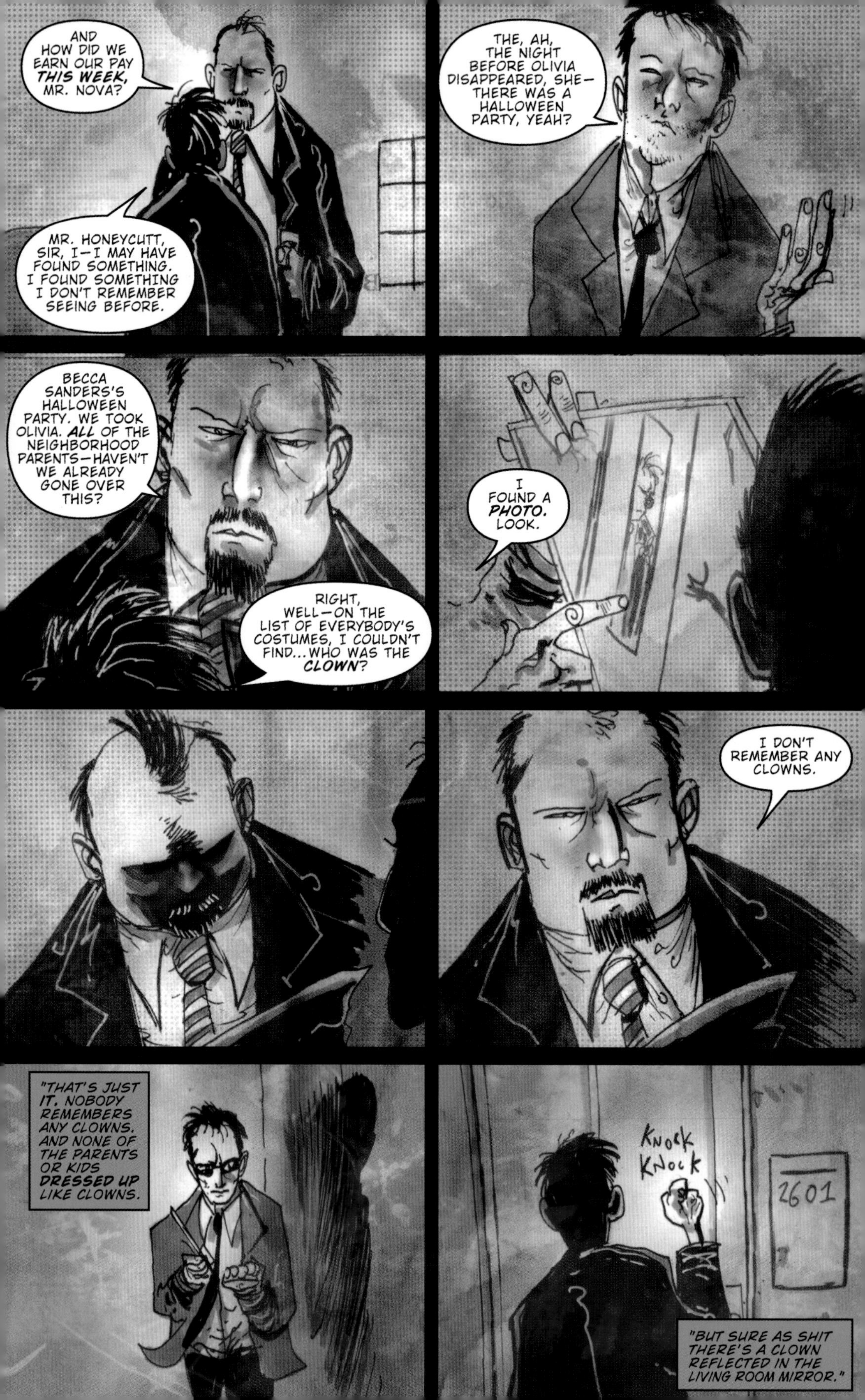

AND HOW DID WE EARN OUR PAY *THIS WEEK,* MR. NOVA?
MR. HONEYCUTT, SIR, I—I MAY HAVE FOUND SOMETHING. I FOUND SOMETHING I DON'T REMEMBER SEEING BEFORE.
THE, AH, THE NIGHT BEFORE OLIVIA DISAPPEARED, SHE—THERE WAS A HALLOWEEN PARTY, YEAH?
BECCA SANDERS'S HALLOWEEN PARTY. WE TOOK OLIVIA. *ALL* OF THE NEIGHBORHOOD PARENTS—HAVEN'T WE ALREADY GONE OVER THIS?
RIGHT, WELL—ON THE LIST OF EVERYBODY'S COSTUMES, I COULDN'T FIND...WHO WAS THE *CLOWN*?
I FOUND A *PHOTO.* LOOK.
I DON'T REMEMBER ANY CLOWNS.
"THAT'S JUST *IT.* NOBODY REMEMBERS ANY CLOWNS. AND NONE OF THE PARENTS OR KIDS *DRESSED UP* LIKE CLOWNS.
KNOCK KNOCK
2601
"BUT SURE AS SHIT THERE'S A CLOWN REFLECTED IN THE LIVING ROOM MIRROR."

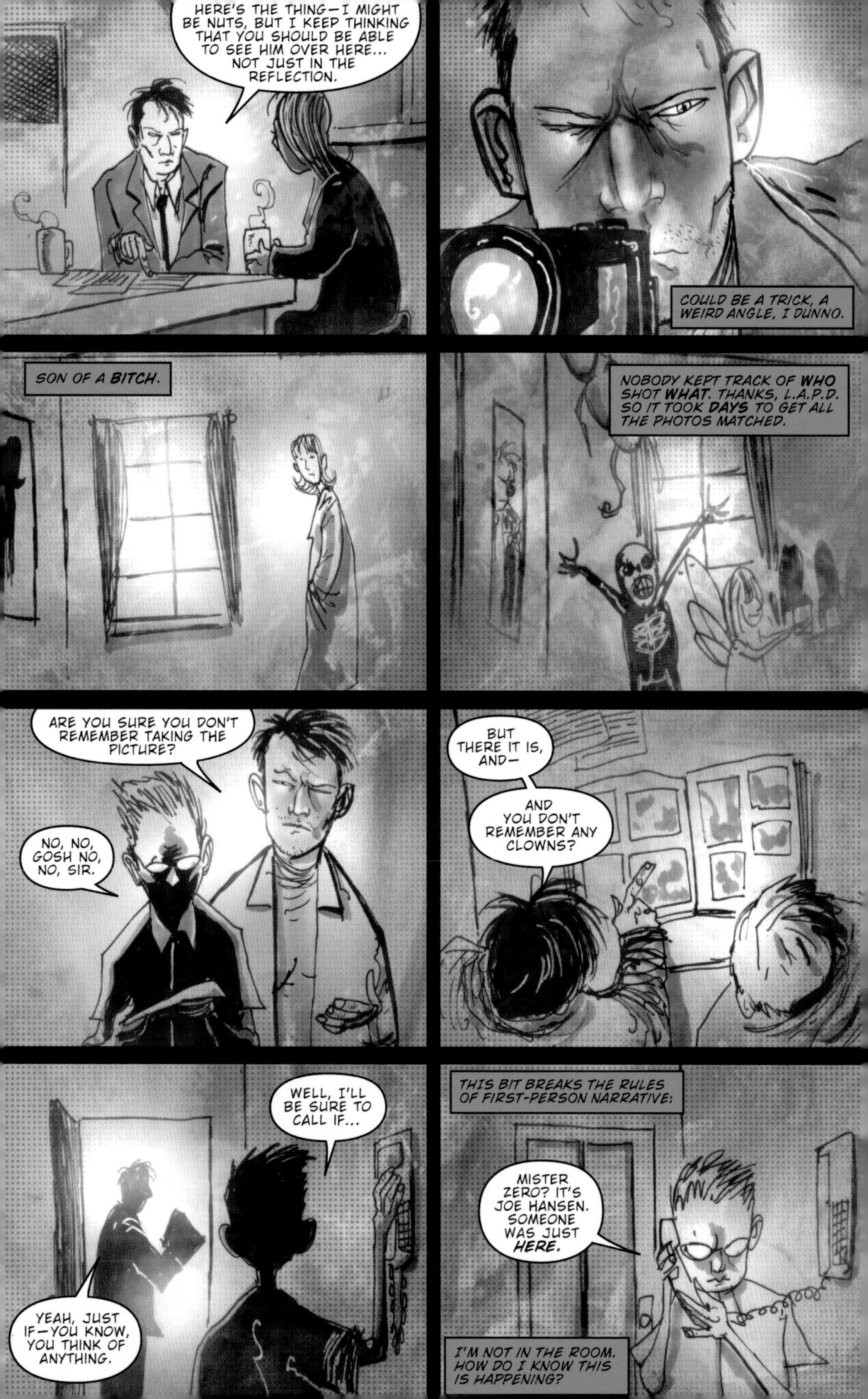
HERE'S THE THING—I MIGHT BE NUTS, BUT I KEEP THINKING THAT YOU SHOULD BE ABLE TO SEE HIM OVER HERE... NOT JUST IN THE REFLECTION.
COULD BE A TRICK, A WEIRD ANGLE, I DUNNO.
SON OF A BITCH.
NOBODY KEPT TRACK OF WHO SHOT WHAT. THANKS, L.A.P.D. SO IT TOOK DAYS TO GET ALL THE PHOTOS MATCHED.
ARE YOU SURE YOU DON'T REMEMBER TAKING THE PICTURE?
NO, NO, GOSH NO, NO, SIR.
BUT THERE IT IS, AND—
AND YOU DON'T REMEMBER ANY CLOWNS?
WELL, I'LL BE SURE TO CALL IF...
YEAH, JUST IF—YOU KNOW, YOU THINK OF ANYTHING.
THIS BIT BREAKS THE RULES OF FIRST-PERSON NARRATIVE:
MISTER ZERO? IT'S JOE HANSEN. SOMEONE WAS JUST HERE.
I'M NOT IN THE ROOM. HOW DO I KNOW THIS IS HAPPENING?

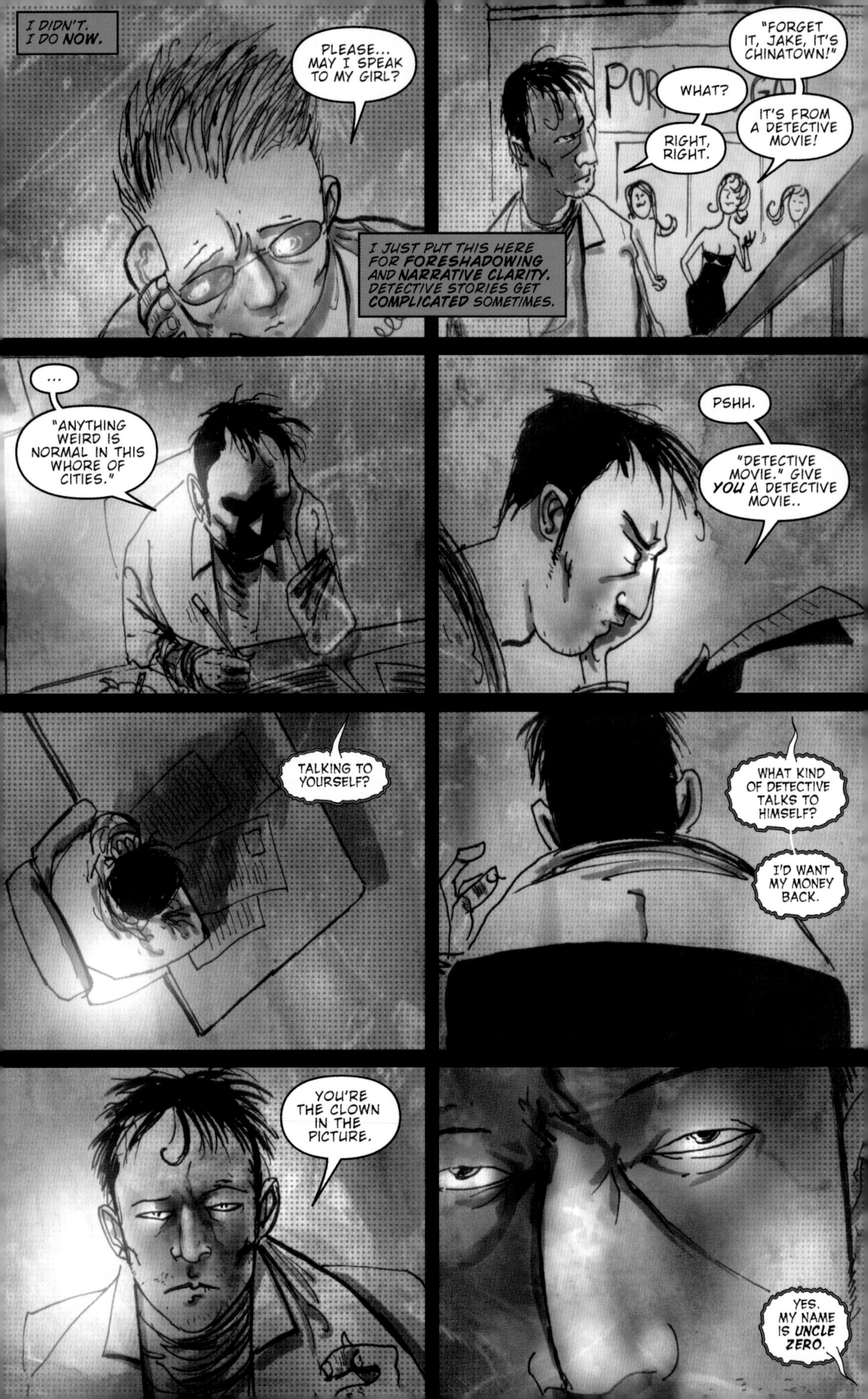
I DIDN'T. I DO NOW.
PLEASE... MAY I SPEAK TO MY GIRL?
"FORGET IT, JAKE, IT'S CHINATOWN!"
WHAT?
IT'S FROM A DETECTIVE MOVIE!
RIGHT, RIGHT.
I JUST PUT THIS HERE FOR FORESHADOWING AND NARRATIVE CLARITY. DETECTIVE STORIES GET COMPLICATED SOMETIMES.
...
"ANYTHING WEIRD IS NORMAL IN THIS WHORE OF CITIES."
PSHH.
"DETECTIVE MOVIE." GIVE YOU A DETECTIVE MOVIE..
TALKING TO YOURSELF?
WHAT KIND OF DETECTIVE TALKS TO HIMSELF?
I'D WANT MY MONEY BACK.
YOU'RE THE CLOWN IN THE PICTURE.
YES. MY NAME IS UNCLE ZERO.

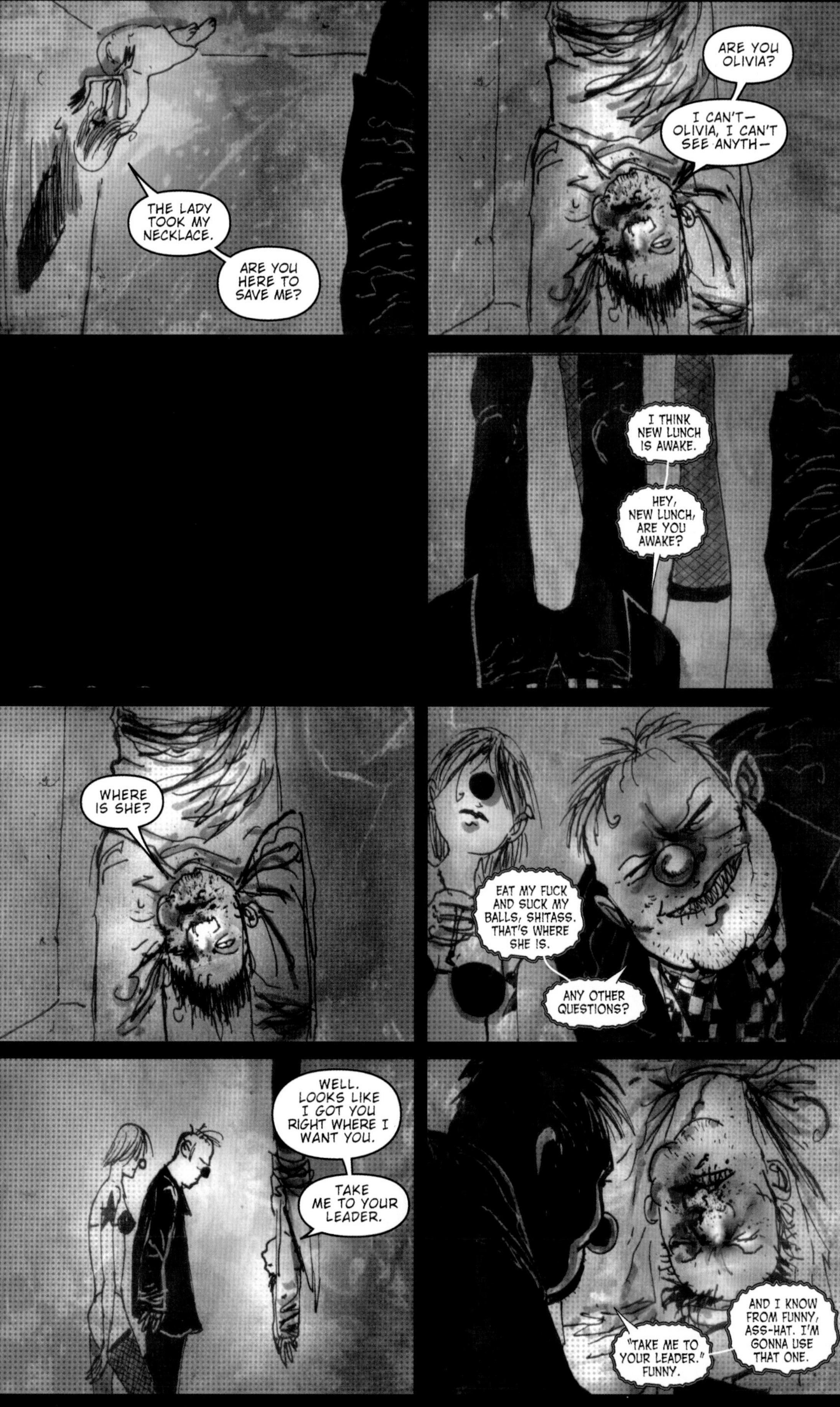
THE LADY TOOK MY NECKLACE.
ARE YOU HERE TO SAVE ME?
ARE YOU OLIVIA?
I CAN'T— OLIVIA, I CAN'T SEE ANYTH—
I THINK NEW LUNCH IS AWAKE.
HEY, NEW LUNCH, ARE YOU AWAKE?
WHERE IS SHE?
EAT MY FUCK AND SUCK MY BALLS, SHITASS. THAT'S WHERE SHE IS.
ANY OTHER QUESTIONS?
WELL. LOOKS LIKE I GOT YOU RIGHT WHERE I WANT YOU.
TAKE ME TO YOUR LEADER.
"TAKE ME TO YOUR LEADER." FUNNY.
AND I KNOW FROM FUNNY, ASS-HAT. I'M GONNA USE THAT ONE.

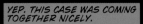
YEP. THIS CASE WAS COMING TOGETHER NICELY.

WHUK
GNNAAAA

WE PUT HER NIGHTSHIRT IN YOUR OFFICE. OLIVIA'S. AND THE HANSEN GIRL'S, TOO.

IT'S NOT THE MOST SUBTLE FRAME IN THE WORLD, BUT IT'LL GET THE JOB DONE.

"NEIGHBORHOOD KIDDIE-KILLER CAUGHT." THE END.

AND THAT'S THE END OF *YOU*, TOO, MR. ALEX ROSCOE GORODETSKI, 5006 WEST PICO, LOS ANGELES, CALIFORNIA.

YOUR LIFE WILL MAKE A MEDIOCRE EPISODE OF *FORENSICS FILES* ONE DAY.

HALO, FETCH OUR SPECIAL LITTLE ANGEL.

GUM

I WANT TO SEE HER FIRST *FEED*.

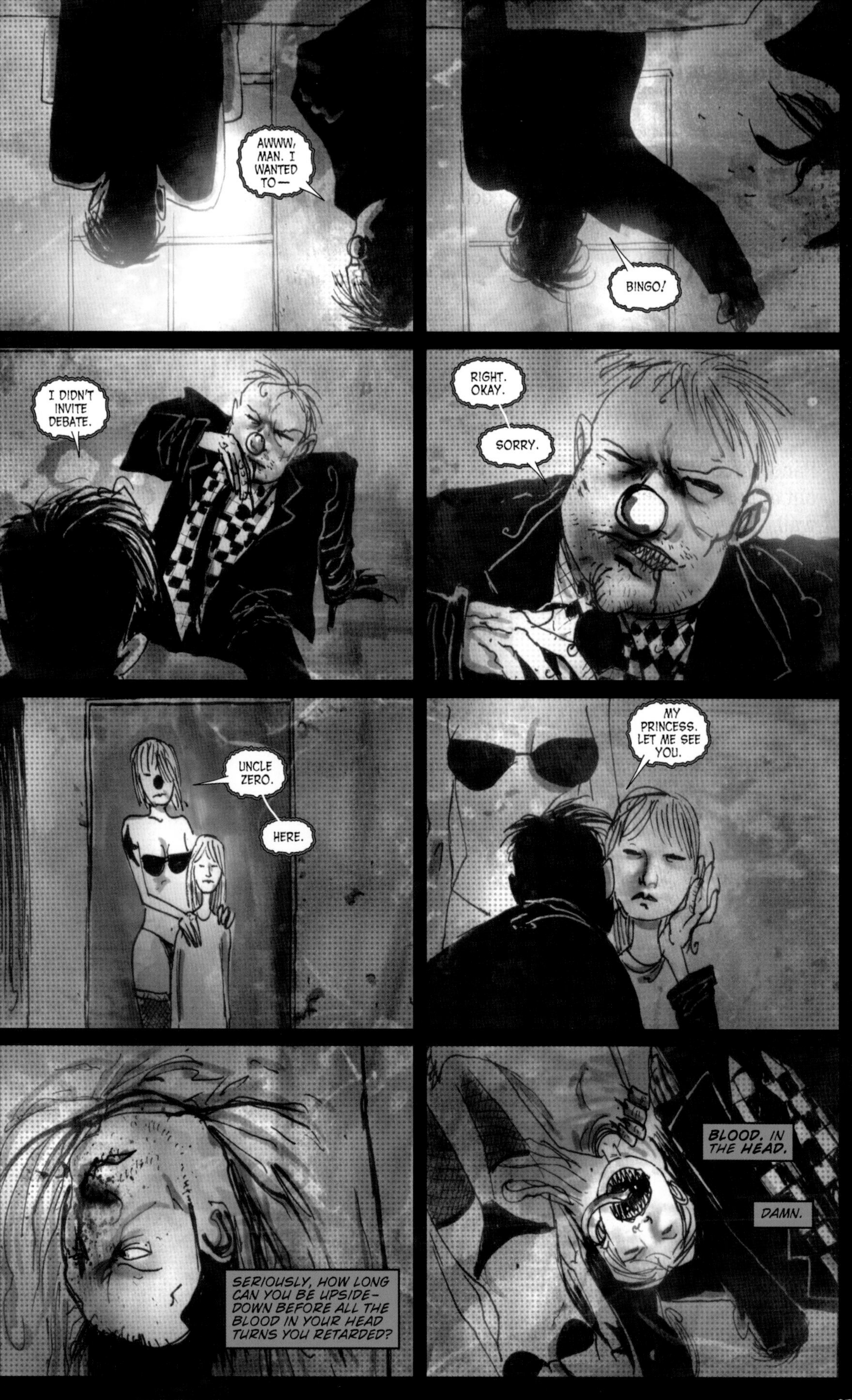
AWWW, MAN. I WANTED TO—
BINGO!
I DIDN'T INVITE DEBATE.
RIGHT. OKAY.
SORRY.
UNCLE ZERO.
HERE.
MY PRINCESS. LET ME SEE YOU.
SERIOUSLY, HOW LONG CAN YOU BE UPSIDE-DOWN BEFORE ALL THE BLOOD IN YOUR HEAD TURNS YOU RETARDED?
BLOOD. IN THE HEAD.
DAMN.

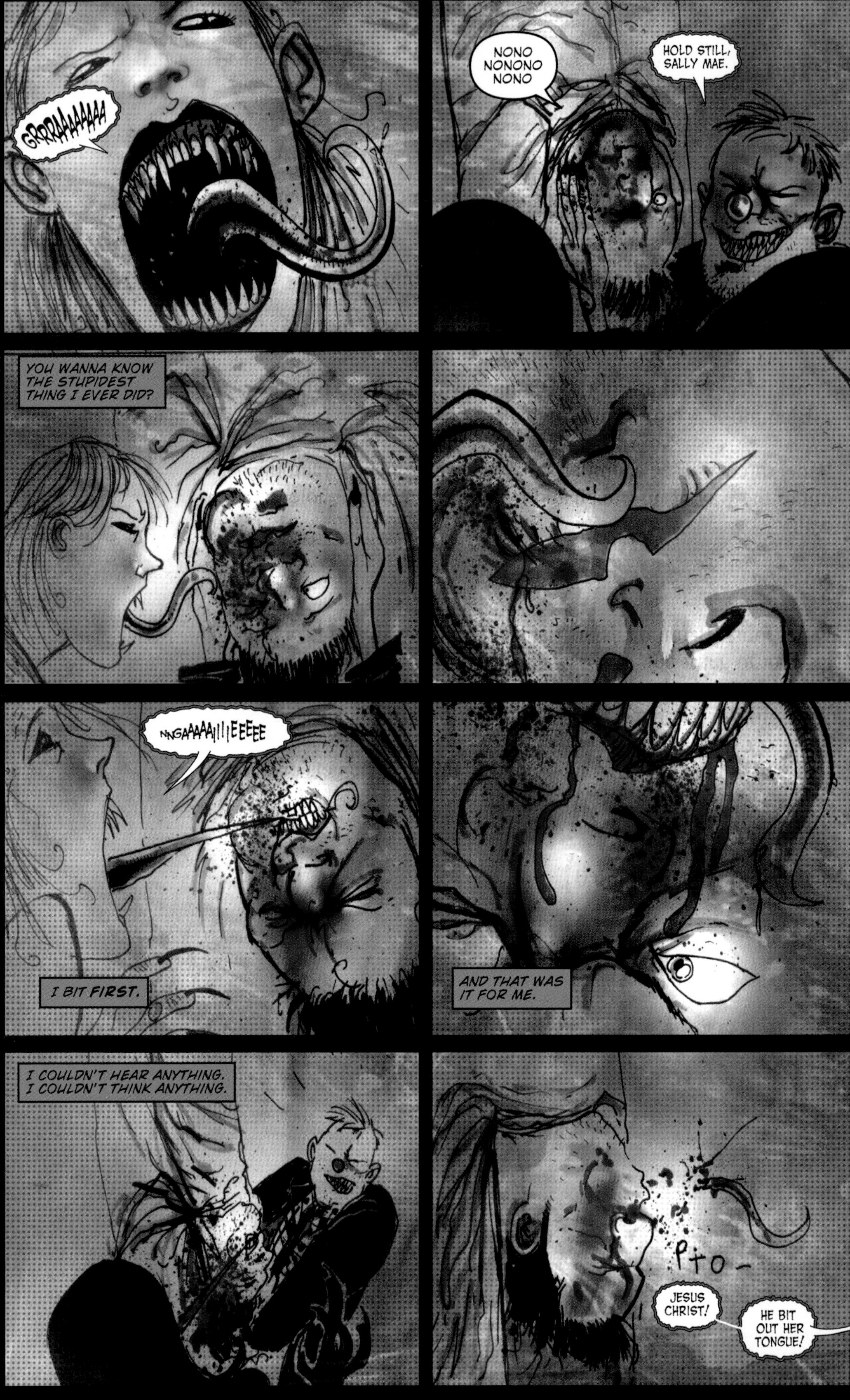
GRRRAAAAAAAA
NONO NONONO NONO
HOLD STILL, SALLY MAE.
YOU WANNA KNOW THE STUPIDEST THING I EVER DID?
NNGAAAAA!!!!EEEEE
I BIT FIRST.
AND THAT WAS IT FOR ME.
I COULDN'T HEAR ANYTHING. I COULDN'T THINK ANYTHING.
PTO-
JESUS CHRIST!
HE BIT OUT HER TONGUE!

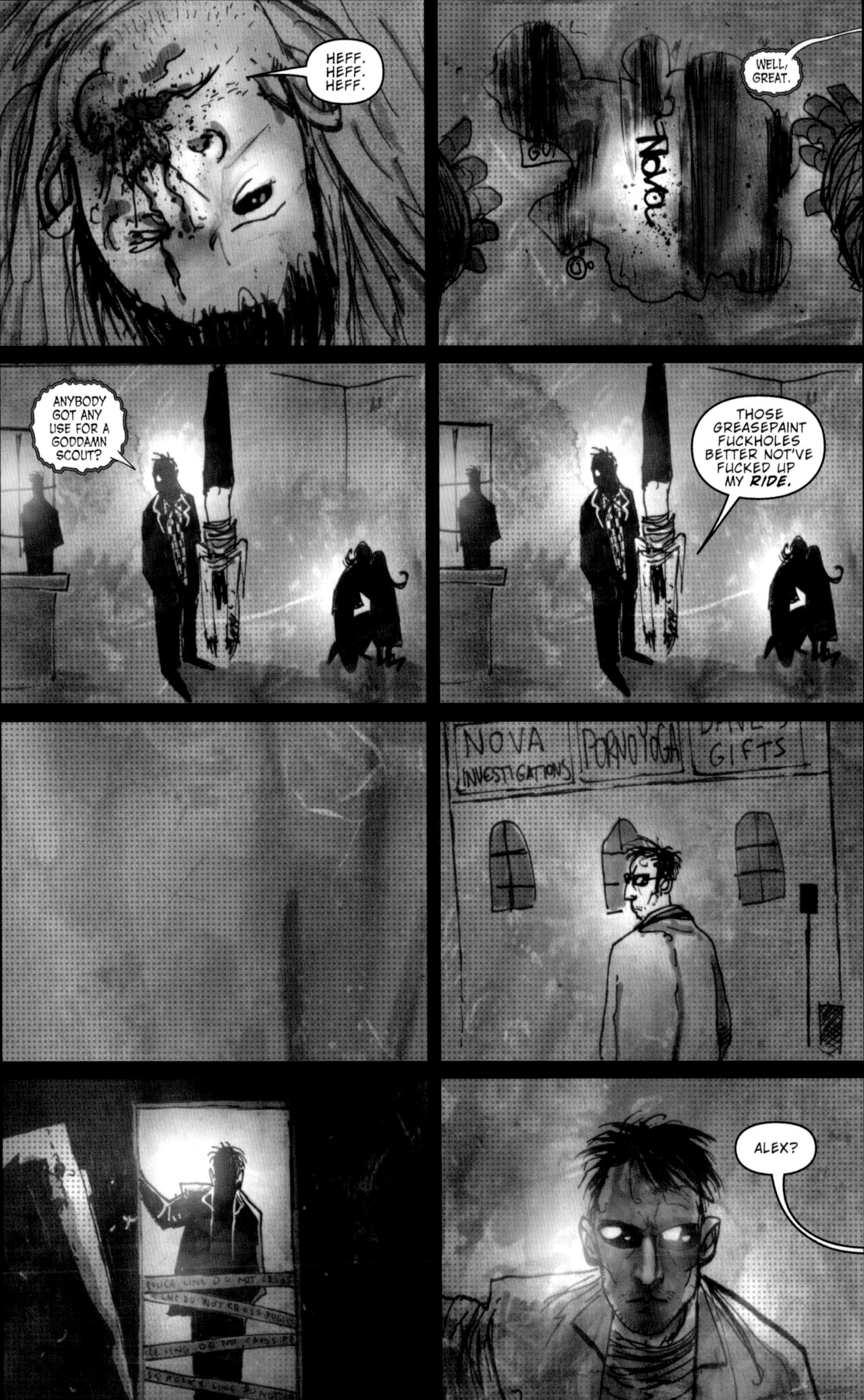

HEFF. HEFF. HEFF.
Nova
WELL, GREAT.
ANYBODY GOT ANY USE FOR A GODDAMN SCOUT?
THOSE GREASEPAINT FUCKHOLES BETTER NOT'VE FUCKED UP MY *RIDE.*
NOVA INVESTIGATIONS
PORNOYOGA
GIFTS
ALEX?

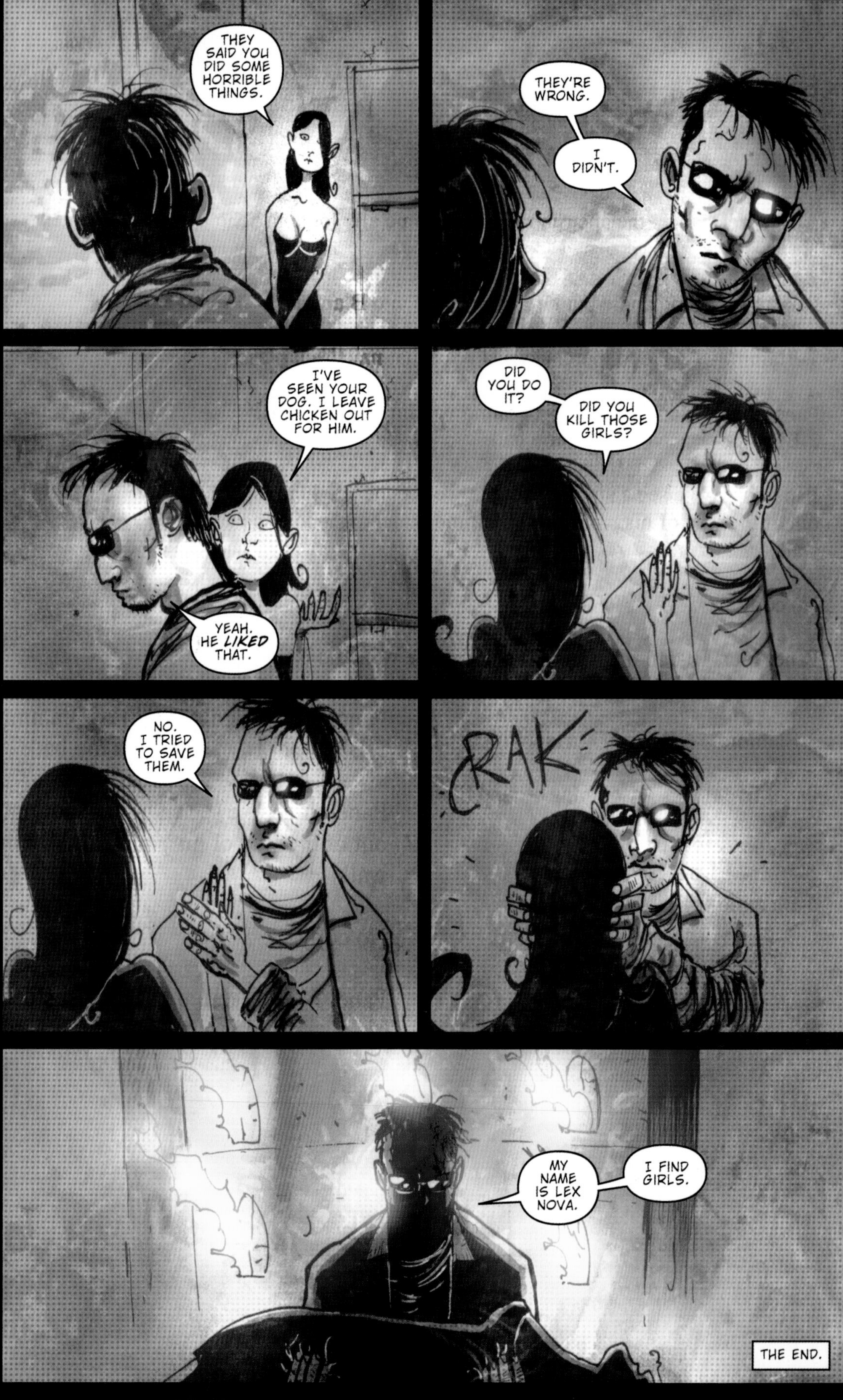
THEY SAID YOU DID SOME HORRIBLE THINGS.
THEY'RE WRONG.
I DIDN'T.
I'VE SEEN YOUR DOG. I LEAVE CHICKEN OUT FOR HIM.
YEAH. HE *LIKED* THAT.
DID YOU DO IT?
DID YOU KILL THOSE GIRLS?
NO. I TRIED TO SAVE THEM.
CRAK
MY NAME IS LEX NOVA.
I FIND GIRLS.
THE END.

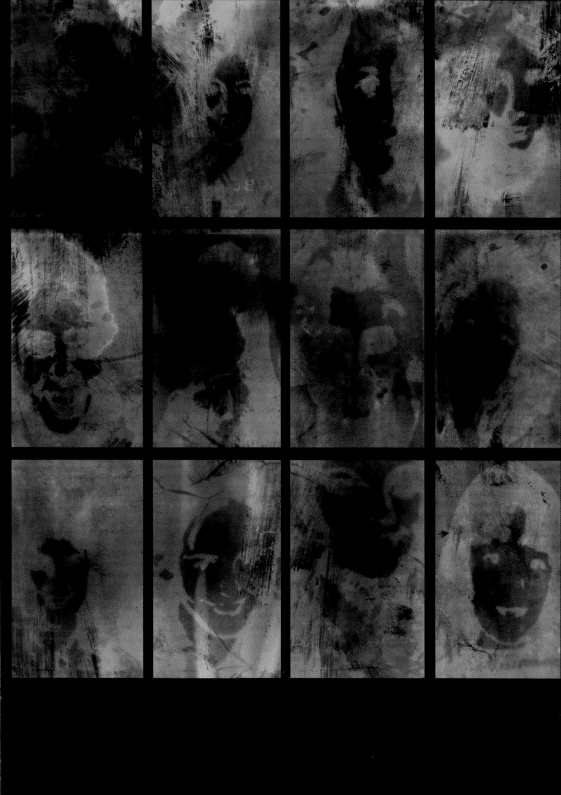

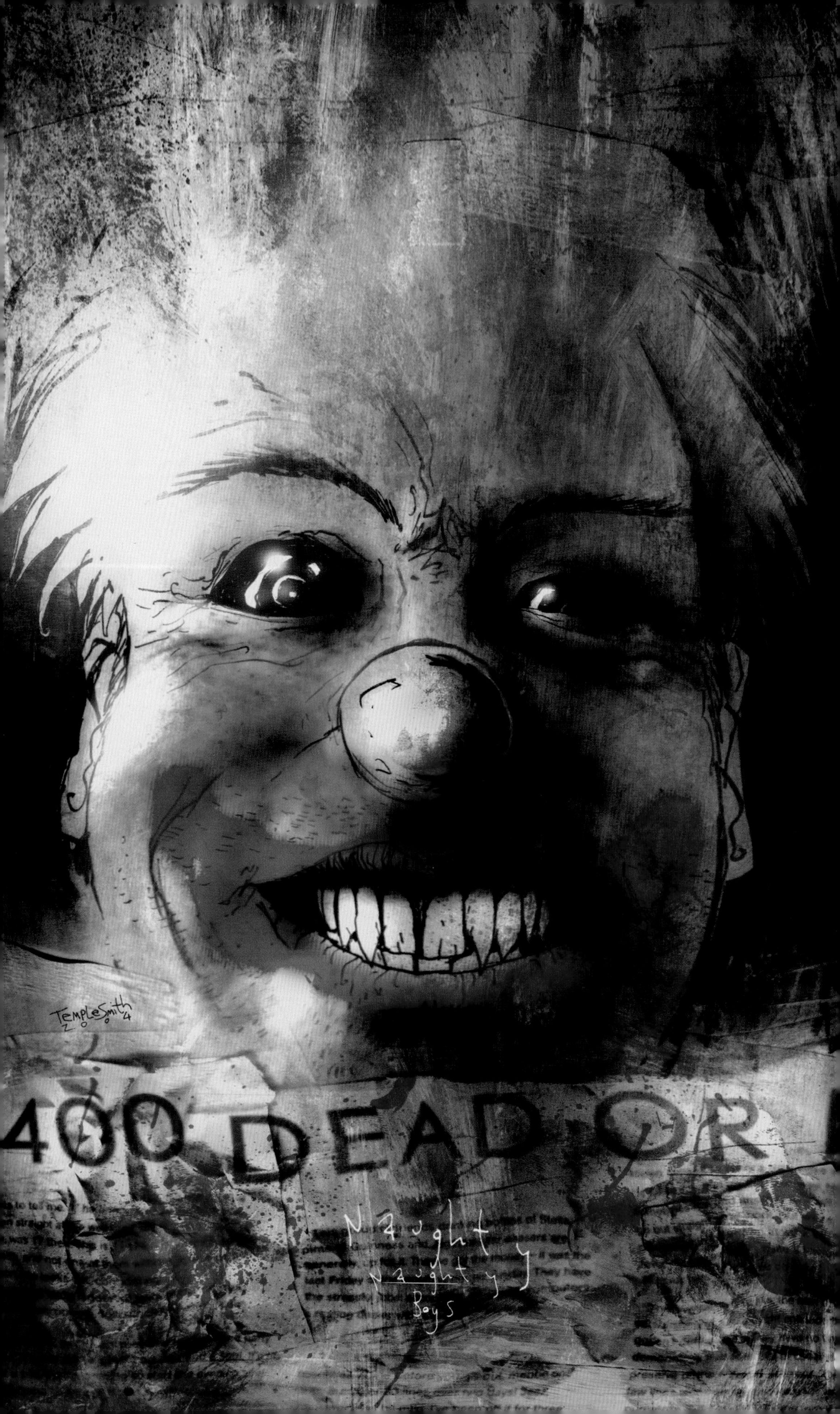
TempleSmith 2004
400 DEAD OR
Naughty
Naughty
Boys

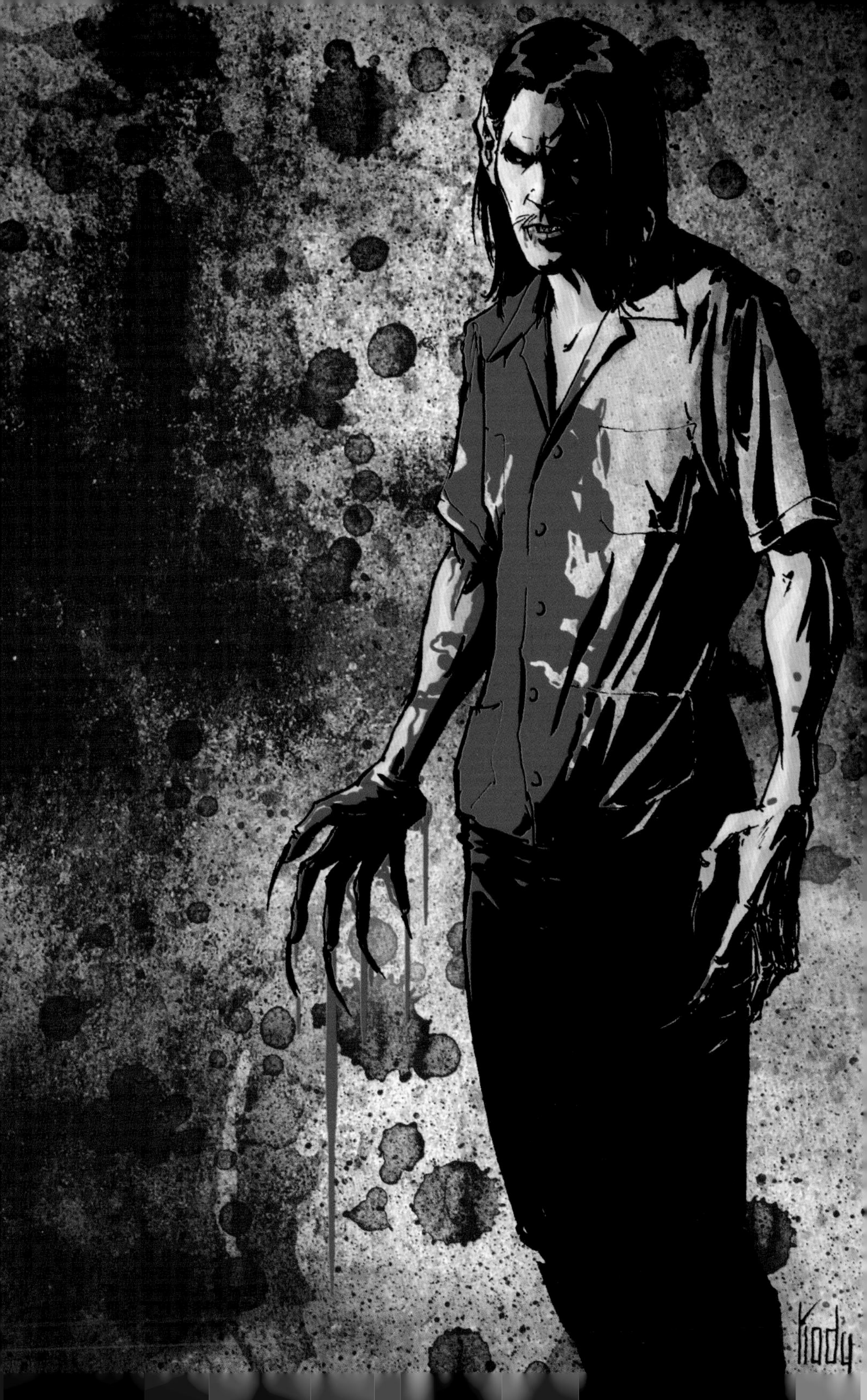

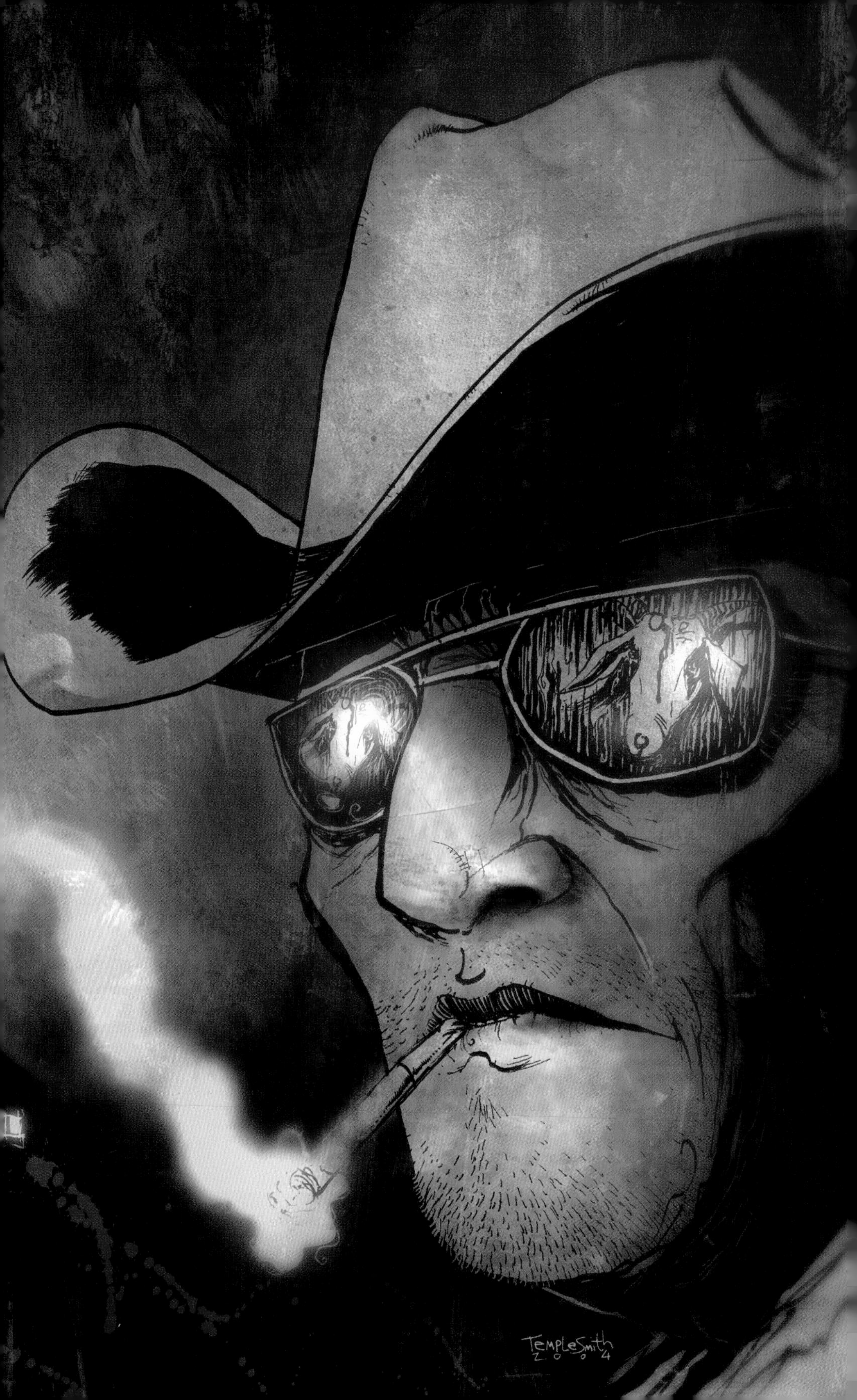
TEMPLESMITH
2004

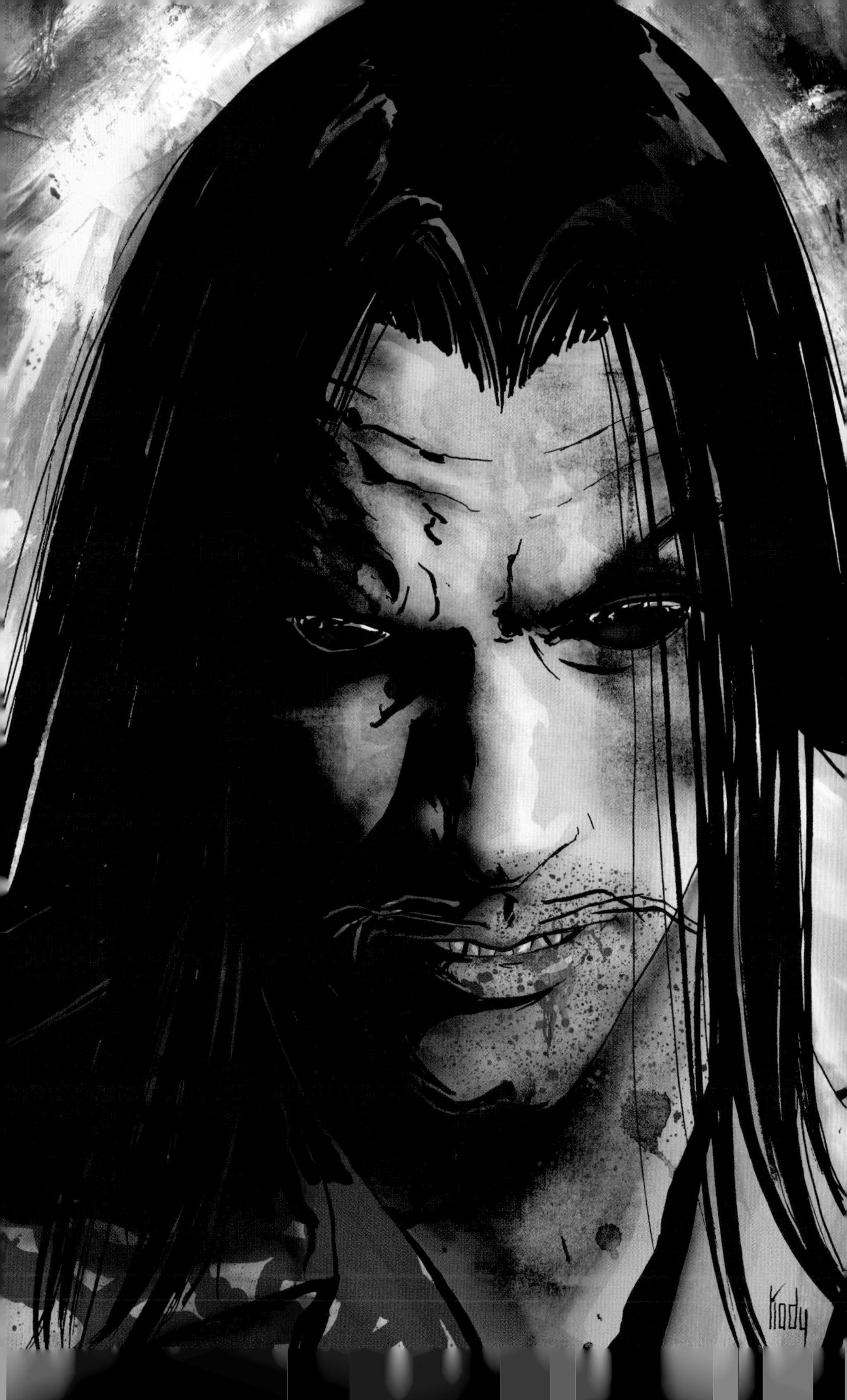

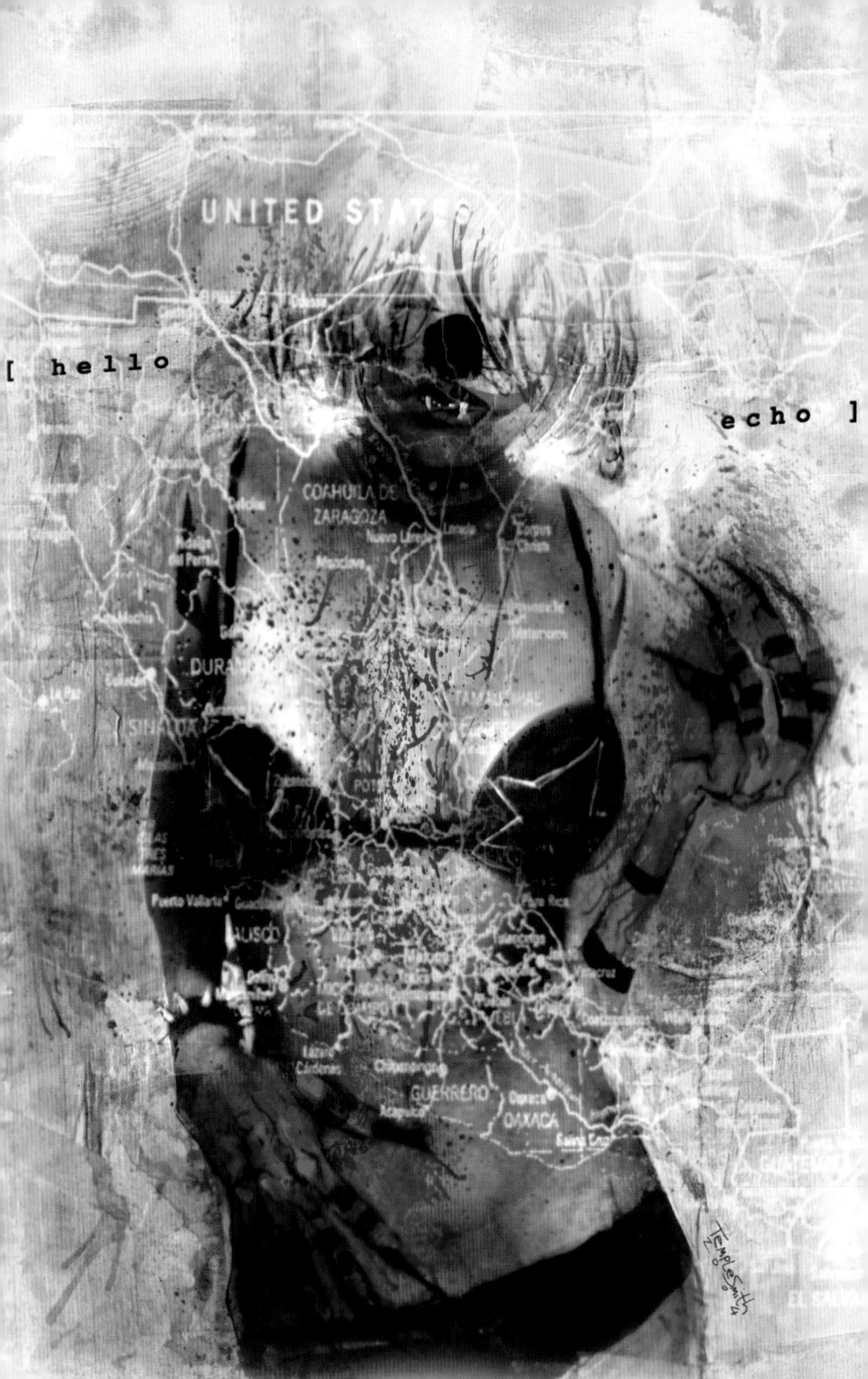
[hello
echo]
UNITED STATES
COAHUILA DE
ZARAGOZA
Puerto Vallarta
GUERRERO
OAXACA

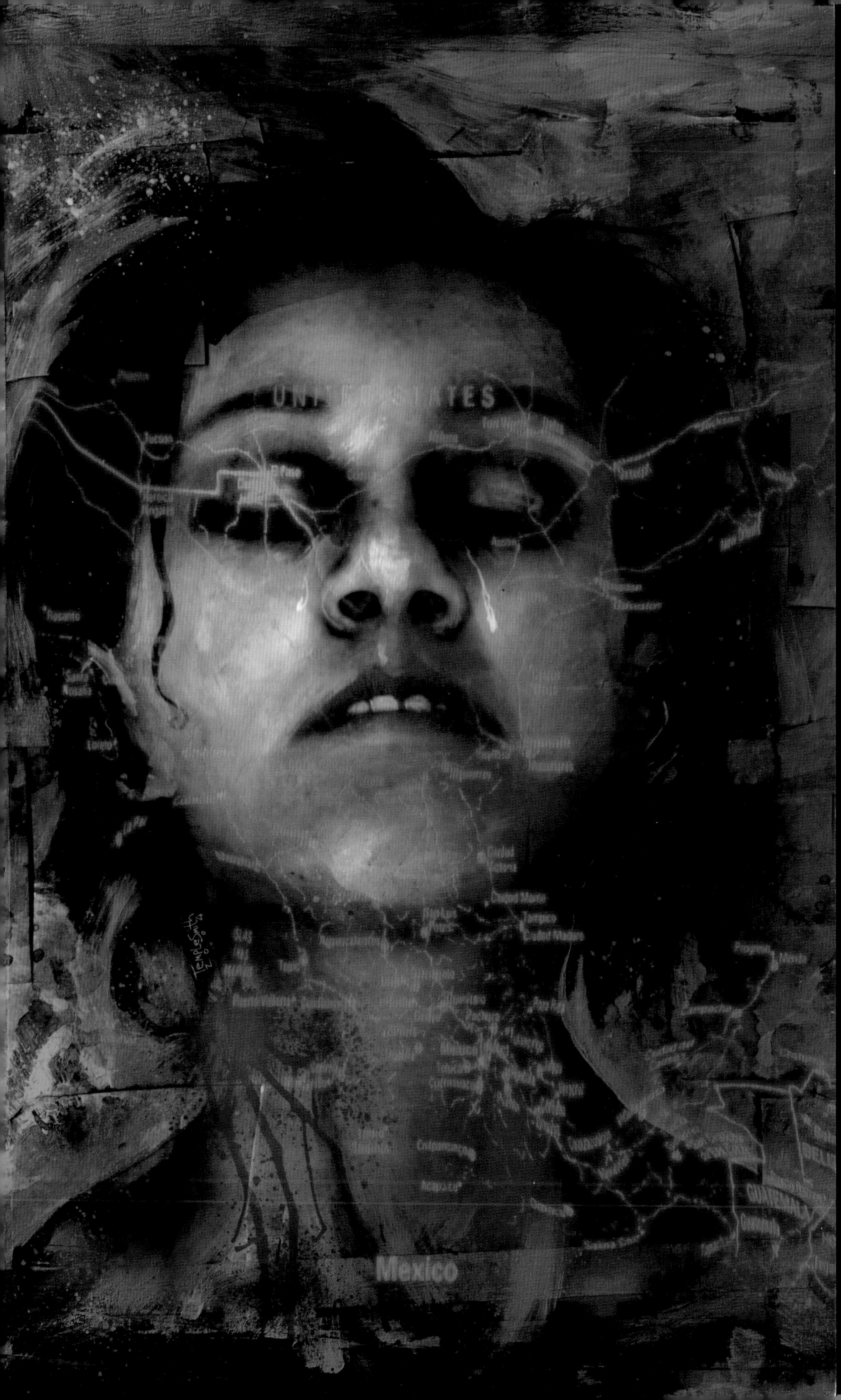
Mexico

STEVE NILES

Steve Niles is one of the writers responsible for bringing horror comics back to prominence, and was recently named by **Fangoria** magazine as one of its "13 rising talents who promise to keep us terrified for the next 25 years."

Niles later got his start in comics when he formed his own publishing company called Arcane Comix, where he published, edited and adapted several comics and anthologies for Eclipse Comics. His adaptations include works by Clive Barker, Richard Matheson, and Harlan Ellison.

He formed Creep Entertainment with Rob Zombie, as well as the film production company Raw Entertainment with Tom Jane.

Niles resides in Los Angeles. Visit his official site at **www.steveniles.com**

Look for these Steve Niles books from IDW Publishing!

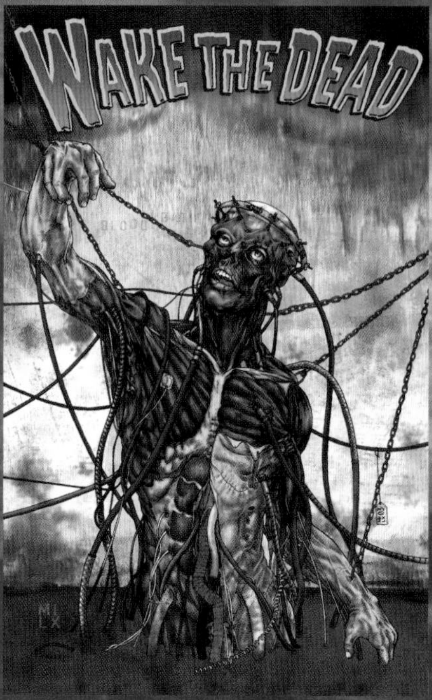
WAKE THE DEAD

WAKE THE DEAD
978-1-932382-22-8 • $19.99

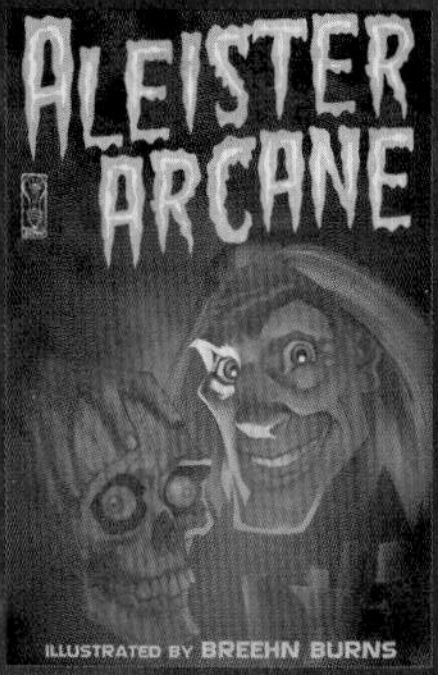
ALEISTER ARCANE
ILLUSTRATED BY BREEHN BURNS

ALEISTER ARCANE
978-1-932382-33-4
$17.99

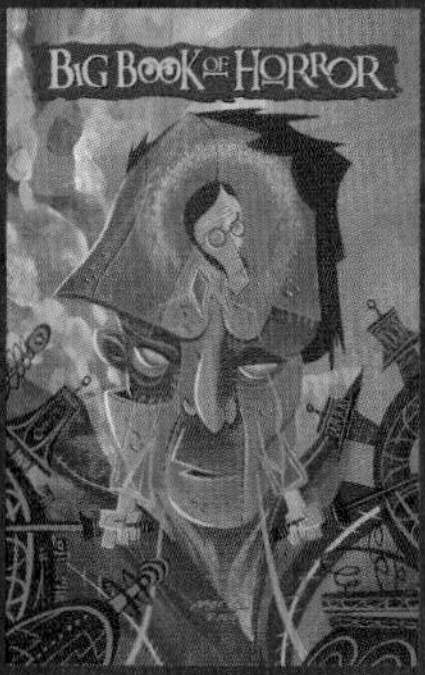
BIG BOOK OF HORROR

BIG BOOK OF HORROR
978-1-600100-14-7
$19.99

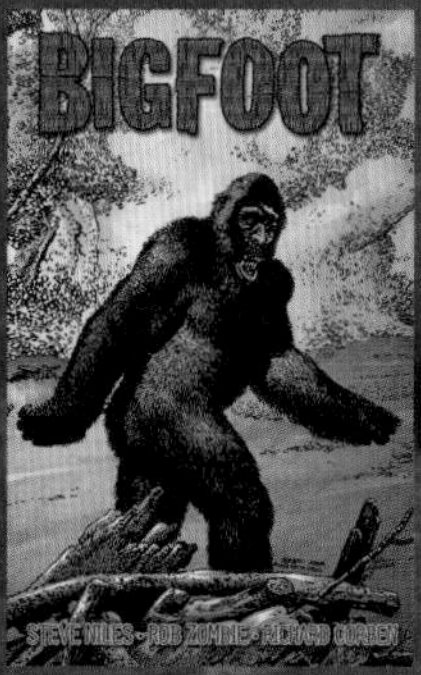
BIGFOOT

BIGFOOT
978-1-933239-13-2
$19.99

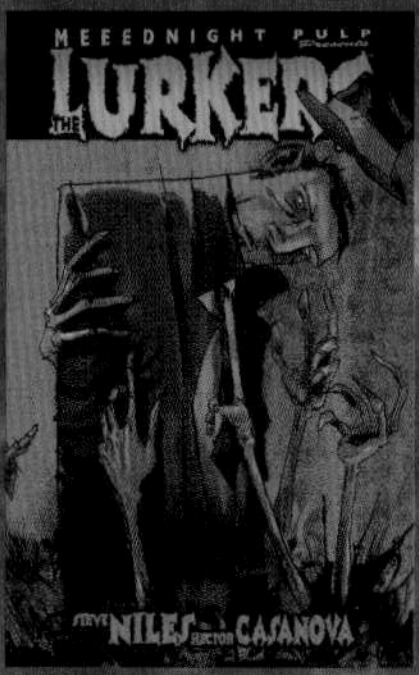
THE LURKERS

THE LURKERS
978-1-932382-80-8
$17.99

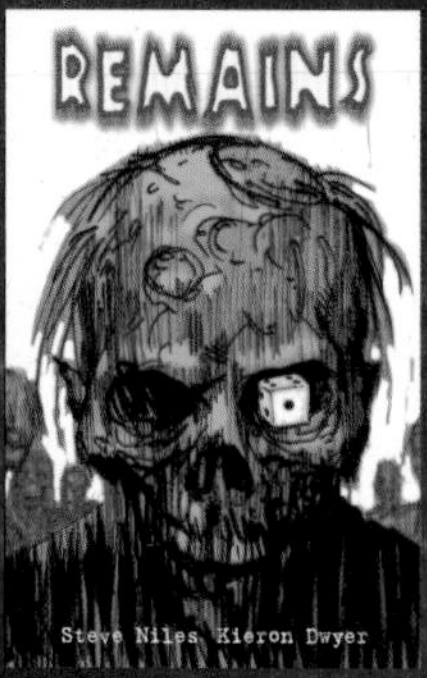
REMAINS
Steve Niles, Kieron Dwyer

REMAINS
978-1-932382-38-9
$19.99

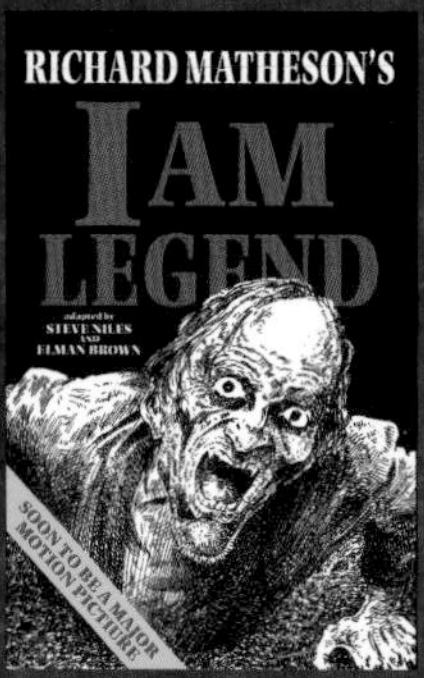
RICHARD MATHESON'S
I AM LEGEND

RICHARD MATHESON'S I AM LEGEND
978-1-933239-21-7
$19.99

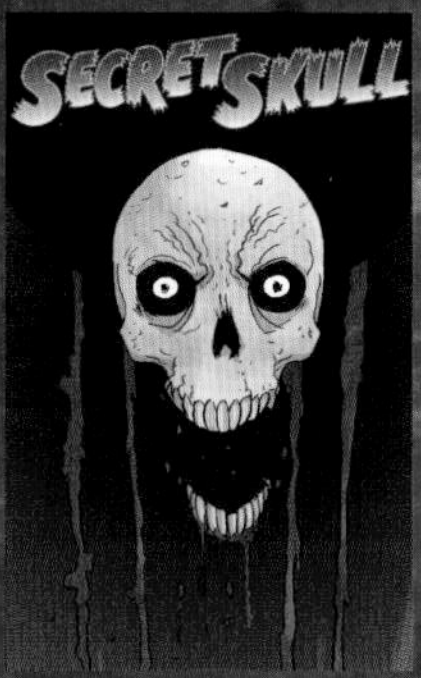
SECRET SKULL

SECRET SKULL
978-1-932382-57-0
$17.99

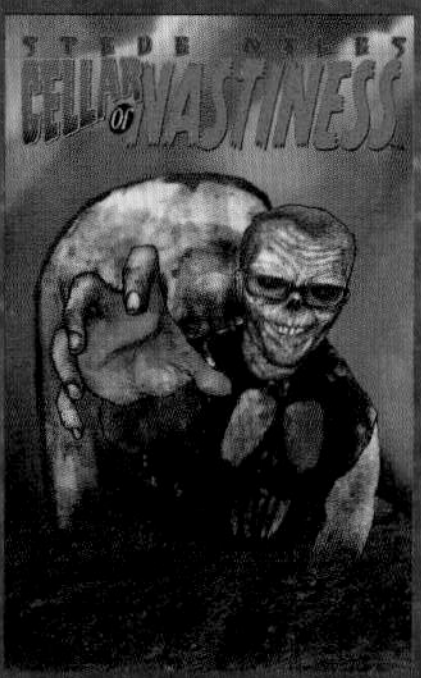
CELLAR OF NASTINESS

STEVE NILES' CELLA
OF NASTINESS
978-1-932382-95-2
$24.99

BEN TEMPLESMITH

Born in 1978, **Ben Templesmith** hails from Perth, Australia where he attended Curtin University of Technology and received a degree in design.

As a commercial illustrator, his works include the widely successful ***30 Days of Night*** and ***Fell***. His first written work was ***Singularity 7*** and he is currently writing and illustrating ***Wormwood: Gentleman Corpse***.

Ben likes Sumo wrestling and, in all probability, can hold more alcohol than you (he is Australian).

These days, Ben lives and works in his studio in Perth where he attempts in vain to get what others call "sleep" at least a couple of hours a day. There's also a strange American lurking around his home, although she could easily be a figment of a caffeine-induced delirium.

Visit his official site at www.***templesmitharts.com***

Look for these Ben Templesmith books from IDW Publishing!

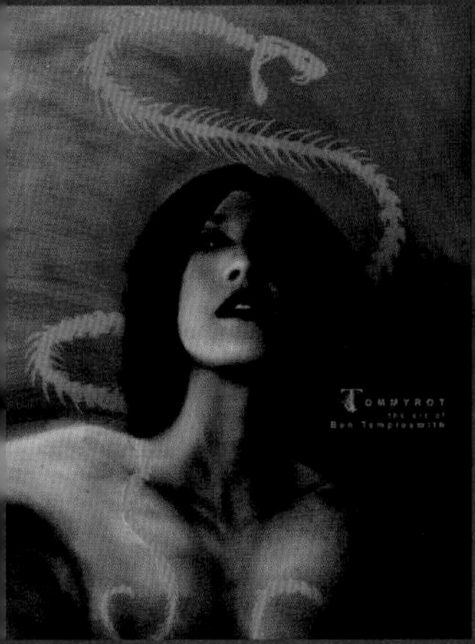

TOMMYROT: THE ART OF BEN TEMPLESMITH
978-1-60010-005-5 • $19.99

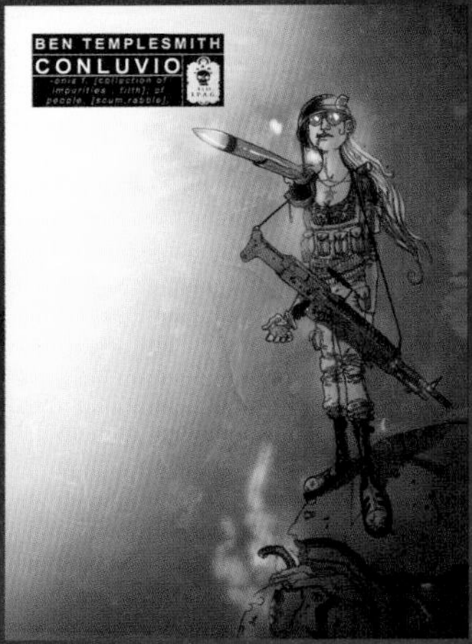
BEN TEMPLESMITH
CONLUVIO

CONLUVIO: THE ART OF BEN TEMPLESMITH, VOLUME 2
978-1-60010-053-6 • $19.99

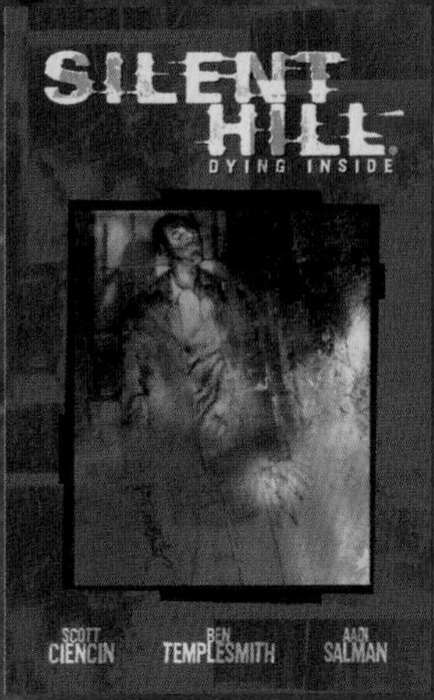
SILENT HILL
DYING INSIDE
SCOTT CIENCIN
BEN TEMPLESMITH
AADI SALMAN

SILENT HILL: DYING INSIDE
978-1-932382-24-2 • $19.99

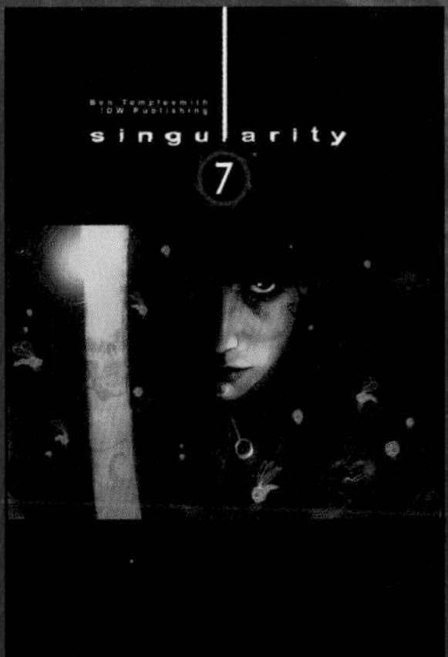
singularity
7

SINGULARITY 7
978-1-932382-53-2 • $19.99

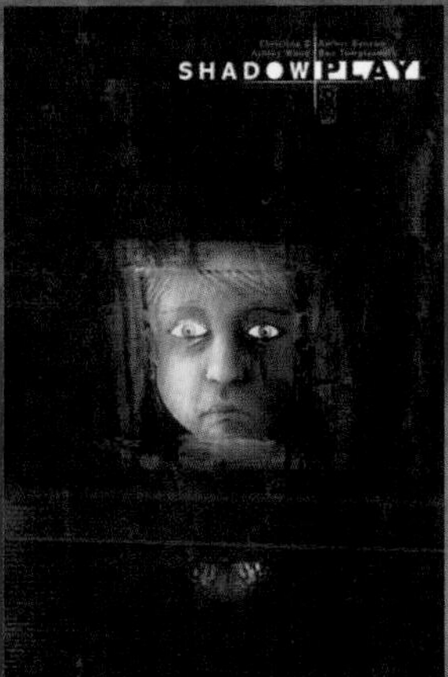
SHADOWPLAY

SHADOWPLAY
978-1-933239-84-2 • $17.99

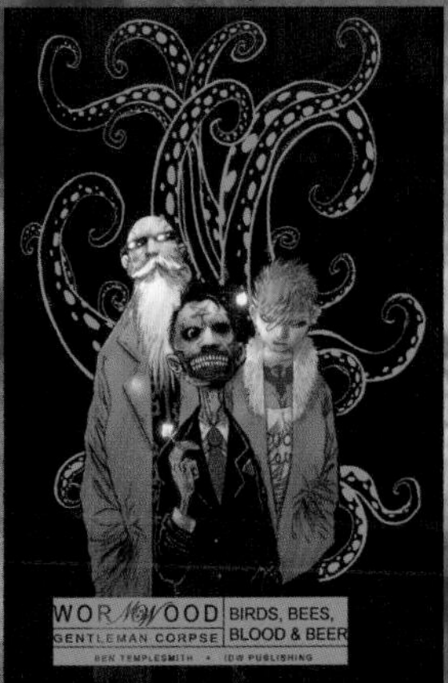
WORMWOOD
GENTLEMAN CORPSE
BIRDS, BEES, BLOOD & BEER

WORMWOOD: GENTLEMAN CORPSE
978-1-60010-047-5 • $19.99

THERE'S EVEN MORE *30 DAYS OF NIGHT* ACTION IN THESE THRILLING TRADE PAPERBACKS!

30 DAYS OF NIGHT: DARK DAYS

30 DAYS OF NIGHT:
DARK DAYS
STEVE NILES • BEN TEMPLESMITH

In *Dark Days*, the action shifts from Barrow, Alaska to Los Angeles, as Stella Olemaun, her life forever altered by the vampires' assault, rededicates herself to wiping out the vampires and alerting the world to their shadowed existence. Along the way she meets new allies and new foes—lots and lots of foes. Intense action and gripping suspense make this a must-have for all fans of *30 Days of Night*!

AVAILABLE NOW!
ISBN: 978-1-932382-16-7 • $19.99

30 DAYS OF NIGHT: THREE TALES

30 DAYS OF NIGHT
THREE TALES

This latest foray into the vampire-centric world of *30 Days of Night* collects three tales of terror. In "Picking Up The Pieces," **Steve Niles** and **Ben Templesmith** contribute a short story about John Ikos and his run-in with the FBI agent-turned-vampire, agent Norris. **Steve Niles** and **Nat Jones** continue the story in "The Journal of John Ikos" as Ikos heads to Los Angeles to track down the undead G-man. What happens when a bloodsucker enters outer space? Found out in "Dead Space," written by **Steve Niles** and **Dan Wickline** with art by **Milx**.

AVAILABLE NOW!
ISBN: 978-1-933239-92-7 • $19.99

ALSO LOOK FOR THE PROSE NOVELS FROM POCKET BOOKS.

30 DAYS OF NIGHT: RUMORS OF THE UNDEAD

30 DAYS OF NIGHT
RUMORS OF THE UNDEAD
STEVE NILES & JEFF MARIOTTE
BASED ON THE GRAPHIC NOVELS FROM IDW PUBLISHING

AN ORIGINAL NOVEL BY STEVE NILES & JEFF MARIOTTE

FBI special agent Andy Gray used to have a grip on things. But that was before the violent confrontation with the terrifying creature that had once been his former partner and friend turned his world upside down. Now Gray is looking for some answers, and finding only more questions, all of which seem to lead straight to the backwater town of Barrow, Alaska—a place that has seen its own share of horror. Andy Gray has no idea what he's gotten himself into—and he's about to find out just how dangerous the stuff of legend can actually be...

AVAILABLE NOW!
ISBN: 978-0-7434-9651-3 • $7.99

30 DAYS OF NIGHT: IMMORTAL REMAINS

AN ORIGINAL NOVEL BY STEVE NILES & JEFF MARIOTTE

The second original novel based on the acclaimed graphic novel series—an innovative expansion of a nightmarish narrative that explores the very nature of ancient evil existing—and thriving—in an unsuspecting modern world.

AUGUST 2007
ISBN: 0-7434-9652-3 • $7.99

www.idwpublishing.com

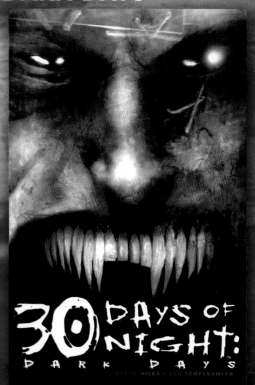